THE
APOLOGY
PROJECT

THE APOLOGY PROJECT

a novel

Jeanette Escudero

LAKE UNION
PUBLISHING

Text copyright © 2021 Jeanette Escudero
All rights reserved.

Published by Lake Union Publishing, Seattle

www.apub.com

Amazon, the Amazon logo, and Lake Union are trademarks of Amazon.com, Inc., or its affiliates.

ISBN-13: 9781542029926
ISBN-10: 1542029929

Cover design by Liz Casal

Printed in the United States of America

To all the women juggling careers and families and who still manage to get up the next day and do it all over again. Thanks, Mom, for showing me we can do it all!

CHAPTER ONE

"Margret!" I just finished reading the transcripts from the first day of Hugh Phoebe's criminal trial, and I'm currently on my hands and knees in my office tossing the cardboard lids off the boxes. "Margret! Where's the other box? I'm missing boxes!" *I can't work like this.*

I can hear the door to my office open and close and my executive assistant's footsteps coming closer, but I keep tossing lids and random papers aside, looking for the box containing day two of the monthlong trial. "Why the hell aren't these labeled? These should be labeled."

"I don't work for the state attorney, Ms. Montgomery. I can't tell you why they were archived this way. I can, however, get someone to organize these for you before you start going through them."

"A little too late for that, don't you think?"

"An intern, perhaps. Maybe a junior associate? I'm sure they'd assist." That's Margret, as even-keeled as ever.

"No. It's fine. It's too late anyway. The partners' meeting is Friday and I need to be ready—oh! Here it is!" I say and sit back on my heels with the thick file in hand. I look up and see Margret, with her sensible shoes and support hose, her arms crossed over her chest, and her lips in a thin line, waiting for my next request or order or tantrum. *Oh, am I annoying you?*

"I need the rest of the team to read through these and give me summaries. Please scan them. We'll regroup tomorrow. Eight sharp." She nods and then walks out of the room. Less than two minutes later my phone dings with the meeting invite for eight a.m., and I'm sure she's already emailed the junior attorneys about summarizing these files. The woman is efficient. Robotic and sometimes downright emotionless, but efficient.

The rest of the day I spend reading the transcripts of the Phoebe criminal trial that occurred two years ago. Sometime in the late afternoon there's a quick knock at my door, and before I can tell the person to come inside, Marc Jones Jr. strolls in.

"Just met with Hugh," he says without a single pleasantry—right down to business. I've known Junior since I started interning at JJF almost two decades ago. He's one of the Js in JJF. The other is Junior's father, Marc Jones Sr., and the F is for Fisher. Junior, much like his father, is a tall man, over six feet, with broad shoulders and a receding hairline. Senior's hairline, however, had fled before I even stepped foot inside JJF; consequently, his head has always been as bald and shiny as a cue ball to me.

Junior manspreads his legs on the chair across from mine, making himself comfortable, uncaring that he's taking up more than his share of the space and that the button on his suit jacket looks like it's about to catapult away from his big gut. I feel my eye twitch in fear of a flying button.

I think this is the first time I notice how much he's aged. I remember the first time I met him, how intimidated I was by his presence. He was in his early thirties and already riding his father's coattails up the corporate ladder while I clawed my way to the top behind him. On my own, might I add. Now, in his fifties and very wealthy, he spends most of his time lording over the rest of the staff. I don't remember the last case he even tried, but I can remember the last time he yelled at someone for losing a case and upsetting a client. His job duties include:

coming in whenever he's not golfing, negotiating our fees on big cases, and leaving early enough to make it to the country club for a drink. Even if I had as much money as he does, I think I'd feel useless. Plus, I love my job, and I would do it even if I didn't have to.

"I'm catching up on the case," I say, motioning to the twelve boxes scattered around the room. "I want to have a preliminary defense strategy ready for you to consider on Friday."

"We've decided that you're going to be the lead on this one." *We* of course being the other partners.

My eyes widen. I was going to be co-counsel, and Junior was going to be lead. He doesn't try a lot of cases these days, but he'll cancel a game of racquetball when a big case pops up. And there are not many civil lawsuits bigger than Hugh Phoebe's.

"Oh, wow. Okay. Sure. Thank you. I've been reading up on the defense already and—"

"We already have a strategy, Amelia. It's going to be a slam dunk just like the criminal trial."

"Well"—I pull one of the files—"I don't know if slam dunk is realistic and—"

"Let's not get bogged down with the details. We'll discuss things further at the meeting on Friday. I just wanted to be the first to tell you. Have to run, my tee time is in an hour." He smiles and stands up, and then I push off my own chair and reach over my desk to shake his hand. His eyes drift to the top of my blouse, which sags a little when I lean forward. Quickly, I let go of his hand and adjust my shirt. His eyes become heated and there's a little upturn on his lips. Wealth doesn't always equate to decency. It's not the first time he's done something skeevy like this, but then again, maybe I'm reading too much into something that's not really there. He's a married man with two grown sons, and he's one of the most respected attorneys in Chicago. He did promote me, a woman, to managing partner, and he's never outright hit on me.

So I wave it off and continue working until my eyes hurt and I can see from the windows in my office that it's way past normal working hours.

———

Where is my freaking team? I'm sitting at my desk at six in the morning the next day. I expected them all to be here already. During my first years at the firm, I was always the first in and last out. That's how you start to make partner. I take a sip of my coffee and sit back on my chair to think about Hugh Phoebe, my defendant, and what defenses we could possibly use. And I'll confess, thinking of Phoebe isn't pleasant.

He is a five-foot-ten white male with three very prominent black moles on his face. One has a hair that sticks out of it. He's balding but refuses to succumb to the loss of hair, so he combs the little he does have over the bald area and uses a lot of product to get it to stay there, which makes his hair (and head) visibly greasy. He is always sweating, and it's disgusting. He does have a good tailor, though. His oversize belly is always well hidden in very expensive designer suits. He wears a big, gaudy Rolex watch with diamonds and a gold ring squeezed onto his pinkie finger. The best way I can describe Hugh Phoebe is a cross between an old-school stereotypical Italian mobster, like Marlon Brando from *The Godfather*, and Felonius Gru, the bad guy from *Despicable Me*.

I shudder at the disturbing visual.

Not to mention, what I've read in the last twenty-four hours is weighing on me. I'm hoping these junior associates have a good take on a defense because, quite frankly, I don't like where I see this headed. I think settlement may have to be the way to go on this one.

Wendy walks in first. She's the brightest of the bunch, sharp but shy, and you can't be shy if you're going to litigate. "Good morning, Ms. Mon-Montgomery." I narrow my eyes and then tilt a brow. She always stutters when she's around me, yet I've overheard her speaking with others and I've never once heard her stutter. Also, she never looks me in the eye. I've never been unkind to her; I don't know why she's so nervous around me. Maybe she just dislikes me. I don't know, and quite frankly, I don't have the time to care right now.

"Good morning, Wendy."

"I took the liberty of asking Chris to move the files to the conference room. He should be here any moment. I thought it—that—you know, that there's more room there. Is that okay? Did I overstep? I can always have them leave—"

"It's fine, Wendy. That's a good idea. We'll meet over there. Tell everyone to meet at CR1."

She bows her head low, almost turning the gesture into a curtsy, and then walks out of the room.

Strange girl.

A moment later, Chris, the maintenance man, walks in with a dolly, and I direct him to the boxes that need to be relocated. By a quarter to eight I'm walking into the conference room with my coffee mug in my hand, a gag gift I received from an old friend, Luanne Chase, when I passed the Illinois state bar. It says, Trust Me, I'm a Lawyer.

I hear laughing and chatting. Matt's drinking something that looks milky. There are some black balls sitting at the bottom of his clear cup. When they see me walk in, all laughter and chatter cease and they jump up to their feet, but Matt momentarily chokes on whatever it is that he's drinking.

Sylvia pats him on the back as his eyes water.

"Are you okay? What are you drinking? They look like marbles." I'm sure I look disgusted, and aside from being worried that he may actually choke, I *am* disgusted.

That makes him cough even harder. "Boba," Wendy clarifies. "It's boba tea. Those are tapioca balls."

Now I'm truly sickened. I hate tapioca. I slide the files away from Matt. The last thing I need is that boba stuff splattered all over the transcripts of the Phoebe trial.

5

After Matt catches his breath and everyone sits down, I begin the meeting. "Let's stick to coffee from now on, shall we? That's revolting." I eye Matt, who wipes his eyes in embarrassment. "I hope everyone had a restful sleep because we have a lot to do before Friday."

I make my way to the head of the table, four yellow legal pads in hand.

"Where's . . . ?" I snap my fingers together. "Tall guy, glasses—"

"Luis," Sylvia says.

"Yes, Luis." He's the newest intern. "Why isn't he here?"

The five of them, three junior associates and two interns, just shrug.

It amazes me how unprofessional and unmotivated these new interns and JAs can be, but I don't have the time or the energy to dwell on the eventual failure of someone else. "All right, let's get started. As you all know, we are representing Hugh Phoebe on the civil matter. There are four victims bringing seven separate assault and harassment charges. The first order of business is to move to consolidate all the cases together." They nod, taking notes, and I continue. "As you also know from every news outlet across the nation and from your reading last night, Phoebe won the criminal case."

"We're essentially retrying the case, but civilly," Wendy says.

"That is correct, and as such, we'll see where the defense attorney in the criminal matter prevailed and where he was deficient. Remember that a jury will be more sympathetic about putting a man in prison than they will be about finding him guilty to the tune of $150 million."

Their eyes widen. That is a sum of money no one at this table will ever see, but Phoebe is a billionaire with a big, fat capital *B*, and he is willing to spend a fortune to save a fortune.

"Alice, what are the charges?" I ask one of the interns who's sitting back nervously. I want to see if she's prepared.

"Sexual assault, sexual harassment, indecent exposure." As she says this, Luis strolls in with a tall coffee in hand.

"Sorry I'm late. The line at Star—"

6

I don't let him finish.

"This is a career-defining case we're about to embark on, and I need people who are ready to put in the time and work hard, not people who prioritize coffee over their careers."

"I am willing to work hard, Ms. Montgomery. It wasn't my fault that the line for—"

"Get out!" I point to the door. I hate excuses.

"But—"

This time I shout. The word *out* reverberates throughout the big room. The rest of the team jumps in their chairs, and Luis's eyes widen as his posture slumps and he walks out.

I push my chair back and pace the room. "I hope you all understand what we're dealing with here. Hugh Phoebe is a public figure. This will be the trial of your career, and I've been asked to be lead. I need a dedicated team, not someone who's going to stroll in with a latte ten minutes late. There will be long days and nights. Sometimes weekends and holidays. Until this trial is over, we will be neck-deep in work. Am I clear?" They all nod. "Okay, so back to the case. Matt, what do you think about Phoebe?"

Matt pulls out his notes, which are on an iPad, and scrolls.

"No. What do you *think*? Forget your notes. From what you read. The defense, the victims' testimony, what do you think? What's your opinion?"

"He's a very successful hedge fund guy. Self-made. Scholarship to Harvard Business School—"

"Raised by a single mom," Sylvia adds. "Donates millions to different organizations. Was named businessman of the year some time ago for his commitment to the environment in all his business dealings."

"Been married for over thirty years and just had an anniversary party in the Hamptons," Alice says as they continue spewing all Phoebe's accolades, until finally, I interrupt.

"Great. You guys read."

They all smile proudly. I pull the chair back and take a seat. "Do you want to know what I think?"

They nod eagerly.

I lean forward, and they lean in as if I'm about to give them the secrets to life itself. "I think that Hugh Phoebe is a despicable human being." Their mouths open wide as I continue. "He got out of jail because he had the equivalent of the Dream Team representing him, and they won on technicalities. But the civil world is different, folks. A lot of the evidence that was not brought into the criminal case *will* be brought into the civil case."

Craig, the other intern, who's been mostly quiet, says, "Well, um—"

"Speak up, Craig. I can't hear you," I say, and sit back and drink some more coffee as I await his inexperienced ideas of the case.

"There's an angle that I think would work," he begins, and I impatiently wave him along with my free hand. *Spit it out.* "In the deposition of one of the victims, I read that she has been in rehab three times and—"

"And what?" I don't let him finish. "And she deserved to be fired from her job for not sleeping with the old man? Because of her drug problem, Phoebe had a right to grope her? Is that what you're saying, Craig?"

"Well, no. No!" He becomes flustered. I'm speaking to them just like opposing counsel or a judge would speak to them. There's no time to dawdle. You have to make decisions and then assertively defend them. No ums, no stuttering, no floundering. If you don't believe in what you are saying, no one else will. "I'm just saying that if she's discredited—"

"No!" I put down the mug, stand up, and start to pace again. I'm a pacer. When I think, I walk. When I talk, I walk. I don't know how to do thinking or talking from a chair. "Listen to me, all of you, and listen carefully. I will not try a case by making victims seem like they asked for it. I don't care how much money Phoebe has. You hear me?" There is a big difference between knowing how to win and being unscrupulous, and I will not taint my reputation for Phoebe. "You have two days." I hold up two fingers. "Two days to think outside the box and figure out another angle. Could the victims have been out of the office? Is it possible he didn't do it? But discrediting the victims to get Phoebe out of the charges is not going to happen. Maybe settlement is the best option? I don't know yet, but whatever it is, I will not put a victim on the stand only to rip her apart about her past. Understand?"

They all nod, and then I take my legal pads and walk out.

By the look of fear in their eyes, I think I've made myself clear.

CHAPTER TWO

It's Friday. I'm supposed to meet with Hugh Phoebe and the partners to discuss the case. Rarely are the three partners all in the office at the same meeting these days, but Phoebe is the kind of client that will get J, J, and F to put on suits and designer shoes and make an appearance.

I have all my notes and I'm ready. I even wore my pristine white Chanel power suit and sky-high Louboutins, the ones that say, "If I can walk in these all day, I can win any case." They make me feel fierce and in charge.

As I head to the meeting, I see Sylvia, Matt, Wendy, and some other interns congregated in the cubicle area planning happy hour tonight. When they notice I'm approaching, they all stop what they're saying and stand up straight. Some give me a fake smile; others avoid my eyes completely.

No one invites me to happy hour.

Not that I'd go. I'm busy, and I don't normally hang out with the staff, but an invite would be nice. No matter, though. I'm about to start preparing for the biggest case of my career, and all attention will be solely on the Phoebe matter. I've never wanted or needed to go out for a night of drinking. In fact, the JAs should take note and stay late and help prep instead of going out to drink. I have an Excel spreadsheet of tasks that is long enough to keep them busy for the next two months.

Fisher, Jones Senior, and Jones Junior are already in the conference room when I arrive. In fact, by the papers strewn about the long table, I think they've been in here for a while. Maybe they had other matters to discuss? I'm not sure, but I push that out of my mind, walk all the way around the table, and pull a seat. "Good afternoon, gentlemen."

"Amelia, hello, how are you?" Jones Senior says, and the other two follow the same script. A secretary comes in with a tray and serves us coffee. I don't know why I'm so aware of this silly mug this week, but it's now right in front of me, filled to the brim with steaming hot caffeine. I remember I left it in here a few days ago when I met with my team. Somebody must've washed it and put it away, like they do every single day. *I wonder who does that. Do we pay someone to do that?*

"Amelia?" Senior repeats while clearing his throat.

"Oh, I'm good. Thank you. You?"

They don't answer. Instead, Junior slides a thick folder across the hardwood table. "So we met with Phoebe this morning, and here are our thoughts."

They met with the client? Without me? "I thought the meeting was now."

"That's not important," Fisher says, waving it off. "We have a PI tailing Rebecca. As you know, she's the one holding the reins on this case." Rebecca had been Phoebe's CFO for ten years. "We've been hearing rumors that she frequents a little bar on Eighth Avenue and often leaves completely inebriated. If we can get her to back off, the others will probably follow suit."

"You're tailing Rebecca?" I parrot, dumbfounded, but they ignore my question.

"And I have good news. During the criminal trial, the judge struck down the testimony of a man named Marcelo McFadden. He was the nurse who worked with Vanessa, Plaintiff B. He has videos and first-hand knowledge of her psychotic episode in 2003. He even has her on tape asking another patient for cocaine. I think if we grab on to—"

"Drugs? Wait. Wait." I shake my head as if I'm actually hearing voices. I pick up my file and then put it back. Did I hear them correctly? Why aren't they correcting me? I pick up the file again, blinking slowly. "Actually, I was not going to go that route." I flip pages in the file, but I don't even know what I'm looking for, so I close it and place my palms over it. I close my eyes for a moment and then start speaking. "The cost to settle compared to a trial will save Phoebe substantial money. Has anyone suggested a settlement?"

"That is not an option," Junior says with an arrogant smirk.

"Fine. Then I think we can show that Phoebe was not present during two of the altercations. I've been looking at the timeline of events based on the allegations and comparing them to the flight plans of his private—"

"No," Junior deadpans with a look of superiority that makes me instantly enraged. "We're not doing that."

I tap my finger on the file a few times, my moves jerky. Three men are staring at me. Why did I not realize the subservient position I'd been put in when I walked in? My back is against the wall, literally, and these three men, the living embodiment of our letterhead, are sitting directly across from me as if I'm on trial here. They're not here to brainstorm. They're here to order. Red flags start to pop up all over the place, and I can feel my heart pick up speed. Not because I'm scared. Not at all. But my temper . . . I feel it begin to approach fight-or-flight mode.

I never flee.

I can feel the skin around my cheeks and on the backs of my arms mottle as heat fills my body. "We are not doing what?" My tone is slow and firm, and I'm fairly certain I bare teeth.

"We are going to crush those victims. We are going to salvage Phoebe's reputation. We are going to win," Junior says. Turns out Junior is the ringleader of this little gang today.

Fisher, in a condescending manner, points his fingers toward the file and wiggles them around. "Everything you need is right there. Junior will be second chair, but we insist on daily updates. Stick with the script, Amelia. Wouldn't it be wonderful to have this victory under your belt?"

I picture Joanne, whom Phoebe allegedly groped during a late-night meeting. She screamed so loudly to get him to stop that she actually tore her vocal cords. Phoebe, the sonofabitch, didn't even deny it, according to the transcripts I reviewed. He said it was consensual. Joanne worked as a cocktail server at a strip club when she was twenty-one. She's thirty-three now with a son and husband. Her strip club days are not relevant to this case, except to drag her through the mud. Rebecca the CFO had worked with Phoebe for years when one evening Phoebe asked her to dinner to talk work. Turned out, dinner was at a hotel room. When Rebecca tried to leave because she felt uncomfortable, he fired her. Claire, Phoebe's personal assistant, is the worst story of all. He cornered her during one of those late-night mandatory meetings and stuck his tongue down her throat and his hands up her skirt. She pushed him away and he slapped her. There are photos of her broken lip and bruised eye. How the prosecutor in the criminal case lost on this one, I'll never understand. She kneed Phoebe in the groin when he unzipped his jeans and took out his penis. She was able to get away.

So whatever these women had going on in their lives is not relevant to the case. My job is to show a jury that Phoebe didn't commit these particular crimes, not that the victims deserved what they got.

"Amelia, did you hear what I said?" Fisher asks.

"Yes. I'm processing," I admit. "No offense, but you are rarely involved in cases anymore, yet you want me to update *you* daily? When's the last time you practiced law?"

With a brow arched high, Fisher replies, "Careful, sweetheart."

I close and open my fists a few times, which I've hidden under the table. "Do not call me sweetheart."

"He's just saying that this isn't just any case. We've strategized and decided this is best for the client," Jones Senior adds. Then he smiles.

It is such an unusual gesture for him that I think his face is actually rejecting it. It looks more like a stomachache than a smile.

The three of them begin to stand. The meeting's over, but I'm left with more questions than answers.

Junior winks at his father in a knowing way that bothers me. Hell, everything about this meeting bothers me, and I can feel my cheeks flame and my pulse quicken. These are my bosses, and I can't very well challenge them, but then again, I also can't in good conscience go through with this.

They may be finished, but I'm not. I push my chair back and stand. "Stop." It comes out assertive even to my own ears. "I want to understand exactly what you want me to do." Junior opens his mouth to say what I'll presume is a condescending and/or snarky remark, but I just keep plowing through. "Hugh Phoebe has been accused of rape—"

"Sexual assault," Senior corrects.

"The CFO of his company alleges that on a business trip he forced her into sex."

"It was consensual. She seduced him. She went to dinner with him late at night. And she's making seven figures." Junior again. I want to strangle him. I can see myself in my mind's eye with my hands around his fat little neck.

"But her allegations are different, and you want me to say that her mental state three years before she even met Phoebe is the reason he rap—assaulted her?"

"No. She is a liar, and her mental state is altered, and it discredits her," Junior says.

"And how about the four NDAs he's signed over the last ten years with four other women?"

"Irrelevant to this case."

Again, they turn to each other as if I'm dismissed. As if that is supposed to answer all my questions.

But I'm far from done. "Why have me as lead in this case if you're essentially pulling the strings?"

The three look at each other, and a thousand unsaid words flash among them.

I know why. I know why. And I hate why.

With a clenched jaw I answer the question that's sitting in the room like a heavy fog. "Because I'm a woman. I'm the token woman who'll get the jury and the media to sympathize with the disgusting pig." These three entitled assholes are too much like Phoebe to ever get a jury to side with them.

"Watch it, Amelia. That's our client. He's paying your salary," Junior says.

I cross my arms over my chest. "I'm not doing it."

"You are. If you value your job, you'll do it," Junior says, taking a step toward me as if he could intimidate me.

"Relax. Let's take a breath. Amelia, you are a phenomenal litigator; that's why we chose you. The fact that you're a woman just sweetens the pot," Fisher says. He's trying to be the voice of reason, but I've known the old man for two decades. I know he's as cutthroat as they come.

"I am a phenomenal litigator," I repeat. Then I lean forward, my palms on the desk. "And because I'm phenomenal, I'll take on this case on my terms or not at all."

Junior slams his palms on the table, causing me to jerk back. "No. You will do this the way the client wants it done. The way we want it done. If not, there's the door." He points behind him as if I needed that clarification.

"Marc!" both Senior and Fisher shout at the same time. I've always had a distaste for Junior, and it's all coming to a head now. His voice sends my temper rising like a pressure cooker. I'm doing everything I can to stop it from exploding.

"I've given you half of my life." I jab my finger inches from his face, seething. "I've made you money. Millions. I've been an exceptional employee, and you're willing to lose me because of one case?"

"No, because you're being insubordinate. I'm not going to stand here and tolerate insubordination. Not from a woman who has me to thank for her entire career. You're being an ungrateful bi—"

"Watch it," I say, because I see the way his lips are drawn together and I know the next word that's coming out of his mouth. "You made me a partner. A managing partner. I'm your equal. I get a say."

"You don't have enough shares to say how this place runs. Your name is not on this building, so you better settle down before you say something you'll regret." This time it's Senior speaking, and he's completely ignored the way his son is speaking to me.

But Junior's ego gets the better of him, and he keeps running his mouth. "You're not my equal, honey. You're just a woman who was in the right place at the right time. When the firm needed a woman, you were the only one available. Don't flatter yourself into thinking you're anything special."

The blood drains from my body. I don't believe him. I refuse to pay him any mind. I'm good at my job. The best. I am special. I've won awards, and not because I'm the damn token woman at the firm. I stand up straight, teetering on my stilettos. He's trying to cut me down, and I refuse to let him. "You are no better than Hugh Phoebe. You should be ashamed of yourselves." I start to walk around the longest damn conference table on the planet, trying to feel triumphant in having kept it professional while attempting to get out of that room as quickly as I can.

"I told you it was a bad idea. They belong barefoot and pregnant, not parading around a law firm trying to play in the big leagues."

I turn to face Junior. "*What* did you say?"

"Marc," Fisher warns, but Junior just keeps going.

"You know what I think? I think you're just jealous that even Hugh Phoebe won't touch you and, secretly, you want him to. How long has it been since you got laid? Because damn, you're wound tight." And to add insult to injury, Fisher and Senior chuckle at idiot Junior's words. *Chuckle!*

I'm speechless and livid, and without thinking I wind my arm back, but as I'm about to land the slap that he deserves, my heel gets caught on the carpet and I make contact with my elbow instead. The weight of my body propels me forward as I keep falling. My hip hits the edge of the table, which stops me from crumbling down on top of him, and my mug comes crashing down on the floor, shattering and sending piping hot coffee onto Junior.

Years later, if I were asked to re-create what just happened, I could only compare it to a slow-motion film with me sitting in the audience watching it all unravel.

First, I see blood gush out of Junior's nose.

Then, I see Senior's and Fisher's eyes and mouths open wide, much like my own.

Finally, I see my career vanish before my eyes, but I can't help but hyperfocus on the way my favorite mug is scattered all over the floor, in a million jagged pieces.

Well, that certainly escalated quickly.

CHAPTER THREE

I've never hit another person before. I would have thought I'd have instant remorse. Stooping low and resorting to violence is not my style. But the only thing I actually felt was a bruised hip and a sore elbow. My teeth do ache, however, when I recall the sound of Junior's nose crunching against my elbow. The same sensation as nails on a chalkboard. I'd have thought bones were harder, but nope . . . it felt like breaking apart two KIT KAT bars.

So now it's a week later and my last day at JJF.

You must be wondering why I wasn't immediately fired. The answer's easy: I'm a damn good lawyer, that's why. *Token woman, my ass.*

Before the words *you're fired* came out of any of their lips, I kindly reminded them about Junior's wandering eye, specifically how it likes to wander to my breasts. And how I was the only woman in a senior position at the firm. And how I could convince any jury that Junior had in fact stated those sexist words, trashing JJF's own client. And then I gently suggested that I could very well speak with the other women in the firm to see if they'd ever had a similar experience. With blood gushing out of Junior's nose and hot coffee soaking through his shirt, we collectively decided that I'd take a week off and we'd all regroup at a later time in the coming week.

Also, I did fall. It's not like I meant to break his face. Not really.

A week and a dozen email exchanges and heated Zoom negotiations later, we've decided to part ways (not amicably).

So here we are; it's my last day.

In dramatic fashion, I always envisioned when you left a job you'd make that walk of shame—classily, of course, weaving your way through the lengthy expanse of the office as your coworkers gasped and stared. Head up high, arms wrapped around that classic cardboard file box full to the brim with all the items you accumulated through the years. *Mad Men*–style.

Except this isn't 1961, and in *Mad Men* I don't recall Peggy ever having decked her boss.

Also, there's no box filled to the brim.

I have only a plant.

My sister, a child psychologist, would say that the prickly little cactus from my desk is symbolic of my character. I'd say it's a freakin' cactus. One that a client gave me and one that refuses to die, so I'm keeping it because the little green sucker is persistent and doesn't deserve to stay in a place like Jones, Jones & Fisher.

"Good evening, Margret. You have my contact information if you have any problems," I say with my purse around my shoulder and the small potted plant in my hand.

Margret smiles a fake smile, says good night, and goes back to typing, her fingers moving swiftly across the keyboard. She hates me. It's obvious. I've always known. Most people dislike me, but Margret probably does more than most since she's been forced to rewrite more than one of my briefs and memorandums and has been on the receiving end of my wrath when I've lost a motion or had a bad day in court. And if you're wondering whether she knows it's my last day . . . she was in charge of redistributing my files to other attorneys in the firm, and she's the one who contacted IT to have my email disabled. So yeah . . . she knows and she doesn't give a shit.

I, however, should give a shit that she doesn't give a shit, right?

I'm waiting for the tears, but they just don't come. Today is, after all, a monumental day in my life.

As I walk into the elevator, Chloe, Jason, and Robin, all from IT, are coming out. They move aside to make room for me. Jason looks down to avoid eye contact. I see them only when I have computer issues, and by the time they walk into my office, I'm usually frustrated and upset.

"Good evening," I say, even though I know one of them shut off my access. But it's their job; they're just following orders.

Chloe looks stunned that I'm speaking to her, and I see her gaze flick back and forth between me and Robin. "Um . . . good evening, Ms. Montgomery."

I smile but they just scurry into the office without a second look back at me. Schmoozing with the staff isn't normally on my list of priorities or in my job description. Today isn't one of those days, though.

It's Friday night, and the lobby is abnormally empty as I leave for the last time after almost twenty years. Surely the staff knows something happened between the partners and me, but they don't know the details, nor would anyone dare ask. Thanks to Junior's mountain-size ego, he hid in his office with an ice pack until the bleeding subsided and then sneaked out of the building using the back exit. I, on the other hand, stormed out so fast no one saw the utter shock on my face from the assault.

I inhale a deep breath, memorizing those last smells of ink from the copy machine, stale coffee from the lunchroom, and the too-strong Axe body spray the new male interns seem to always wear. It's repugnant, but it's also home. I'm going to miss it.

Once I'm in the basement, I walk straight to my car, my heels clacking and echoing loudly in the empty parking garage.

As I'm getting into my car, my phone rings and I let the Bluetooth activate before answering.

"Hello."

"Hi, honey, how was your last day?"

"Hi, Mom. It was fine. Uneventful."

"You were there for so many years, are you sure you're making the right decision? You're too young to retire."

"Yes, Mom," I say, as if I really had a choice. The moment I hit Junior, I kissed my job goodbye. Actually, that's not really true. The moment I kissed my job goodbye was when I decided that I couldn't represent Phoebe the way they wanted me to represent him. Everything after that was just icing on the toxic-work-environment cake. Just thinking about the spiteful words that spewed from Junior's mouth repulses me. Has there ever been a cruder, viler sentence uttered? I think not. Which is why I lost it.

Big. Time.

Go big or go home, I always say.

I don't regret anything I did. He deserved more than that, and the other two deserved something just as painful. They have daughters, wives, mothers. But that didn't stop them from joining Junior.

I gave the firm my blood, sweat, and childbearing years, and Junior is a misogynistic, money-hungry pig who thinks he's above the law. The other partners aren't much better, especially because they sat idly by and allowed this kind of behavior. In my book, that makes them just as culpable. And not just because they laughed at Junior's foul behavior, but also because they agreed to represent such a foul man.

"Did they throw you a big send-off?" Mom asks.

My poor, sweet, naive mother. She doesn't know the entire story. I think of all the blood that poured out of Junior's nose and the stained carpet in the conference room that must've been professionally cleaned. So, no. I did not get a big send-off.

I did, however, get a big eff-you from Jones, Jones & Fisher as I signed an agreement not to sue, not to disclose the terms of the separation, and not to talk negatively about the firm. I could still practice law if I wanted, but for the next year, I could not practice within ten miles of the firm. The biggest win for me wasn't even the money. It was the fact that I was able to get Junior to attend a series of sexual harassment trainings and added a caveat on the NDA that if any other woman ever came forward with allegations of harassment or assault, my NDA would be void and I could serve as a witness for that victim.

If I told my parents the entire story, I'd be violating the terms of the NDA, and there's no way my parents would not tell everyone they know. So the story is: I was having differences with the partners, and we all thought it best that we part ways in exchange for a nice severance package.

Nice is a very discreet way of saying millions.

"No, Mom. No party."

"Maybe it's a surprise party. You never know."

A surprise? Ha! Yeah right.

I turn out of the parking garage and head home. My mind starts to wander, as it normally does. I analyze and then overanalyze everything, which makes me a great attorney but a bad everything else.

Well, there wasn't anyone at work tonight. Could it be? No, it couldn't be. I mean . . . ? Could it? A surprise party?

Yeah, no. Never going to happen. There wasn't even one person there to wave farewell. Or even care about a farewell. That's depressing. I need a drink.

"Mom, let me call you back," I say and hang up to call my sister, Nina, who's dating Kevin, one of the Axe-wearing guys. He's not an intern but acts like one, and works in the firm's accounting department and whose JJF-employed face I don't want to see right now. But I would like to grab a drink with Nina, alone.

"Hello!" It's loud in the background and I can barely hear her. "Millie? Is that you?"

"Hi, yes, it's me!" I yell back as if I'm also in a loud place. "Where are you?"

I hear muffled sounds. "Millie? What's up?"

"I'm leaving work. Where are you? You want to grab a drink?"

"I'm actually out with a friend celebrating her promotion. Why don't you join us?"

Of course she's celebrating the success of someone else. That's what friends do. Except me. I go home alone and sulk. I can hear Kevin in the background.

"Oh, nah, that's okay. Maybe some other time," I say, gulping down an unrecognizable emotion that I feel brewing in the pit of my stomach. "Have fun."

"We're still on for breakfast tomorrow, right?"

"Yes. See you." And I hang up.

I reach my apartment building ten minutes later.

There's silence as I walk down the hall. People are out for the night or home enjoying a nice evening with their loved ones.

I, on the other hand, enter my empty apartment, and I'm greeted with a bored look and judgmental meow from my cat.

This is my new life.

CHAPTER FOUR

So . . . guess what.

It turns out I'm not a robot after all.

I do have emotions. A lot of them, in fact.

How do I know this? I googled it.

According to the World Wide Web, not getting out of bed for forty-eight hours while crying and eating Nutella straight out of the container (with my finger) is a form of depression. I thought I would enjoy my new employment status—retirement. That's how I'm now referring to it. Retirement. Sounds pleasant, right? Anyway, I'm not enjoying it. I feel lost, like I'm floating out into space, up and up and up with no end in sight and nothing to anchor me back to Earth. There's no noise, no air, no people, just darkness, quiet, heaviness.

To make matters worse, I woke up today determined to get myself out of this funk. "Amelia Montgomery doesn't cry." I chanted this to myself as I brewed coffee. "Amelia Montgomery doesn't lose." I chanted this out loud while I fed William, my cat. "Amelia Montgomery is a winner, and I'm going to get up and out of bed today and do what I do best: win." I chanted this as I started getting dressed to conquer the new day. Instinctively I grabbed a suit—a navy Dolce & Gabbana pant set—and before I finished fastening the last button, I realized I have no job. I have no need to wear a suit. I have no purpose.

That sent me into a fit of anger, and now all my suits (three-quarters of my closet) are flung around my bedroom, making small hills of clothes. And then I got back in bed.

I'm still in my Dolce & Gabbana suit, by the way.

My front door opens and closes. It's Nina. It's only ever Nina. "Millie, get your ass out of bed. First you cancel breakfast and then you stop answering calls. Mom and Dad are going crazy and about to drive over to check on you. And what the hell happened here?" She looks around the room at all the clothes scattered about.

"Why do I have to get out of bed? I have everything I need right here. You can tell Mom and Dad to relax," I say as I take a fingerful of Nutella and stuff it into my mouth. "I don't need any of those suits."

"And so you just threw them around your room?"

I shrug. "Spring cleaning?"

She moves a little pile over and then sits down on the foot of the bed. "When you quit your job, what was the plan? To eat and vegetate?"

"I retired. There was no plan." She doesn't know the entire reason I left either. She knows I had issues with one of the partners, and I even went as far as telling her that I didn't agree with the way they were handling a particular case. But I didn't give her details or the full extent of the argument thanks to my confidentiality agreement and my sister's JJF-employed boyfriend.

"You plan everything, Millie. Everything," she says. "You planned each one of your science fair projects a year in advance in order to have a one-up on the other third, fourth, and fifth graders. And you've known you were going to be a lawyer since first grade. You planned exactly what classes you could take in order to get in and out of college and into law school quickly, while you were still in high school! So don't bullshit me. What's the plan?"

"What good did all that planning do?" I say, thinking of the fact that I have zero friends. That not one person even said goodbye to me on my last day. Hell, Margret assisted in my quick departure in her ever-so-efficient way.

"Don't be all *woe is me*. That's not you. You are a multimillionaire. Who else do you know that can retire at forty? So get your ass up and talk to me. What's going on?" She yanks the covers off me.

"I am not forty. I'm thirty-nine." I groan and try to reach for the covers, but my fingers are brown and sticky, so I decide against touching anything else for a moment.

"You turn forty in two weeks."

"Ergo, I'm thirty-nine."

She rolls her eyes. "What's the plan, Amelia?"

"The only plan was to relax," I say, the roof of my mouth still full of Nutella. Everything I say comes out with a lisp. Could anything else be more relaxing than what I'm currently doing?

"You're not acting like yourself at all. I'm worried."

"Stop worrying. Everything is fine." As I say *fine*, I can feel my eyes getting watery and the words sticking to the back of my throat. Or maybe it's the Nutella. It must be the Nutella because I don't get lumps in the back of my throat and I don't cry.

"Millie," she warns. "If you don't tell me what is going on right this instant, I swear, I'll sic Mom and Dad on you."

"Google treats me better than you do." Google is my go-to therapist and diagnostician. My sister is just a judgmental pain in the ass who is also technically a therapist, but that's beside the point. I love her, but the truth is the truth: Google is better. Nevertheless, I sit up, sucking my fingers clean. She cringes and then disappears to grab some wet paper towels and hand sanitizer and offers them to me—judgmentally, I might add.

"Let's not get chocolate on the designer clothes, sis," she says, but I don't care about the clothes. "I need the Nutella, Millie. Hand it over." I huff out a breath and finally place the jar in her hand when she continues to wait on me, her palm up. I love my sister. She's ten years younger than me and my best friend. Apparently my only friend. The thought makes that water thing happen to my eyes again. Does Nutella contain pineapples? Pineapples give me watery, itchy eyes.

"Are you crying?" she asks, sincerely shocked. Maybe I need to see the ingredients in Nutella because I have to be having an allergic reaction. "Holy shit, you are crying. Do you think it's because you've gone a whole forty-eight hours without yelling at someone? Maybe your body is rejecting relaxation or jonesing for an argument?"

"You're an ass, you know that?" I clear my throat and wipe my eyes. "No one even said goodbye to me. Twenty years and it was like I didn't matter to one single person in that office. I know I'm being silly, but . . ."

"Oh, Millie. I'm so sorry. I should have left the bar Friday night and met you for drinks," she says as she sits down on the bed.

I wave her off, but she continues. "It's not silly to want friends. You've always been so independent, it didn't occur to me that you were lonely. I should've seen the writing on the wall."

"I'm not lonely," I say with a bite in my tone. *That's absurd.* "I was perfectly content with how things were. There was no writing and no wall. It's just a lot of changes happening all at once, and I think that for a second, a tiny little moment, I thought it would be nice to have a few people wish me luck, give me a hug, say, 'Goodbye, it's been great.'"

"A tiny little moment? Then why are you crying?"

I don't have an answer for that one. It's a trick question. A psychology mind trick.

"Because my mug broke." I sniffle. "I loved that mug. Luanne gave me that mug."

She eyes me. "A mug? You're heartbroken over a mug?"

The mug. The job. What Junior said about me. Everything. Was I really just a token woman? Did I let those bastards win by accepting their money and walking away? But I don't say any of that. I just nod. "I really liked that mug."

"When's the last time you spoke with Luanne? Maybe it's a good time to reach out. She gave you that mug and it broke. It's as if the universe is telling you—"

I sit up and hold out a hand. My sister is on a different plane. She sees signs in things and has feeling words. "No. No. I'm fine. I'm not reaching out to anyone. There's no universal whispering. I just . . . it's a lot of changes all at once. I'll be okay. I'll order a new mug on Amazon later."

"To think that you don't need anyone or to be perfectly content with not having any friends is just plain stupid and extremely arrogant," she says.

"Therapist of the year."

She rolls her eyes and then scoots up closer to me on the bed. "You used to have friends, Millie. You and Luanne were thick as thieves, and there were more than a few others in high school and in law school."

I shrug. "I like my cat. We're friends."

She shakes her head, unamused. "I'm being serious, Millie."

"So am I, Nina."

I push myself off the bed and stand up, unbuttoning the suit jacket. "It's too late. I've been working and working and, well . . . working. There's no one. What am I supposed to do? Call Luanne? Call Brenda? I was busy making partner in my firm and people moved on. It is what it is. I can't go back and change things." I toss my suit into one of the piles and pull on a T-shirt.

"You can make new friends, you know? You can call old ones. You're acting like this is the end of your life and you're going to stay in this room until you wither away and die, and then William will have to eat your body because no one will be around to feed him."

"That took a weird and very dark turn, Nina. Jesus."

"I'm trying to show you that today is the first day of the rest of your life, not the beginning of the end of your life. You can do anything. You have money, time, and health."

"And a personality that causes people to run the other way."

"That's just at work. That's not you all the time."

"But no one knows me as anything other than Amelia the attorney."

"Well, sister, it's time that people met the real you."

"Too late for that. Amelia is 'retired,' remember?"

Nina mulls that over as she starts to move all the clothes in my bedroom to the corner of my walk-in closet. "Yes, Amelia retired, but what about Millie, the funny, smart, cool chick? She's not retired."

I start to help her tidy up since I can't stand to be in a messy home, notwithstanding my current mental state. I'll have to figure out what I'm going to do with all that clothing at a later time.

"Oh, I know!" she says, and I almost crash into her since she stops so abruptly. "Your birthday!"

"Yes, I know. Forty in two weeks. Why do you keep reminding me of my big, life-defining birthday? It's not helping at all." I take the pile she's still holding out of her hands and move it into the closet.

"It's a big birthday and you've just had a major life change. I think we should have a party to commemorate the occasion. It's the beginning of your new life."

"We?" I ask.

"You should have a party and I should plan it. It's the first time since I can remember that you won't have a case, a trial, a memo, or something else standing between you and fun. You wanted a farewell, right? So make it happen instead of wishing someone would have done it for you. You're not the kind of woman who sits back and wallows. You're a doer. So let's do!"

"Absolutely not."

"It's happening. You can't say no."

"Actually I can. Watch: no."

"Mills . . ."

Just to indulge her, I ask, "Who will come?" I've had enough disappointment to last a lifetime. Between the argument with JJF, the subsequent termination, and the fact that not one employee from JJF has even reached out to see how I'm doing, I'm good for a while.

"Everyone will. People are busy living their own lives, but if all they have to do is get dressed and show up—plus, enjoy free food and drinks—no one will say no. And Kevin still works there. He'll make sure people will come." I shake my head and eye her. We both know that Kevin has absolutely no pull at JJF. But she continues. "Trust me. I'll make it happen."

"I don't know . . ." Why am I even contemplating this?

"Come on, it'll give them the opportunity to see you outside of work and get to know the Millie that I love, not the She-Demon they worked with."

I hate that moniker. When Nina started dating Kevin, she told me about the nickname they all called me behind my back. It started the year that I went through eight secretaries. Why does wanting a competent secretary make me a She-Demon? But the name stuck.

"I admit, I could use a fresh start." I would love everyone to see another side of me. Millie, a fun woman who can laugh and make small talk and . . . not yell or argue or make people generally scared by my mere presence. They only know me as Amelia, the woman who made an intern cry for spilling coffee on a stack of depositions while on the way to court. And who made another associate have a breakdown after losing a court case I could have won in my sleep.

"That's the theme! New beginnings. A butterfly burrowing out of her cocoon." She mimes a butterfly being released. "Or a baby being birthed. A—"

I put my palm out. "No! No themes!" I can just picture the very graphic and very literal hippie-dippie decorations she'd use.

"So that's a yes!"

"To the party, not to the theme. I guess it could be fun."

"It's going to be more than fun, Millie. It's going to be epic." We both sit back on my bed, and she scoots close to me, finds the Pinterest app on her phone, and starts searching for party ideas.

Well, at the very least, it can't be worse than the last two days.

———

I text Nina a few days later while I get dressed to meet the event planner at the venue. I found the perfect location for my party. Easy Street has a private room and the food is delicious.

I thought I was planning this, Nina writes back.

You're busy with work and I thought I'd take on this one task. You can do everything else.

Crap. I take off the button-down shirt and pencil skirt I put on without thought and toss it onto the pile of business suits that still sits in the corner of my closet. Instead, I pull a maxi dress that I haven't worn in years off the hanger.

Okay, fine. But I'm handling everything else. Just send me a list of guests.

About that. I've been thinking about what you said. What do you think about inviting some of my old friends? Luanne, for example. I haven't spoken to her in ages, but maybe this is a good time to reconnect. She used to live nearby. I wonder if she still does? Or maybe it's weird to contact her after all this time. What do you think?

I think that's a great idea! Go for it. Oh—gotta go. A patient's walking in, Nina replies, and with that final text, I email the restaurant and
go ahead and book the venue.

I have about fifty-five people on an Excel spreadsheet consisting
mostly of my former coworkers, old friends, and my parents and
Nina. Once I'm done, I create another web-based Excel worksheet
with a checklist of everything that needs to be done for the party so
that we can both track the items and check them off. I like lists. They
show progress made and what's left to do.

I email both to Nina, and almost immediately she replies, Wow. A
spreadsheet. You are a real party animal, sis. I ignore her comment
and spend the rest of the evening binge-watching *Cupcake Wars* on
Netflix while trying to ignore the pang of anxiety that has taken hold
in the pit of my stomach over the last couple of days. I need to find
something to do. I need a purpose. Otherwise I'm going to completely
fail at this retirement thing and end up once again crying in bed, eating Nutella with my fingers.

———

"Whatcha doing?" Nina calls me a few days later.

"I'm in a fitting room trying on dresses for the party."

"Ah yes. Item number seventy-six on your to-do list," she says.

"Don't make fun of my list. It is the only way to avoid forgetting
something."

"You've done it all, Millie. There is nothing left for me to do."

"That's . . . not . . . true . . ." I think hard about what is left on
the list. "Oh, I know. The bartender asked what kinds of vodka and
whiskey are preferred. Why don't you make that decision? His number
is on—"

"The Excel worksheet. Yeah, yeah, I know."

"I like Belvedere, but really, I'm good with whatever you think—"

"Oh my God, Amelia. You are a control freak!" she says. "I'm hanging up, and I'm booking mariachis and telling the bartender Smirnoff and bourbon!"

"Don't you dare!" But the line's already dead. The thought of five mariachis singing loudly to me while everyone watches is giving me hives. She's obviously kidding. She has to be, right?

———

It turns out things could always be worse.

Exhibit A: I look around the empty room for my sister. I'm looking for her because once I find her, I'm going to kill her.

"You can't kill Nina," my mother says, reading my thoughts. "Your dress was too expensive, and blood is too hard to get out of silk."

"What a disaster," I admit to her. "I'm sorry you and Dad drove all the way here for this."

"Don't be sorry, honey. It's only a two-hour drive. Besides, you're our daughter and this is a special day. A milestone birthday. You only turn forty once."

Ugh . . . "You're not helping, Mom."

We look around the room: black and gold balloons fluttering about, clear square vases filled with water and a haphazard (but very carefully arranged) bunch of red roses in the center of every high-top table, dozens of lit votives. The room is dimmed to add to the elegant ambience, and soft music plays in the background.

"I have something that'll put a smile on your face," Mom says and then turns and grabs a box from the table and hands it to me. "I bought you something I think you're going to love. You're so hard to shop for, but I thought this would be fun. We can do it right now if you want!"

I furrow my brows. "Like a puzzle or something?" She's actually piqued my curiosity. And, at this point, a puzzle is just what this party needs.

"Not quite. Open it."

I place my glass down on the table and rip open the pretty wrapping and take a look at the box. "23andMe? Is this one of those mail-in genealogy things?"

"Yes!" She practically hops in excitement. "Your father and I already sent ours in, and we're waiting for our results." She doesn't stop there. She starts opening the box and then takes out a test tube. Is this really happening at my party? "Aren't you curious about your dad? I certainly am, even if he isn't." My father was adopted, so we know nothing about his biological side of the family. Every time we've brought it up, he just shrugs it off. We didn't even know that Nana wasn't Dad's biological mother until I was in my teen years. It wasn't meant to be a big secret; it just "never came up" according to Dad. I'd be lying if I said I wasn't curious.

I used to wonder about it, but he always seemed uncomfortable discussing it—he said that as far as he was concerned, Nana and Bill were his parents. Years after they passed away, I asked him more questions, but all I got from him was that Nana and Grandpa Bill, who couldn't have children, took him home straight from a hospital in Miami. He doesn't know more than that, nor does he seem to care to find out. "All you have to do is spit into this," Mom says. And she holds a tube up to my lips.

"Mom!" I shriek incredulously. "While this is . . . interesting, I'll take it home and do it some other time."

"No. You'll toss it in a corner. Eventually you'll start researching and overthinking it. Then you'll call me and lecture us on giving the government our DNA. Spit, Amelia," she says with firmness.

I look around the empty room. Maybe it's a good thing no one came because here I am, in my party dress, spitting (a.k.a. an unrefined dribble down my chin) into a tube, which my mom then carefully repacks into a box that I assume she'll take back home with her. "You do see how strange this all is, right?" I ask.

She waves me off. "I can't wait to get the results. It's also a great little project. You get updates, you know? I'll make sure you're all signed up. Check your emails."

"Uh . . . thank you, Mom." I'm not sure about this quirky gift, but it's right up my mom's gift-giving alley. Three years ago, she gave my sister and me sets of fine china for Christmas. Nina gave me her set, and both are in my storage closet collecting dust until the day the queen comes to visit and we can take them out and use them properly. One birthday, about seven years ago, my mom set me up with a farming co-op, and I received fresh fruits and vegetables on my doorstep weekly for an entire year. I had kale and fresh eggs coming out of my ears and felt guilty every evening when I came home too late to make something with all the parsnips. The rest of my neighbors, however, were very grateful once I started to give it all away.

So yeah . . . genetic testing sounds about right.

She finishes repackaging the box, and we both look around the room. "The party really did come out beautiful, dear."

"It really did," I lament. The guest list had had about fifty-five carefully curated people on it, and two hours into this little disaster (a.k.a. my big fortieth birthday party), there are my mom and dad, my sister, and me . . . so four people. Even Kevin failed to make an appearance. Allegedly he had to work, which I know for a fact is bullshit.

I'm never taking Nina's advice again.

I should have listened to my instincts and nixed this crazy idea. I need to take those rose-colored glasses off my sister's glass-half-full face.

"Well, at least that server is enjoying the canapes," my mom says as if she knows exactly what I'm thinking and is trying to defuse my murderous thoughts.

My mom and sister are both optimists. My dad and I are realists. And this is a *real* crappy birthday party.

I turn and see a man dressed in a black suit similar to that of the servers holding a champagne flute in one hand and reaching for a canape with the other. He shoves it into his mouth in a most unrefined way.

"We're going to head to the hotel, honey. Your dad is complaining about heartburn." She kisses my cheek, looking sad on my behalf, and brings me in for a hug. We're not the kind of family that hugs a lot. It feels awkward, but I squeeze her back.

"Love you, Millie. Don't worry about this. I bet the invitations got lost in the mail."

They were e-vites, but I don't correct her. Instead I say, "Yes. Probably."

My parents leave, and after I see Nina on a heated cell phone call with her boyfriend (probably about not attending the party), I decide to address the intruder eating all my food and drinking my alcohol. I put my empty glass down and march toward this trespasser.

"Excuse me. Those are for my guests."

"Well, lucky me. I'm a guest," he says, and swallows another canape whole.

"You are not a guest because I've never met you and I would know who *I* invited to *my* party."

He has the decency to use a napkin to clean his sticky hands and wipe crumbs from his face. When he finally swallows, he extends his hand. "Oh, finally. I get to meet the great Amelia Montgomery."

I hesitate before extending my own hand to his. "And you are?"

"Sorry. Sorry. John Ellis. I'm the new associate at JJF. Margret forwarded the invite to me, and I thought everyone from the office would be here."

Yeah, so did I.

"Margret shouldn't have sent you the invitation. I don't even know you."

"Well, that's easily fixed," he says, and I notice a dimple on his right cheek. Dimples are a weakness of mine, but I ignore it and continue to glare at the intruder. His salt-and-pepper hair is combed neatly back, his suit immaculate and fitted perfectly. This is a man who's used to wearing fine clothes, notwithstanding his dreadful eating habits. "If you stopped shooting daggers at me, I'd love to buy you a drink. Come on, have a seat."

That earns him a smile. Not because of the drink, but because I like people who say what they're thinking. Beating around the bush is not my style. With my arms crossed over my chest and a hip leaning against the bar, I say, "I'm paying for the open bar, so that's not exactly a worthwhile invitation."

"Since you already paid for them, may as well enjoy one with me." He looks around at the pitiful room. "Unless, of course, you have a more pressing invitation."

This stranger is teasing me about my guestless party. I don't know whether to laugh or cry.

I pull out the chair next to him and sit. Why not? There's no one else here anyway.

"What can I get you to drink?" he asks.

"I can get it myself." I signal for the bartender and ask for champagne.

"I wonder why there are so many no-shows. You're so pleasant."

I exhale loudly and slump forward. "Sorry," I murmur. Damn. I'm being a bitter cow, aren't I? This man is not the cause of my anger. In fact, he is the only person who bothered showing up. I should actually thank him. He orders a gin and tonic, and this time I don't question him since he may as well enjoy it. Someone should.

When the drinks arrive, he holds up his glass. "To Amelia Montgomery. A woman who throws one helluva party." I reluctantly chuckle as I clink my glass against his. It's the first time I've smiled all evening. "You have quite the reputation, Amelia." I open my mouth to say something, but he adds, "Professionally speaking. Not when it comes to party planning."

I smile again. This man is funny. Or perhaps it's all the alcohol I've consumed thus far.

"I'm obviously not very popular," I admit.

"Obviously." He smiles and then sits back casually, his leg crossed in that way that men cross their legs, ankle to knee, his baby blue polka dot dress socks peeking out. "It's weird that no one says you're beautiful. That should really be the first thing out of people's mouths when they describe you." It's a subtle way of telling me that people *do* in fact talk about me, but his segue is pretty effective.

I tilt a brow up. "You're already getting free drinks and food, Mr. Ellis."

"John," he quickly corrects.

"You're already getting free drinks and food, *John*. No need to butter me up."

"I'm not buttering you up. I'm just stating the truth. You're beautiful, you've earned the respect of your colleagues, and you have opposing counsel pissing themselves. If you had a full house tonight, you'd be too perfect, and who wants perfection?"

I don't even bother sipping my champagne. I down the rest of my glass in a gulp. I'm not sure how to respond. He's actually left me a little flustered.

"And you? What's your story?" I fumble out. "Do you make it a habit of crashing parties?"

"Only every first Saturday of the month. That's when you get the best booze." He winks and I chuckle. "Nothing to tell, really. I just moved here from Portland."

"Wife? Kids?" I'm forty. May as well get right to the important questions. No need to waffle.

"Ex-wife and no kids. You?"

"Never married and no kids either. Life of an attorney, I guess."

"Nah . . . not all attorneys, just the successful ones," he says.

"Perhaps." I think of my failed relationships. "I'll admit, not many men can handle a successful, assertive woman."

"Ahhh . . . so you've had a broken heart."

"I wish," I say. "It's more like a lot of wasted time." Marcus Worthington, my ex-fiancé, the biggest waste of them all.

"Ahh . . . so you've sworn off dating because of a few insecure men?" He smiles. "I'm not insecure, just in case you were wondering."

"I wasn't wondering." I move in closer. "I find that most men wouldn't admit that they're insecure, which, by definition, makes them insecure." Damn. The way he speaks, he is practically Marcus Worthington 2.0. I need to steer very clear of this handsome man.

"I have many faults, but feeling threatened by a strong woman isn't one of them. In fact   ." He smirks. "That's the only type of woman I'd want to be with. Who wants boring?" Now he leans closer, as if he's trying to figure something out. "And you are definitely not boring. Two months after being named the top litigator in the state by *Lawyers Weekly* you just walk away from the top civil firm in all of Illinois. The job most attorneys would give their right arm for. I'm definitely intrigued."

I swallow. I don't like how that sounds, so I don't answer, even if he isn't really posing a question anyway. Instead, I wave the bartender over for another drink.

"Margret used the term *retired*, but Junior said you quit."

I almost bleed from biting my lip so hard. I wonder what else Junior said. He's treading dangerously close to violating the NDA.

"Which is it?" he asks. "Retired or quit?"

"What's with the interrogation? This isn't a courtroom. Retired, quit, fired . . . all of it has the same end result, right?"

"Just trying to figure you out. I've heard about you. You don't seem like the kind of person that would just walk away."

"Well, you don't really know me, John. I'm pretty close to walking away right now."

He tilts his head back and laughs heartily. The deep, rumbly sound makes me laugh with him.

"No, please stay. I'm enjoying your company," he says with a flirty wink as he, too, orders another drink. This witty, intelligent man is making an unbearable evening bearable. I'm glad this stranger is here.

———

"So let me get this straight." We've been chatting now for about an hour and a half. Nina left a while ago to deal with her boyfriend. She apologized a dozen times before giving me a big hug and walking out while yelling into her cell phone at Kevin. "You're a new attorney at JJF, and you were forwarded my e-vite, and even though you don't know me, you decided to come to my party?" I'm repeating what he told me earlier like I would when cross-examining a witness who is clearly lying to me. It's a good tactic to get the witness and the jury to hear the absurdity of the lie.

I ask the bartender for a glass of pinot. I've had enough champagne. It's time to change things up. This party is costing me a small fortune, and I'm going to drink the alcohol I paid for. All of it. All the fifty-five people's worth of alcohol. Liver failure doesn't seem all that bad at this point in the evening. Or rather, at this point in my life.

"You invited the entire office. I thought I'd be welcome. But I also thought the entire office would be here." He shrugs and takes the glass of wine from my hand.

"W-what are you doing?" I pull my arm back, and some of the liquid dribbles over the rim of the glass and onto my fingers. "There's plenty of alcohol. You don't have to take mine. I already told you you could stay and shove as many canapes into your mouth as you want," I say.

He smiles. "I think you should have some water between drinks."

"Oh . . . You think because you're a penis owner, you've got the right to tell me what to do. Well, John, I am a grown woman. I don't need you or anyone telling me when I need water," I say indignantly.

"Penis owner?" He laughs. "You are too much, Amelia. I'm a nice guy, and it's not a gender thing. It's an 'I think you may regret it in the morning' thing."

"Well . . . whatever. It's the principle of the matter." I'm tired of men trying to tell me what to do.

"Isn't that the story of our life?" He taps the rim of my glass with his, as if he's toasting his own cleverness. "All our cases begin the same way. I'll pay an attorney $30,000 in fees to divorce my wife because she cheated on me, and dragging her to court and having her stoned on the stand is what I need to do because . . . it's the principle of the matter. Then I end up with a crappy apartment and a seven-year-old sickly bulldog."

"Ohhhh," I whisper, dragging it out slowly. "You're a bitter divorcé. Ouch. What's the name of the bulldog?"

He laughs. "It was just an example. Not my story."

"Sounded quite detailed for just an example."

"It really wasn't an anecdote of my life. As an attorney, how many cases did you think could have been avoided by coming to terms with the fact that it's just not worth it? Letting shit go is more cost-effective than fighting for one's principles sometimes."

I wince. "I believe in principles."

"Yes. Of course. But our clients . . . it's usually a business dealing that's gone wrong. Not all battles need to be fought."

"You picked the wrong career path, my friend." I take my glass back from his hand and finish *my* pinot. Another full glass awaits, but beside it is also a glass of water. I drink some of the water before diving into the next glass of wine. "I mean, fighting is what we do. It's what we studied. It's in our DNA. You do know that JJF is a trial firm, right?"

He laughs that hearty laugh, and I see the crinkles around his eyes. He must be in his early forties. "I love a good fight. But I've fought enough to know that sometimes it's just not worth it."

"Yeah, yeah, yeah. Tell me about the dog. How sickly is it?"

"It really wasn't my story. I don't have a dog and I didn't fight my ex. In fact, we're friends."

"So, what happened? What went wrong?"

"She cheated on me."

"Ohhhhh." I scrunch my nose. I hadn't expected such a genuine response. "How could you possibly be friends?"

"It wasn't easy. After a lot of bitterness and anger, one day I just woke up tired of it, and we talked."

"She must've groveled."

"Not at all. I actually apologized to her."

My eyes open wide. "I'm gonna need more information."

"Here's the CliffsNotes version. I met my ex in high school. We married young, and by the time I was twenty-five, we were divorced. I was bitter and angry for many years. How could she betray me that way? I just couldn't wrap my head around it. Then one day I realized that my ex had actually done me a favor. Who wants to be in an unhappy marriage? I was still young enough to move on, and so was she. We talked and I ended up apologizing. I have to tell you,

Amelia. It's the most liberating thing I've ever done. She's one of my best friends."

"Wow," I say, because . . . wow. He is nothing like Marcus, and he's not the insecure alpha male I'm used to dealing with. But it may be too soon to tell, since I did just meet him. "You're a better person than I am."

He shrugs and smiles. "What can I say? Life has a funny way of flipping you on your ass sometimes." That one dimple in his right cheek is really deep and quite sexy. I've never seen a dimple that high on a cheek. They're normally closer to the corner of the lips. And his eyes are green, but not green like mine are green. Green like the bottle of Tanqueray that the bartender is holding in his hand. John's taken off his suit jacket and has rolled up his black shirt cuffs. I stare at his forearms. I've always been a lover of forearms. His are brawny enough to indicate there is some muscle underneath that lean-looking physique. Hmmm?

"Pardon?" he says with a smirk.

I look up, the wine sloshing over the rim again. "Pardon what?" Did I say something?

"I thought . . . no. Never mind. I just thought you purred."

Shit. I did, didn't I?

I laugh way too loud. "No. No. It's just . . . you're actually quite attractive."

"Why, thank you. I should tell you you're beautiful again, but I've already said that, and I don't want you to think that I'm desperate."

"But you have to say something nice to me now. It's the proper thing to do. Especially since I've had an epically bad day. You are, after all, the only guest at my birthday party, which I organized and paid for. And, ironically, you weren't even one of the fifty-five invited."

"You are something else, Amelia Montgomery."

He slides another glass of water to me as soon as it's placed on the bar. I think he is in cahoots with the bartender to bring me water between drinks. Without arguing, I down the glass and wipe my lips with the back of my hand.

"What are people going to say when they hear you had drinks with the She-Demon?"

He frowns. "She-Demon?"

I roll my eyes. "Oh please. It's the worst-kept secret in the office."

"I can honestly say I have not heard anyone call you that before."

"Well, you will. But in my defense, it's not my fault that I can't find a decent assistant or secretary. Fisher has gone through more staff than I have, just so you know. I bet they don't call him She-Demon for firing so many people."

I bet he's picturing Fisher, too, a short, rail-thin man with thick glasses and unruly gray hair. "I'm sure they don't." He laughs some more. "You never did tell me why you left the firm. Was it because of that interoffice pettiness and name-calling?"

I lean back and run my finger around and around the rim of my wineglass contemplatively. "Do you really think I'd leave the firm because of a few catty people?"

"No, I don't. So, what was it?"

I shrug. "I retired. It was time." I hate lying to him. I hate lying to everyone. But I'm sticking to the retirement story since it's partially true and the most I can disclose. I wish I could tell him all about Junior. I wonder what he'd think. Would he say I acted rashly, that I failed at my job by not defending Phoebe? Maybe he'd think I was a badass and get all the employees to join me in standing up to Phoebe and the three partners.

Or maybe I've drunk too much and I'm acting crazy.

One of his brows shoots up and he looks at me with a knowing smirk. He's about to call me out, but instead he says, "It was time? Really? At the ripe old age of . . ."—he looks around the room and sees two gold balloons in the shape of a number—"forty. A mere babe."

"Yep. And this party was supposed to be the beginning. A way to get people acquainted with Millie the person, not Amelia Montgomery the attorney. But now that they've all stood me up . . . screw 'em all."

"Very mature stance on your part."

"I don't need them to show up, drink my alcohol, and eat my food. They're not worth it. I don't care about them." My voice grows a little louder. "I lost my way for a moment is all. I let my guard down for one stupid party and *I'm* the one swimming in a pool of regret? I don't even recognize myself. No. It ends here." I punctuate the last word with my palm against the countertop of the bar. *Ouch.*

"Are we still talking about the party?"

I wave him off. "The point is . . . I'm not letting some idiots ruin my special day."

"For what it's worth, I don't find you to be a She-Demon whatsoever."

"Clearly you're a terrible judge of character." Because I know I am that and a bitch and not in the pejorative way that women are referred to, but in the mean and petty way that makes me sad. When did I become mean and standoffish? I wasn't always like this. I started off wanting to conquer the world. I wanted to be a great litigator. I wanted to be respected by my peers, and I wanted to be successful. Somehow that translated to bitchdom.

He chuckles.

I lean closer, my elbow on the bar and my chin on my palm. "So, tell me, John. How can I fix this? Maybe you are exactly what I need. A stranger's perspective."

"Not that you care, though."

"Right. But if, let's say, hypothetically, I wanted to fix this, what should I do? I wanted friends, a great big party with lots of people. You know, I was even planning to apologize to some of these people. Apologize! Can you imagine?" I guffaw. "I was weak. Got a little sentimental and now I'm over it. I don't need to apologize for being good at my job."

"No. You absolutely don't."

"You're good at your job, right? Do you have a lot of friends? I bet you do. You're a nice guy, I can tell. When I was an intern, I used to bring the other interns coffee and chat about the trials after work. I was liked. I was probably just as nice as you are."

"I'm not that nice. In fact, the Portland superintendent of schools would say I'm the opposite of nice."

"Superintendent? Portland?" I snap my fingers while I think. "I read an article recently about an attorney who went head-to-head with the school board for something about desks. Was that you?"

"It *was* in Portland, but it was about chairs, not desks. My client's son broke his arm in the middle of algebra when his cheap plastic chair broke. We uncovered that, in the district, some of the funds for the school were being misappropriated. It was a big scandal, and more importantly, I won," he says with an arrogance only an attorney who had uncovered a money-laundering ring inside a school board could pull off.

"That was a great argument. I read some of the clips of the cross-examination while researching case law for a file. It was skilled lawyering. And you were brutal in your cross-examinations. I think I remember reading that the superintendent cried at one point." When I had read that case, Brenda had come to mind. She was a friend of mine from law school who wasn't in it for the money, but to help the less fortunate. This is the exact kind of case she would have loved.

"Thank you." He grins and I chuckle. That's the difference between us. He's a pit bull in the courtroom and a well-adjusted, regular guy in the real world, as far as I can tell, at least. I, on the other hand, am known as a bitch both in the courtroom and out. I don't say any of this, though. Not because he continues to speak, but because I want to go home and fixate on that. Why do I have to be my work? Why am I defined by that?

Or maybe it's all the drinks making me philosophical.

"*Roland v. McAllister,*" he says. "I just read some of the depos, since I was assigned to close up some of your cases at the firm. I have to say, I would not have had Roland testify. Bold move, Millie."

"But it paid off. I made the firm $1.3 million in legal fees with that case."

"And yet you walked away."

I hate that he keeps saying that. "Retired," I correct him.

"Oh yes, retired. Of course, excuse me."

I wish I could tell him that I would never just walk away. I would never "retire" unless it was on my terms. I don't quit on anything. But I had no choice, and now I can't even defend myself since I can't discuss it.

"I'm unpredictable that way." I swat him and go to take a step away, but he grabs me by the wrist so quickly it catches me off guard. Then in one swift movement he pulls me against him. I mean, *against him*. His entire chest is pressed against mine as I'm tucked between his thighs.

"Unpredictable and sexy as hell," he says in a whisper against my neck. My body erupts into goose bumps.

For a moment, I'm intrigued and possibly a bit . . . hot. Is it hot in here? I can feel my cheeks blaze. It's his nearness and sexy words. He's so close that I can smell the gin on his lips, and I can feel the small splay of hair on his arms against my forearm. I'm heady with alcohol and John and what were we talking about . . .

"Millie?" At his whisper, I realize I've been staring at his lips.

"Uh . . . what?"

He grins and signals for another drink at the same time as I lift my glass of wine and the entire thing comes tumbling down on my white silk dress.

"Shit!" I shriek. "My dress!"

"Um . . ." He looks down at my chest and then up at me. "It's a little see-through."

I look down at my chest and then quickly cover my breasts with my hands. "Crap. Shit. Damn."

He reaches behind me. He is so close his breath tickles my neck. I wonder if he feels the same heat I do. Is he going to kiss me? I close my eyes in preparation for the kiss. But it turns out his jacket is on the back of my chair, which he pulls off and then helps me into. *Damn* . . . I feel my cheeks flame red.

"I live very close by," he says. "I'm sure we can do something about the dress before, you know . . . it gets wetter."

At the moment, I couldn't care less about his lack of creativity in the innuendo department or my dress casualty. I just want him to kiss me. "Perfect. Let's go." I grab my purse and my cake, which they packed up for me to take. I sign the final credit card slip for my failed party and follow him out of the restaurant.

CHAPTER FIVE

My tongue is thick and dry, and my head feels like there is a drum line rehearsing where my brain should be. I try to open my eyes, but something is holding my eyelids shut.

What the hell?

Memories of bad decisions start flooding in almost immediately.

Champagne. Champagne. Champagne.

Wine. Wine. Wine.

Maybe a little water.

More wine.

Perfect white teeth and a dimple on the right side. *A server? No, not a server—a man.* A very attractive and very arrogant man.

More wine.

My body aches in a hangover kind of way, but also in a deliciously satisfying kind of way, mostly between my legs.

I shoot up into a sitting position and moan as my brain tries to come out of my skull with the motion. I rub my eyes and find a pair of false eyelashes sticking together, which is why I can't open my eyes. *Ouch,* I think as I pull them off and toss them aside.

Before I turn my head, I extend my arm to feel around for another body. Luckily, the bed seems empty. But I also realize it's not my bed without having to look. My lovely pillow-top mattress and five-thousand-thread-count sheets are missing. I open my eyes—one and then the next—bracing myself for what I'll see. But just like I suspected, it's empty. Unfortunately, I know it wasn't empty earlier, and even more unfortunate is that I know exactly who's been there . . . not just there beside me on the bed, but inside me. I cringe.

Regrets, awkwardness, alcohol. Exactly how a one-night stand is supposed to be.

I just never thought I'd be the one experiencing it. I'm much too old for a drunken one-night stand.

Carefully, I lift the gray comforter away from my body to check and . . . yep, I'm naked. I've never done something like this before. All my lovers have been boyfriends that I've carefully vetted. I'm no prude, but I'm also not one to sleep with a complete stranger. One-night stands with strangers aren't usually planned, and I'm a planner.

My panties and bra rest on the lamp on the other side of the bed, and there's one pair of men's shoes by the window, but my dress is not in sight. I remember sleeping (not the sex kind, the "closing your eyes and snoring" kind) with him, but I don't remember much of the rest. *How much did I drink?* God, I hope we used a condom. A lifetime of constantly using disinfectant spray and antibacterial lotion, and I let a stranger put his germy penis in my very clean vagina. Who knows where it's been? I shudder at the thought.

Without lifting the covers, I clumsily roll to the side and pull my undergarments away from the lamp, almost tipping the lamp in the process. I slide them on, still hiding underneath the comforter. It's not much, but at least I'm not buck naked. I quietly and gently lift the covers from my body; one foot and then the other gently hits the floor, and I tiptoe around the room trying to locate the rest of my clothes.

I see only one of my shoes and a pair of polka-dotted men's socks. I look under the bed. Nothing.

"Shit shit shit," I whisper. I stand upright and look around the large room. There's a modern, black, leather-and-metal chair overlooking a large floor-to-ceiling window. Oh God . . . that chair. I remember we had sex on that chair. "Oh . . . ," I groan, feeling the heat on my face as I remember how I sounded last night.

Argh. *Focus, Millie. It was sex, it happened. Happy birthday to me.* Now I need to focus on finding my clothes and getting the heck out of here. I can't even fathom what I'd say in the harsh light of day to my one-night stand.

By the foot of the bed, there's a flat sheet, the kind that's supposed to go above the fitted sheet but instead normally gets tossed into the linen closet and never used. Nina and I have had major debates about this in the past. I'm a flat-sheet kind of person. If it's too hot in the room, the flat sheet gives the perfect amount of coverage, and if it's too cold, you just add the comforter. Nina disagrees. She says it's useless. Nina says normal people keep the fitted sheets and the pillowcases and toss away the flat sheets. What kind of uncivilized heathen just tosses away a flat sheet?

Not me and not this man. This man, being a mature, responsible adult, also seems to be a flat-sheet kind of person. That tidbit of information makes me somewhat relieved. I didn't sleep with a complete degenerate. Ignoring the feeling, I grab the sheet from the floor and use it to cover the (sex) chair. I don't need that kind of judgment staring back at me while I search for my things.

Unfortunately, there is no sign of my clothes anywhere in the room. Aside from the other clothes strewn throughout, the room is neat and very masculine. The modern wooden armoire matches the bed and nightstands. There's some abstract art on the wall, and there's a charging station with the cables neatly hidden. The dark gray carpet feels plush underneath my feet, and the room smells faintly of men's cologne.

There are two doors in the bedroom. One obviously leads to the rest of the house and the other to the bathroom, I presume. I feel like Morpheus from *The Matrix* is asking me, "Red pill or blue pill?" Red pill, I have to face the truth and consequences. I slept with a stranger, and now I have to have a civil conversation and pretend he hasn't seen me naked.

Or I could take the blue pill, where I can hide out in the bathroom and pretend that last night never happened, regardless of whether it felt good or not. And the more that I think about it, the more I realize how good it felt.

Blue pill is my safe and secure dull life. It's the lane I've always traveled in.

Blue pill it is!

I pull the door open and lock myself in the bathroom.

I place both palms on the sink and loll my head forward, taking deep, soothing breaths. *Why am I being so ridiculous? There is a simple solution to this problem, Amelia Montgomery. Just find one of his T-shirts and gym shorts in a drawer, slide them on, and walk out of the room, head held high with the confidence of a woman who just had casual sex. Then you give—shit shit shit—what the hell was his name?* Oh God, when I mess up, I mess up big. *Anyway, names are irrelevant. You say, 'Thank you so much for a lovely evening,' ask him where the dress is, put it back on, find your phone, and request a Lyft to take you home. Easy. The entire process should take no more than ten, maybe fifteen, minutes. Then I can put this entire debacle, including the epic failure of a party, behind me. Great plan.*

I exhale and stand up straight to face the mirror. Except when I confidently lift my head, a crazy clown-person is staring back at me. My confidence melts into an internal shriek.

This is the thing about most women—whether we're four or forty, attorneys or teachers—we get a lot of our confidence from our looks. It's a sad reality, but a reality nonetheless. And after a man has seen you naked, no woman wants to look like a troll the next morning.

"Holy hell!" I silent-screech. I tamp it down quickly. My red lipstick is smeared all around my mouth and I have eyeliner and mascara dripping down my face, and . . . I lean in closer to the mirror. The other damn eyelash is now stuck to my cheek. I yank it off my skin and toss it in the little wastebasket by the toilet. In a panic, I try to find something to wash the makeup off my face. Water and soap aren't the ideal way of removing red lipstick or waterproof mascara, but it's the best I can do. I scrub and scrub until about two layers are gone and what's left is mostly a pink tinge of lipstick around my mouth.

My hair is next. It's all over the place, part of it sticking up. I take out some of the bobby pins that are still in my mane and gather it all in a ponytail and—crap—no ponytail holder. There's a black comb on the counter, so I use it to try and manage the poof, but alas, the only way of controlling my hair is with a shower and shampoo. It is what it is. There's nothing else I can do. I shouldn't care anyway; I'm never going to see this man again.

I look into the mirror one final time. God, how the mighty have fallen. There's mouthwash by the sink, so at least I won't kill him with my breath, I think as I gargle and spit it out. This is the best it's going to get.

I just can't walk out with a bra and panties. I mean, I'm pretty confident in fact, many people might call me arrogant—but even the arrogant need clothes. Power suits and high heels, and I can conquer the world. Put me in a bra and underwear and I'm a wimp. Hopefully, I can find a shirt and pair of shorts quickly and stick to my plan.

I open the door of the bathroom and yelp again. Well, it's less of a yelp and more of a "Motherfu—"

"Good morning to you, too, sunshine," he says with a big grin on his face.

I point a finger at him and blurt out, "John. Your name is John! I remember!"

"You'd forgotten my name? That's a first." He shakes his head side to side and gets more comfortable on the bed. He's just sitting there, a half-eaten bagel in his hand, chewing without a care in the world. "Bagel?" he asks, extending the half-eaten baked good toward me nonchalantly.

I'm leaning against the doorframe trying to look just as lackadaisical as he does, except, unlike him, I'm slightly hunched over trying to hide my seminakedness and I have my right hand over my heart because he scared me half to death. So, in actuality, instead of looking relaxed and cool, I look like a crazy person with a stomachache and heartburn.

"Uh . . . no, thank you?"

He tilts his head. "You okay? Why are you standing like that?"

I put my arms down and stand up straight. To hell with it. There's nothing I can do at this point but stand up straight and own this disaster. *It's not like he hasn't seen me naked.* Flashes of kissing and touching flood my mind, but I shake my head trying to get them out.

"Why'd you cover my chair with a sheet?" He uses his thumb to point over his shoulder.

I don't want to answer that, so I just shrug as if I have no clue what he's talking about.

"I don't remember you being this quiet last night," he says, and I wish I could remember as much as he does. "Especially when we were using that chair." And he winks. The sonofabitch winks. I narrow my eyes and he has the decency to change the subject. "Are you sure you're okay? You did drink a lot."

"So did you," I say defensively, hoping that I'm not making it up. I don't remember exactly how much he drank, but I do recall drinking at the bar with him. So I'm assuming he drank as much as I did.

"I did. I have a headache, but I also have a great hangover cure. I can go grab—"

I take a step forward to stop him, but as my hand is about to make contact with his, I pull it back. If I touch him and I like it, I may want to touch him again, and then things will escalate and before I know it I'll be left brokenhearted. It's been a tough few weeks. Why add more heartache to the pile? "No. No. That's okay. I'm okay. Where's my dress?"

He takes a huge bite of the bagel, too big. For a moment, I think he's going to choke, but he just chews. I tap my foot up and down as I wait. It takes him forever to finish chewing and finally swallow. And since I'm in his house mostly naked, all I can do is stand there and wait. I decide, at that moment, that I don't like him. He's too comfortable and too calm, and he doesn't care that I'm impatient to leave.

Seven years later, he stands up, brushes the crumbs off his gym shorts, and walks toward a chest of drawers. He opens the top drawer, grabs a T-shirt, and tosses it my way.

"This is not my white silk Chiara Boni La Petite Robe."

His brows furrow together. "I don't know what you just said."

"My dress. I was talking about my gorgeous dress. This is not it."

"Oh. Your dress was still wet, so I put it on a second cycle in the dryer."

"*Dryer!*"

"Yeah, that thing that dries clothes after they've been washed."

"*Washed!*" He eyes me with amusement as I take a step toward him and then another. "You put my Chiara Boni La Petite Robe silk dress into the washing machine?"

He grabs my finger, the one I'm using to poke him, and stills me. I'm standing half-naked, a T-shirt in one hand and his fist wrapped around the index finger of my other hand. *Am I being pranked? What has my life become?*

"No," he says and then uses his other finger to point at me. "*You* put *your* Chiara Boni whatever-the-hell in the washing machine last night."

"I would never do such a stupid thing!" I pull my finger away from his grip. "That was a very expensive designer dress."

"Except that you did. How do you think we ended up at my apartment?"

I plop down on the edge of the bed and try to remember the events that led to me being at John's house.

Crap!

I remember.

He wrapped his hand around mine and pulled me out of the restaurant while I followed close behind, barely registering that I was wearing his way too large and delicious-smelling jacket around the hustling, bustling Chicago night-life crowd. We walked silently around the corner and crossed two streets before we stopped in front of a swanky apartment building.

It was quite the walk home! I've never been more aware of my nerve endings. The slight brush of his thumbs against my collarbone when he helped me into his jacket, the way my wet dress clung against my heated skin, sending tingles through my body. And the anticipation. Anticipation can be a very sexy thing. The headiness of wondering what would happen when we were alone in his home. I'm sure that the fact that I hadn't had sex in a very, very long time or that I really, really liked his big hand enveloping mine or his witty banter and all the things we had in common made me even more hypersensitive. I don't know what it was that possessed me to take his face in my hands and plant a big, wet kiss right on his lips the moment his front door closed behind us.

It shocked us both, but he didn't let the surprise deter him. He stalked me the two steps back so that I was plastered against the wall as he pressed his body against mine, kissing me back until I was whimpering. I don't remember words being spoken, but I do remember feeling dizzy from his touch. I remember being lifted up and then wrapping my legs around his hips as if I'd done it a hundred times. As if I were preprogrammed to be held this way by this man. And I remember . . .

"Millie. Hello."

Damn it. I was having naughty thoughts about the man standing in front of me and the hot sex against the door.

"Uhh . . ." *Super eloquent, Millie.* "I spilled wine on my dress," I say, remembering how he asked me to lift my arms and then slid my dress over my head. *He tossed my clothes to the side and then went to the kitchen, his button-down shirt untucked and the top button of his pants undone, and brought me a big orange bottle of Gatorade. "Am I going for a jog? A naked marathon?" I asked, seriously dumbfounded.*

"You're not naked. You're wearing a bra and underwear. A rather sexy set," he said, watching me. "I think you need to hydrate. You drank a lot." He took a big gulp from another bottle. "I have to hydrate too." Then he signaled for me to drink. I smiled and sat on a stool at the counter in his kitchen. He leaned on the other side of the counter while we drank our sports drinks and sobered up and got to know each other a bit more.

At some point, I demanded to see his laundry room, where I proceeded to toss my very pricey designer dress into his washing machine, throw two or maybe even three detergent pods in it, and press start. I didn't even bother to put it on delicate or on a cold spin. Just the regular hot load. The one that shrinks all my T-shirts.

I gasp and cover my mouth with my hand.

"That's the look of recollection." He smirks.

"How could you let me do such a stupid thing?"

"Are we talking about the sex or the dress?"

"Mostly the dress." I can't seem to regret the spectacular sex, even if it's completely uncharacteristic of me.

"I don't know anything about laundry and dresses. Plus, I was just as drunk as you were by then. You could have said you were going to stick your entire body in the washing machine for a bath and I probably would have joined you."

"Then why do you look so fresh and all . . ." I point a finger toward him and wag it around. *Handsome* is the word that almost comes out of my mouth, but instead I say, "Smug. You're all smug while I sit here half-naked, thirsty, and with a headache. And how many times exactly did we have sex, anyway?" Shortly after the laundry room debacle, I recall kissing each other again, followed by sex in his room.

"You got a shirt in your hands, sweetheart. Don't get me wrong, I'm not complaining. You can stay half-naked or completely naked all day if you want. As for the sex, are you asking me how many times you came or how many times we actually had sex?"

I roll my eyes. "Cocky sonofabitch," I whisper. And then I remember the third time. On his bed, sometime in the middle of the night.

And it was sublime.

CHAPTER SIX

"I can do something about that headache and thirst," he says and reaches out to help me up. I look at his hand as if it's a grenade. I stand and walk around him. I don't need his hand; I can get up all by myself, thank you very much. I slide the shirt over my body and walk out of his room, looking for the kitchen.

"Yep. That's the woman I met yesterday," he says, but it's almost a whisper. I'm not sure what that's supposed to mean, but right now I don't care. I need water. That Gatorade from last night would be perfect right now. I also need an aspirin and pants or shorts or something so that I can grab a taxi and get the hell out of this nightmare without having my ass on full display. Speaking of my ass, I can feel his eyes on it as I walk out. I have a fairly small frame except for my butt. When I was younger, I didn't particularly like it. It's not proportional to my body, but there's not much I can do about it and I've grown to accept it. Right now, however, I'm inwardly smiling that John's a butt man.

"So about that water and aspirin?" I look at my wrist as if there's a watch, but there's no watch because I don't own one. I'm not even wearing my Fitbit. But that's not the point. The point is that I'm in a hurry to get out of here. "I have somewhere I need to be, so if you would be so kind as to maybe lend me some shorts to go with this T-shirt? I'll make sure to have it washed and returned as soon as I get home. I'll pay you for it, if you want."

Instead of answering, he walks around me into his open-concept kitchen, reaches into a drawer, and takes out a bottle of aspirin and hands it to me. Then he turns to his fancy refrigerator, which has a touch screen (for what I have no idea), and takes out a water bottle.

Why would you need your refrigerator to have a computer? Not my problem. Again, I need to focus on getting out of here.

I'm struggling to open the bottle of aspirin when warm hands brush against mine. He takes the bottle from my hand. With his thumb, he flips open the cap from the container, takes out two little pills, and hands them to me. Quickly I swallow them down and then look up expectantly. *Shorts, sweatpants, a damn kilt . . . anything to cover the lower half of my body will do,* I think as I wait for him to make a move.

"So, what exactly is it that you need to rush off to?" He's leaning across from me on the counter in that too-calm way that I'm starting to realize is his way of doing everything. It probably unnerves the hell out of opposing counsel. He's just too damned relaxed. I don't like it.

His elbows are on the granite countertop, and his chin is resting casually on his knuckles. There's some sort of smirk on his face that I can't read. Of course I can't read it; he's a stranger. Nevertheless, he's waiting for an answer, one that I don't have. But if I'm good at one thing, it's bending the truth. I am a lawyer after all. "I have some work to do."

"I'm calling bullshit on that. You are"—and he uses air quotes—"'retired.' Why don't you try that again?"

"Let's not pretend you know me, John. I can have other things pending that do not relate to JJF." Now I'm getting a little ticked off.

"You're unemployed. There is nothing else. You said as much last night," he says. Damn it. I guess I was chatty last night.

"My reason for leaving is not your concern. I just am. Last night was fun, I'll admit we made the best out of an awkward situation, but it's over and now it's the morning and I need to get home. I have a cat to feed." William has an automatic food and water dispenser since I worked long, irregular hours, so this isn't exactly true, but John doesn't know that.

He reaches into his pocket and takes out a crumpled napkin and slides it my way. My brows furrow. It's full of writing in blue ink and looks vaguely familiar. I bring it up to my face and squint as I see name after name after name on it. There must be a dozen names on there. Most but not all of them are names of people I know.

"How about this?" he says, motioning for the paper. "You made me promise to do this with you."

"Do what? What's this?" I turn the napkin over and see more names.

"Your 'I'm sorry. Can we be friends again?' list. Don't you remember? That's what's on the agenda for today."

"What?" My voice comes out high-pitched, but even as I say the words, I remember the conversation. Apparently alcohol, sex, and self-pity make me extremely talkative. I look up and I know that he knows that I'm remembering the conversation because those annoyingly beautiful teeth are gleaming, and if eyes could twinkle, his would be twinkling with amusement. Damn him. I try avoiding his gaze and his handsomeness and look down at the list in my hand again.

The list is written on a napkin, the light-blue flower painted on it a bit distorted from the heavy, blue ink that seeped onto the back of the paper. "Did you use a quill and inkwell?" I say, trying to make out the words.

He smirks and points to the pen on the kitchen counter. It's one of those inky pens that easily smear and leave the side of your pinkie finger full of smudges. It has the logo from Jones, Jones & Fisher on it.

"You stole a company pen? What will they say?" I ask and feign a shocked expression.

"Deflection isn't going to work with me."

I roll my eyes and look back at the list. There are misspellings, smudges, words crossed out, a few hearts, sad faces, stars, happy faces . . . It's a disaster, is what it is.

I'm so confused. I remember holding my fingers out and naming these people one by one.

"Your 'I'm Sorry' list. Remember? You want to apologize, make up, and be friends with all these people again."

Up to the sex part, I thought I remembered everything.

"I am one hundred percent certain that I really don't want to be friends with these people again." I didn't even invite the Jennys to the party, and they're not even part of our office. They weren't my friends to begin with.

"That's not what you said last night." He points to where I actually drew a heart.

"I remember the sex, and then after that, everything is just hazy." And I think I'm okay with leaving some of it out of my permanent memory bank.

"We both passed out. But while you were drinking, between wine and Gatorade, you were very informative. You talked about each and every person on that list."

I bring the list closer to my face. I turn the list around, and there are more names, but it's even harder to read because (*a*) his penmanship sucks, (*b*) the ink is seeping from one side to the other, and (*c*) he used the shittiest napkin to write on.

I read the names on the back out loud. "What's all this?" I point to a black blob.

"Oh, the boyfriends. There was a Marcus something or other, an Alex, I think . . . There were about four different men you said you scared off with your success."

"I did not say that!" My eyes widen in sheer horror as I remember saying exactly that. "Oh God . . ."

"But then you made sure to cross them out because you said you refused to apologize to stupid boys who were scared of assertive women. It was a real 'I am woman, hear me roar' moment."

"No. No. No." I cover my ears, and he takes the list from my hand and starts to read the names out loud in a high-pitched voice. I think he's trying to impersonate me, which just adds to my embarrassment. He's too amused by my humiliation.

"No more talking," I say. I take the list back and ignore the black blob and read through the legible names. "These people, the ones I invited, did not come to my party," I say with righteous indignation.

"Yes. But that's not what the list is about. It's about *why* they didn't come to the party and *how* you're going to make amends. That's why you threw the party after all."

"Amends? They need to apologize to *me*, not the other way around. And I didn't throw the party to make amends. I threw it to celebrate my birthday."

"That's not what you said last night."

"You can't hold me to what I said under the influence. I was going to apologize to them at the party in order to start fresh, and hopefully they'd want to get to know me. But that was before!"

"Before what?"

"Before they stood me up! Now they need to apologize!"

"Don't you remember sitting right on top of this very counter, eating cake, crying, and begging me to help you?"

"What?!" Now I really shriek. He opens his fridge and takes out the cake, which looks like it's been mauled by a bear. And damn . . . I do remember. I did cry. "I didn't beg," I clarify, which causes him to chuckle. "We brought the cake back here, and in the middle of the night, after all the sexing, we ate it. We didn't even get plates. Just picked at it with forks." I recall him laughing while I tried not to drop the cake as we walked to his apartment. At some point, he took it from me and carried it.

"Yep. And you ate it sitting on top of the counter because you kept saying something about Samantha and Jake and *Sixteen Candles*," he reminds me, and I cringe, my hand going straight to cover my face. It was my birthday, and I got nostalgic and sloppy. Leave it to me to get drunk and embarrass myself by paying homage to my favorite childhood movie after having sex with a man I just met while having some sort of existential crisis and documenting it with a list. "Please stop talking."

He laughs loudly. "I don't think they had so much wine in the movie, and I'm fairly certain her ass wasn't bare on Jake's table."

"Oh no, no, no. Kill me now."

He hands me a fork and slides the cake over. "Don't be shy now. You were adorable last night." I want to dig a hole and bury myself in it, but instead I take a huge bite of my delicious raspberry and chocolate cake. He takes a fork and joins me. We're leaning against his counter eating cake for breakfast while I try and forget my horrible, embarrassing display of ridiculousness last night.

"So about the other thing," he says.

"There's more? I guess nothing you can tell me at this point would surprise me."

"The crying. You cried a lot. And that's what propelled that list."

"You're still talking," I say and shove cake into his mouth with my fork. He swallows it with a hearty laugh. "I had a bad night, and the alcohol made me weepy. There's no way in hell that I'm going to go through with that list. It's absolutely absurd."

He places his fork down, and in a somber tone he says, "It's shitty that you were stood up by everyone, and I'm sorry that it happened to you. No one deserves that."

The empathy he's showing me warms my heart, and my eyes water again. What is happening to me? In the weeks following my "retirement" I've cried more than I have in the last decade. All these feels are foreign to me, and it makes me uncomfortable, especially around this virtual stranger. "At work, I'm the She-Demon, but it's my job, you know? I can't just walk around being Suzy Sunshine when someone is paying me a fortune to help them. I have to do my job, and that sometimes means I have to be assertive. I was going to try and show them that I'm not like that outside of work, but they didn't even bother showing up. I can celebrate my next forty birthdays with Nina and William."

His brows furrow, so I explain, "My sister and my cat."

"Good times," he says.

"Better than the epic fail of last night." I grab a napkin and wipe cake off his chin. "Thank you for being sweet. What happened yesterday . . ."—I shake my head from side to side—"I'm glad I wasn't alone. But I think I'm on humiliation overload."

"You're welcome, Millie. I'm glad I was able to spend that night with you." He smiles and then reaches across the counter and squeezes my hand. I try to ignore that stupid list on the napkin that's just lying in the middle of the counter.

I remember thinking it would be a fantastic idea if I apologized to all these people. But . . .

"I don't even know what I would apologize for," I say, as if we were midsentence. "Most of it was petty. If they're that mad about something that stupid, then screw them."

He holds his hands up defensively. "Hey, it's not my list. You don't need to explain it to me. But it might make you feel better."

"Nothing done under the influence of that much wine can be a good idea," I add, grabbing the list and looking at it again.

"In vino veritas."

Oh, wow. Okay, that *was* sexy. I'm sure I found him attractive last night, too, but now in the light of day (and sobriety), the man is not classically handsome. He has a crooked nose and his hair is more gray than black and he's wearing black-framed glasses. There are wrinkles around his eyes and a lot of morning stubble on his cheeks. He's also wide—not overweight, but strong, like someone who spent a lot of time in the gym at some point in his life. Or maybe like he played some sort of sport, something I never found attractive. I always preferred men who were slim and tall. John's not exceptionally tall, although he's taller than me. Regardless, the way his tongue rolled with the *v* in *vino* and then again in *veritas* is sexy. That's the perfect word to describe him: *sexy*. Not handsome, necessarily, but sexy.

"That's the same look you got yesterday when you pounced on me."

"Pounced? On you?"

"You kissed me first. I'm not complaining, don't get me wrong, but I was trying to be a gentleman. So, are you going to pounce again? I'm game if you are." He smiles.

"As enticing as that sounds"—it actually does sound enticing—"I'm trying to figure out how to get out of here."

"That's a shame. I was looking forward to watching you attempt those apologies."

"You sound amused. As if you think it's going to be a disaster."

"Didn't say that. I was looking forward to watching the great Amelia Montgomery work her courtroom charm on a bunch of angry people."

"That's pretty sadistic."

He chuckles, and that dimple, less pronounced this morning from his stubble, winks at me. "Do I still get a copy of your client notes? You promised me that if I went with you this morning as support, you'd give me notes on your clients so that I can win them over. They're not happy that you're out of the firm, and it would help a lot if I knew what it would take to win them over."

"I have zero interest in helping JJF win over my clients." I can't poach them, but that doesn't mean I have to butter them up so that they stay with my ex-partners.

"It wouldn't be for Jones, Jones, or Fisher. It would be for me. I'm new to the firm and to Chicago, and I'm still trying to build my local client list. You'd be helping me out."

I narrow my eyes.

"We discussed this, remember?"

"Obviously not. I can't believe I would agree to help JJF by proxy. You do know that they've been taking on some shady cases lately." I can't divulge too much because of the NDA, but I want to warn him against taking on the Phoebe case.

"I wouldn't take on any cases that I'd find unethical or questionable, but I do believe that everyone has the right to their day in court."

"Hmph," I say, unsure whether I should trust him.

"I think we should avoid shop talk for now."

"Fine with me. It's your conscience, not mine."

"So, are you going to go through with the apologies or not?"

"I don't see where I'm getting anything out of this deal."

"Are you kidding me? With my help, your forty-first birthday will be a hit. Nina and William plus all of these." He waves the list around. "Your nearest and dearest and their significant others."

"I think this is my last party for the foreseeable future." Although a year with no friends and nothing to do does sound exceptionally boring.

"All kidding aside, Millie, I don't know you that well yet, but what I do know, I like. You don't seem like someone who lets her guard down often, but last night, you did. You were pretty shaken up, and my day's free. I really don't mind helping you."

"Because you want my help with your client list."

He shrugs. "Because I'd like to spend the day with you. Your help would be appreciated, but I'm bringing major clients to the firm from Portland. I'm pretty sure I can schmooze my way into meeting new clients, too, if I have to."

This man is going to make partner soon. He is not just a lowly associate. He is a known litigator with his own clients and a sharp tongue. It would have been fun to go against him in court.

He's making me a very interesting proposition. Instead of getting angrier at people who hurt me by standing me up, I would apologize. I look at the list. There are a few people on it that meant a lot to me at some point, and my heart does ache to reconnect with several old friends. There are others to whom I was a jerk and should apologize now that I have a little more perspective. And there are others who don't deserve anything from me. I don't know why I keep talking to John as if I've known him for years, but I think his sincerity makes me vulnerable. Or maybe it's the hangover. Nevertheless, I open my big mouth and say, "When I was in my twenties and early thirties I used to be more careful of people's feelings. I didn't want to make anyone uncomfortable, and I'd tiptoe around anything that would hurt anyone's feelings. But as I became successful and realized that no one was tiptoeing around my feelings, I hardened. John, it's not that I want to be mean, it's just that I am."

"You don't seem mean to me." I let out a long breath, and he continues. "Let me see if I understand," he says and points to the list. "One of these office jerks spills coffee on a final order that I need to give to opposing counsel to sign by five in the afternoon. I now have to explain to my client, who's already spent over $500,000 in legal fees, that he will have to wait an additional day for the judgment to be signed and for the case to be closed because my secretary, a.k.a. office jerk, spilled coffee on it? What would you do, Millie?"

"I can assure you, there would be cursing and yelling because I'd have to take the brunt of that blame, not to mention the yelling and cursing I'd get from the partners at the firm because ultimately it's my case and the person who spilled the coffee doesn't matter. I'm the one who's screwed in that scenario."

"And in your head that makes you a She-Demon?"

"No! That makes me the boss. The person responsible for the case. But I could have said things a bit less harshly. In your example, that is . . . and in my day-to-day interactions. I could have skipped the cursing and yelling, and I probably should apologize for that."

"You could have." He shrugs, as if whether I curse or not is irrelevant. Clearly he doesn't have the same hang-ups I do. I exhale and take the list from his hand. "There must be . . ." I start counting, but he interrupts me.

"There are thirty-four people on that list," he says.

I turn the list back around and then to the front again. "There are only thirteen people on here," I correct him.

He points to where it says *office*. "There's about twenty people in the office. We counted yesterday."

Damn. We sure were thorough last night. "You want me to apologize to thirty-four people?"

"No, I couldn't care less. I'm not the one who had zero people at my party," he says, and I roll my eyes and glare at him. "But *you* wanted to apologize because *you* wanted to start your new year fresh so that *you* didn't have a shitty forty-first birthday. Your words, not mine. *I* just want to spend time with you."

"And watch me be mortified."

"You did call me sadistic," he says with a wink.

CHAPTER SEVEN

Luanne
Gary
Lindsey
Jenny O.
Jenny M.
Jenny Z.
Mary
Office
Brenda
Margret
Jimenez

I rewrite the list. Neatly. It needed to be done. If I had been home, I would have probably typed it up into a nice Excel spreadsheet, but alas, I'm not home and it was difficult enough to find a real piece of paper in John's house because he's very neat and tidy. There wasn't even a junk drawer, which not only surprised me, it made me a little jealous. I close my eyes and point to a random name. I hope it's not Luanne; she would be the most difficult one on the list. When I open my eyes, my finger is right over Brenda.

Brenda Neilson.

When I was in law school, Brenda and I became very good friends. We bonded over late nights at the law library and our mutual hatred of our properties class. She was the bright light in days and evenings filled with classes and lectures and studying. Even when the work seemed daunting, she always made it better with her positivity. While I was the overachiever who cried over a B, she was the glass-half-full girl who was content with just passing the class and keeping her dream alive of helping everyone who needed help pro bono. I would tease her about how she'd pay off her student loans and how she'd afford her daily lattes if she worked for free, and she would always tell me that I'd have to buy her lattes with my big paychecks while she saved the world. She was the dreamer while I was the realist, and it worked.

In fact, during our first spring break, she invited me to go back home with her to Wyoming. The relaxing mountain retreat she described was the perfect escape for my first real break from school.

And then I met Evan, her brother. He was an unexpected little surprise and a fun and wild spring fling. When Evan and I weren't sneaking off to make out, Brenda and I were hiking and enjoying drinks and talking about everything except school. It was a wonderful break, exactly the escape I needed from the intense life of a law student. Unfortunately, it didn't last long, because a few weeks after I returned to school with Brenda, I received an unpleasant call from Evan's girlfriend. Brenda denied having known he was dating, but I was so furious with Evan that I stopped speaking to Brenda too. She tried reaching out to me throughout the semester, but I ignored her every attempt until she stopped trying. Years later, we went up against each other in a trial and she won. It was one of the two trials I ever lost.

Now looking back at it, she had done a great job with the case and deserved to win. At the time, I wanted to shove that little smirk right up her own ass.

"She works at a boutique firm downtown. I would have no way of reaching her today, on a Sunday," I tell John.

"You can social-media her."

"What? Like look her up on Facebook? I don't have Facebook."

"Who doesn't have Facebook?" he asks incredulously. "Do you have any social media at all?"

I shake my head and he looks dumbstruck. He finds his phone and starts scrolling. "Her full name is?"

"Brenda Neilson. At least that's what it was back then. Not sure what it is now. She could've married or—"

He turns the phone around and Brenda's face greets me. "Oh, well yes. That's her. Wow, that was remarkably fast." I'm suddenly very glad I don't have social media. I wouldn't want someone to have such quick access to me.

"We're in luck. She just posted a photo of her and some other people at Saint Mary's. It looks like a wedding or something?" He scrolls through the photos on her Facebook, and I look at them from behind him.

"I'm not going to find her at a wedding, if that's what you're thinking."

He exhales and then takes the napkin with all the names and says, "Jenny M. Let's find her instead. You can leave Brenda for another day."

"Uh. No. None of the Jennys. I'd need wine and patience to speak with them, and I'm still partly hungover, so no to the Jennys."

He looks over the list. "How about Luanne Chase?"

Luanne Chase. She's the hardest person on that entire list. She was my best friend since kindergarten. Because of the big age difference between Nina and me, I was closer to Luanne than I was to my own sister for most of my life. Losing her left a big, huge black hole, and not knowing why made it infinitely harder.

"Fine. Let's find Brenda." The thought of confronting Luanne in any capacity gives me hives. Church it is.

"Maybe I didn't think this thing through. This is silly," I say an hour later. "My self-worth isn't linked to whether others like me. But I can do a quick 'I'm sorry,' cross her off the list, and move on. Easy."

"You are not going about this with the correct intentions, Millie. Maybe you shouldn't do it."

Damn it. He's right(ish). "Saying sorry is always a good thing, right? My intentions may not be honorable, but the end result is still good. That is the point, right?"

He doesn't answer. I don't care. His opinion doesn't actually matter. We just met.

I've been fiddling with Facebook since I got into John's car thirty minutes ago. Well, first I downloaded the app and created an account and then used it to look up Luanne. I couldn't help myself. I know that I don't need friends to make me happy, but the truth of the matter is, I miss Luanne and she's been on my mind nonstop since the mug she gave me broke into a thousand pieces. I'll admit there was a smidgen of envy when I saw her Facebook, how wonderful her life had become and how mine was devoid of friends and laughter. And it saddens me that I didn't even know she had children. I would have liked to have seen her pregnant and bought her a ridiculous stroller and . . .

"You shouldn't stalk people on that thing," he says, looking over to my phone from the driver's seat. I move the phone away. "It's a slippery slope."

"I'm not stalking. I'm just . . . researching."

He chuckles. "Why didn't you just start with her? You mentioned her often last night."

"Let's stop discussing last night. I'm not ready to talk to Luanne. I wouldn't even know what to say." I keep scrolling through her pictures as we drive to Saint Mary's. "It's not like she invited me to her baby shower. I mean, I didn't even know how much I missed her because she didn't call me. *She* stopped being my friend, not the other way around. She actually owes me an apology if I'm being honest," I say. "We grew up together. We were friends since we were five, and she stopped calling me. I may have to remove her from the list altogether."

"So you hold no fault in any of it?" he says as I look out the window.

"I hate you, you know?"

"But do you?" He laughs.

No, I don't hate him. But I don't tell him that. Instead, I watch as he gets out of the car and runs around to open the door for me. I'm not sure if he's being chivalrous or if he knows that if he doesn't help, I may chicken out. John is the most annoying person I've ever met, but we're in it together for the moment and I'm glad he's here.

Oh, and let's discuss my wardrobe in this possibly monumental point in my life. When I finally decided to go through with this idiocy, I took my dress out of the dryer and almost wept. My stunning Chiara Boni La Petite Robe dress is now half its original size and almost completely unwearable, not to mention no one would dare assume that the wrecked piece of fabric once had another life as designer clothing.

To his credit, John did let me borrow a pair of gym shorts, but they were so big, every time I took a step, they'd fall down and I ended up having to hold them up even when I tightened the cord on the waist to its full length. I couldn't very well go see Brenda holding up my clothes up with my hand, so I went with option two, which I'm currently regretting. Big-time. He suggested I go home and change first, but the church was closer to his home and I just wanted to get it out of the way. If I'd gone home first, I probably wouldn't have left for a week.

I'm wearing my "dress." I use the word *dress* loosely since it doesn't resemble any garment I've ever owned. If I pull it up to cover my boobs, then my butt is exposed. If I pull it down to cover my behind, then my boobs are exposed. So, I pull it down and use it as if it's a skirt, almost like an awkward-looking pencil skirt, and then pair it with one of John's Penn State T-shirts that's too long, so I tie a knot in it at the side. I want to say I look shabby chic. Like, I don't care that I'm wearing a peculiar ensemble because I'm so cool, it works in a bizarre way. Like when the Kardashians wear those outrageous biker shorts and sports bras paired with ridiculously high heels, expensive jewelry, and a face full of makeup. Except I'm not a Kardashian and there's no paparazzi around. I look like Punky Brewster meets homeless vagrant. I'm apologizing to someone I haven't seen in years, at a church, and then I'm going home and forgetting this ever happened. Everything! The party-that-never-was, the drinking, the dumb list, and most definitely what I'm about to do.

"There." He points to the progression of people exiting the church. All dressed to the nines.

I had been hoping that they'd be gone by the time I arrived, but the fact that everyone is still here is a testament to the luck I've been having lately. *The universe hates me.*

I teeter out of the car in my high heels. The dress is so tight around my knees, I'm walking like a penguin. "This is so stupid. I can't believe I let you talk me into this," I say under my breath as John leads me toward the side entrance where people are coming out.

"This is all you, sweetheart. I suggested you apologize. I didn't suggest you start now and definitely didn't suggest you do this for the sake of getting your to-do list done. Somehow you've turned what could have been a nice gesture into a treasure hunt with the win of 'getting it out of the way,'"

I ignore him. "Oh shit, that's her!" I wince, not intending to curse in front of a church and also surprised at how easily we found her.

"She's not in white. Probably just a guest."

"Thank God," I whisper as we walk toward her. The last thing I need is to make a grandiose and extremely odd gesture to the bride on her wedding day. As I approach, I see Brenda do a double take when she sees me. She squints and then looks up at a man who then looks back at me. Now they're both watching me approach, confusion on their faces.

"I can't believe I'm doing this," I whisper to John, and then, when I'm closer to the confused couple, I say with a little too much excitement in my voice, "Brenda, hi. Long time no see!"

"Oh, please God, tell me you're not here to break up the wedding?"

I furrow my brows and look around me. "What? No . . . I . . . what?"

"You heard Evan was finally getting married and you came to break it up?"

"Evan? Your brother? Oh God, no!" I practically snort out a laugh, although there is nothing funny about this except my impeccable timing. Of all the places to meet Brenda, it's at her brother's—my ex-fling's—wedding. A few weeks ago, I received one of those spam prayer-chain emails that said I had to send it to twenty people within twenty-four hours. I didn't do it. This must be my punishment.

"Okay . . . then what's going on?" She looks over to John behind me and then back at me, baffled. John extends his hand, and she hesitantly takes it.

"I'm John." As if that's supposed to mean anything whatsoever.

"Brenda," she says, then turns her attention back to me. "I have no idea what is happening right now. I know you weren't on the guest list because I helped with the wedding planning."

"I wanted to speak with you for a moment. I know you're busy, clearly." I point to the mayhem of photographers and people around us. "Just five minutes, please."

She excuses herself and we walk (I mostly waddle) a few feet to the side, where there are fewer people. Her husband, I assume, walks to a nearby group, leaving us to ourselves. "You see, I drank a lot last night, and somehow that brought up old memories, and that led to some realizations and—"

"Oookay . . . ," she says, her arms crossed over her very pretty sapphire dress. She has no interest in hearing the backstory. I don't blame her.

"Anyway, I wanted to apologize. I owe you an apology. I was a jerk in law school, and you didn't deserve it."

She looks over her shoulder and then back at me as if she's waiting for a *Candid Camera* situation to spring up on her. Again, I don't blame her.

"I'm not sure if I'm understanding," she finally says.

"Nothing to understand, really. I was not very nice to you, and we were good friends back then. You deserve a long overdue apology, so I'm sorry. There's nothing you need to say or do. I just wanted to say that."

"Well, um . . . okay."

There's more unease as we just stand there waiting for more words, but there's nothing left to say. "Well, then if that's all . . . I think I'm needed." She points to the group being photographed.

"Yes. Okay, of course. You look great, Brenda, by the way. It was nice to see you."

She looks me up and down and then does a weird wave and walks away.

I cover my face with my hands and grumble. "That was so awkward," I say through gritted teeth. "And she didn't even accept my apology or anything. What the hell?" I turn and start penguin-walking back to John's car.

"It was a little uncomfortable," he admits and opens his car door for me.

"A little? A little? John, it was mortifying. She probably thinks I'm on drugs or something."

"But it's done. I'm sure it feels good to get that off your chest." He starts the car.

"No, it really doesn't. Not at all. Please take me home. I have to reconsider some very recent life choices and maybe go back to sleep and wake up when I'm forty-one, because forty hasn't been great thus far."

"It wasn't that bad. Maybe the next person will be easier."

"Listen, John. The sex was good, but not good enough to have you witness any more of my humiliation. Every decision I've made in the last twenty-four hours, including the stupid party, has been awful and uncharacteristic, to say the least. I think I need to sleep or to get a lobotomy."

The light is red, and he turns to me. "I'm sorry if *everything* has been awful."

I consider that over trying not to chip a tooth at how hard I'm clenching my jaw. Because damn it, he's right. Not everything was awful. The conversation with John and then the sex—that was far from awful. Nor was my family's support. None of this I say out loud. Instead, I give him my address and we drive because—damn it—I'm mad, I still feel gross from all the drinking last night, my clothes are stifling my circulation from the waist down, and I've apologized (or contemplated apologizing) enough for one day.

CHAPTER EIGHT

Luanne
Gary
Lindsey
Jenny O.
Jenny M.
Jenny Z.
Mary
Office
~~Brenda~~
Margret
Jimenez

The shower is fantastic. I almost, *almost* forget about John. He dropped me off about thirty minutes ago, walking me to my door but barely speaking to me except to say goodbye. After I check on my cat, who was completely fine without me, I shower, taking my time blow-drying my hair, moisturizing, and then putting on a comfortable pair of plaid lounge pants and a matching T-shirt.

As I'm taking everything out of my small clutch, I notice John's business card inside with a note on the back that says, "I hope you call."

I wonder when he slid it into my handbag. Was it before I insulted him on the car ride over by saying last night was terrible or after? I stare at it for a moment. *John Ellis.* His card is practically still hot from the printer, and I wonder if he was given my office. Is he friends with the partners, particularly Junior? If he is, then there is no way he's not an asshole, too, regardless of the mind-blowing sex and amusing conversation. I crumple the card and toss it into the trash. I don't want any connections to my old life. After the epically failed attempt at trying to reconnect with others through a stupid party, I've found it's better to start a new life.

Except that it's Sunday, the middle of the day, and I don't have anything else to do but overthink my cringeworthy interaction with Brenda. I'm bothered that she didn't accept my apology. It was so long ago; had she still been holding a grudge? I know I don't have a right to be mad, but I can't help it. I was the bigger person and went in search of her and apologized. That must count for something, right? I try and distract myself with television, but one of those entertainment shows is talking about Hugh Phoebe and the "scandal" that is "unfolding." There's even an attorney giving his opinion on the case and saying how this trial could be the biggest of the decade if all the women who signed NDAs or victims who never came forward start to give interviews to the press, or if they decide to testify or join the lawsuits. The TV attorney is speculating about all the possible outcomes, and there is a photo of Junior walking out of the courthouse with Phoebe and Phoebe's wife, who are holding hands sweetly. It is so obviously a photo op that I immediately turn off the TV. It makes me nauseated and so very mad.

With television out of the question, I finally succumb to my curiosity and decide to scroll through Facebook.

It doesn't happen immediately, though. First, I swipe open my phone and start surfing through the news feed. Somehow, that leads to Goodreads. It's not exactly a social media app, although I do search for Luanne in the "find friends" section. I can't find anything there, so that leads me back to Facebook, where I hesitantly click the newly added icon on my phone.

"Is this creepy, William?" My cat looks at me, judgment written all over his face. I'm a forty-year-old woman stalking an old friend on Facebook instead of trying to see if the phone number I have for her still works. It's pathetic and it makes me feel foolish, but, as the internet tends to do, it sucks me in. By the time my eyes drift closed hours later, I know more about Luanne and everyone else on my list than I care to. I've also installed Twitter, Snapchat, TikTok, and Instagram. I have no idea how they work, but I'm totally hooked and I don't think I like it. I hope that Big Brother doesn't find me as easily as I've found everyone else.

The next morning, I wake up to a text from Nina: You're on Facebook now? Who are you and what have you done with my "I'm too mature for Facebook" sister?

I never said I was too mature for Facebook. I just never had the time, I reply while lying on my belly, William purring next to me.

So it is you? You joined?

Sort of.

Sort of? Just like you can't be a little pregnant, you either are or you're not, she types back.

Fine. I am. But mostly because I was doing a little research, not because I'm going to start posting selfies or taking pictures of my food.

"Research" is social media code for "stalking," and the fact that you just used the word "selfie" and that you know about the obsession with food pictures means that you, dear sister, have in fact been sucked into the social media vortex. 😂😂😂😂😂

I can't wait to see you dress up William and start a page in his
name.

I chuckle, sit up, and dial her number because I feel like hearing
her voice and telling her everything that's happened.

"I have to tell you about Saturday night," I start.

"Why do I feel like this should be an in-person conversation? Either
at my office or at a bar," she adds.

"I'm never drinking again," I say.

"So at my office, then," she says with a laugh. She's probably right
about seeing a medical professional.

"I slept with John."

"The hot man at the bar? Who was he?"

"One and the same. He's a new associate at JJF."

"You're not a 'sleep with random men' kind of person, so I'm thinking you feel . . ." She's waiting for me to use my feeling words. When I
don't answer, she suggests, "Regret, embarrassed, excited, fulfilled . . ."

"Confounded." Yes, that's what I feel. I stand up and pad to the
bathroom. Holding my phone with my shoulder and head, I start to
brush my teeth.

"Wow. Okay. Not one of the words my kids normally say in therapy, but a good word nonetheless. So, what are you confounded about
exactly? That he isn't going to call you again? That the sex wasn't good?
Whether you should call him first?"

I gargle and spit and I can hear her rummaging around in her
kitchen. I'm sure she's making eggs. She eats an egg-white omelet for
breakfast almost every single day. "No. Nothing like that. It was strange,
sleeping with someone I didn't know, but it was oddly satisfying and
liberating."

"Good feeling words."

I laugh and continue. "The conflicted part is what happened after."

"Uh-oh. You met his wife?"

"No!"

"Girlfriend? Boyfriend?"

"You are not normal, you know that? It's nothing like that. Jesus, Nina, you are on a different plane than the rest of us here on Earth." I shake my head and then continue. "Anyway, as I was saying, we were talking, and I was a little drunk and a lot chatty. Apparently I wrote a list with a bunch of names of people I need to apologize to."

"You? What? I'm not following."

I exhale and start brewing coffee. "My party was a complete failure. I'll kill you another day." She grumbles into the phone, but I continue. "I guess I was feeling a little sorry for myself, and I confessed that perhaps I've been a little bitchy to some people, which explained why no one showed up to the party, and I actually made a list."

"You are a barrel of fun, aren't you?" She sounds like John. "What did you do to the people on the list that would make you feel a need to apologize?"

"This and that. It varies."

"Well, maybe then you do need to apologize. Well," she backtracks, "to a few people, not people who were wrong, like those ex-boyfriends of yours."

I roll my eyes and continue. "Of course. Originally, I made the list in a drunken state, which I immediately regretted in the morning. But now I'm starting to genuinely think about it."

"Apologizing is never a bad thing." She pauses for a moment and then adds, "When there is something to apologize for."

"Right! My thoughts exactly. I had a failed party. Then I thought, maybe if I set things right with everyone, I could have an actual successful forty-first birthday for the cost of only two little words."

"Oh, Mills . . . ," she says, and I can picture her shaking her head side to side. "Walk me through your thought process."

"Simple. I apologize. They like me. I invite them. They come. I have friends. Super easy. Except that it wasn't super easy. I found Brenda and I apologized. It was uncomfortable and it left me feeling shitty, Nina. She didn't even accept my apology. It was mortifying."

"Brenda? From law school?"

"Yep."

"Maybe you feel bad about it because it wasn't sincere?"

"I know! How messed up am I?"

"You are not messed up, Millie. You're just a little lost right now. You just stopped working after going nonstop for your entire life. You're very standoffish because you've been hurt and you're scared to open your heart. These are normal reactions. You need to figure out what it is that you want to do. Forget other people. You need to figure *you* out."

"I'm not scared to open my heart!" I say huffily.

"Millie, you were engaged to a man who broke your heart when you started to become successful. The last man you dated broke up with you when you couldn't go to his office Christmas party because you had to prepare for a deposition that week." I remember Warren. He wanted all my time and couldn't deal with not being my priority. There've been so many like that.

"I never looked at it that way," I tell her. "I just thought they were jerks."

"They *were* jerks. Probably still are. The question is, why do you continue to pick jerks?"

I roll my eyes and let out a deep breath. "I don't do that on purpose! They're pretty great when I meet them."

"You need to open your heart and let your guard down a little, Amelia."

"I don't know . . ."

"I can't even picture how that apology went down. You just found Brenda, knocked on her door, and said, 'I'm sorry'?"

I grab a mug—more bowl than mug, really—and pour coffee to the rim, then go sit on my balcony. The day is gorgeous. I inhale deeply, sit back, and take in the warmth of the early morning sun. How I wish it

84

had been as easy as Nina described. We would have met at a coffee shop or had lunch; I'd have worn something presentable, maybe brushed my hair, removed all my lipstick; we would have laughed it off, reconciled, and become great friends again. I would have then tackled the apology list with the zeal of someone who won a reconciliation award. Amelia Montgomery, World's Best Apologizer. Alas, it went nothing like this. Finding Brenda and then being vulnerable(ish) left me discombobulated. I'm mortified by what I did almost twenty years ago and by the actual apology debacle. I cringe just thinking about it. And the worst part is, it didn't do a damn thing. I don't feel better, we're not friends again, and she didn't accept (or reject) my apology.

"Sort of. There was more to it than that, but yes. I found her—well, John found her—on Facebook, and we went together and I apologized. That's where Facebook came into play."

"What exactly did you drink at the party?"

"Everything," I say and she laughs. "Do you think it would be weird if I actually went through with it? Apologizing to everyone on that list, I mean. Not because of a future birthday party but because they may actually be owed apologies?"

"It's not the craziest thing I've ever heard . . ." There's silence for a moment. "Do you feel as if they deserve apologies?"

"Yes," I say quickly. At least I think so. "The party was bad, Nina. I think it was a wake-up call. Not one I wanted, but maybe one I deserved."

"I don't want to believe that."

"Because I'm your sister and you love me, but it's true. I've messed up, and it's time I atone. Right?"

She sighs. I think I've left my sister speechless. That has to be a first.

"If no one likes me, Nina, then I'm the common denominator. I need to do a bit of soul-searching here."

"It can't hurt."

"That's my thought too."

"And this guy, John? He went with you?"

"Yep. It was pretty humiliating."

"Are you seeing him again?"

"I threw away his number."

"That's not a no," she says.

"It's a no, Nina. A big fat no."

She laughs. "Well, keep me posted on the Apology Project. Let the record reflect that I'm on the fence about it."

"It's not a project, and I'm not a hundred percent sure if I'm going to go through with it yet. But I do need to do something to get out of this funk. Amelia took over for too long, and I'm scared I've lost Millie along the way."

It is devastating to admit, and honestly, I don't think I even saw that point until right this very moment. It took a series of crappy events for me to realize how different I'd become. Or rather, how much my work life had dominated my persona. And it scares me to death that this will be my life forever. Alone. Jobless. Friendless. I feel hopeless.

"Don't say that," Nina says. "Just like you evolved into Amelia, you can evolve right back into Millie. You're not changing, not really. It's you, the same you you've always been, but with less work and more time and self-awareness."

I wish I was as optimistic as she is. I exhale with all the heaviness that has filled me over the last couple of weeks. She continues. "You'll find her. I see her, and in time you will too."

"I hope so," I admit.

Then our conversation breaks down into small talk and pleasantries.

"Well, keep me posted," Nina says. "I'm on my way to end things with Kevin. Any advice?"

"Yeah . . . don't break up with him."

"Har har. See you later, sis," she says and hangs up. Kevin and Nina have been on and off again for years. I doubt that this is a permanent off.

I place my mug on the table beside my lounge chair and close my eyes for a bit. I think of my broken work mug scattered all over the floor. Luanne gave it to me when I began at JJF, and it broke on the last day. Shattered and irreparable—the mug and myself.

I inhale and exhale, trying to find calm in the chaos. I've owned this apartment for almost fourteen years, and I've sat on my balcony a handful of times. As I breathe in the fresh air and feel the breeze from Lake Michigan, I vow to sit on this balcony and drink my coffee slowly as often as possible because doing this has been the most sublime moment I've had in a long time.

Coffee consumed, mood somber, mind less confounded.

I can't say that the moment of relaxation has completely cleared my mind, but it does make me feel more grounded. I need to find a purpose. I don't even know what I like to do for fun anymore. I'm blessed to not want for money. Between my career, investments, lack of major expenses, and now my big, whopping settlement with JJF, I could choose never to work again. But I don't think I'm built to be a woman of leisure. It's just not in my DNA.

Speaking of DNA, did I spit into a tube for my mother? I send her a quick text about that, which I'm sure will be answered in about a week once she realizes she even has a text.

When the soft warmth of the sun starts to feel like blistering coal on my skin, I decide to amend my earlier balcony proclamation to maybe a nightcap before bed. Otherwise, I'm going to have to wear four layers of sunscreen before walking outside at midday.

I go back inside and plop down on my sofa, and William settles in close to me. William is an ornery cat, as most cats are. He either cuddles close, needing my touch, or hides on the highest shelf, avoiding any contact with me whatsoever. Today he wants to be petted, and I oblige happily.

As I'm about to doze off into a siesta, something completely uncharacteristic for me, I hear a new and unfamiliar sound coming from my phone. There's a Facebook notification. I click on it, and it turns out to be a Facebook friend request from Brenda Neilson. I click "Accept."

What exactly does this mean? I can see her profile now, and she can see mine. If she still hated me, she wouldn't have gone through the trouble of looking me up and then requesting my friendship, right? I mull this over for far too long.

I wish I understood the nuances of social media better, but I do go to sleep with a sense of peace I haven't had in days. I can feel some tension roll off my shoulders, making me lighter, as if this tiny, silly digital interaction is, in fact, a major victory for the Apology Project.

CHAPTER NINE

"Have you lost some weight?" is my mother's brunch hello. "Are you exercising?"

"Hi, Mom. Dad," I say, hugging them both and then sitting across from them in the warm and stuffy restaurant booth. It's been about a week since my birthday, and summer is at its peak. I'm in a new pair of jeans that go to my calves and a cute white-and-blue tank top that matches my blue platform espadrilles. I had to put my hair in a ponytail so that it didn't stick to my neck during the walk from my car to the entrance of the restaurant. I'm surprised my parents didn't ask to be seated outside since they're always complaining that it's too cold, even when it's eighty degrees out. I almost roll my eyes at the cardigan my mother is wearing. "I took up Pilates and I've been walking."

"You look wonderful," Mom says.

"Pila—what?" my father asks.

I explain Pilates, and they both seem even more confused. "So, in other words, you are exercising."

"Yes," I reply, which is what I should have said from the start.

"That's great, dear. Maybe you'll meet a nice young man there," Dad says.

I exhale. "Maybe."

"Is that why you joined? Are there men there?" my mom asks.

"I joined because I wanted to do something new. Also, it is really good exercise. I don't think there are men there."

"You should look around. Make yourself available, Millie."

I bite my lip and my father changes the subject, thank God. "So, is that what you've been doing with your free time? Stretching and walking?"

"Honey, your father has a jacket in the car. Would you like him to go get it for you? You'll catch a draft like that," Mom says.

"I'm fine, Mom."

She shrugs as if I'm completely off my rocker, and I turn my attention back to my dad's question.

I'm trying not to get annoyed, so I smile instead of throwing a bread roll at them. "I'm attempting new things. I tried tennis, but I was no good. I also went to a needlepoint class last week, and that was a fiasco. I think I'm going to take some cooking classes online. I've always wanted to learn how to cook."

"Oh! That reminds me. I have the results of your 23andMe test." She pulls out her phone and scrolls through the page while my dad and I look at each other in amusement. "I've been analyzing and comparing yours with ours—"

"Why do I feel like that's some sort of privacy issue or HIPAA violation or, basically, just inappropriate?"

She shakes her head and continues scrolling. "It's fine. It's just your DNA. I think you're going to be shocked at the results."

I doubt that. I have brown hair from my dad, I presume, but my fair complexion and green eyes are definitely from my mother's Irish stock. I look American—whatever that means. I always mark the "White" box on all documents when they ask about race. I doubt I'll be very surprised by any of the results.

"What did you learn that is *sooo* surprising?"

"Well, your father's are even more surprising than yours and will help explain yours," she says. "He is 52.5 percent from Spain and

Portugal, specifically Canary Islands, Spain, and 19.7 percent unassigned is from Havana, Cuba."

"Huh? What?" I try and take the phone from her hands, but she pulls it away.

"Yours. Because of me and my Irish background, you have all that Irish and European from my side, but you also have 31.1 percent Spain and Portugal, specifically Canary Islands, Spain, and 7 percent unassigned, Havana, Cuba."

Now I take the phone from her hand and skim through the color-coded results: one section is Irish and splatters from different parts of Europe, which is similar to my mother's side, and then a big chunk is Spain and parts of Cuba.

"Dad's family is from Spain?"

"Or Cuba," he says. "We've been researching it. Many immigrants from Spain or Africa headed to the Caribbean or were taken there by force. In terms of 23andMe, at least, they can't tell that it's Cuba, per se. They use the results of other people who've taken the test to come up with the Cuban identity."

I could be Cuban American? I'm still Amelia Montgomery, but this somehow feels like a major deal. "What do you think about this, Dad?"

"Doesn't change anything. I am who I am."

"Yeah, and you're Spanish," I say. "Your entire identity is not what you've thought it was." I'm befuddled, by both the results and his lack of reaction.

He shrugs as if he really doesn't believe this means anything.

"That's all you have? A shrug?"

"I'm not as enthusiastic as you are."

How is that even possible? If this is a surprise for me, it must be life-altering for him. He should be interested, even if not enthusiastic. I want to shake him into an appropriate emotion. "Jeez, Dad!" I rein in my snark. "Well, I'm excited. What if we have family in Spain or Cuba?"

"You always knew that you had family somewhere, even if we didn't know who they were," Mom says, referring to my dad's biological parents.

"I know, but I always thought that the person would be in the United States somewhere. Maybe I've even interacted with a long-lost cousin at Whole Foods. It never occurred to me that I may have some family abroad. Family that I wouldn't even be able to speak to because I don't speak a lick of Spanish."

"Maybe you can learn," my dad says just as the server comes by and leaves us menus.

"Spanish? Learn Spanish? That seems like a pretty big undertaking, doesn't it?"

"It has to be better than needlepoint, honey," Mom adds.

"Would you want to learn, too, Dad? We could do it together." It is, after all, major news for him too.

"No, no. I'm too old for that."

"You're not," I say, but it makes me excited to think that maybe I could learn Spanish. Maybe the thing that's been missing in my life is that half of myself, my genetic makeup, has been a mystery. As an only child, my mother doesn't have much family, and the family she does have is scattered throughout the world; we have no communication with them. This new side from my father is all I have to cling to.

"Eh." He shakes his head. "I'm not really interested in taking that on."

"What if your parents are alive, Dad? Or you have an opportunity to meet a relative?"

"It would be interesting, I suppose," he says nonchalantly. "But I'm not learning Spanish at my age for that."

"But you've never even tried looking for them?" My frustration mounts. Why isn't he curious or excited? Something.

"Honey, I'm sorry if I'm not giving you the reaction you want. I can see you're getting irritated. A long time ago, in my early twenties,

I did try and look for information, and I didn't get anywhere. It's not that your grandmother was trying to keep it a secret, it's just that there was no information about my biological mother. All I know is that I was born in a hospital in Miami, and I lived in Miami for just a few months because Dad got a job at a plant up here." I actually already knew that. My grandparents moved often because of work, and finally when they adopted Dad, they settled in Chicago. "I've lived a wonderful life, sweetie. I don't need to find her; I am not as curious as you are, I suppose. Maybe at one time I was, but I'm not anymore. I think it would be hurtful to my parents' legacy if I went digging. It's hard to explain why I feel that way, but I just do."

Fair enough, I suppose. I can't force him to have a particular reaction. He's old. Set in his ways. And that's that.

"Would it be okay if I did more research?" I don't want to hurt my father or my grandparents. "Not on your biological parents, but on our lineage. Cuba, Spain . . ."

My mom eyes me warily; she sees my mind racing. "Amelia . . ."

"It's not like I was going to start searching right this instant."

"You never know with you. Once you get something in your head, you're like a dog with a bone."

My father laughs and then winks at me sweetly. "Sure, honey. I'm fine with whatever you want to do."

"I bought you the test because I thought it would be fun, but I can see you're going to make it into a project. As it is, you've done more in the month you've been retired than your father and I have done in twenty years, Millie. Are you going through some sort of midlife crisis?" Mom asks.

"No, Mom. I'm fine." *Have I taken on a lot?* It's not like I've done much with the Apology Project since Brenda. Although I have taken a glance at it a few times, I quickly look away; I'm not in a rush to humiliate myself again. "I'm just trying new things. You're the one that got me that test, and now I'm intrigued."

"Is this one of those new-age things I've heard about? Like . . ." She snaps her fingers together and turns to my father. "What's Selena and Ramon's daughter's name? Remember? They told us over canasta last month how she'd up and moved to India and became a yoga instructor and a vegan when her husband divorced her."

I don't even ask who Selena and Ramon are because that would lead us down a rabbit hole, but by her comment about canasta, I'm assuming they're from the country club. "Does her name really matter, Mom?" I ask.

"Melanie? Melissa?" my father starts.

"Morgan!" my mother finally settles on. "Poor thing. Selena's broken up over it. It's her only child, you know. To lose a daughter like that, it's horrible." My mother shakes her head and tsks. "Is that what you're going to do next, Millie? Because that would not be wise. You moving to another country in search of long-lost relatives, not knowing the language, afraid of flying, and—"

"She's not dead, Mom. She just moved. I'm sure she can come back if she wanted to. Plus, I bet there's much more to that story. Not that any of this has anything at all to do with me."

My parents are absurd sometimes. Their view on things is antiquated and sometimes off-the-wall. Unfortunately, with all the crap that's been running through my head lately, I couldn't sit with my own thoughts for a minute, let alone sit in a foreign country. "How did this go from me learning a new language to moving to a foreign country?"

"It's just that we're worried about you. You left your job and you've lost weight and you're not doing anything with your life except trying out new hobbies every other day."

"Mom, I'm trying to find what it is that I like. I haven't ever just done *nothing*, and I feel like it's time I took a moment to myself."

"*We* never did nothing. Not until we retired, and you're too young to retire, Amelia," my father says. "Are you looking at new firms? Maybe you can try a different kind of law. Family, criminal, divorce—"

"Relax." I'm trying not to lose my patience. "I'm not looking for a new job. Not right now, at least. I'm just trying to make some changes is all. If you see me booking a trip to India, then you can send help. Otherwise, please just give me some time to figure things out, okay?" I mean, I took the leap, made the apology to Brenda, and nothing came from it. I'm not exactly having a life-changing *Eat Pray Love* moment here. Brenda didn't accept my apology, and I didn't have a deep desire to make amends with everyone like drunk me assumed I would. But maybe drunk me was onto something. Maybe it doesn't matter whether Brenda accepted it. Maybe I should at least give the Apology Project a second chance. I didn't love Pilates the first time, and I'm going back. My first baking experience was a huge flop, and I tried that again.

"Change is good, sweetheart," my father says and squeezes my hand from across the table just as I'm thinking that I owe it to drunk Millie to give the project a second chance. My father looks at me, bewildered. He knows me well enough to know that my mind is elsewhere, but his concerned expression disappears when the server brings another basket of buttered rolls; all the love my father has for me is forgotten because I'm pretty sure there is nothing in the world my father loves more than carbs—buttery carbs.

As we eat, my parents tell me all about their recent cruise and how they plan on taking another cruise in the winter. They love to cruise, and they love to talk about their cruises. My father basically gambles while my mother plays bingo and drinks martinis. It's always the same stories.

"So about your birthday party . . . ," my mom begins, and I sigh loudly. "It wasn't a great success."

"Ya think?"

"Maybe they didn't receive the invitations?" She said this at the party too.

"Email broke for only these fifty-five people? How about Nina's boyfriend? You think his email broke too?" I say, the sarcasm rolling off me.

"Nina says that you're not everyone's favorite person at work," my mother says. "Kevin says that they call you the devil's wife."

Water almost comes out of my nose, since I have just taken a sip. "She-Demon, not the devil's wife."

"That sounds worse, honey," Dad says.

"Maybe that's why no one came to the party," my mother adds.

God, my parents are great, aren't they?

"I don't want to talk about it. Let's just enjoy brunch, okay?"

"Fine," my mother says. "But I just want to say one more thing, then I'll let it go."

I let out a long breath, and my dad snorts. We both know she's not going to let anything go.

"You're forty. There's still time, but not much. I'd like a grandchild and your father would like to walk you down the aisle one day. Take this retirement to find a nice man and settle down, honey."

She says it as if I'm single out of my own choosing. And as if it's just that easy to get hitched. But I'm not going to argue with her, so instead I say, "I'll get right on that, Mom."

Maybe leaving the country for a little while isn't such a bad idea.

———

I pause the *Great American Bake-Off* episode when I hear a knock on my front door. I've been binge-watching cooking shows, trying to avoid social media, and focusing on things I want to do with my newfound freedom. I'm sure it's the new set of cooking equipment I ordered. I basically spent a great deal of my new fortune purchasing every single product in Rachael Ray's cookware line (everything is red). Turns out that, after working sixty-five-hour weeks and never cooking, I don't own much in the cookware department. It also turns out that I find cooking fascinating. Yet I can't start learning if I don't have the proper equipment. I open the door to find a box, but it's not big enough to fit an entire set of pots and pans.

My brows furrow as I place the package on my dining room table, scooting William off. I peel off the tape and open the box to find another box inside, but this one is wrapped. I carelessly rip the gift wrap off and open it. I gasp as my lips curl up into a smile. I pull out a new white silk Chiara Boni La Petite Robe that is neatly and carefully folded with a satin hanger. There's a card.

I open the envelope to find a cheesy birthday card with the cutest puppy on the cover. It has a birthday hat and a sad little black-and-white puppy face. The card says: *Sowwy for the late birthday wish.*

Inside it continues: *But I hope it was doggone great.*

I laugh out loud. Literally snort out a big chuckle. In his messy chicken scratch, John wrote:

A belated birthday present. I'd like to see you again. I enclosed my card with all my phone numbers just in case you tossed out the other one. I promise we'll only discuss highly personal things. No work talk. No apologies.

John.

PS: Did you know that the circle symbol on the laundry tag means dry clean only? I googled it, so it must be true. May I advise that you stop sticking silk dresses in strange men's washing machines? It'll ruin the dress.

Now I'm doubled over laughing. During the last week, I had moments where I regretted throwing away his card. I could've easily gotten his work number from the JJF website, but I just didn't know what I'd say.

I've been out of the dating game for a while, choosing my career over a personal life, and I'm rusty. Not to mention how embarrassing the hours we spent together were in hindsight. Nevertheless, I'm glad he reached out. He's charming and so very funny. Plus, he replaced a $900 dress! That's too much.

I find my phone and send him a text. Thank you for the card and the extravagant present. It was very sweet of you. I really can't accept it, however. It's too much.

A moment later he texts back. You're very predictable, which is why the tags have been removed. You must accept it. Otherwise, I'd just have to keep it and it doesn't fit me.

I let out a breath, laughing some more, then type back, In that case, thank you. I love that dress.

I'd like to see you again, he says.

I want to see him too. He makes me laugh. "What do you think, William?" My cat yawns, then hops onto the top of my wall unit, where he likes to hide. I think that's a yes from William.

I'd like that too, I type before William and I can think about it too much.

John sends me a quick text to meet tomorrow night for dinner at Mint, a little Indian restaurant downtown, and then tells me he's running to a meeting.

I've been slowly adding to my wardrobe, and I've stopped accidentally putting on business suits in the morning, which means that I have something perfect to wear for my date with John. I'm not sure if it's because I broke the habit of wearing suits or if it's because they're still piled up in a mountain in the corner of my closet. Nina suggested donating the pile, but I can't bring myself to get rid of them yet. I don't know—somehow no suits means no job. Intellectually I know I don't have a job and don't need one. Whether I have my clothes or not doesn't change anything. But there's an entire chapter in my life connected to those unworn suits, so I just try and ignore them.

Also, the new sporty clothes and Pilates are doing wonders for my figure. Or maybe it's the newly discovered Cuban side of me that has somehow given me a new perspective on my booty. It was always something I loathed. Wider hips made it hard to find clothes because they're not proportional to my thin frame, which is why I usually had to alter the waist of my pants and skirts. I find myself trying to remember if my maternal grandmother was curvy. She passed away when I was just a little girl, and my mother doesn't have these curves either. Do I have family somewhere with these same curves?

I don't know if it's boredom or John's text, but I think about the list as I get ready for Pilates later that day.

Nothing has transpired between me and Brenda since the awkward apology except that now I have access to her Facebook profile and I've "liked" her most recent photo. I think that's the modern-day equivalent of an olive branch.

Which of course reminds me of the apology list. When I had brunch with my parents, I told myself I'd give the list a second go, and seeing Brenda's profile reminds me that it's time to follow through with my promise.

I take out the list and unfold it. Brenda was a complete disaster. I picked her name randomly, and I wasn't prepared to meet with her. This time, I really look through the names and decide I'm going to try the easiest person first and do the apology with the correct intention. Immediately, I think of Gary.

Gary.

That's an easy one. He was my first boyfriend. We dated for three years. I scroll through my phone and find his number. The only reason I still have it, more than twenty years later, is because years ago I ran into his parents at the grocery store and they told me I should reconnect with him, giving me his number. I saved it thinking I'd never have use for it but not having the heart to toss it away. I don't even know whether the number they gave me is still the same, but I'm compelled to dial it anyway.

It rings and rings, and when I'm about to hang up, there is a breathless "Hello?"

"I . . . um. I'm looking for Gary Lee."

"This is he."

Oh, wow. I wasn't actually expecting him to answer, and I'm genuinely caught off guard.

"Hello?" he says again.

"Gary. Goodness. I didn't expect you to answer. I . . . um, it's Millie. Amelia Montgomery."

"Millie? Oh my, wow! Uh . . . hi. It's been a long time."

"I know. It has."

There's silence. It's beyond awkward.

"Is everything okay?" he asks.

"Yes, sorry. Yes. I'm actually calling because, well, this is weird." I giggle nervously. I'm scared that he'll give me a big eff-you and hang up. Or maybe he won't even remember me. *Maybe this wasn't a great idea,* I think for a moment, but then decide I've called, I'm already on this train, better make the best of it and say what I intended to say. "I wanted to apologize to you."

"Apologize? For what?"

"For kissing Melvin Rogers during freshman orientation."

He's quiet, and then I hear a laugh, a sincere, loud laugh that reverberates into the phone. I don't know what to make of it except that it puts me at ease. Laughter is better than a hang-up.

"Okay," he says after a moment. "I mean, I think you already apologized for that when I saw you and then broke up with you."

I had apologized, but it wasn't sincere. I remember saying, "I'm sorry," but mostly because I was caught, not because what I'd done was wrong. Gary was a good guy, the kind of guy who held doors open for me, made sure I ate lunch when I was in the library studying, and often left me a single bright yellow sunflower on my car for no other reason except that I liked sunflowers. He really liked me. We had been together since high school, and I broke his heart.

"Maybe I did, but I've been thinking about things recently. I feel bad about how I behaved back then, about how I treated you when we broke up, and about how dismissive I was about your feelings. I was so inconsiderate and immature. I'm truly sorry, Gary." It feels very freeing to say those words. It didn't feel like this with Brenda. I was caught off guard, embarrassed, and unprepared. John sort of pushed the apology on me. It may have been my idea, but had he not been there with me, I would not have done it. This one, however, is all me. I chose to call Gary and I knew he deserved an apology, which is probably why it was easy to do. It had been years since I thought of him, but every once in a while, when I'd think of high school and those first months of college, I would think of sweet Gary. There had been times in my life that I thought the jerks who came after him were my karma for the way I treated him. "I hope you can forgive me." And I really mean it. Truly. With Brenda, I just wanted to say the words, get out, and cross her off the list. With Gary, I want his forgiveness.

"I forgave you a long time ago, Millie. There are no hard feelings. We were kids. You wanted to break up with me before we graduated high school, and I think I pressured you into staying together. I knew you didn't love me anymore, and yet I was too selfish to let you go. It's my fault as much as it was yours. I think I owe you an apology too."

"No. Really. I was old enough to make my own decisions, and it's time I own up to my screwups."

"Are you sick or something, Millie? What's all this about all of a sudden?" He sounds genuinely concerned. Jeez, it didn't occur to me that I would sound like I was making amends before I passed away from some terminal illness.

"No!" I quickly reply. "No, not at all. I'm perfectly healthy. There's no agenda, just wanted to apologize is all."

"Well, that's very nice of you. I accept your apology then, and I'm glad to hear you're doing well."

We talk for a few more minutes while I open a can of cat food and pour it into William's bowl. He jumps down from his hiding nook and licks the plate clean before I've even finished the conversation with Gary.

Gary tells me he's living in Fort Lauderdale now and is an architect. He has two kids, and he's married to a nurse. He asks about Mom and Dad, and I tell him how they're always on some cruise or another. I don't tell him about leaving JJF even though he does ask me if I'm still practicing law. I say yes and then change the subject.

Am I still practicing law? My license is active, but I don't know if I'll ever see the inside of a courtroom again. I don't even know if I want to.

Even though he wasn't holding a grudge, I don't like that I treated him this way—even if our breakup was years ago and it's been forgotten. My palms start to feel a little sweaty, and I'm feeling uncomfortable. I've said my piece, and I think it's time to end the call. I don't want him to think that we need to be friends who call each other on a regular basis. I don't want my uncomfortableness to make him uncomfortable. "It was nice catching up, Gary. I'm glad you're doing great. I know this was a strange call, but I'm happy you answered and that I had an opportunity to talk to you."

"Likewise, Millie. Goodbye."

"Bye, Gary."

That felt cathartic. Not only apologizing, but reconnecting with someone I was very close to at a key point in my life. But it makes me wary. Why am I doing this exactly? Is this to become friends with people I haven't seen in decades, or is this just something I need to get off my chest? Should I care that I might make someone uncomfortable?

I call Nina.

"Hey!" she says on the first ring.

"Hypothetical question for you. Apologizing to someone out of the blue and getting all touchy-feely with my emotions—that may make people uncomfortable, right?"

"Maybe."

"So I shouldn't do it?"

"Who's the one who's uncomfortable, Mills? Is it you or the other person?"

"The other person?" It comes out more like a question.

"I'm thinking it's the person who's all weird about sharing her feelings who's uncomfortable," she says.

"I'm not weird about sharing my feelings."

"Oh, really?" I can practically see that perfect eyebrow of hers shoot up.

"Whatever," I reply, the queen of maturity.

"Anyway, it's okay to make people feel a little uncomfortable. You're not hurting anyone. Don't overthink it, Mills. Do whatever *you* are comfortable doing. Stop thinking about what the other person may or may not be feeling. Trust me, if someone doesn't want to hear it, they won't."

"Got it. So ignore everyone's feelings."

"That's not what I said!" I know it's not, but I like to mess with her.

"Love you, sis." And I hang up.

Humph . . . I try my luck again without wasting a moment by overthinking. Overthinking is my superpower after all.

I turn the paper over; there are some names on it of people who would be difficult to confront. I can't jump into the deep end of the pool yet.

Professor Jimenez, my properties teacher in law school. She gave me a C, and I wrote a seething letter to the administration about her poor teaching skills. Looking back, she wasn't terrible; I was just overwhelmed with my course load, and properties was a difficult class. I have always wondered if she was reprimanded as a result of my letter.

I have an hour before my Pilates class begins. I've fed William, my house is spotless, and I just finished reading a novel and binge-watching a TV series, so I have nothing but time. I grab my tablet and begin searching the university site to see if she is still a teacher there.

Luckily, I find her bio under the professors' tab on the website. Right below her photo is her email address. I press the hyperlink, and it takes me to my Outlook, where I start to draft an email.

Professor Jimenez,

You will probably find this email highly unusual, but very overdue. You were my properties professor about twenty years ago, and even though you surely do not remember me, I have not forgotten you. You gave me a final grade of a C. It was my first C ever. I was young, entitled, arrogant, and, apparently, overdramatic. I thought that C was the end of the world and I would never be hired to a top-tier law firm because of it. Consequently, I wrote a letter to the administration about your teaching skills, imploring them to terminate you or at the very least to reevaluate your credentials. I now understand that it was immature and utterly ridiculous, and I am embarrassed by my behavior. Seeing as you are still at the University of Chicago and have since achieved tenure, I'm sure my letter was ignored. Thank God. Nevertheless, I'd like to take this opportunity, late as it may be, to apologize for my behavior. It was uncalled for and I sincerely regret my actions. I am very sorry.

Yours truly,
Amelia Montgomery

I'm embarrassed that I would even do such a petty thing. *What was I thinking?* I'm not sure what else to say, but I end my email with that word. *Sorry.* And as with Gary, I *feel* sorry.

I read the email twice and finally decide to hit "Send." I don't wait for a response because I don't need it. I didn't apologize because I needed her to accept it; I did it to convey my sorrow for something ugly I had done. And now I've said it, and there's a lightness in my soul whether she accepts it or not.

I take a pen from my purse and cross out Gary and Professor Jimenez.

Luanne
~~Gary~~
Lindsey
Jenny O.
Jenny M.
Jenny Z.
Mary
Office
~~Brenda~~
Margret
~~Jimenez~~

———

After Pilates, as I'm taking my car keys out of my purse and checking my phone, I see that Professor Jimenez replied to my email. I'm scared to open it. Now I understand what an awful thing I did to her. I'm sure she's going to send me to hell. It would be deserved, but I don't know if I want to read that. I need to prepare for the worst and not lash out if I get a nasty response. Maybe I shouldn't even read it. I apologized and the rest is not important, right?

Yet my curiosity gets the better of me, and I open the email.

Dear Ms. Montgomery,

I hope you are well. I did not know anything about your letter to the administration, but am not surprised by it. I have always been a difficult teacher, and most of my students would have been grateful for a C, seeing as the passing rate in my class was always very low. Regardless, I thank you for your apology. There are no hard feelings. I'm sure you were not the first nor the last to write a letter to the administration about me. I bet, however, you learned a lot about properties from me. Good luck in all your endeavors.

Angela Jimenez

She's right. I did learn a lot from her, and some of my cases did have underlying real estate issues that I was able to handle because of Jimenez.

I reread her email.

Simple. It was more my problem than hers. I have had that worry for nothing. Nevertheless, it makes me feel pleased to have apologized.

I decide to try and make a nice dinner using my new cooking techniques with my new pots and pans. I load up my tablet for some background music and instantly see Hugh Phoebe plastered all over my news feed.

My skin crawls at the mere mention of his name and his photo on my screen. Nevertheless, I click on the link. It's a feel-good article on the scumbag billionaire, which makes me want to throw up. Phoebe and his team must be spending a fortune in publicity to show him as an upstanding human being, but I know better. I can barely finish reading it when I see photos of his family and two kids on the bottom, the caption praising Phoebe. I see words like *great man* and *best father*. Then I read: According to Phoebe's new counsel at Jones, Jones & Fisher, "I have no doubt that Mr. Phoebe will prevail. He is an upstanding citizen and justice is on our side."

It's such a high-profile case that I have no doubt that Junior took it upon himself to handle it after I left. I'm eager to find out but also hesitant to know. I need that part of my life to be over and done with, and knowing details about Phoebe and the trial will not do me any good.

My stomach churns when the story ends with:

> High-profile defense attorney Amelia Montgomery withdrew from the case over a month ago, almost ruining Phoebe's defense and forcing a last-minute scramble to find suitable counsel. The firm has confirmed that the case was too complicated for Montgomery and a more seasoned and reputable attorney within the firm would be a better fit. An anonymous source has reported that Montgomery even physically attacked some members of the firm during a tumultuous mental breakdown. The firm did not press charges, even with clients left unrepresented. Ms. Montgomery seems to be recovering, as photographs have surfaced of her leaving a wellness spa.

My Pilates class is in a spa, but it's not a wellness spa, and I am certainly not having a mental breakdown!

I knew that Junior was a despicable human being, but to call Phoebe an upstanding citizen is completely ludicrous. Even if Junior defends him in court, he doesn't have to go that far out on a limb for the vile man.

I would bet my new fortune that JJF leaked the story about my fake meltdown. Sonsofbitches, I can't even go after them for the breach of the nondisclosure since they will deny having said anything. Anonymous, my ass!

I also wonder if John's read the article and whether he will cancel our date tomorrow. Does he believe I had a meltdown? I did get a bit unhinged during my birthday party and the subsequent morning. I'm sure it's not easy for John to be linked to me while hearing the rumor mill in the office about what went down between me and the partners at JJF.

The article's left me feeling despondent. There's no way I can start my life anew if my name gets dragged through the mud. Should I even bring this up during the date? He does work at the firm; pretending I didn't read the article would be bizarre. I'm also curious about his take on Phoebe. Even if he's not handling it himself, does he agree with the way Junior wants the case tried? And—oh my God!—what if he's helping Junior with the case? That hadn't even crossed my mind, but now that it has, I can't unthink it. What if he agrees with Junior? This would be a worst-case scenario.

I decide to enlist Nina's advice. Again. "It's me again."

"Twice in one day? All the therapy I couldn't get you to do, you've decided to do it all today?"

"Sure feels like it, doesn't it?"

"I'm about to walk into a therapy session with a new client. I have five minutes," she says.

"Would you date someone who is morally reprehensible?"

"Jesus Christ, Millie. Of course not."

"I mean, this is all hypothetical of course. I don't know how much John knows or doesn't know. But if he does know, can I date him?"

"Stop. Explain. You have three minutes. I have zero idea what you're talking about."

"John works at JJF. I doubt he has anything to do with Phoebe because the vile bastard would never settle for John, a meager associate. I'm sure Junior is representing him. But for argument's sake, if John did help out on the case and if John did think that Phoebe wasn't a scumbag, could I date him?"

"Who the hell is Phoebe?"

"The pig I didn't want to represent, remember?"

"Oh. Okay. I didn't even know his name until just now." The only thing Nina knows is that I had a difference of opinion on how to handle a case. I was probably yelling and crying into the phone, and it is very probable I never disclosed the name of the defendant. Her confusion is warranted.

"Got it," she clarifies. "And that makes John morally reprehensible?"

"I don't know. Maybe. We have a date tomorrow, and I'm not sure what he knows about me and JJF or what he knows about Phoebe."

"And could you perhaps discuss this with him like a normal person? Perhaps without leading with the words *morally reprehensible*? Maybe compartmentalize the lawyer and the person, and then reconcile the differences in a nonconfrontational manner? And then maybe, just maybe, you'll find out that you're overreacting, and the guy has no idea what you're talking about."

"That would be the reasonable thing to do, I guess." Unfortunately, there's an NDA in the middle, which means I can't do exactly what she's suggesting, but I can ask in a way that doesn't disclose too much but still gets me the information that I need.

"You guess?" She laughs. "Are you trying to tell me I'm right? Is that what is happening right now?"

Now it's my turn to laugh. "I'll try the reasonable approach you're suggesting. I'll try not to jump to conclusions."

"So . . . you are going to go out with him?" she asks, confused.

"Yes. I'm not going to talk to him about his work. Focus solely on personal conversation. I'm going to pretend he's not even an attorney. Just like what you said. Compartmentalize."

"Uh . . . no! That is not at all what I said."

"Well, more or less. I get the drift. You're late for your patient. Thank you again! Love you. Bye." And I hang up feeling much more decisive.

CHAPTER TEN

Hugh Phoebe and Marc Jones Jr.

Two wealthy and powerful men. It's hard not to see the similarities between them, and how they played a part in my current conundrum, the conundrum being: I am about to go on a date with John, who works with Junior, who represents Phoebe. My two nemeses. Though it's difficult not to think John's like them in any way, it's hard for my mind not to make that connection. Especially since it has been my experience that you don't always see a man's true colors until you really get to know him. Case in point, all the victims in the Hugh Phoebe case were women who worked with him for years. They trusted and respected him. He charmed and seduced them with job security and money, not unlike Junior, who gave me a career and an opportunity to be a partner at one of the most prestigious law firms in the nation and then bam . . . the other shoe dropped.

And then there's Marcus Worthington who, if he is even a smidgen like his father was, has probably grown up to be just as vile, entitled, and sexist as Phoebe and Junior.

For a brief moment, a tiny little second, when I was writing the apology list, I thought that maybe I should have added Marcus to it. He was, after all, my first and only love, my fiancé, the man I almost married. He was also the man who broke my heart. If I'm trying to figure myself out, I'd have to admit that I was also at fault for the relationship falling apart. That's how therapy works. You figure out what role you played in the situation and you take accountability for it. At any rate, that's what Google says. But even in my drunken state I had scratched his name out with a thick, black mark and never added him back.

I've never sat back and reflected on my life. I just worked and got shit done, slept, woke up, and did it again, holding no accountability for any of my actions. People have been just part of, or a hindrance to, accomplishing a task. Now, however, I have all this time and nothing holding me back from thinking of everything that's led me to where I am today. A lost woman.

And I find myself finally, after all this time, reflecting on the years I spent with Marcus.

We met in law school. Him: six feet tall, lean, blond, wealthy. Me: only telling you this because he had the kind of wealth that defines a person. The kind of wealth that paves the way, gets you into the best restaurants, buys you $100,000 cars, takes you on spontaneous trips to Bali, and makes you inherently lazy and entitled. Marcus never had to get a job to pay bills or wash his own underwear or cook his own meals. He also never had to study for the LSAT to get into a top law school because his last name and huge donations got him in.

Marcus swept me off my feet our second year of law school, something that I'd never experienced. Sure, I'd dated, but I usually lost interest quickly. He was the first man in a sea of boys. In retrospect, what I loved most was how direct he was. From the moment we were paired together in a mock trial, he had absolutely no reservations about letting me and the entire class know how he felt. He bought me flowers and weekends at a spa and charmed his way into my heart. I'm not sure if it was because of the immaturity of the guys I had dated before, or perhaps my expectations were low, but I had never had someone give me so much of themselves as Marcus. It was as if his entire world revolved around me and my happiness. And he did make me happy. Very much so. When I was sick one week, he brought me soup, cared for me, took notes for me, and didn't let me move even after I whined and tried to go to class. We were practically living together by the end of our third year of law school, and by the time we had to take the bar exam, we were engaged.

To this day, I've never been in a relationship where a man wanted me so completely. His world revolved around me, but what I didn't realize at the time was that that kind of obsessive love came with reciprocity.

Don't get me wrong, I love being pampered and swept off my feet as much as the next girl, but school was a priority, not Tahiti, not partying. After a while, the attention he gave me became overwhelming.

I was being selfish and ungrateful. How could I possibly turn down what he was offering? The guilt chipped away at me little by little, but I never told him. If he wanted me to go out for drinks instead of studying, we went out for drinks, and I'd later spend all night cramming for the test.

Unfortunately partying has a way of catching up with you, and at one point Marcus was barely passing classes. But when I tell you that he came from money, I mean there was a wing in the school named Worthington Hall. His father was an attorney, and so were his uncles and grandfather and great-grandfather and so on and so forth.

But Marcus was not cut from the same cloth, and money can only do so much for you. At some point you have to sit at a table with three hundred other students and take the Illinois bar exam, and no one is going to change that.

I passed the first time around.

Marcus did not.

His father did not like this. Marcus did not like this. The pressure from his family started to take a toll on our relationship. He resented me for passing and finding a job immediately upon graduating. He told me so every day and made me feel awful when I couldn't make time for him. I was already an associate at JJF, and I was working long hours and I just couldn't be there for him and work simultaneously. I could not cut myself in two and make everyone happy.

Meanwhile, Marcus was still partying instead of studying for his third attempt at the bar exam. He demanded constant attention. But how do you toss away someone who's so in love with you that they just want your time and attention? Turning that away would make me a terrible person. That was the true definition of a bitch.

Well, it turns out that it wasn't really my attention that he needed. He just needed attention. Any warm body would do.

One evening after a very long day doing the partners' grunt work at the office, I raced home hoping he was still up so that we could grab dinner and spend a little extra time together. Instead, I walked in on Marcus and some random girl having sex in our bed. Needless to say, that was the end of Marcus and me.

After arguing on my part, and by arguing I mean throwing a few pieces of a hundred-year-old bone china serving set against a very old and very ugly family portrait and stomping on his bullshit Yale diploma, I took my stuff and left. He begged me to stay. I wish I could say it ended there, but after the breakup, Marcus's father blamed me for his son's inability to pass the bar exam (and probably for the damage to the china, the portrait, and the diploma). Evidently, my leaving Marcus made him stupid. Of course, his dad didn't call his son stupid, he said that Marcus was too depressed to study. But we all know it wasn't the breakup that caused Marcus to fail the exam. I endured months of calls from Marcus and his father, Marcus still begging and his dad impatiently demanding I make things right. Because sometimes men with money think that they hold all the power.

But I didn't bend to their will. Eventually, I threatened to file a restraining order on both of them, which, as a matter of public record, would bring shame to the Worthington name. If I were to analyze myself a little deeper—Nina-style—maybe it's why I felt so adamant that Phoebe should be held accountable for his actions. The victims in the case didn't provoke Phoebe into becoming a vile human being. Phoebe is a vile human being because he has never needed to take responsibility for a single wrongdoing in his life. He has the money to make things just go away. Poof! Just like Marcus and just like Marcus's dad.

So, no, I feel no need to add Marcus or his father to my list of apologies, and I feel 100 percent justified in my decision.

Marcus was the most significant of my failed relationships, but there've been others. Always the same formula: a meet-cute followed by nothing but rainbows and butterflies, then a plot twist summarized by "I'm too busy to give them all my attention," which makes them feel emasculated. The dark moments of my relationships vary from cheating to dumping to ghosting, but there's always the same epilogue of my crushed heart hardening even further. So you can see why I'm not too eager to jump into a new relationship. I'm not Cinderella, and there's no Prince Charming. There are women and there are men. There is affection and maybe even love, and then, if you're lucky, you find someone with similar interests, and you live contentedly ever after.

The thing is, I like myself enough to not settle for contentment. I'd rather stay single and do the things I love without having to compromise anything for someone else. And I will not be blinded by money because when I had none, I didn't settle, and now that I have a lot, I have even more reason to be particular in choosing whom to spend my time with. But I do miss having regular sex, and sex with John was phenomenal. I also wish I had companionship, someone with whom to share funny stories and hold hands while watching scary movies.

And here I am, heading to a date. A date with a man I thought was very charming and witty but who may or may not be representing Satan and working with my nemesis. A man much like the men I've been avoiding.

This is going to go great!

———

I'm in a pair of ankle-length fitted trousers with a crimson-and-white sleeveless floral top. I've let my hair down and put on some makeup. I feel pretty good about myself as I walk into Mint, a well-known Indian restaurant in the area. It's not pretentious or high-end. It's middle-of-the-road, not too loud, not too intimate, but cozy with its dim lighting and dark decor. A perfect place for a first date.

I spot him the moment I walk in. He sees me, too, because he stands right up and holds the chair out for me as I walk toward the table at the back of the restaurant. He's shaved, so his face is smooth, and his hair is combed in a way that I know took time to style, even though it's messy, as if he's attempting to convey that he woke up this way. Except I know he didn't just wake up that way because, well, I've woken up with him.

I like it. It's shiny and dark, and it makes his eyes look greener. The gray sprinkled in makes him look a little mysterious. He's wearing black pants and an untucked pink polo. He looks extraordinarily handsome. I wonder how old he is. When I met him, I thought he was in his early forties. Then when I woke up the next morning and he had those glasses on and that stubble with mostly gray hair, I thought maybe he was closer to fifty. Now, I'm unsure again.

"You look gorgeous," he says as I near, and he kisses me on my cheek, lingering a little by my face. "You smell even better."

Those butterflies . . . damn it.

"I remembered your love for red wine, so I ordered a bottle. I hope that's okay."

"Yes, of course," I say, guarded. I'm still not sure about him, and I will not let those eyes and that dimple sway me. The server comes to our table with the wine and hands John a little to taste, but John slides it over to me. I taste it and give my approval, and the server proceeds to pour us each a glass.

"There was a wonderful Indian restaurant by my house in Portland. I used to go at least once a week, but I haven't had Indian food since I arrived in Chicago."

"You picked the best one in town. I was here once a long time ago and it was very good."

"Great. I'm starving." We both look over the menu before the server gets back to us.

"Can I ask how old you are?" I take a mouthful of wine.

"Forty-four."

"Do you date much?"

"You're cross-examining me already?" He chuckles but gets right into it. He puts the menu down on the table and sits casually back, ready to answer any question I may have.

"Just getting to know you. I'm a little rusty."

"No, it's fine. Ask me whatever you like. I'm an open book, Millie. And to answer your question, no, I don't date much. You?"

"I used to date more, but between work and the awkward, uncomfortable dates, I just stopped. It's hard dating when you're so busy."

"Here's to avoiding awkward and uncomfortable," he says, lifting his glass, and we clink them together. I take a sip and let it slide down my throat, feeling my limbs start to relax. "So now you have all this time, so dating's back on the schedule?"

"Do I have that much time? I mean, between my recuperation from the mental breakdown and all my trips to the wellness spa, I'm booked!" My ability to compartmentalize lasted all of twenty minutes. "The less I know, the better" went straight out the window.

"You read that, too, huh?"

I sit back, arms crossed. "It was all over the news. Hard to miss."

"If it means anything, I don't think it's true. You're clearly sane, and you don't seem like a person who'd lose her mind over a case. But . . ." He takes a sip of wine. "I did see you walk into a wedding to apologize to a total stranger, so who knows." He winks and shrugs.

"And you decided to go out with me anyway. Maybe you're the insane one here." I chuckle.

"All kidding aside, I know you're not insane, but I would be lying if I didn't tell you that I'm very curious as to why you left the firm. And please don't say you retired. I know that's bullshit. Retirement is something someone ordinarily chooses, and they do so at a certain age. You were either forced to quit or left on your own. But why? That's what intrigues me because I can't figure out a reason."

"And you've put a lot of thought into that."

"You've got no idea. I know you want to tell me; I can see it in your eyes. But you can't, either because that reason will paint you in a bad light or your hands are tied. An NDA, perhaps?"

Ack . . . he's so close to knowing. It makes me anxious that it may slip out of me because I really want him to know the truth, or that he will find out somehow and it'll be a violation of the NDA because we're dating. It would be difficult to prove that I didn't disclose it. That he just guessed. And if he guessed, what would he do with that information? Would he be mad on my behalf and say something? Could he keep it a secret to protect my NDA? There's countless reasons why dating John could become a mess. Still, I can't help but nudge him a little because it's my reputation on the line.

I put the glass down and inch closer to him from across the table. "I didn't go crazy. I didn't have a meltdown. I haven't been in a spa. I'm doing Pilates, and it's inside a spa, but I'm not in a wellness treatment center because I've lost my marbles as the article suggested. I'm just exercising."

"I believe you," he says without missing a beat, and I decide right there and then that that is enough for me for now. I don't need to know that he's a flat-earther or antivaxxer (not yet, at least). I just need to get to know him and trust that my ability to weed out the good and the bad in people isn't broken. He read the trashy article and made his own decision, and here he is, on a date with me.

For now, that's enough.

But then he screws it up by adding a *but.* "But I don't know you all that well and you are not forthright at all. You're not giving me much to work with, Millie, and I don't think you retired. In fact, I have no doubt that you did *not* retire. You don't walk away from things. You're not built that way. I just met you and I know this without a doubt."

I sit back and sip my wine. My eyes narrow on him. This is a thin line, as I can't say anything about why I left. Regardless, I want to know what he thinks the reason is.

"Why do you think I left JJF, John?" I ask.

"I know what I've heard from people at the firm: you just decided to quit one day. The office talk is all over the place since no one seems to know what exactly happened. I even heard you're the love child of Margret and Jones Senior."

I chortle loudly at the ridiculousness of that conspiracy. "I can honestly say, without hesitation, that that particular rumor is unequivocally false."

"You didn't have a meltdown, and you look healthy and sane. If I was a betting man, I'd wager that you had some sort of falling-out with one of the partners. If I had to bet on it, it would be Marc Jones Jr. His father isn't there enough for you to argue with, and Fisher always has his head up his ass, so unless you're on the golf course with him, he probably doesn't even know you're alive."

I don't deny it, but I also don't agree.

"I believe you signed a gag order and you can't talk about it."

He's going to figure this out all on his own. I can't even confirm or deny what he's saying because part of the gag order is not to acknowledge that there's a gag order!

"Marc's a jerk on his best day, and I can imagine he's worse to an assertive woman like you," he continues. "Although, I have to say, and don't take this the wrong way, I've worked in other firms, and the partners are usually jerks. Old, white, entitled men. It's part of the job.

Which is why I can't figure out why now, after all these years, you'd leave because of a jerk. It doesn't add up."

"So a woman should just put up with that kind of behavior? Is that what you're suggesting?"

"It's a paycheck. We work, we get paid, we suck it up, and eventually we become the boss and become a jerk to our subordinates. It's the circle of life," he says.

"Except in that scenario I never become an old, white, entitled male."

"No. But things aren't the same as they were ten years ago, and those dinosaurs are slowly dying, and we're taking over," he says, watching me closely.

"We? Are we analogous?"

"No. I'm just saying that I'm an open-minded, unbigoted person. Not a walking antique. I wouldn't be a dick to my female subordinates."

"You'd be a dick to everyone."

"A nondiscriminatory asshole, perhaps." He raises his glass in a mock toast, and I can't help but laugh.

He'll never understand what it's like to be a woman in a man's profession. He may want to understand, and he may be empathetic, but he doesn't know.

"And you don't feel bad about that?"

"About what? About doing my job? No, I don't. We argue for a living. We can't let our guard down, or someone will swoop up and crush us. That's what we're paid to do. To fight. Are you having a crisis of conscience?"

"No," I say quickly. But maybe I am. In all the years I practiced law, I'm sure I represented some unsavory people, but mostly in a business capacity. Not that that made it right, but I never stopped to evaluate the ethics behind any of it. It all felt very transactional—two businesses fighting it out or two people fighting about business. Never had I been handed a case where the client was an accused rapist. He had not been convicted, but there was very strong evidence provided by many women that led many to believe he was wrongly acquitted.

I think that's why I ultimately snapped. It just felt too close to home, I suppose. I don't know, but what I *do* know is that John hasn't said anything about Phoebe and I really, really want to know if he's assisting on the case. But I also really, really don't want to know.

"By the way, just to put it out there, I have zero doubts that you were capable of representing Phoebe. I'm certain, in fact, that no one is more capable or has more trial experience than you." My heart melts. There's something so utterly sexy about being acknowledged by a colleague. That article suggested I wasn't equipped to handle the case, and he understands how fabricated it all is. If he was representing Phoebe, he would have told me so right here and right now.

"Let's not talk about work anymore." I smile at him, feeling flushed from the compliment. Maybe he's being sincere. Maybe he's trying to get into my panties. Maybe he's still hoping to get my client list. Whatever the reason, the tactic is working.

"Sounds good to me," he agrees. "So, have you had a hard time finding another firm or are you going to try going solo?" I think this is his attempt to change the subject, but it's still straddling the same line of conversation even if he doesn't know it.

"I'm not looking for another job."

"Really?"

"Really," I say and watch him take a sip of his wine with confusion etched all over his face. Now he is the one assessing me. The server comes back and tells us the specials. I order the butter chicken, and he orders the lamb curry and an order of naan.

"I hope it's good," he says. "I'm starving."

"I ordered the curry last time, and it was delicious. And, back to the question, I think I'm going to explore other options for the time. Law isn't calling me back, at least not right now."

"I can admire that, although I don't know if I could stop practicing. Don't you miss it?"

Do I miss it? It's not like I just walked away; I was forced away. That makes things different. "I do miss it. Some of it. I miss being in court and the adrenaline rush of finding a good argument when everything feels hopeless and, of course, the trial. The argument. The show of it all."

"But . . . ? There's a *but* in there somewhere; I can tell."

I sit back, relaxed, the awkwardness melting away as we talk about the thing we both love. We shouldn't talk about work, but it's such a huge thing not to talk about.

I ponder his question. I haven't had this conversation with anyone, partly because I don't think anyone else could possibly understand. Not that I've had that many people to chat with.

"Have you ever been on a sugar-free diet? You need that sweet taste so bad, but after a few days, the craving starts to subside, you stop getting headaches, and after a week you feel wonderful. Then one day, a few weeks later, you have a piece of cake and it's delicious, but it gives you a stomachache or a headache. When you think of just the taste and the sugar rush you can easily become addicted to it again, but the indigestion and migraine come along with the high, so do you want to have a piece of cake?"

"So you're saying you've had your fill of arguing," he says.

John fills my glass a bit more, and I take a sip, starting to feel its effect. My muscles have loosened, and apparently so has my tongue. He tops off his own glass and sits back as I continue. "Maybe. I don't know for sure, but right now, I'm good. I've been finding it rather fascinating not having to argue every day. Even if it's the thing I loved the most, not doing it has also made me realize it's the last thing I feel like doing these days. I think that is why I'm not rushing the Apology Project. The last two apologies went very well, and they helped me feel great, but also it makes me hesitant to move forward quickly. Our job is exhausting, John, and I don't want to start arguing with people outside of work because of the silly list. Work took a toll on me I hadn't even realized until I cut it out of my life, and I don't want to do anything that messes with my Zen. That's not to say that I had a meltdown and couldn't handle it," I quickly add.

"I know. I know. I get it. I suppose I'm not at that point yet. I still need chocolate cake and welcome the indigestion."

I laugh loudly. "And maybe you'll never get sick of it."

He shrugs, and when the naan arrives, we pick at it as we chat. "On another note, I am glad to hear you've been tackling those apologies, even if it takes you years to finish it."

"I called one person on the list after you and I met Brenda, and I have to admit, it went very well. He didn't even know there had been a problem to begin with. His response propelled me to email another person, and she accepted my apology too. But I've been thinking about a few others on the list I've been avoiding. I'm not even sure I want to apologize to them."

"Then don't."

He makes it sound so easy. I'll have to overthink that later.

The server brings the food, and we begin to eat in companionable silence. It's delicious. While we're eating, he tells me all about Portland, and that eventually brings the conversation to all the pro bono work he did for the community.

I'm impressed with all the work he's done. All his passion projects just cement the fact that he has integrity, a trait I need in a man. I'm relieved because the more I talk to him, the more I like him. "The jury's still out on you, John Ellis. I must be rusty because I can't get a good read on you."

He chuckles. "I'm easy. I'm an open book. What is it that you can't read?"

"You seem like a genuinely nice person, and then you move across the country to work in a trial firm like JJF, the kind of firm that does not do anything at all to help the community unless they'd be profiting from it somehow."

"I like a challenge, and JJF is the best trial firm around. I also like money, and they made me an offer I couldn't refuse. I'm not that selfless, trust me. I'm driven by success just like most people."

"But at what price? How can you sleep at night? You're better than JJF." Even as it comes out of my mouth, I realize I'm attacking him.

"You experienced it yourself. A pretty awesome cotton duvet and fluffy pillows." I've pissed him off. He's clearly deflecting, and his tone has a bite to it I hadn't seen before.

"John . . ."

"Listen, Millie, I'm neutral. This is work. Everyone has a right to representation; you know that as well as I do. It's my job, and that's all there is to it. I can separate work from my personal life. If you came here to argue with me about my career choices, you can save it. You're overthinking things."

"I've recently been told that I do that."

"Well, I can overlook it if you can overlook that I'm working at JJF."

I don't know how long I'm sitting there in thought, but when I look up, most of his food is gone and he's watching me intently.

"It's not that difficult, you know?" he says, that smirk back on his stupidly handsome face. He knows that if I haven't gotten out of my seat and walked out by now, I'm not going to.

"What's not difficult?"

"Those three little words that you hate to say. If you want, I'll walk you through it. Repeat after me: *I am sorry.*"

I snort out a laugh. He has an uncanny ability to make me laugh and to keep me on my toes even when I'm upset or frustrated or want to wring his neck. "First, I'm not opposed to apologizing to you or to anyone. I'm just tired of throwing around apologies to undeserving people."

"And I'm undeserving?"

"You want me to apologize for voicing my opinion? Junior is a dick and you're working in a place surrounded by dickheads. I don't see why I'd need to apologize."

He laughs too. "I want you to apologize for making our first date uncomfortable and for coming here not to enjoy my company but to give me a piece of your mind. You could have just said all this over the phone, you know. Mind you, I took the job at JJF before I even met you. You can't crucify me for past indiscretions."

I roll my eyes. "Isn't a first date about getting to know one another? I think they're supposed to be a little uncomfortable."

He puts his fork and knife down and gives me that lawyerly attention he probably uses to get the jury on his side. "You can't put all your cards on the table on a first date. You don't just walk into a nice restaurant and vomit all your beliefs. You work into it. Slowly. So as to not scare off said date."

"So I scared you off?"

He guffaws. "Not at all, Amelia Montgomery. Not. At. All."

I can't help but be amused.

"I thought we had agreed to table any conversation that involves morality, ethics, politics, and religion until a later date. Say, third or fourth?"

I smile. "That's right. A separation of church and state. Work stays at work and we don't discuss it." This may be good, the more I think about it. I can avoid questions that could violate my NDA while he avoids discussions about cases or about Junior that could upset me. "We can just agree to have a nice time together."

"You're the one that keeps bringing it up."

He's right. Damn it. "Well, now that we've set up the rules, I won't be making that mistake again."

He smirks and shakes his head. "First date and you're giving me rules?"

"Not rules, just rule. Singular. There's just one. No shop talk. Simple."

"Deal," he says. "I'm sure we will have many more uncomfortable dates. I can't very well sleep with you again without at least a semblance of gentlemanly decorum. Today I wine and dine you, and then next time maybe we handle first base or second, and so on and so forth."

This time I actually laugh out loud. "So this nice dinner is just a pretense for your ultimate plan of seduction."

"Ultimately, yes. I won't lie, I want to sleep with you again. The great conversation and animosity are just icing on the cake."

I try not to smile so big; I wouldn't want to inflate his ego further. "I will not be sleeping with you tonight. I don't do that on first dates. Just for the record."

He laughs. We already slept together and we're doing this completely backward. But he's a nice guy and I appreciate his honesty.

We do put a pin in all work-related conversation, and even though I'm still super curious to know whether he's on the Phoebe case, the rest of the night we get to know one another.

Turns out, he's been living in Chicago for only a few short months. He moved here for the job. My job. Well, not exactly my job because they haven't made him a partner yet, but he's on a fast track since he has more experience than all the associates at JJF. He was born and raised in Portland. He has one sister, like I do, and he misses her terribly. I tell him how Nina is always trying to psychoanalyze me, but I love her more than anyone in the world.

I look around, and there is a bartender leaning over the bar, fiddling with his phone. The server, the poor, nice man, is yawning and looking like he just wants us to get the hell out of there so he can go home. All the other tables are clean and their chairs have been stacked on top while a woman sweeps the floor.

"Uh-oh . . . I think the restaurant is closed. What time is it?" I ask and he looks at his watch.

"Twenty past eleven. I think they closed at eleven." We both look around again and wince.

"Oh, damn," I say, genuinely surprised we'd been so into the conversation that we both missed everything happening around us.

He looks at the server apologetically and then takes the bill that is placed on the table. "Let's split it," I say as I grab my purse.

"No," he says, and just places his credit card into the little leather envelope without even looking at the bill.

———

We're standing in front of the restaurant, and the valet brings my car first and hands me my key, then jogs off to get John's car. The weather is warm even this late at night. I can see a small drop of moisture gathering on John's forehead. I'm sure my face is becoming shinier as the minutes tick by.

"I had a great time, Millie," he says, kissing me tenderly on the cheek as he opens my car door and helps me inside.

"I did too."

"I'll call you," he says and closes the door. I put on my seat belt and am startled by a tap at my window.

I press the button, and the window lowers. John crouches down, resting casually against my window. "I took a chance coming here tonight after that article came out. I chose to give you the benefit of the doubt, Millie. Try and do the same for me. I promise you won't regret it."

My lips form a small O shape.

"You're a brilliant woman, Millie, and even when you're being antagonistic with me, I find myself smitten. It was a good night, and I . . . I don't know. I wanted you to know that even if the jury's still out on me, it's not out on you. I've already formulated my opinion of you."

"Okay," I say softly.

He leans into my car and kisses me softly on the lips. It's not sexy and it doesn't even involve tongue, but I feel it all the way down to the tips of my toes. It's quick but it's tender and sweet and damn . . . I think I like John. I know I don't like his employer.

Please, Lord, let his worst flaw be that he took a job at JJF.

CHAPTER ELEVEN

Luanne
~~Gary~~
Lindsey
Jenny O.
Jenny M.
Jenny Z.
Mary
~~Office~~
~~Brenda~~
Margret
~~Jimenez~~

Good luck on your first day of school! John texts me. It's been two weeks since our date at Mint, and we've had lunch once and another dinner date since. I admitted that I was nervous about starting Spanish at the local community college, but he cheered me on.

An hour into class later, I realize I'm in over my head. School's meant for young people, especially when it comes to learning a new language.

I place my Spanish textbook in my oversize purse at the end of class.

Yes, I signed up for Spanish because it's the only concrete thing I could do to feel closer to that side of me that I didn't even know existed.

I have a bunch of baby photos of my father that I looked at with new eyes. I don't know what clue to our Hispanic genes I expected to find, but I keep looking through them. Of course there are no hints. No clues. Just a baby that looks like every other baby.

"This class is going to be the pits," says the man who's been sitting next to me for the last hour.

I laugh, feeling relieved that someone else is as lost as I am. "Tell me about it. I don't know if I'm capable of picking any of this up."

He zips up his TUMI bag and extends his hand. "Z Alfonso."

"Your name is Z?" I ask, trying not to insult him. Maybe I just didn't understand the pronunciation.

"No. It's Zacharias, but most people call me Z. It's easier."

"Zacharias." I try to pronounce it the way he just did, with the *z* in that Spanish accent that sounds like an elegant lisp and the *ch* pronounced like a *k*. I think I've butchered it. "Z it is. I'm Millie. Millie Montgomery. It's nice to meet you."

"You too, Millie." He holds my hand a little longer than necessary. Midthirties, tall and lean, he has a lovely smile. He has a crossbody bag where he keeps his textbook and a thin laptop, which he used to type his notes.

We walk out of class together and he continues talking. "Why Spanish?" he asks.

"It's a little silly, but my mother got me one of those 23andMe tests, and it turns out that I have a lot of Spanish blood I had no idea I had because my father was adopted. Now I have this desire to learn Spanish. Maybe I can connect to those roots." *Why am I babbling?* I stink at making friends.

"You sure you're not in one of those commercials for 23andMe?" he says, chuckling.

I laugh. "I know. It's a little insane how weird it is to find out you have this entire lineage that you didn't know about. Anyway, how about you? Why'd you sign up for this torture?"

"My parents are from Colombia, but I was born here in the States, in Connecticut. They've always been on my case about not speaking Spanish. They'd talk to me in Spanish, but I'd always answer in English. But at work they're opening a branch office in Puerto Rico and I got the job. I'll move there next year, so I guess it's time I learned the language. Both for work and for my parents' sake. I do know *un poquito*." He holds his thumb and pointer finger together.

"Seems like a much better reason than mine." I laugh. "What's work for you? What do you do?"

"I'm an account executive for a marketing firm. You?"

That explains his expensive suit and tie. Why did I ask about his job? Now he's asking about mine. "I was a lawyer—well, I still am, but not currently employed. I'm in between careers at the moment." Telling him that I'm retired seems like it would elicit too many questions. "It's complicated," I finally say because I sound as if I don't know what my job situation is. Then I point to the end of the parking garage. "That's me."

"It was nice to meet you, Complicated Millie. See you next week." *Complicated! Ha! Ain't that the truth.*

"See you next week, Account Executive Z." He waves as we part ways to our own cars.

I think I just made a friend.

As soon as I get into my car and the Bluetooth connects, my phone rings. "You want to grab dinner tonight?" Nina asks instead of saying hello. Nina and I try to have dinner together at least once every other week, though we talk on the phone all the time. Even when I was swamped with work, I'd always make time for Nina.

"Sure. My house at six?"

"Your house? Are you ordering?"

"No. I'm cooking. I'm excited to try out one of the recipes I learned from my online class." I want to try making braised short ribs. My mom used to cook almost every day when we were kids. She had go-to recipes that she'd stick with, like meat loaf, lasagna, a stir-fry, and a few others that were in the rotation. As a busy office manager at a doctor's office and as a mother of two, she was usually running home to get food on the table. There was never a time for fancy new recipes, though that's not to say that she wasn't a good cook. I don't need to be the best cook, but I would like to expand my cooking portfolio beyond spaghetti and scrambled eggs.

"I think you forgot that you don't cook."

"I do now. Prepare to be impressed."

"Okay. If you say so." And she disconnects and texts the green queasy emoji and Don't poison me.

I reply with the devil emoji.

In sneakers, leggings, and a T-shirt that has a cactus on it that says, NOT A HUGGER, I head out to the grocery store on foot. An hour and a half later I'm in a foul mood as I open the door to my house; I hate to sweat, and just walking out the door this month causes perspiration. I also didn't account for all the crap I'd buy, so lugging it back home was a huge pain in the ass.

I drop all the groceries on my kitchen island as my phone dings with an incoming call.

"How was school?" John asks.

"Hard. How was work?"

"Exhausting."

"Want to grab dinner?" he asks.

"Can't. I have plans. How about tomorrow?"

"Tomorrow's no good for me," he says. "Friday, lunch before I fly out to Vegas?" He told me in one of our late-night conversations that he has a new case and the defendant's based out in Vegas, which means there will be some traveling in the foreseeable future.

"Sounds like a plan," I say.

"Meet by the office at one?"

"I'll be there."

"Great. See you soon and don't have too much fun with your 'plan' tonight," he says before disconnecting. I look at my screen. Does he think I have another date? I should correct him, but he also has plans tomorrow and he didn't give me any details. I don't owe him an explanation, right? I try to put that out of my head as I shower the sweaty morning away and then get started on making dinner for Nina. While all the food is cooking, I log into 23andMe, something I've been doing lately. It's interesting how much information they give you as people join and data is inputted. I wish I had a way of finding out more information about those "unknowns" in Cuba, but there's nothing I can do but wait. Meanwhile, I decide to purchase a Spanish cookbook. Maybe it's time I take my cooking to the next level.

———

Turns out—I might need more practice.

"Mills, honey, it's a little soupy. Is it supposed to look like that?" We both look down at the pot as I stir it one last time before serving it.

"I followed the exact instructions. I don't understand."

She takes the spoon from my hand and tastes my braised short ribs. I wait for a reaction. "It's not terrible."

"But it's not great."

"I wouldn't say great, no. I would say . . ." She takes another taste or, rather, another slurp. "It's a start."

"Well, if I had told you I was going to make a stew, would this have been up to par?"

"Yes. For a stew, it's good."

"Then, Nina, I'm making stew for dinner."

She laughs and I serve us bowls of hearty, meaty stew. I have some french bread that I bought, and I cut it into thick crusty slices and serve it along with the soup. The rice I made to eat with the short ribs, I'll save for tomorrow.

"I want to try making paella next," I say. "Do you think that the reason we like paella so much is because of our Spanish DNA?"

"No. I think most people like paella," she says as she eats. "You're really into this 23andMe thing, aren't you?"

"Yes! How are you not?" I yelp. "I keep just looking online, but I don't know where to start. Maybe I should hire a genealogist."

"Wow. I mean . . . wow," she says. "Seems like overkill, but if you're really that curious, I guess it makes sense . . . sort of." She's very supportive of everything I do. "Mom's been on my ass to do that 23andMe thing, too, by the way."

"You should! You know you can loosen up the privacy settings so that people who may be related to you can contact you and vice versa. No one's contacted me, though."

"Are you looking for Dad's biological mom?"

"Not actively, no. I'm just looking to see if there are any matches. Someone we may be related to. I wonder if we have close family somewhere. I can't believe you're so blasé about this."

"I'm not trying to be blasé, I just don't see what difference it makes. What would change in our lives by knowing all this information?"

"Nothing, I suppose. But it's our identity. I was researching Cuba, and I found out that Cubans are very generous and also they're generally very good at chess. That's you, Nina! How cool, right?"

She shrugs. "I liked chess because Mom liked chess and she taught me. You weren't patient enough and wouldn't sit down long enough to learn. And I don't think I'm that generous. Either way, I don't see why it matters why we do what we do. Why you're a neat freak and I'm not. It just is. Well, if you want to get really into it, we can go back and discuss major traumas in your life that—"

"No, no! Don't." *I do not want to be psychoanalyzed!* "I just think it would be interesting to connect with someone with similar qualities."

"Big-butt quality?"

"No!" I laugh.

"And what if you find these people and they are nothing like you? There's genes and then there's learned behaviors from your family and society. You could have absolutely nothing in common with them."

"Perhaps," I say. I've thought of that too. "But I still want to find out. Maybe it would explain my weird pineapple allergy or why you can roll your tongue and I can't and neither can Mom or Dad." *Or maybe by finding this missing side of me, this lost feeling will go away. Maybe I'll find people who get me. Who understand my need to win, to work hard, and to overthink everything.* I don't voice any of this, though. I don't want to concern Nina or for her to put on her therapy cap and start digging further.

She shrugs. "I can see why you're into it, I'm just not."

"You sound just like Dad."

"Maybe you'll go to Spain or Cuba," she adds. "For research."

"Learning Spanish and flying across the world are two very different things."

"Well, I'm voting for a trip. Cuba, the Bahamas, Europe. Anywhere. Live a little. Enjoy your retirement."

"It would be kind of cool to meet some of our cousins, wouldn't it?" I say.

"So you *are* thinking about it?"

"No. Well, maybe. I don't know. You know I don't like traveling. For now, I just want to learn Spanish and maybe try making some tapas or some flan."

"I guess it would be so cool if there were a bunch of Montgomerys somewhere that we don't know anything about."

"Well, they wouldn't be Montgomerys, but yes, it would be very cool. Either way, this Spanish thing seems hard. I wouldn't last one day in Spain."

She giggles. "Are you going to quit?"

"Absolutely not! I'm going to double up on studying."

"Everything doesn't have to be so intense, Millie. It's not a competition. You went from taking a 23andMe test to taking Spanish classes to actually considering going to Cuba or Spain."

"I never had time to *do* anything. I have no idea what I like or even dislike; I've never done anything but work. I feel like this is my chance to try everything I've ever had any interest in and see if it'll lead to the next chapter in my life. And now there's an entire part of me that I want to discover."

"That's good, Millie. I like how self-aware you're becoming."

"I've been listening to you all these years, it turns out." And I wink. "So enough about me. What's new with you?"

"Nothing much. Kevin wants to get back together."

I roll my eyes. "I've heard this before. And?"

"And nothing. It's really over this time. I gave him plenty of opportunities to take this relationship to the next level. He didn't want to, and I'm not going to sit around waiting."

"And you're okay?"

She shrugs. "I'm okay. I'm trying online dating."

I open my eyes wide. "Really?" Unlike me, my sister has a ton of friends and is a risk taker. She is a perfectly balanced person, which I'm not, apparently.

"Really! You need to try it, Mills. It's fun and very enlightening."

"Enlightening? Poor fools. Do they know you're psychoanalyzing every single thing they say and do?"

"Like you could have a conversation that doesn't sound like an opening statement or a cross-examination?"

"I'm trying to stop doing that."

"I'll believe it when I see it. So, tell me more about John. Anything new on that front?"

"As long as I avoid any topic about work, things are great."

"How great?" she says with a very dramatic eyebrow waggle.

"Unfortunately, not that great. After that drunken night, he hasn't tried anything other than a good night kiss, and I'm not too crazy about moving too fast. He works at JJF and I want to give him the benefit of the doubt, but I also want to get to know him a little better."

"At some point, Mills, you need to start trusting your gut instinct. Not every guy is going to be a jerk."

I sigh. She's right, but I'm still so hesitant. "I don't think I can handle one more rejection or disappointment," I blurt out. "I think I'm the one hesitating. He's not making any moves, but I'm also not giving him any indication that I want him to. What if he's trying the case? I altered my entire life over this stupid case, and I can't possibly date someone who doesn't believe in the same things I believe in."

"Wasn't he behind the Apology Project too? He brought that out of you, and you felt a connection with him that night at your birthday. You're not forthcoming, Mills, especially not to a stranger, yet you were vulnerable with him. You may have been drunk, but you weren't oblivious. You trusted your gut that night. Why not do it now?"

"Ugh. You make a good point," I agree. I hadn't thought of it that way.

"And anyway, how do you know he doesn't believe in the same things you do? Have you even asked him?"

"He can't give me details on what he's working on. Not directly anyway."

"And you're not pressing it either." She knows me so well.

"If I know, then it has to end, and I guess I'm not ready for things to end yet."

"That might be the most honest thing you've ever said to me, Mills." I sigh.

"So you'd rather be in this limbo status? One foot in the pool and one out? That sounds stressful, Millie. If you're not asking him because you don't want to know the truth, then commit to whatever it is you two are doing. Otherwise, move on. But don't half-ass this. It's just making it unnecessarily stressful for all parties involved."

I've come to realize in this short time of mostly talking and texting each other that it's not just about wanting to be intimate with John, it's about putting my heart out there and then . . . no one showing up at my party, leaving me disappointed, even though, until now, John's done nothing but impress me. But, just like I did with the Apology Project, I need to take the leap of faith and hope it pays off.

I toss a napkin at her from across the table. "Lately, every time I talk to you, I leave feeling exposed. Stop making me think so much about feelings. I don't like it."

She laughs. "It's because you don't have work to obsess over."

Huh. Interesting. "Let's talk about something else."

She smirks. "How is the Apology Project coming along?"

I take the bottle of wine and pour us some more. "The Apology Project? It's not a project." Although that's exactly what I've been calling it these days. "It's just a thing I'm doing, and it's going okay. I apologized to two other people and it felt nice. Unlike Brenda, the other two accepted my apology."

"But I saw that Brenda liked your Facebook profile photo last week."

"So?"

"She friended you on Facebook, Millie. She liked a photo."

"How is one thing connected to the other? I swear, sometimes your logic is so illogical it makes me dizzy."

"We're living in a world where you're considered an item based on your Facebook status. If you don't post a photo of where you are, it's as if you weren't really there. If you argue with someone in person, you get blocked from their page, and if you want to connect with someone, you request their friendship. It's her way of making a grand gesture."

"By pressing 'Request'?"

"Yes. And then you accepted; that's it. That one little button is a huge deal. If you don't accept, it's a metaphorical slap in the face, and if you block her—oh God, that's like peeing in her chicken soup. I had a patient the other day, sixteen years old, who didn't get out of bed for five days because the boy she had a crush on didn't like a bikini photo she posted, but did like a photo her best friend posted of a dog."

I roll my eyes. "I'm not sixteen, and that girl needs to toughen up. If she's hiding out at sixteen for a boy, what's going to happen to her at twenty when her boyfriend's in her bed screwing another girl?"

"Jeez, Millie."

I shrug because that's life and she knows it.

"You never talk about Marcus or any guy you've dated. It's something I've always noticed. You break up and it's over."

"That's the definition of a breakup."

"Being sad doesn't make you weak."

"Who has time to wallow?"

"Everyone. Maybe if you wallowed you would open up your heart instead of closing it tighter."

"Oh no, don't even think about doing that. None of this has to do with Marcus or Alex or Levi or any other guy. There are no unresolved issues. We're talking about Brenda and you brought in some crap about social media. How did we even fall into this rabbit hole?"

"I was just pointing out that the internet makes us all obsess over stupidity, and if Brenda is a social media ho, like most of us are, she grand-gestured you."

"I guess that somehow makes sense. And the two other people I apologized to were nice about it . . . What if the next one doesn't go as well? I'm not looking forward to getting a door slammed in my face."

"Well, yes. It might happen. But who cares? Are you doing the apology for them or for yourself?"

I thought it was for them. By saying I'm sorry to them, I'd be mending fences and hopefully creating new relationships. Maybe I've been looking at this all wrong. "I'm giving them the apology they deserve. Maybe it'll fix things."

"But who or what is it you're trying to fix, honey? You or them?"

Hmph. It's for me. "I'm doing this for me."

"Then does it really matter if people accept your apology?"

Even if doors get slammed in my face, it doesn't matter. I may deserve some of it, after all.

Damn it. I've been psychoanalyzed again.

CHAPTER TWELVE

Luanne
~~Gary~~
Lindsey
Jenny O.
Jenny M.
Jenny Z.
Mary
~~Office~~
~~Brenda~~
Margret
~~Jimenez~~

I'm sitting on my couch just watching television, wondering what I'm going to eat for dinner but too lazy to do anything about it, when my phone dings with an incoming email from 23andMe. They send updates often, so I'm not that curious except that this one says that I have a "DNA relative." I turn off the TV and turn on my tablet. I'm not twenty years old anymore, and I find myself holding my phone away from my face because of the tiny letters. So I find the email and click it. It's someone named Rosa, and she's from Cuba. My curiosity escalates, and I want to email her right away. I want to know everything.

But I'm interrupted by a knock at my door, which startles me. It's seven p.m. on a Tuesday, and I'm not expecting anyone. I stand up and pad to the front door. When I look through the peephole, I see John's face. *What the hell?*

During the last week, I've compiled a list of reasons it's okay to let my guard down with John. It's how I evaluate cases and what I do when making a decision. I weigh the pros and the cons.

John's kind, smart, and sexy. He works at JJF and has a big caseload, some of which are cases that I know for a fact I would have handled had I still been there. He's still an associate, so there's no way an egotistical man like Phoebe would accept John as his counsel. Phoebe specifically requested me to be the lead in the case because he believed having a woman represent him would send a message to the jury—that message being: my attorney is a woman and therefore I can't be a misogynistic, sexually harassing pig. He vetted firms for weeks. Even though there are hundreds of female attorneys in the Chicago area, there are not many with my trial experience and even fewer who are managing partners at such a well-known law firm.

Even though we never had a formal meeting, mostly because of the brawl I had with the partners, I briefly met Phoebe when he first came to our office. I'll admit, I was excited our firm was going to get such a high-profile case and that I had been hand-selected to be lead. I had to push aside the skin-crawling feeling I had gotten whenever I had watched him on television. I was Amelia Montgomery, badass lead attorney who doesn't get those weird "feelings." I'm not "that" woman. Or rather, as a woman in a man's world, I've always felt the need to be likable to them, to the men who were the ones ultimately in charge of my career. Pretend that those roaming eyes and creepy vibes didn't faze me. But it's one thing to put those feelings aside for my own selfish reasons and an entirely different thing to let him, or anyone else, destroy others.

Like Marcus Worthington's father years ago, Phoebe has the kind of money that gets him whatever it is that he wants. And he wants to win, but more than win, he wants to drag his victims through the mud in the process. He wants to humiliate and destroy them as payback for speaking out against him. The partners at JJF were okay with that. I was not. Would John be?

Phoebe vetted me very well before hiring the firm, and with John's background and all his pro bono work, he would never fit the bill.

It says a lot about me that I did. I'm not proud of it.

But back to my overanalyzing: John is not representing Phoebe. All he's really doing is working at a place that I hate. But I didn't always hate it, and I can't fault him for that. And maybe John is friends (or friendly) with Junior and the other partners. Maybe he's not. Regardless, being friends with your enemy doesn't necessarily make that person your enemy, right? Or is that the complete opposite of the saying? Anyway, the facts as I see them are clear. If I was making a rational legal conclusion, all evidence pointing to John being a sexist human being would be completely circumstantial, but unfortunately most in our profession work with sexist, despicable humans. There's no way around that. So I'm done driving myself crazy over something that isn't even a thing. John works at JJF. It's a job. I can live with that.

After the talk with Nina last week and my "list," I decided I'm going to assume that the facts that I have on John are the ones I'm working with and I'm tossing out all extra assumed and/or imagined evidence. Because we have rules, rules I put in place, and I'm not going to break them just because I'm still not over being furious at the way I was treated at the firm.

Anyway, that was my thought process after talking to Nina. My thought process may be skewed and this may all come back to bite me in the ass, but the alternative is to walk away and I'm not sure I want to do that just yet.

After I made that long-winded conclusion, things have been less stressful on my part at least. I feel more at ease in letting down my guard with John. I've even stopped thinking about the upcoming trial that had been a thorn in my side. When the trial is splayed all over the media in a few months, I'll just ignore it.

And now, John's at my house unexpectedly.

My pulse races and I run my fingers through my hair.

"Open up, Mills. I know you're there. I can hear you breathing."

I unlock the door and open it to find him holding two brown bags with the logo of my favorite Thai restaurant. He kisses me on the lips before walking in as if he's done this a thousand times.

"Uh . . . hi?" I say.

"I was in the neighborhood and thought I'd bring dinner. I'm assuming you haven't eaten yet since you had a late lunch."

I texted him something about Anthony Bourdain around three o'clock. He got me hooked on *No Reservations* and I got hungry while watching Anthony trek through Thailand. I told him that I was eating a peanut butter and jelly sandwich because I had forgotten to have lunch and that I wished I knew how to make pad thai because I was craving it but was too lazy to leave my house and too hungry to wait for delivery.

"Nope. Not yet. If there's pad thai in there, you're officially my hero. I'm starving."

"Call me Superman, sweetheart." He sets out the food on my kitchen island, and my stomach rumbles. "Did I interrupt anything?"

"Remember that I told you about the 23andMe thing? I just received an email saying that I have a 'DNA relative.' Her profile name is Rosa R. and she lives in Cuba now, but apparently she lived in Miami for about twenty years."

"Is that real? Why would you think she is a relative?"

I shrug. "I'm not sure. The database said so. I guess we have DNA in common. I just got the email. I need to look into it some more, but

I'm so excited. I think I'm going to respond. It would be interesting to find out more. Don't you think?"

"Absolutely. It must be weird to find out this whole new side of you."

"You've got no idea. It's interesting but also makes me feel a little guilty, like I'm somehow betraying my nana, my dad's adoptive mom. I'm forty years old; knowing this shouldn't change anything. I'm a fully formed human being. Yet I feel like it changes so much."

"I get it. It's a lot of changes in a short amount of time."

I let out a big breath. It is a lot. It feels sort of silly to me that I'm so hyperfocused on the DNA results at my age. I'll obsess over the email when he leaves and I'm alone.

"Anyway, enough about me. How was work?" I ask John. It's the first time he's been over, but you wouldn't know that by the way he rummages around, taking out plates and utensils. "I'm a mess. You should've called first."

I wish I hadn't grabbed the oldest T-shirt I own. It has a small rip on the bottom, and my pajama shorts aren't much better. But he stops what he's doing and reaches over the counter, cups the back of my head, and pulls me to him for a second, and even better, kiss. "You look perfect," he says with a wink and then goes back to serving us, unaware of how my heart just fluttered.

"It was a busy day, but your text got me craving Thai too." He portions out all sorts of Thai goodies. He's made himself very at home in my kitchen. "I have depos in Portland coming up, and I've been preparing all day. I'll probably be gone for a week. I want to visit my sister while I'm there." He slides a plate over my way.

"Sounds lovely. You must miss her. I can't imagine moving that far away from Nina."

"Very much," he says and then sits down across from me. I've poured him a glass of wine, and I'm sipping some when he says, "Why don't you join me?"

I almost choke on my wine.

"Join you?" We're nowhere near traveling together and definitely not at the "meeting the family" stage. "Go on a trip? Together? That seems a little more than what we've been doing so far. I literally just decided to date you. Like, two days ago, and now you want to go on a trip? How would we even handle sleeping arrangements?" I ask, maybe too frankly.

"You just decided to date me?" He sort of laughs and coughs simultaneously. "We've been dating for almost a month now. I know I've been busy and we haven't seen each other as often as I'd like, but we talk all the time. What do you mean you just decided to date me?"

"Long story." I wave him off but am also surprised (pleasantly) that he is already in full-on relationship mode with me. Neither of us is a teenager. We've had relationships. We're fully functioning adults, and we know what we want and don't want. Well, maybe I don't since I'm currently unsure about everything, it seems. But, John, he knows what he wants and he's not playing games. He likes me and has no qualms about letting me know. Admittedly, this sends butterflies fluttering in my belly, especially since he knows I'm currently under construction, and instead of running away, he's trying to get closer. "Apparently, I have trust issues and I wasn't so sure about you. I thought I was honest about that during our dinner at the Indian restaurant."

"You were worried about me working at JJF, but I thought we settled that."

"I thought we settled it, but then I wasn't so sure."

"And now you're sure?"

"I'm not so unsure anymore. If that makes sense." I hope it makes sense because I want him to keep liking me. I want him to keep trying to make headway even as I fight it.

"No. It really doesn't."

"I weighed the pros and cons and extrapolated all the superfluous crap that I may have assumed and then decided to focus on facts and feelings."

"This is about work, I'm guessing."

"Of course. I want you to understand that leaving JJF was a big, enormous, life-altering decision and I'm still getting used to this new life. But I'm not going to judge you based on where you work."

"Okaaay. Thank you?"

"You're welcome," I say, and he chuckles. I'm sure he thinks I've lost it, but I know what I'm saying and that's what counts. "Don't disappoint me."

"I won't," he says confidently.

"So maybe we don't have to take things that slow anymore." I fork some noodles into my mouth.

He lifts his shoulder and then drops it. "The ball's been in your court. I want you to feel comfortable."

"Me?" I practically shriek. "I'm not the one who set the pace of this . . ." I point my fingers between us, back and forth. "Whatever this is."

"Relationship," he quickly adds. "We're in a relationship, I thought. Although apparently you just decided that. I've been in one with you since . . . Mint." He puts his fork down and takes a big swig of his wine before standing up, walking around the table, ridiculously slow. He then turns me around so that I can face him and places his hands on the arms of my chair, essentially caging me in. "Millie. I'm not a patient man, but with you I'm trying to be because you are indecisive as hell." I start to argue, but he just keeps talking. "And as far as sex is concerned, last time you used the alcohol as an excuse that you didn't remember and perhaps our inhibitions were down and yeah, we slept together without putting much thought into it, but that day and every day since I've wanted to sleep with you again. So if the lack of sex is what is making you unsure of the status of this relationship, it's because I am patiently-ish waiting on you. You can—and should—be clear on what you want and make the move here." He starts to push off the chair now that he has made that very clear, very sexy, and very sweet declaration, and I stop him.

The food is forgotten, the fact I'm wearing white-cotton, high-waisted, unsexy, practical underwear is also forgotten. I wrap my arms around his neck and pull him down for a long kiss. This time, there's no alcohol, no excuses, and definitely no overthinking.

———

"You were killing me, sweetheart," he says as we lie in bed together, tangled in my five-thousand-thread-count sheets, sated and content. "I'm very happy you finally made a move."

"Are you staying over?" I begin, but then I pause because I think our relationship has been lacking clarity on my part. "I'd love for you to stay over."

Damn it . . . I do like him and I'm already pretty invested, so I'll close my eyes and hope for the best.

"I'd love that, too, but I'll have to leave early to grab clothes at home before heading to work."

"I can always wash your suit for you. Let's see." I sit up and press my index finger to my lips and look up at the ceiling. "Silk suit, so definitely hot water, two, maybe three detergent pods, and then a few cycles in the high-intensity, ultra hot dryer."

He laughs and, with his arm around my waist, pushes me down on the bed, and I shriek in surprise as he kisses me over and over again. This time, we don't do any talking or laughing afterward because we're not just content, we're blissed out and exhausted. I fall asleep in his arms feeling wonderfully happy. And I realize that intention is everything.

With the Apology Project, apologizing to Brenda felt disjointed because I did it for the wrong reasons. I didn't think it through; it was just something I wanted to do to get it out of the way because I had made that list and felt that I had to follow through with it. Sleeping with John that first time was much the same. I wasn't intending to sleep with him, it just happened, and I didn't enjoy it as much as I did this time because I'm the kind of person who needs to do things with intent, with thought. I need to put my whole heart and mind into everything that I do. I can't just go through the motions anymore. I did that for twenty years at JJF, and I was miserable. The silly Apology Project doesn't seem that silly anymore. It's gone beyond apologizing; it's teaching me a lot about myself.

The next morning, I open one eye when I feel John getting out of bed. I'm sated, I'm sleepy, and most importantly, I'm relaxed. "Do you want me to put on a pot of coffee?" I ask him, but I'm cocooned in my sheets and I really don't want to put on a pot of coffee. I just want to close my eyes again and stay in my blissful state for as long as possible. These moments of pure contentment are few and far between.

"Yes." But he laughs, sleep still in his voice. "I'm kidding and so are you because you don't look like someone who's going to make anyone anything."

He's right. He kisses me on the forehead, and then I think he's gone. I'm not sure because I'm asleep again too.

Later that morning, when I do get up and walk to the kitchen, I see all the evidence of Thai food is gone. He picked up. That makes me smile wide. There's also a note.

Thank you for last night. I made coffee. I need to bring over creamer. Who doesn't have creamer? (You are weird, but it turns out I like weird. Think about Portland . . .

I pour the warm coffee into my big mug, and since it's still early enough that I won't get sunburned, I have my morning coffee on my balcony.

And I don't think about Portland because I'm not the kind of person that dives into things. I'm not ready for that yet. I need to slow things down a bit. I do, however, decide to tackle more apologies, but I find myself torn. I think the people I really owed an apology to I've done. Except for Luanne Chase. The rest . . . I'm not so sure.

Apologizing to Brenda, Professor Jimenez, and Gary made all of us feel better because they deserved it, but that's not the case with everyone on this list. Mary, for instance—she is not ever going to be my friend. Mostly because we weren't ever friends like I was with Brenda or Luanne. Mary and I were friendly, but that's not the same thing. Still, I wronged her, and I feel she deserves an apology. The Jennys, on the other hand, that's a different story.

Jennifer Oliva
Jennifer Malkovich
Jennifer Zafer

Picture it. One year ago. A trial involving a contract dispute. I represented a well-known global company. I was cross-examining three different witnesses, all general managers of different branch offices for the company. One was here from Brazil, one from Turkey, and another from Russia. Because I don't speak any of these languages and neither did the opposing counsel, the jury, or the judge, interpreters were brought in. All three witnesses were questioned at different times of the day. Two were scheduled early in the day, before lunch, and the last one later in the afternoon. That was the plan, at least. The questioning lasted three days, and the interpreters, coincidentally all named Jennifer (a.k.a. the Jennys), came from the same agency.

I won't go into boring details, but by the end of the third day, all three interpreters, not the witnesses, ended up crying. It was a disaster that cost my client more money. Needless to say, the translation agency was not happy. Losing JJF as a client must've made a huge dent in their pockets.

I've made people cry before. I ask questions, usually hard questions, and some people are more sensitive than others. Apparently the Jennys are as sensitive as they get. In fact, if I ever have children and any of those children are female, I'd never name them Jennifer, Jenny, or any other derivative of the name.

Jenny O. said I was too harsh on the witness and refused to interpret some of the fouler words I'd been using. The words I'd used were words said by the witness in her deposition, and I was merely reading them aloud. After a heated exchange with Jenny O. in English, Judge Sullivan agreed with me and instructed her to say exactly what I was saying, without any deviation. If there was a deviation of any kind, the judge would hold her in contempt. She cried.

Jenny M. had to take her son to a cross-country meet. The trial ran over through no fault of my own; my work involved asking four hours' worth of questions. Jenny M. asked the judge if she could be excused early. The judge said no. No qualms. Flat-out no. The interpreter was contracted and paid handsomely to do her job. Without her, the trial would have had to be stopped, and the judge was not going to allow Jenny M. to be the cause of his judicial calendar piling up. So he denied her request.

Jenny M. missed her son's meet and cried while answering all the questions. It was absurd and pissed me off.

Regardless, that one wasn't my fault. The judge makes the rules.

And Jenny Z. Well, that one *was* totally my fault. Turns out that my intern grew up in Saint Petersburg and was fluent in Russian. During a quick recess, my shy intern hesitantly pointed out that Jenny Z. wasn't translating all the words I was asking. Apparently, she was sugarcoating some of it. This is why I hate to use translators. Part of the art of questioning has to do with inflection, tone, and pausing at very specific times. It's no different from a comedian and the way he tells his jokes. You can have ten comedians all say the same joke, and if one's comedic timing is off, they won't be as funny. Same thing with questioning a witness. All lawyers have their style, and I have mine. But I don't know Russian, or any other language for that matter, and there are times I have to use an official interpreter. The one job of that interpreter is to say *exactly* what I say. Granted, they may not say it with my inflection, which already hurts my strategy, but they at least have to use my exact line of questioning. It wasn't up to Jenny to rephrase my question.

After recess I had the court reporter read back the questions, and after going back and forth, Jenny Z. was reprimanded in open court. I even cringed at the judge's tone. The testimony was thrown out and questions had to be asked again, another reason why Jenny M. missed her son's meet.

I was harsh with them, but so was the judge. But they're not going to give the judge an attitude. I'm the easier target, even though I was just doing my job. They were not. I mean, I did go to their office, personally, and tell their employer that I never wanted them on any JJF cases and I may have used some expletives when I said it, but again, I was pissed off and I was reprimanded myself for the extra expense my client had to incur. I probably should have stopped at the judge's reprimand. Maybe I could have said things a little differently. After the trial was over, I could have greeted them when I saw them in the halls of the courthouse—it's just business, after all—but I didn't. Yes, I'm no-nonsense; yes, I used very colorful words when I spoke with the interpreters, the judge, and finally the agency. I almost lost the entire trial because of their inability to do their job.

So, no, I'm not apologizing to those three. They owe me a damn apology. Hell, they owe my client a damn apology. But they also weren't my friends, which is why I purposefully excluded them from my party invites.

It's my understanding that Jenny Z. was suspended for two weeks and Jenny O. and Jenny M. were given final warnings from the agency. I felt very vindicated by this.

I cross them off my list without a second thought. Then I decide I'm only going to go through with the apology if the person truly deserves one and not just as a means of making myself feel better. I'm tired of feeling guilty for being me. For my profession. It's not fair, and it's not something a man would feel. It's not something I should have to do. Maybe the idea of the project was well intentioned—*in vino veritas*, after all—but it wasn't well thought out. Now, in the sobering light of day, and with my new perspective, I'm going to rethink and revise.

CHAPTER THIRTEEN

Luanne YES!
Gary
Lindsey ✓
Jenny O. NO!
Jenny M. NO!
Jenny Z. Absolutely NO!
Mary
Office MAYBE
Brenda
Margret Undecided
Jimenez

The next day, while I'm sipping my morning coffee, I decide to try my luck with this Rosa R. person from the 23andMe email. The system says not to give out too much information but that a little digging into family trees and timelines is always a good idea.

Dear Rosa,

My name is Amelia, and I think we might be related. My father was adopted almost seventy years ago. I do not know anything about his biological parents, but I received an email from 23andMe that said we may be related. I would love to have a conversation with you, if you are open to it, or if you have any idea why we may have some DNA link. I don't have any relatives outside the country, so this is a surprise for me.

Best regards,
Amelia

I press "Send" nervously. What if I never receive a response? What if I receive a response from a crazy person? What if I expect a certain reaction from her that I don't get, like with my father and my sister? Or worse, what if there is some sort of nefarious reason why my father was given up for adoption? I cannot help but think that my quest to find this unknown part of me will also open a can of worms. For a moment I panic and try to unsend the email, but then I think of all I've done since that fateful day in the conference room at JJF. I've apologized to people, something I would never have done. I've found that, of all the hobbies I've tried, I've liked cooking the best, even if I'm not great at it (yet). I've met a man and opened my heart. Why not also take this leap? It's not like I'm giving Rosa any of my personal information

With my mind made up, I get ready for the day. It's a couple of days after the wonderful sex with John, and I'm dropping him off at the airport, then going to Starbucks to study.

"You sure you won't change your mind and come with me?" John says as I pull over at the terminal.

"I can't. It's too much too fast," I tell him again.

"Next time then."

"Next time," I say noncommittally, and he gives me a kiss on the lips before stepping out of the car.

"Don't do anything I wouldn't do," he says with a wink.

"I'll try. Have a great trip!"

As I drive off, I realize I'm happy. Really happy. It's not just John; it's everything. It's the challenge of learning a new language, the peace I feel in the mornings when I wake up—even the frustration of not getting any recipe to work has been fun.

The failed birthday party slithers into my mind every once in a while, and I try to ignore it. Phoebe and the trial creep up once in a while, too, and I try to ignore that as well. It's not my business, and I don't want to know more than I need to. And even though I am enjoying John's company, I'm also very much enjoying my own company.

I like that I'm trying new things. I like that I'm doing things outside my comfort zone. In fact, the moments of solitude, when I'm alone, at home, with nothing to do, nothing pending, just me and my thoughts, they've been some of the best days I've had since leaving JJF. I never had that before.

While I was working, the moments I was alone were just breaks. Even sleeping at night felt like a break. Breaks from deadlines, from the meetings, the trials, the depos . . . If I could have worked 24-7 without causing myself physical harm, I probably would have done it. When you spend every waking moment of your life thinking of work, there's no space for cooking lessons, walking, relationships, inner peace. There's just the constant hum of stress.

I walk into Starbucks a short time later with my textbook in my hand, ready to conquer my Spanish homework with a brand-new zeal. Damn, I should have probably sent that email to Rosa R. in Spanish. Maybe I'll work on translating it, which will also serve as a good way of studying. I'm about to sit down when I trip over two kids, a little boy and a little girl, fighting over a cake pop.

"Oh my!" a familiar voice shrieks as she extends her hand to help me up. "I'm so sorry. Are you all right?"

I stand up and run my hands down my jeans and then pull my shirt down as I turn my head. "It's fine. I'm fine. Oh—Luanne?"

"Millie! Shit. I mean, shoot. It's you. Wow."

"Mommy! Olivia isn't sharing."

Luanne and I are still staring at each other stupefied when she breaks the eye contact and looks down at her two quarreling children (at least, I assume they're her children). She takes a bag out of the little girl's hand and takes out two cake pops. "One for you and one for you. I don't want to hear either of you argue one more time."

"Sorry, Mommy," both children chorus. They look so cute with their little impish faces. The *r* in sorry sounds more like a *w*.

"Go sit," she says, pointing to a nearby table. "And eat that fast. We need to go soon."

"Oh my God . . ." It's mostly a whisper. "I can't believe it's you. I've been thinking about you and then bam—here you are."

She looks flustered at seeing me again after all these years.

"Do you live around here?" she asks.

"No. I live downtown, but I was in the neighborhood and needed a change of scenery," I say. "I'd offer to buy you a coffee, but—" I point to the coffee she already has in her hand. "Can you spare a minute? I'd like to catch up."

"I . . . uh . . . ," she says, looking around, her words drifting off.

"Just for a minute. Please. They're still working on their cake pops," I say with an anxious little laugh. Because now that I have her standing in front of me, I realize I'm nervous. I didn't prepare for this moment, and I have no idea what to say. "How old are they? They're adorable, Luanne." I pull out a chair at the table right beside her kids, and she hesitantly drops her big purse on the floor and sits across from me, her eyes moving back and forth between her kids and me.

"Five. They're twins. Mikey and Olivia."

"Twins, yikes. Must keep you busy."

"You have no idea."

"I've been wanting to reach out," I tell her.

"Really? Why?" The snarky way she says it takes me aback.

"Why?" I reply with indignation. I make a mental note to tone it down. "Because you were like a sister to me. Because I've known you forever. Because I cared about you; I still do. And I miss our friendship."

She makes a noise that sounds like a *hmph*.

"What's that supposed to mean?" I ask.

"You didn't seem to care much about our friendship. You rarely called. Every time we did talk it always became about you and your problems."

"That is absolutely not true."

"It really is. When I needed you most, I called, and you didn't answer. If it wasn't about you, you didn't make time."

"Oh my God, are you serious? You stopped calling me. Not the other way around."

"Listen, I need to get the kids home. I don't really have time to talk about all this right now."

"Make time. Please. This is important to me."

She stands and grabs her purse. "To *you*. It's important to you."

I stand up, too, as I realize what I said and how bad it sounded. "*Us*. It should be important to both of us."

"It was. It's a shame it took you all these years to figure it out. You are not a bad person, but you are a busy person. My boring little suburban life didn't fit into your busy corporate life. I'm sorry, Millie—I don't hate you even if this sounds harsh. I really do wish you the best. We just grew apart. Nothing more really to discuss."

"No," I say. "I refuse to accept that."

"Mommy," the little girl says, "I'm all done."

"Come on, kids," she says, herding them to her. "It was nice to see you, Millie."

"No, wait. I just . . . Please, can we catch up? *Really* catch up. I don't want this to be the end of us, especially since maybe this was a misunderstanding. We can fix this. I can fix this."

She looks at me like I'm crazy. It seems she's already made up her mind and there was no misunderstanding. I'm an asshole and I've thrown her aside. But that's not true. Not at all. I mean . . . is it?

"Please." I find myself almost begging. "Can I call you?"

She takes out a pen from her oversize purse and scribbles her number on a brown napkin. "I did love you, Millie, but I didn't always like you. Especially when I needed a shoulder to cry on or someone to talk to. Things have been very rough the last few years. Very, very rough."

"I'm here now. We can get back to that."

She lets out a deep breath.

This time it's Mikey. "Mommy . . ."

"We're goin'. We're goin'." She turns to me. "You have my number." It's almost a challenge, the way that she says it. As if she really thinks I'm not going to call her.

"I'll call you."

She takes one child in each hand. "I'll answer."

"Bye, Lu."

"Bye, Millie," she says as her kids pull her out of the Starbucks.

I sit for a moment, completely discombobulated. "Well . . . ," I say under my breath. Immediately I pull out my phone and text Nina. I just ran into Luanne Chase.

Is this part of your apology project?

She's on the list. But that's not why I saw her. She just happened to be at the same Starbucks.

Did you apologize?

No.

Are you guys okay now?

No.

Millie? It's the middle of the day and I'm about to see a patient. You need to use all your words, not just no.

The conversation was quick. I'm rattled. She gave me her number. I think . . . I think . . . Nina, am I self-centered? Or selfish?

There is no immediate response. Even the three little dots have stopped.

I take your silence as a yes. I'm a self-centered bitch who deserves to have a guestless party. I am the She-Demon.

Slow your roll, Mills. I was thinking.

Well . . .

You are self-centered, yes. But not in the "bitch, I don't give a shit about anyone but me" kind of way. You are busy and never have time for chitchat. And you're definitely not selfish. Maybe selfish with your time but not with your actions.

Damn.

So you're flawed. Big deal. Is that what Luanne told you? That you're selfish?

Not in so many words. But what the hell, Nina? She's flawed, too, right? And so are you and so is everyone. I was busy, but it didn't mean I didn't care about her. I think she's at fault here too. Looks like my job here is done, she types.

You didn't do anything. I did all the work here.

LOL. I have to run. We'll pick up right here, later on.

Thanks, Nina . . . I think.

She sends me a kiss-face emoji, and then I'm left in Starbucks with my thoughts. A moment later, I pack up and leave, feeling dejected.

———

As soon as I walk inside my house, I go straight to bed feeling like I did on my last day of work. I almost pull out the Nutella, but then I think, *What did I do to Luanne? What was my part in all of this?* Instead, I pull out the apology list and read it again. The brief interaction with Luanne has left me questioning everything. She didn't even give me a chance to speak, not really. She was defensive and quick to blame me for everything. She's flawed, too, just like I told Nina. Why do I have to do all the apologizing? I cross out her name with such ferocity I almost make a hole in the paper. Maybe this Apology Project is stupid. It certainly is embarrassing. Putting yourself out there usually is.

CHAPTER FOURTEEN

Luanne No!
Gary
Lindsey ✓
Jenny O. NO!
Jenny M. NO!
Jenny Z. Absolutely NO!
Mary
Office MAYBE
Brenda
Margret Undecided
Jimenez

I'm not going to let Luanne dictate what I had already decided to do. It took me two days to decide this. I felt good when I apologized to Brenda, Gary, and Jimenez, and they felt good receiving that apology. It isn't stupid. Maybe it's unorthodox, but it's not stupid. So I'm not going to let a little setback, and my temper, cancel out what I set out to do.

After I finish making dinner, I'm going to pull out the list and keep moving forward. As I'm chopping onions for a recipe I'm trying out, however, I hear the ding of an email. I wipe my hands on my apron and scroll through my phone. It's from 23andMe. I'm excited. I was hoping I'd receive something back from Rosa R., and here it is.

I stop all kitchen activity, pull out a chair, and click on the links until I'm reading the email. It's long, but it's in English, thank God.

Amelia,

It was such a surprise to get your email. I cannot be certain that we are in fact related, but I think there is a good chance we are. I will explain. My mother's sister Mercedes fled Cuba at fifteen years old when she found out she was pregnant. You must understand it was 1950 and a pregnant girl did not have much options at the time. She was scared and hid on a fishing boat that was headed to Miami. The only reason we know this information is because she left a note, which my mother found far too late. That was the last we heard of Mercedes. My mother, may she rest in peace, looked for her for years. I fled to Miami in the sixties during the revolution and I lived there for almost twenty years. I searched for Mercedes as a favor for my mother, and after a lot of research I found a death certificate for a Mercedes Roybal, that was her name, by the way and it was due to complication at childbirth. If your father's birthday was March 26, 1950, then I am certain that his mother was Mercedes Roybal, my aunt, who died at childbirth. Because there was no next of kin, the child was put up for adoption. We did not even know if the child survived, but this email gives me great hope. I hope you help me fill in the gaps and I will do the same.

Rosa R.

I am in a state of shock when I read and then reread the email. My father's birthday is March 26, 1950, and he was born in Miami, Florida, but was quickly adopted and then moved to Chicago with Nana and Papa Bill. We have family in Cuba, and I have so many questions!

Immediately I write back.

> Rosa,
>
> That is, in fact, my father's birthday. We may be related. I cannot tell you how surprising this all is. May I ask why you live in Cuba now? And is English a good way of communicating with you or are you having this translated? Also, on my DNA results, a high percentage was Spanish. Would you be able to give me more information? And who was the father of the child?
>
> Sincerely,
> Amelia

I still don't know whether it is proper to give her more of my information. Could this be a hoax? I call my father right away and tell him everything. The fact that his mother didn't want to give him up must mean something to him. She wanted him. She wanted him so much she fled the country. At his silence, I think I've overwhelmed him. I've just given him a lot of information, including that his biological mother is not alive. "Okay, well, okay." That's his answer.

"Should I have not told you?" Now I feel as if I've opened a wound that I shouldn't have opened and I feel terrible for doing so.

"No, it's fine. I'm glad you told me. It's a lot. I have to process it."

I completely understand. Of course he's going to take time and process it. Slowly. Methodically. I didn't get that habit from my mom after all. But, after a bit more conversation in which I tell him the very little information I have thus far, he seems fine, and I'm relieved. Though he doesn't want to meet or connect with Rosa himself, I forward the emails to Nina so that she can read them. Her response, an hour later, is simple: Whoa!

I reply to her email: That's all you have to say? Our biological grandmother was so afraid of what her family would think about her pregnancy that she stowed away on a boat at fifteen years old! And she died during childbirth.

She replies: I don't know what else to say. Is that even true? Who is this Rosa person? Be careful.

I ignore my sister's negativity. I'm so excited for this information that I must have checked my emails a thousand times, waiting for Rosa.

———

A week later, with no response, I'm looking at myself through the big, beveled, floor-to-ceiling mirror in my bedroom. It's Halloween. I don't know if they have that in Cuba. Usually I'm working or stressed out about an upcoming trial. This year, however, I'm getting ready for a party. I adjust the short, black, severe bob and undo the top button of the white blouse. Except for the wig, I look absolutely nothing like Uma Thurman, mostly because I'm short. When John convinced me to go to a Halloween party that many of my ex-coworkers would be attending, my first reaction was no. My second reaction was hell no. But then I softened because maybe this could be a way to apologize to some of the office staff. So here I am, all *Pulp Fiction*-ed out, waiting for John to pick me up.

After decades of arguing in front of some of the state's fiercest attorneys and judges, I'm rarely nervous. However, here I stand, with butterflies and pangs of nausea in my belly.

"Here goes nothing." I exhale loudly to William when John knocks and I walk to the front door.

I open the door and stifle a laugh. John's in the iconic long wig with the sides coming loose. He's even wearing a clip-on gold hoop on his ear. He looks more like Travolta than I look like Thurman.

"I like the wig," he says, reaching over to finger the tips. "Very cute."

"You need a chin dimple," I say. When he smiles, my heart briefly skips at the sight of the dimple in his cheek.

"This one'll have to do," he says, winking. He walks inside, closing the door behind him. Over the last month, we've continued to see each other, and with every conversation and date, I like him more. Every time I see Hugh Phoebe's face on the news, bile rises up my throat, and the urge to ask John what Junior is doing with the case almost overwhelms me. I'm sure John knows. During the weekly case reviews at the office they discuss the big files. He must know something. But this new Millie, she's not going to get involved.

"Glad you agreed to come with me," he says.

"I don't want to ruin the party."

His brows furrow.

"If people hate me and I show up, maybe it'll ruin everyone's good time," I clarify.

"Babe." Yeah . . . he calls me *babe* sometimes. It always does squishy things to my insides and makes me feel like a teenager. "You overestimate your impact."

I gently swat his shoulder. If there is one thing I love and hate about John, it's his honesty. He isn't one to beat around the bush.

"Seriously, Millie. You are important and special to me, and I'm glad you are coming with me tonight. But these people . . ." He hesitates, which must be bad. He's not the hesitating kind of person.

"I'm not that important," I finish, helping him out.

"Sorry. Sounds harsh." He grabs me by the waist, pulls me toward him, and gives me a soft kiss on the lips.

Damn . . .

"I'm trying to be more aware of other people's feelings. Also, I want to make a good impression," I confess. This is the first time I'm seeing everyone in a while, and the last interaction I had with most of them may not have been great.

"Be yourself and I'm sure they'll love you."

I side-eye him.

Then he quickly adds, "Well, maybe more Millie than Amelia, and then I'm sure they'll love you." I smirk. They're not going to love me. They may start to thaw, but we're light-years away from love. My apology could be a good start.

———

John was wrong(ish). I don't ruin the party, but people do stare when I walk into the house. I hear the proverbial record scratch when the door closes behind us. All eyes are on us, but it's only for a second and then everyone's back to talking among themselves. John pulls me deeper into the home. It's Liam Walker's house. He is a partner of JJF, and I've known him for years.

"They knew I'd be coming, right?" I whisper.

John shrugs. "I just replied with a plus-one. I didn't tell them your name, but I haven't kept you a secret. Don't worry. It's all good."

It's *all good*? I could kill him right now.

Sara, Liam's wife, walks up to us first. I've met her a few times throughout the years when she'd come to meet her husband for lunch.

"Hi. Glad you could make it," she says, and kisses my cheek and then John's, her witch hat bobbing as she leans in. "Thank you for having us," I say.

"Make yourself at home. There're drinks in the back and food in the kitchen."

She then walks off to greet other people. I can still feel eyes on me.

"Be yourself," John says. "They'll love you."

"I was myself for twenty years, and that didn't do me much good."

"This is the perfect opportunity for them to get to know you," he says as we smile and shake hands with a few people that I don't know too well.

My only salvation is that Jones, Jones, and Fisher are not the kind of people who attend their employees' parties, so at least I'm safe from running into them. Because if there's one thing I know for sure, it's that no matter how much I've been trying to work on myself, if I see any of the three—J, J, or F—I will not be able to control my temper. Unfortunately, I also realize that until this very moment, I wasn't the kind of person that attended the parties of my employees or colleagues either. I recoil inwardly. I never even realized I was that kind of person until now.

"Margret?" I'm surprised to see her here. She's in an eighties punk sort of outfit, which is completely surprising. I've only ever seen her in ill-fitting knee-length skirts, sensible shoes, and a white, cream, or beige blouse. And always with a scowl or fake smile.

"Hello, Ms. Montgomery." She smiles (fakely) at me and then smiles (genuinely) at John. "John. How are you?"

"Please, Margret, call me Millie."

Again she smiles, but her lips are pressed together. The woman clearly dislikes me, and she looks like it's taking all her self-control not to slap me.

"Nice costume, Margie," John says.

"Thank you."

I watch the interaction in complete awe and confusion. Margie? *What the hell?*

After she walks off, I turn to John. "Margie?"

"She asked me to call her Margie." He shrugs.

In the next ten minutes we're bombarded with some other employees of JJF and two attorneys I know from cases I've gone against. They are all very nice and make me feel completely at ease, but I'm still thinking of Margret. I've known her for nearly two decades, and we're still very formal in our relationship. John's known her for five minutes, and they're on a nickname basis.

Sometime later, I bump into Margret while I'm pouring myself a second glass of wine.

"It's nice to see you out of the office, Margret."

She does that fake smile thing. An awkward silence stretches, so I try again to make conversation.

"Red or white?" I may as well pour her a glass.

"Uh . . . white. But I can do it, Ms. Montgomery."

"Please, call me Millie," I say again as I pour her white wine.

"I don't know if I feel comfortable doing that. After almost twenty years, I'd feel strange."

"Well, Amelia then. 'Lady,' 'Hey, you.' Anything but Ms. Montgomery. We don't work together anymore, and it makes me feel old. Hell, even She-Demon is preferable," I say, trying to lighten the mood, especially since Margret is probably fifteen years older than me.

Her eyes widen, and when she realizes I'm not upset at the secret nickname, her grimace begins to shift to more of a smile. *See? I can joke too.* Nina once told me that Kevin told her that they were afraid if I found out about the nickname, I'd fire them, which was why they used She-Demon instead of plain ol' bitch. To me, however, they're both just as bad, but I don't say as much. It's time to let that go.

"All right . . . Amelia," she says, taking the offered wine from my hand. "I like your costume, by the way. *Pulp Fiction* is a favorite."

"Mine too. Thank you. You look pretty cool yourself. It's strange seeing so many people outside of work, wearing regular clothes, having drinks."

"You should have done it more often. We had a monthly happy hour, you know?"

I did know. But I never went. I was always too busy or too pissed off by someone who would be at the happy hour.

"I'm sorry about the She-Demon thing. Have you always known?" she asks somewhat hesitantly. She quickly adds, "I didn't make it up, by the way!"

I chuckle and give her shoulder a friendly pat. "It's fine, Margret, really. I know it wasn't you. I've known about the name for quite a while."

"And you aren't mad?"

I shrug. "I don't exactly love it, but . . ." I don't finish the thought. What is there to say, really? "You're being summoned," I say, pointing behind her to a woman calling for her.

"It was nice seeing you, Ms.—I mean, Amelia. Retirement suits you." She smiles with a hint of sincerity.

"Wait!" I reach for her before she turns. Her eyes are wide as she waits for whatever I'm going to say. "I want . . . I want to apologize to you." Her eyes get even wider, if that's possible, and I smile. "I'm sorry if I was rough to work with. I know I raised my voice and cursed—"

"And on a few occasions threw things," she adds, but it's with a soft smile. It was a stress ball, and the other time it was a pen. And I didn't throw it *at* anyone.

I pinch my nose. "And threw things. I'm sorry."

"It's okay, Ms.—Amelia," she corrects herself. "I've been working there since before you even graduated high school. I've been the secretary to most partners in this office at some point. I'm used to it. You're all busy and trying to do your job."

"Yeah, but so are you and you did great work. I didn't have to be so mean, especially not to you. You were truly a great assistant."

"Well, thank you, Amelia. It's nice of you to say. There are no hard feelings. You don't sign up to work at an office like this and expect afternoon tea breaks and morning yoga classes."

"I appreciate that." I smile, she smiles; it's all very civil and awkward, but cathartic too. And then she walks away.

I finally apologized to Margret, while dressed like Uma Thurman, of all things!

———

That night, John and I lie together in bed. I'm on my back watching the ceiling fan whirl around and around.

"You hated tonight, didn't you? You said you had fun, but I can tell you didn't," he says, and I turn to face him. His head is resting on his hand, and he's turned toward me, rubbing circles on my belly.

"I didn't hate it. I got to know some people outside of work. Hopefully they got to know me a little too. It was nice, and I apologized to Margret. Interestingly, she apologized too. For the She-Demon thing, which wasn't even her doing. She didn't need to do that."

"That's what women do. They apologize too often. Isn't that what you said to me?"

"Ugh . . . we need to stop that."

"But there's something else going on in that head of yours, I can tell. What's going on? Talk to me."

I exhale and get a little more comfortable. "For the last twenty years, Margret's been nothing but nasty to me. Yet to you, she's perfectly delightful. Except tonight—tonight she was fine toward me."

"She's not nasty. She's just not overly nice."

I look at him skeptically. "John . . . who do you think you're dealing with here? She's never smiled, never even tried to make small talk. I don't even know if she's married or has children. 'Not overly nice' is the understatement of the year."

His face contorts in a way that makes me think he isn't sure whether to tell me something.

"Oh, for Christ's sake, John. Just say it. Let me guess: 'the pot calling the kettle black' kind of situation here? Yes, you're right, but at least I'm aware that I come across standoffish and mean during business hours. After work, I'm a perfectly agreeable person if anyone ever takes the opportunity to get to know me. She's nasty all the time. It's not the same."

"She has a disabled adult son at home. She has to relieve the day sitter when she gets home and has to bathe and feed him and, well, I think that's why she is how she is. She's *tired*."

My jaw drops. "Whoa. Was he born this way? How is he disabled? Was it an accident?" I have so many questions, I don't know where to start.

"She's not that forthright, and I didn't want to pry. But, from what she told me, it seems that he got into an accident when he was in his early twenties, broke something in his spine or neck, I'm not sure. He is a quadriplegic now."

I put my hand over my mouth. "Oh my God . . ."

"I know. Horrible."

"How long ago did this happen?"

"I'm not sure. But I think he's in his thirties, so it must've been some time ago."

Oh my God, did the accident happen while I was already working at JJF? How did we not do more to help her? Was I nasty to her on that particular day? "I didn't know, John. I had no idea." It's almost a whisper because I'm so shocked.

"I know. I just happened to find out." He's trying to brush it off as if it's no big deal. Not Margret's circumstances, but the fact that he knew and I didn't. He doesn't want me to feel bad about it. It's obvious.

"How did you *happen* to find out? Because I worked at JJF for most of my life and you just started."

"I asked her. One day, she was particularly unpleasant, so I asked her to lunch. We chatted, and she told me."

"I am a horrible, horrible human being. I didn't know. How many times did I make her day worse? Damn . . ."

"Hey. It's fine. I didn't want to say anything. But if she was doing a crap job, you had a right to let her know. It doesn't make you a horrible person, Millie. It just makes you her boss."

I turn to my back and look up at the ceiling. There's a golf-ball-size lump in my throat. How did I not know about her son? Hell, I don't know much about anyone at the firm.

"I ruined the evening. I'm sorry," John says.

"You didn't. Not at all. I'm glad you told me. I was living in a bubble where all I could see was work and more work. Now I'm starting to see things that were right in front of my face all along. Poor thing. She should've told me. I could have done something."

"Like what, Millie? What could you have possibly done?"

"I don't know. Given her some time off. Helped her with expenses. Something."

"She doesn't need anything. She just needed to talk, and tonight, she just needed an evening away from it all."

"I'm unapproachable. That's what people think of me. That I'm going to bite their heads off if they get close. Maybe Luanne wasn't being bitchy to me at Starbucks. Maybe she was just irritated by her kids and who knows what the hell else was going on with her and I'm so direct and . . ." I groan, turn, and take my phone off the nightstand.

"What are you doing?" he asks.

"Being the bigger person," I say and find Luanne's phone number and send her a quick text.

Luanne, it's Millie. I'm sorry that I caught you off guard the other day. I was caught off guard myself. But I'd really like to see you. I'd hate to think that our friendship ends on a misunderstanding, and I do not believe that we just drifted apart. Please, call me or let me know when we can meet.

Usually I'm not the bigger person. I'm the "hold grudges and seek revenge" kind of person. But I really need to understand what happened with Luanne, and if it's fixable, I want to try and fix it.

"You just sent her a text at two in the morning?" he says, and I scrunch my face. I didn't think that through, which is very uncharacteristic of me. But I don't regret it (not yet, at least). Things with Luanne can't possibly get more estranged than they are now.

"So you think you're unapproachable? Did Margret say that to you?"

"No."

"You're definitely direct, but . . ."

"I yelled a lot at Margret and others when they interrupted me in the middle of drafting something. Just flew off the handle sometimes. But . . . you know with this stupid apology bullshit, I think that maybe some people owe *me* an apology. Did I tell you I crossed out some people from the list? Maybe I'm a little more passionate than other people, maybe there were ways of saying things that didn't involve cursing, but I've been thinking about it and some of my anger was justified. My delivery may have been off, but not the sentiment. We women are programmed to feel like we need to apologize for everything. If I bump into someone, my automatic response is 'Sorry, sorry,' but why? Maybe *they* weren't looking. Maybe *they* should've been watching where they were going!" I become more indignant as I speak. "Have you ever laid awake in bed analyzing and reanalyzing a conversation? 'Was I too harsh? Did they take me seriously? Was I showing enough cleavage? Not enough?'"

"The cleavage part, no?"

"Any of it, John? Have you ever dissected a conversation in your head and felt terrible about it?"

"Honestly? Not that I can think of."

"Exactly! I used to do that and then I stopped and became callous and desensitized and trampled over everyone who got in my way. Now, I can't stop thinking of every single conversation I had with every single person at JJF. Like a movie reel I can't turn off."

He nods and then yawns.

"Oh, is my major life epiphany boring you?" I swat his hand and start to roll to my side, but he stops me by quickly shifting to his stomach and using one of his legs to hold down my own legs. He's half on me, half still on his side of his bed.

"Truth?" he asks, cupping my chin, forcing me to meet his eyes. I nod somberly. "I'm not you. Maybe it's a male thing? Maybe it's a me thing? I don't know. I just say what I have to say, and I try and say it from a good place. If it hurts the other person, it's on them, not on me. So I don't dissect it later because I don't regret most things I do."

"Hmph" is all I say.

"Look, I thought you were unapproachable when I saw you across the room at your party. I didn't even know it was your party at the time. You're an intimidating woman, Amelia." I start to open my mouth, but he continues to talk. "You're opinionated as hell, have zero qualms about saying what you're thinking, and you don't sugarcoat anything."

"If you're trying to make me feel better you are failing—big-time."

"I'm not done."

"Fine. Continue," I mumble through his finger on my lips.

He chuckles. "But now that I know you, you're actually a big softy."

"I wouldn't go that far."

He laughs. "You're right." And then he starts laughing and reminds me of my reaction last week to the guy who tried to cut me off in traffic. "Okay, so you're not Suzy Sunshine, but who's that happy all the time? You're Amelia Montgomery, a tough litigator who's had to claw her way to the top in a chauvinistic world. Would Jones, Jones, or Fisher apologize to their assistant for not meeting a deadline?" he asks rhetorically. I shake my head no. "So, why should you?"

"Because Jones, Jones, and Fisher are pricks and I don't want to be like them."

"You're nothing like them," he says, and kisses me. "Babe, I'm definitely not the best person to give you advice on how to be easygoing and friendly, but I can tell you this: all you can do is be cool with yourself. If the thing with Margret is weighing heavily on you, then call her up and do something about it. If you did your best by her and you're good in your soul, then stop thinking about it and move on."

"You just want me to stop talking and kiss you."

He winks, and this time I kiss him slowly and thoroughly.

My forty-year-old-lady heart really likes *babe*.

CHAPTER FIFTEEN

~~Luanne No!~~ *Luanne Attempt #2*
~~Gary~~
Lindsey ✓
~~Jenny O.~~ *NO!*
~~Jenny M.~~ *NO!*
~~Jenny Z.~~ *Absolutely NO!*
~~Mary~~
Office MAYBE
~~Brenda~~
~~Margret~~ ~~Undecided~~
~~Jimenez~~

Winters in Chicago are not that delightful. As a native Chicagoan, you'd think I'd be used to it, but no one gets completely used to that first big snowstorm of the year.

Today is that day. The kind of day where the winds howl and the snow seems to be falling from above and from the sides. There's no winter gear available to keep you from being pelted by ice or the cold from seeping into your bones. I'm saved from going to Pilates when I get an incoming email from Rosa. I mean, I could put on four layers of wool and go to class, but this email gives me the very needed mental justification for not moving from the warmth of my bed.

Amelia,

The internet is not always great here. If I take long to reply, it is not because I am not very interested in our conversation. I moved back to Cuba five years ago to care for my mama, MariRosa, your father's aunt. She is too old to fly. My English is good. We can continue corresponding in English, as I assume it will be easier for you. To answer your question about the baby's father. We do not know. She never told us, and unfortunately, that secret went with her. Perhaps one day with technology you will find out, just like you found me. Although I will say, the idea of 23andMe is not something that exists here. I did it while in Miami after seeing so many adver-tisements. I thought it would be fun. Which brings me to your question of Spain. I believe that my great-great-grandfather was from Spain and immi-grated to Cuba. There may still be a family line over there. However, I do not know much more than what we've been told through generations. Amelia, I have been wondering how this must feel like to your father. I would like to one day share all the stories of Mercedes that my mother told me about her. Is your father still alive? Did he have a good life? I would very much like to give this information to my mother. Her memory fades, but I believe she will find it comforting to know this.

I do hope that I will get to meet you one day. Perhaps you could travel here and meet Mama, me, and all your distant cousins—and there are

many! I would fly there myself, but with Mama sick,
I cannot.

With affection,
Rosa

My eyes water. I have family. I've known this now for a few weeks, but it's becoming more than a piece of paper. Could I be getting catfished? But the site is legit and the connection of the DNA is legit. The dates all add up. Deep in my soul, I know this is real.

Rosa,

My father has had a wonderful life.

I hesitate in providing too much identifying information, so I'll leave out names.

He's been married to my mother now for forty-five years, and I have a younger sister. Unfortunately, I do not have extended family since my parents are both only children. That is, until now. Tell me more about my cousins! Tell me more about Cuba! Tell me more about everything!

Millie

I wish she would write me right away, but alas, I know it does not work that way. She is in a country that has limited resources, and I cannot expect her to be ready to email me back at a drop of a hat. Since Pilates has now come and gone, I decide to read a book under the covers of my thick, fluffy duvet. William seems to be on board with this not-leave-the-house plan since he is snuggling next to me as I try and relax. It's hard. I think relaxing is a learned behavior. It definitely doesn't come naturally for me.

I find myself reading off my phone because I'm too lazy to look for my Kindle. Why is this a problem? Since discovering social media, I've lost a countless number of hours and brain cells to the mindless vortex of Buzzfeed, YouTube makeup tutorials, and life hacks for things that do not need hacks. Sometimes I find myself just surfing mindlessly through all of my "friends'" pages. I now have twenty-one friends. Exciting, right?

It's seventeen more people than came to my party, but who's counting?

Fortunately, my waste of time is interrupted by the ping of an incoming text. Luanne never replied to my sober, middle-of-the-night text three days ago. Now, there's an incoming text from her that says, Sorry. Apparently, I replied to your text in my head. I guess I forgot to actually type it out.

I laugh. That used to happen to me all the time. I would get a text, read it, and forget to reply even though I could have sworn I had. How many "friends" did I lose because they thought I was ignoring them? Or is that the actual definition of ignore, since I never actually replied? Damn.

No problem. You're busy, I understand. Are you free this week to grab dinner?

No. Dinner is out of the question if you want to have actual adult conversation. I don't have a sitter most days.

How about Mitchell? I wonder. I don't text it, though, since her husband and I weren't the best of friends. I don't want her to think I'm being snarky. Then lunch? Or breakfast? I don't mind the kids; I can go

180

over to your house if it's easier. I hesitate in sending. It sounds desperate. I contemplate for a few more seconds before finally just hitting "Send." Screw it. I *am* pretty desperate when it comes to Luanne. I want my friend back. That's all there is to it. Sometimes one person has to take that leap. I'm willing to be that person if it'll salvage our relationship.

> I can meet you for breakfast tomorrow after school drop-off, if you'd like. Maybe at the same Starbucks?

Yes, I respond, perhaps too quickly, and then add, What time?

> I can be there by nine.

Sounds great. See you tomorrow.

> See you.

The interaction makes me giddy. Nothing's resolved, but she answered and that's a start. Since the conversation took me out of my social media rabbit hole, I decide to study one final time for my Spanish test this afternoon. As with everything I do, I put all of myself into it. When I was studying for the Illinois bar, I focused only on that exam for three solid months; everything else was sidelined. Admittedly, I'm not putting the same effort into this class, but I'm still putting a lot of time into it because failing is not an option. For the next hour, I find myself trying to repeat the words over and over, hoping that my pronunciation is improving. I can't help but think that one day I'll meet my extended family or maybe just Rosa. It would be nice if I could speak with them in Spanish or at least understand what it is that they're saying. I have a very difficult time rolling my *r*'s. And just in case you were wondering, the fact that there's Spanish in my gene pool doesn't help me with my pronunciation one tiny bit. It is not a natural thing to roll one's tongue that way! I sound better than Google's robotic pronunciation of the words, though. Or at least I hope I do.

During class that afternoon, I'm the first one to finish the exam. I know I did well. I knew most of the basic words, and the teacher approved my advancement for the next level during the winter term, which makes me very excited. Now, if I need to find a dog, cat, or mat in Spanish, I think I'll be able to do so.

"Do you think you can recommend some easy books for me to read?" I ask Professor Gonzalez. She's an elderly woman in her late seventies or possibly early eighties. A retired high school teacher, she now teaches Spanish at the local community college for some extra income. She smiles often, especially while laughing at our diction.

"*Sí. Sí.* Yes. I will email you some recommendations later," she says, thrilled that I'm taking such interest. I've been in this class now for a while and haven't spoken to anyone other than Z that first day, but we always sit next to each other. Today, we're parked in the same building and end up walking to our cars together while complaining about how hard the class is, especially now that we've started working on the accents, or diacritics, which go above some letters as I've recently been taught. Apparently, their placement determines the entire meaning and pronunciation of the word. *Te* is a form of the word *you* while *té* means *tea*. That's a pretty major difference for a two-letter word. I got that one wrong on the test.

Most people come in right before the class begins and leave the second it ends. It's not high school. Everyone here is an adult with other demands on their time. I, on the other hand, am never in a hurry.

Even though I'm trying to work on myself, there are some things that will never change. I've always been punctual even when I'm rushing around getting everything done. I've always been overprepared and I always overthink things. I try to go that extra mile, and even if I'm not currently working, I don't think that will ever change. I don't want it to.

"You want to grab dinner?" Z asks as we get to my car. It's the first week of November, the first big snow day of the year, and my teeth were chattering until he just asked that question. I wonder if he's asking as friends or as a date. We basically just met, so this catches me off guard.

I like John too much, and I couldn't do that to him. Z must notice my hesitation because he adds, "Just dinner," putting both hands up. "It's late and I haven't eaten. We can talk more about class while eating a nice meal—or not. It can be fast food." He chuckles.

"I'm dating someone, and I don't think he'd be okay with it. I'm sorry."

"It's cool. I understand," he says. "Maybe I should've asked if you were dating anyone first." So he *was* asking me on a date.

"But I'd love to grab coffee or something. Study together? I'm having a hard time with . . . well, with all of it," I admit.

"For sure. Let's forget I even asked."

I smile. "Good night, Z." I don't want to forget it. He is an attractive man, and it's very flattering to be asked out, so no, I don't want to forget it, even if I don't want to take it further with him. But I hope this interaction doesn't make it awkward moving forward since he is my only friend in this class and I like him.

"Night, Millie."

By the time I get home, I have an email from Rosa, which makes me unbelievably excited. I pour myself a glass of red wine, and I sit on my favorite chair, as if I'm about to dig into my favorite novel.

The email is three pages long, and she gives me the names of my thirteen cousins. I find it amazing that only one of the female cousins, Marta, has gone to school and is a nurse. Rosa tells me how her husband left her when he found out she was studying and now she's single with a child but has refused to give up. I can tell Rosa is most proud of Marta. Then there's Lorena, who is happily married with three grown children, and Fabiola, who is unhappily married to Rey. She is the youngest of my cousins. She's pregnant with her first child, and her husband is demanding that she stop working. She works at a local nail salon, which from the description seems like it's in someone's home, but she doesn't want to quit. Rosa doesn't see high hopes for the job.

I don't see high hopes for the marriage.

But I suppose that's the difference between me and Fabiola. I allowed men to dictate my life for far too long. Ironically, anyone from the outside looking in would have thought me an assertive, successful, independent woman. Hell, that's what I thought of myself. But I wasn't. I was a pawn in a law practice where men were making all the rules and manipulating all the moves to their benefit. They were using me. I get enraged when I think of Junior telling me that I was just the token woman. I think that's been on my mind more than the other sexist things he said.

Rey may be trying to control Fabiola, but Fabiola is doing whatever she wants to do, regardless of what Rey decides. And I admire that. I wonder if Fabiola feels guilty for defying her husband. Or maybe she feels triumphant? I'm reading too much into a relationship I know nothing about, but still, it's amazing how she's taking this bold stand of work over family life like I did with Marcus years ago. Except for me, it didn't end up well. I hope Fabiola's fate is different. Somehow, I want to communicate this to my cousin overseas.

I write back, and this time I ask for an address and for permission to send a care package. I hope I haven't overstepped. I suppose she could also think I'm catfishing her.

For now, all I can do is wait to see if I get a reply.

The next day, I arrive at Starbucks early. As I wait for Luanne, I scan the *New York Times* that was left on the table by a previous customer. I inhale sharply when I see Phoebe's face posted right on the front page. It's not front and center and doesn't trump whatever political issue is headlining the news, but it's still there, in a corner with his unattractive photo and the title, A Win for the Billionaire.

I fluff the paper open and read.

> A big victory for Hugh Phoebe in court today. Phoebe is being sued in civil court by four different women for sexual harassment and battery. Chelsea Harmon, the key witness for the plaintiff, failed to appear at a court-ordered deposition. The longtime personal assistant of the real estate mogul is not one of the women suing. Throughout the lawsuit, it has been uncovered that Phoebe paid Harmon over $750,000 as a "severance" package. Phoebe's attorney has held firm that the money was a token of appreciation for her fifteen years of service, but there has been speculation that the large amount of money was actually hush money for sexual assault. Records of Harmon's hospital visit along with pictures of her with a black eye and torn clothes have recently surfaced online. Harmon has failed to comment on the case and has been deemed a hostile witness by the plaintiff's attorney. This is the second deposition Harmon failed to attend, and the judge has now held her in contempt of court.

The article continues, and I'm shocked—shocked!—at the rest. There is even speculation that Harmon has fled the country.

Fled the country!

Junior is as horrible as Phoebe. I knew that, but this article confirms it.

I dial John because I need to talk about this. Yes, we have a rule about not talking about work, but we're also dating and these are the type of feelings and things you share with a partner. At least I think they are. I just . . . I need to get it off my chest.

"Hey," he answers. "I'm about to walk into a meeting—"

"Phoebe is terrorizing Harmon. You have to talk to Junior. He can't allow Phoebe to threaten her."

"Millie." His tone says everything. He isn't going to discuss it.

"Listen, I know that we don't talk about your work, but you're friendly with the partners, you're about to make partner yourself, and you can have this conversation. Please. I just saw the piece in the *Times*, and John, Phoebe can't win based on making the victims too scared to testify. He just can't."

There's silence on the other end just as I watch Luanne walk into Starbucks.

"John," I plead in a whisper. All of Starbucks doesn't need to hear our conversation.

"I can't talk to you about the firm's cases, Millie. You know that," he says, and I can't quite gauge if it's regret in his voice or something else.

"John!" I say it louder. A man sitting at the table beside me looks up, and I wince, shifting my body and cupping my mouth and the mouthpiece of the phone to stop my voice from carrying so much. "John," I whisper-shout.

"You made the rules, Millie, and you're breaking them. You said you'd be able to handle me working at JJF, and now here we are."

It's not only about working at JJF. It's about Phoebe and this damn case. But I don't tell him any of that. I just sigh loudly. "I hate this. I just can't seem to get over you working there."

"It's just a job," he says again. He considers it just a job, and I don't understand how he can separate one thing from the other. I never could.

"I have to go, Millie. I am about to meet with a new client; I really can't talk about this now. But I do need you to think about us because I'll tell you now, I like you, but I don't want to have an argument every time work comes up. This new case I'm taking on you may not like either. In fact, I don't know what it is that you think is acceptable or not. Regardless, I can't choose my caseload based on your preferences. You said you can handle it. Has that changed?"

"I don't know . . ."

"Well, you need to figure it out. I have to run," he says and hangs up.

He hung up on me. Sonofabitch. He's sort of right. He doesn't even know what my problem is with JJF, and I'm expecting him to just "do the right thing" when I don't even know what that is anymore. I mumble a few choice curse words underneath my breath as I stand and wave to Luanne, trying to pretend I'm not preoccupied with Harmon and the Phoebe trial.

"Hi," we both say at once. It's very awkward.

"You want anything?" she asks, pointing her thumb over her shoulder toward the baristas.

"No. I'm okay," I say, lifting my large, black Americano. She drops her purse on the table, taking only her wallet with her.

My mind is jumbled. I'm livid with John. Worried about Harmon. Uneasy about this conversation with Luanne.

She comes back and takes a seat. She places her bag on the back of the chair, and it falls. She does the same thing again and finally tucks it under the table. She has grabbed too many packets of raw sugar but doesn't use any as she starts to sip. Then she makes a face of disgust, opens two, and dumps them inside. All of this happens in a few seconds.

"I'm nervous, too, Luanne," I say, hopefully breaking some of the tension.

She lets out a sigh. "I guess I'm not sure what this little meeting's about. Are you here to argue with me? Full disclaimer, the kids slept terribly last night, which means I slept terribly last night and I'm too tired to argue back."

"No. I'm not here to argue with you. Why would I be?"

She shrugs. "Why are we here then?"

"Because I haven't seen you in years and I miss you."

"Oh." She seems genuinely surprised by that. I guess she doesn't miss me. Damn, that hurts.

"I'm still stunned you have kids. I can't believe I didn't know that. And Mitchell? How's he doing?"

She looks down at her hands and then up. There's definite sadness in her eyes. "Not sure. Probably still sleeping from a fun night out with his girlfriend."

My mouth opens and closes almost on its own. I did not see that coming. I had not noted the absence of a wedding ring. "You . . . you aren't married anymore?"

"Divorced. About a year now."

So that explains her exhausted look. She's raising two kids alone. "Shit. Sorry, Lu. I'm so sorry to hear that."

"Are you? Sorry, that is?" She sits back and takes a sip of her coffee.

"Of course," I say with a bite in my tone. "Why wouldn't I be?"

Now that I'm sitting in front of her, I find the words clogged at the back of my throat. I'm not exactly sure what I'm supposed to be apologizing for, and Luanne looks at her tall coffee as if it holds all the answers in the world.

"I don't know. I always thought you didn't like him or maybe you didn't think our lives were interesting enough."

"What? That's not true." I'm shocked at this revelation, but I'm here to lay it all out and hopefully get my friend back. May as well be honest, right? "Maybe I didn't capital-L love Mitchell, but I never got the impression he liked me very much either. And it was fine. He and I didn't have to love each other. I wasn't the one marrying him. But we were always cordial, I thought. Is that why you stopped calling me? You and I were inseparable. It was very hurtful."

"Did we stop talking?" she says. There is ire in her tone. "Or did *you* stop talking to *me*?"

She said that last time, too, and I haven't been able to stop thinking about that. I've been trying to think back to that time in my life, maybe six years ago. I was working on a huge trial and traveling back and forth to New York for the better part of a year. I may have missed events, but I didn't stop answering her calls. My head shakes side to side. Her recollection is wrong. That's not how it happened. Not at all.

"The last time we communicated in any way was when I sent you a text after I left you a message. You never returned either." I pause. She looks at me as if she's waiting for more. "Ergo, you stopped talking to me."

She rolls her eyes. "You wanted to talk to me? Or did you want to talk to me about yourself? Are you that self-centered or just not self-aware?" she says, and her words actually burn like a poison down my throat.

"Ouch," I mumble. My temper builds. "I didn't realize I was such an ogre. Why were you even my friend for so long?" I say with a bite in my tone. "You weren't always roses either, but as friends, we take the good with the bad. I thought there was more good than bad."

She doesn't say anything, so I continue. "If you felt like I was self-centered, you could've told me. You knew me enough to call me out."

"And get the wrath of Amelia Montgomery? No, thank you."

"Oh, please don't sit there and act like an innocent little wallflower. You could handle yourself. If I was being an asshole, you could've told me. And if I lost my temper and we stopped talking for a day or two . . . so what? People argue. We argued before and got over it."

She doesn't say anything back and also doesn't look at me.

One night over drinks a few weeks before her wedding, she confessed that she was having cold feet. Maybe I was supposed to convince her to go through with the wedding. Maybe a "good friend" would've cheered her on and given her all the reasons why these feelings were "normal" and they meant nothing. Instead, I told her if she didn't want to go through with the wedding she didn't have to. I may have even told her she was too good for him anyway. She was beautiful and could find another man in an instant if she didn't want to marry him. She cried, I cried, we drank some more. Two weeks later, she was walking down the aisle to Mitchell and that conversation was forgotten. Maybe that wasn't the support she needed from me that night. It's haunted me to this day. Playing back the conversations we had before she just stopped returning my calls, all this time, I thought maybe I should have been more supportive, but now, I'm realizing that what actually made her (and Mitchell) mad was that I had been right after all. Mitchell was a jerk.

"Was it one particular thing I said, or was it me in general that you hated?" I ask.

She looks so defeated when she speaks. Her shoulders slump, and she puts the coffee down on the table. "I didn't hate you, Millie. I don't hate you now. There was not *one* thing. There wasn't even a lot of things. People just grow apart sometimes. We grew apart. We were living different lives. I didn't fit in yours, and you didn't fit in mine. Nothing has to necessarily happen, you know? Friendships fizzle out."

"But you just said I was self-centered, so there was obviously something that you didn't like about me."

She shakes her head and sighs heavily. "I shouldn't have said that just now. It's not true. I mean, it is, but that's not the reason. You've always been you, and you didn't change. I didn't hate that about you. It's your personality to be driven and intense. Since we were little, that's just how you've been. Maybe I just couldn't compete or maybe it's my own insecurities. I don't know, Millie. You want answers that I just can't give you because I guess . . . there isn't one."

I drop my defenses. "Can I just be honest here? My life is a disaster."

"Huh?"

I don't go into any major details about my failed party and my lack of a social life, but still, I'm honest with her. "I'm forty and unemployed. The one thing I thought I wanted to do for the rest of my life doesn't sound appealing anymore. And now I look back, and the things

I sacrificed to be successful weren't worth it. Losing you as a friend because I was too busy was just not worth it. I'm sorry, Lu. I don't even know why I'm sorry, but I am. Whatever I did to you to make you not want to be my friend anymore, I'm sorry about that." And it's true; from the depths of my soul, it is true. Whether it was my fault, her fault, or both of our faults, I am truly sorry. Unlike the other apologies, this one isn't going to have a perfect little bow at the end of the conversation, with everyone walking away as if everything's rainbows and butterflies. This one is messy, and there's been real, deep hurt and regret and also time missed that we'll never get back. Regardless, I'm glad we're here, getting messy and trying to figure it out. Unlike with the others, I'm willing to say *I'm sorry* even if I wasn't completely at fault because sometimes you just have to admit you played some role in the mess, even if you can't pinpoint what that role was. It's irrelevant.

She shakes her head, and I can tell she's holding back tears. "Don't apologize. You didn't do anything wrong. I should apologize to you. You're right; I stopped calling you. I should've been more honest with you. I could've yelled at you about your one-sided phone calls and I know you would've stopped. Instead, I just gave up and immersed myself in Mitchell and his friends and their stupid, annoying wives. Then when the kids were born it became all about the kids and . . ." Tears start falling down her face. "And now I have a jerk for an ex-husband, no friends, and two wonderful but very time-consuming children. I messed things up too."

I reach out and take her hands in mine, sniffling hard. "We're idiots."

She nods with her nose running a little, and I think it's coming down from mine, too, but I don't care. This is Lu, my best friend who's seen me at my worst. "I wish I'd seen you pregnant. Big, fat belly and swollen feet. I would've thrown you a really grandiose baby shower."

"And then you would've missed it because of some trial thing," she blubbers, and I nod because that is exactly true. "I know you had a party. I got your invitation. I'm sorry I didn't go. I didn't have a sitter."

"Liar. You just didn't want to go."

"Yeah." She sniffles. "That's true too."

I can't help but chuckle even though I'm also crying.

"I'm sorry," we both sob at the same time. The people around us are watching our spectacle, but I don't care.

"Can we be friends again?" I say.

"I hope so."

You can't go from zero to a hundred in an instant, and I know that even if we are connecting right now, after the emotional crap of today wears out, there'll still be a chasm between us, one that we can't cross overnight.

CHAPTER SIXTEEN

~~Luanne No! Luanne Attempt #2~~
~~Gary~~
Lindsey ✓
~~Jenny O.~~ NO!
~~Jenny M.~~ NO!
~~Jenny Z.~~ Absolutely NO!
~~Mary~~
Office MAYBE
~~Brenda~~
~~Margret Undecided~~
~~Jimenez~~

"What's that?" Nina asks.

I pat the corner of my lips with a napkin as I swallow a bite of the Cuban dish I made for dinner. I turn my head to see what she's looking at.

"Oh. Ha. So I took some pottery classes. That was one of our projects."

"Any Patrick Swayze / Demi Moore moments?"

I shake my head. "Not even close. Most of my classmates were retired women looking for a hobby. Not a lot of hot men at Tuesday morning pottery classes."

She laughs. "What's it supposed to be?"

"A vase. It sucks. I sucked. I actually managed to break two pieces and get the turning thing stuck. I've been picking clay out of my fingernails for a week."

"So you doubled down on classes, I bet? Make pottery your bitch, huh?"

"Nah, I gave up. Pottery's not my thing. Neither is painting or needlepoint. Basically, anything art-related is out."

"Whoa! You've never given up on anything."

"It's just pottery."

"It's just AP Chemistry, it's just a game of UNO, it's just Spanish." She mimics my voice. "Like I said, you hate to lose. Who even are you? Where's my sister?"

"Har har."

"I'm serious. This is not very Amelia Montgomery."

"It's very Millie Montgomery, though. It's just that Millie has been working too long and too hard, and forgot that some things just aren't that important."

"Have you been cheating on me with another shrink?"

I laugh and shake my head.

"So, when do I get to meet John?"

It's been three days since I called him from Starbucks about the Phoebe case. I think it's over. He texted me yesterday morning with a link to an article about Harmon. Literally, it was just the link. Not even a hello. Turns out that she'd been in the ICU for the last month for complications with the flu. The news had sensationalized the entire thing. I have no doubt he knows something about the case. Hell, everyone who watches the news knows about this case. I hadn't even given him the benefit of the doubt.

That same day, I had replied, We need to talk.

He responded with, Yes, we do. I'm in trial. When it's over, we'll talk.

"I don't even know if I'll see him again," I say to Nina.

"Why?"

I tell her about the "Starbucks Scuffle," which is how I have been referring to it in my mind.

"Ohhhh, Millie."

"Yep. The worst part is, he didn't tell me to go to hell and mind my own business, which is exactly what I would have told him if the roles were reversed. He calmly waited until the truth came out, like it always does, and sent me the article."

"But you just got pissed off without letting him explain. He didn't even know how you felt about that trial. He doesn't know why you're not working at JJF. I barely know and I'm your sister."

"And you don't even know most of it," I say, almost underneath my breath. She knows about my NDA, which is more than she should even know.

"Exactly. You know what happens when you tell someone part of the story? Their imagination runs wild with the rest of it. You have no idea what I've imagined, Millie."

"About me?"

"Yes, about you! I know you left on bad terms, but I also remember you calling me hysterically that day. Then suddenly you're walking away with millions and you can't even tell me about it. You're super passionate about a case where the guy raped women and got away with it. If I put two and two together, Mills . . ."

"No! Oh my God, Nina. No. That did not happen to me. No amount of money would have kept me quiet if Junior had physically assaulted me. He's just an asshole is all. A big, huge one." I exhale and think of how I would have felt assuming that of my sister for months. "Jesus, Nina. I'm sorry that even crossed your mind."

"Well, it did; then it sort of shifted to you maybe having an affair and you caught Junior cheating on you."

"Nina!"

"You see. Half truths. You assume shit that isn't there!"

"Like I did with John. Point made."

"You're waging a war on him that he doesn't even know he's in. Listen, if he knows what your ex-boss is up to, using these victims in a malicious way, and he's cool with it, then I'm all with you. Tell him off. Kick him to the curb. Key his car. But don't do any of that unless you're sure."

I bite the side of my lip.

"Millie. This was your mess-up. You know he can't talk about the case, but you can talk about your morals. Your principles. What you think of the defendant. Then it's up to him to do the right thing or not. You knew that when you decided to date this man, that being on this case or other cases you didn't agree with wasn't an option. You both decided not to talk about the job. He held up his part of the bargain."

"Ugh . . . damn. Maybe I owe him an apology. I flew off the handle. This stupid Apology Project has my 'sorry switch' all screwed up."

"Ha! I love that you're calling it the Apology Project. You're welcome."

I roll my eyes.

"I'm not trying to apologize to every Tom, Dick, and Harry who crosses my path and does something to me that *they* should apologize for, i.e., the Jennys." Then I tell my sister all about the Jennys and why I crossed them off the list without an apology. Their mistakes are their mistakes, and I don't need to apologize to them.

"Well, sister, you better change the filter on that sorry switch because your boyfriend deserves an apology on this one. If he actually ends up screwing up, then that's a different story."

"I know." I wince and then blurt out, "Either way, I have this niggling feeling that it'll be over soon anyway. It would've never worked. He's literally working for my nemesis, and it's his dream job. I could never ask him to stop working there or make him choose, not that I think he'd choose me anyway." Saying the words out loud gives me a strange pang in my chest.

"Don't say that, Mills. Again, you're assuming."

"How long do you think two people can be in a relationship and avoid talking about the single most important thing in their life? It's always going to be an issue."

"Maybe after the trial's over, it'll get better."

"I hope so." I sigh. "In other news, have you been reading the emails from Rosa?" I have been forwarding them all to Nina to see if she gets as excited as I do.

"On and off. Why?"

I shake my head. "It's beyond me why you are not into this. You're definitely your father's daughter."

"That's a plot twist, since you two couldn't be more similar," she says, and I smile because my father and I are two peas in a pod. We have the same fiery temper, and we can both hold one mean grudge. But we're also hardworking and very analytical, which is why I can't for the life of me understand why he's not champing at the bit to find out more about his ancestors.

"Anyway, I'm sending them a care package. It's costing a small fortune, but it's fine." I point to the stack of books.

"Aren't people in Cuba in need of food and clothes and stuff like that? I don't think they need some romance novels."

I roll my eyes. "That package"—I point to the other large bulk—"is full of essentials. This one is for Marta. It's some updated medical journals and magazines because she understands English. These are for Fabiola."

"Sylvia Plath? Margaret Atwood?"

"I found them in Spanish!" I say. "Maybe it'll give her the courage or at least the encouragement to stand up for herself. She wants to keep working. She should! I even found *The Devil Wears Prada* in Spanish just in case the books were too heavy—emotionally, I mean."

"I got that, Mills." She snorts.

"Anyway, I couldn't find the book, but I found the DVD version along with a bunch of other movies, and Rosa told me they have an old DVD player. Something'll stick, right? She should not quit."

"Is this about Fabiola?"

"Oh, hush," I say and stuff everything back into the packages. "You don't understand how difficult it is to send this to Cuba. I had to find an agency, and it's by weight and . . . it's been a mission, Nina."

"Well, then it's right up your alley. You can't resist a challenge."

"Don't rain on my parade. I'm really happy about this. Rosa thinks I should fly out myself and meet them all."

"Did you tell her that you don't fly?"

"I fly. It's not my favorite pastime, but I fly."

"So you're actually going through with it?"

"No!" I say far too quickly. "I'm just chatting with her."

"And learning Spanish and cooking Cuban dishes."

"I'm happy, Nina. Really, this Rosa thing and now reconnecting with Luanne, it makes me happy. I'm going to have breakfast with Lu and her kids tomorrow."

"I'm happy that you're happy, Mills. Were you not happy before the 'retirement'?"

"I thought I was. I mean, I wasn't *not* happy. But there were things missing from my life that I hadn't noticed until I stopped working. Until all the noise from my everyday life came to an end."

"Hmmm . . ."

"No, not hmmm." She knows that talking about feelings isn't my thing. The last thing I need is a vague *hmmm*.

"Maybe you were lonely."

"I was rarely alone. I was either at work with dozens of people around or in court with even more people around." I had not thought of that. Not at all. "Nah, I wasn't lonely. Regretful is more like it."

"You can be the most popular girl in school and be lonely, Mills."

I shrug. "Yeah, I hear you. But . . . I don't know."

"What do you regret exactly?"

"I wish more people would've gotten to know me," I admit. "Hell, I wish I'd known me."

"That's deep, sister!"

My doorbell rings, which surprises me.

"Are you expecting company?" she asks. I shake my head and walk to my door. From the peephole, I see John standing on the other side.

"Looks like you're going to meet John sooner rather than later," I say as I unlock the door and open it. John's standing there, a beautiful woolen scarf and gloves paired with his work clothes, which I know he's been wearing since early this morning. The only thing out of place is his tie, which he's pulled down and loosened up. He has a hand behind his back.

"Hi. Judge ruled one hour ago, came straight over. You're avoiding my calls, and we need to talk." He's a bit reserved, serious, a side of him I haven't seen before. Except then he brings his hand forward, and there's a familiar logo on a familiar-looking lime-green box.

"Crazy Cleo's Cookies!" Nina says excitedly behind me. It's a well-known bakery downtown that only makes cookies. The cookies are the size of fat pancakes, and they're usually stuffed with something delicious. "Come in. Come in," my sister says, walking around me and pulling John inside, ignoring the tension in the room. "I'm Nina, Amelia's sister. You must be John."

"I've heard a lot about you, Nina. It's a pleasure to meet you," he says and puts the cookies down on my kitchen counter. My sister opens the box as John takes off his suit jacket. "Hey," he says, and leans over and kisses me briefly on the lips, but it's formal and not John-like at all. I'm glad he's here—we need to talk—but I don't want to have this conversation with Nina around.

Thank God my sister gets the hint. After she takes a cookie, she blurts, "I'm going to run to the store real quick. I think we need wine, but I'll be back in . . . twenty minutes or so?" She looks us both over as if that should be enough time for us to quash the problem or clean up the dead body from the epic argument we may or may not have.

"How about thirty," I say, and she gives us a thumbs-up, grabs her coat, and makes herself scarce.

"Before you say anything, I need to say something," I begin, and he tilts one eyebrow up, waiting. I pull out the chair from the counter to sit and then signal for him to take the other one, but he doesn't sit.

"I'm sorry. For the scolding. I jumped to conclusions and got mad without even explaining myself. I can't expect for you to read my mind, and I should have talked to you first."

He releases a deep breath, and I can see him begin to thaw. He strolls over to the hook by my door, hangs up his jacket and scarf, and then sits down, moving in a bit closer. He must've expected me to be angry or to yell and scream because he definitely came here with his defenses up. It doesn't go unnoticed, however, that he came over. Prepared to argue or not, he came over. This relationship must also be important to him; otherwise, he would not have gone through the hassle.

"You accused me of things I have no control over. I had nothing to do with the article."

"I know. I'm sorry."

He eyes the glass of wine I had with dinner. "Are you drunk?"

"No!"

"I expected you to be more argumentative," he admits.

"It just upsets me that Junior wants to rip Harmon and the rest of the victims apart in order to make Phoebe look like the innocent party here."

"I can honestly tell you that I don't know the defense tactic on Phoebe. I only know about the cases I'm handling, Millie."

"If you did know, would you tell me?"

"No," he says honestly. I wouldn't tell him either if I were in his shoes. He can't. He could lose his license. The attorney-client privilege extends to the firm, even if it's not his particular client. "I just had a two-day trial I didn't tell you anything about. I've had depos on four other cases that I haven't talked to you about either. We avoid talking about work, and I didn't think anything of it. I'm not intentionally trying to keep it from you."

"Maybe I overreacted. From now on, I'll keep it all bottled up inside and talk about my feelings and opinions with a therapist like most sane people do."

He smiles with a flash of sadness. "How about you just come and talk to me instead of jumping to conclusions?"

"I can do that."

A loud knock on the door makes me jump. Nina has the keys, so I know she's doing this on purpose. "I'm coming in," she says, a hand over her eyes. "Get dressed or let me know where to hide the body."

Now there's no doubt in John's mind that she knows we've been discussing him. "You kids drinking?" she asks as she tries to assess the room. I give her a little smile and a wink, letting her know it's okay to stay and that John and I are not going to kill each other. Not right now, at least.

"Yep. Why don't you pour yourself some more wine?" I say, pointing to the nearly empty bottle on the table and taking the one she just purchased out of her hand.

"I need to assess the cookie situation first."

John slides the box over. He may have been mad, but he still made a stop to bring me cookies. Damn him and all his mixed emotions.

"Mills, you better hurry. There's only one Nutella cookie." She looks up at John. "Nutella's her favorite."

"I know," he says. "There was only one left at the shop; otherwise I'd have bought more." He reaches into the box and hands it to me.

"Did you eat? There's leftovers," I say, and he looks concerned.

"It came out good. It's . . . what is it, exactly? It's like a beef stew," Nina says.

"It's called *ropa vieja*. The literal translation is 'old clothes.'"

They both look at me, then each other, then make a disgusted face, which causes me to chuckle. "That's just the name. It's like a Cuban beef stew. Forget the name and just trust me, it's delicious. Rosa sent me the recipe."

"It really was," Nina reassures him.

"You sure?" he asks her, and then they get deep into a chat about my food.

"Hey. I'm standing right here!" I say, feigning anger as I prepare a bowl for him. The next hour is surreal. John, Nina, and I are sitting at my kitchen counter talking, laughing, but I can't stop thinking of the case that's looming and how involved he is exactly.

———

The next morning, I leave John still sleeping in my cozy, warm bed. Admittedly, I was close to canceling on Luanne. Why would she venture out of her house on a snowy day at nine in the morning when she could make pancakes or order them? These better be some damn good pancakes. I tremble as I step out of my warm apartment into the freezing city. I hail a cab for the one-mile trip to a hole-in-the-wall breakfast spot she says her kids love. And even though I'm prickly, inwardly I know that meeting her for breakfast is a major step in mending fences. Also, the restaurant, even from across the street, smells like cinnamon and vanilla and homemade chocolate all wrapped up in a little gingerbread-looking storybook house. I instantly know why the kids would love waking up to have breakfast at the world's cutest little bakeshop.

I easily find them because there's only three tables in the entire place. I smile when I see the chair saved just for me. "Hi!" I say, and Luanne stops whatever fussing she's been doing with the napkins and turns to see me. She smiles wide. "Hey, glad you made it," she says and motions to the empty seat.

"Hi! I remember you from Starbucks," Mikey says.

"This is my friend Millie. Millie, this is Olivia and Mikey," Luanne says.

They grin at me, and it warms my heart to see their crooked little smiles, much like Luanne's at that age. "It's very nice to meet you both. I heard this was the best restaurant in all of Illinois!"

"They have chocolate chip pancakes!" Mikey practically jumps up and down in his seat, and Luanne reaches over and gently pushes him back down.

"And strawberry," Olivia says. She is absolutely adorable.

"Oh my gosh, do they have blueberry pancakes too?" I ask, and they both make a disgusted face, which causes Luanne and me to laugh loudly. I remember when we were kids and we'd make faces at the lunch ladies in the cafeteria every Wednesday when they'd serve creamed spinach for lunch. It was the same face her kids just made, and I'm sure Luanne is thinking of the time we got detention for getting caught. We swore we'd never make our own kids eat things they hated when we grew up. "Okay, so blueberry is out. I can't believe I didn't know this place existed," I say to Luanne when the server brings the kids some paper menus and crayons.

"It's one of those places you don't know about unless you have kids."

For some reason, reasons I will not allow to intrude on this lovely morning, that hits me hard. I'm forty and I don't have kids. Hell, I don't have a husband or a job, and I hadn't even put much thought into having children. I'm not part of, and may never be a part of, this society of mothers that knows of special places like this. I've missed out on so many things I didn't even know I wanted. She must see the change in my face. Though I've swallowed it down and stuck that smile back on, Luanne knows me. We may not have seen each other for a while, but where it counts, she knows me.

"I didn't mean anything by it," she quickly backtracks. "It's like Chuck E. Cheese and things like that. Why would you know about it without kids? Heck, why would you want to know about it unless you have to go?"

I wave her off. "It's fine. Really. I get it. Although I think I'd want chocolate chip pancakes with or without kids." I wink at Mikey and Olivia, who now have turned their attention to us. "So, what do I get, guys?" I change the subject like the expert litigator that I am, turning the conversation to where I'm most comfortable. The kids yell out their preference just as the server comes to take our order. We compromise: they'll share their pancakes with me if I get the sprinkle ones and share those with them.

This is not a lengthy breakfast with mimosas and heartfelt conversations. This lasts the amount of time that it takes the kids to eat and get sleepy, then cranky. I try to slip in some conversation, and so does Luanne, but it's virtually impossible. Regardless, I enjoyed breakfast. We all hug each other goodbye over my stuffed belly. This time I walk back home since I'm wide awake and some of the frost in the air has dissipated.

Mostly, I enjoyed how easy it was to fit into Luanne's life again. I'm probably being overly optimistic, but this feels like a huge shift.

Dear Rosa,

I haven't heard from you. I hope everything is okay. I'm really enjoying our chats. I woke up this morning thinking that I should have tried searching for you sooner. I'm sorry I didn't do that. I don't know if I would have even known where to begin, but still,

I wish I had. Anyway, I sent you a care package, I hope it arrives safely and that everyone is well.

Affectionately yours,
Millie

Inwardly, I know there's nothing I could have done and that it is in no way my fault that we have only just now connected, but I woke up feeling sentimental and wishing I'd received a reply from Rosa. When there was nothing in my in-box, I felt the need to tell her exactly how I was feeling, so I did. Sometimes I suppose it's easier opening your heart to strangers than to someone you know.

But I refuse to let this melancholy overtake me, so I'm going to venture out and try something new.

I've been eyeing everyone around the city riding bright green bikes, and I've also seen the kiosks where they get them from. While I was in my big office at JJF, I missed all these changes going on around me. This seems to be one of those things I've missed out on. It's nice out, chilly but sunny, and there's no snow on the ground.

I'm supposed to have lunch with John before he flies to Vegas for a few days, and we're meeting at a café across from my old office. Because I'm trying new things and because it turns out that nice, long bike rides are a good form of relaxation (thank you, World Wide Web), I'm going to pedal there on one of those bright green bikes.

I stand by a rental bike with a fat tire that is locked at the front wheel. I have a juris doctor; I can figure this out. I've seen kids do it, so it can't be that difficult, right?

But where exactly can I place my handful of quarters to unlock that wheel? I walk around the contraption and the seven other bikes and see nothing. A kid—no more than nineteen, with wireless earbuds—walks by me, gives me a chin nod, and just pulls out a bike.

"What the f—" I whisper to myself and try and pull just like he does, but the damn thing won't budge.

"Do you need help, ma'am?" the kid asks as he takes off the earbuds. *Ma'am? Sonofabitch.*

"No. I got—actually, yes. If you don't mind showing me how you just did that, I'd really appreciate it."

"Sure," he says, and pushes out the kickstand on his bike. "Load up the app on your phone."

"Oh. You need an app?"

He looks at me like I'm my mother when she comes over and can't figure out my remote control. "Like, of course, ma'am. How else did you plan on paying for it?"

"I had quarters." When he looks at me with furrowed brows, I add, "Those metal coins that you mostly get as change and throw in your pocket and forget about."

He laughs. "I know what quarters are, but these machines don't take money. Plus all that change will weigh you down. It's better to travel light, don't ya think?"

"I suppose that's true."

"I normally pay for everything through my e-wallet," he says, swiping through his phone. *Oh God. I'm an old dinosaur who has a small coin wallet in my purse, like my grandmother used to carry.* I can't deal. But he's friendly and willing to help, so I go along with it. "So yeah, you need to download the app. Please tell me you have an iPhone or even an Android."

I'm not that ancient. "Of course I do," I say, taking out my phone, which happens to be the newest iPhone available.

"Awesome," he says. He takes it from my hand after I've unlocked it and goes to the App Store, finds the app, and then tells me to press my fingerprint on it in order to get access to download. We wait a half a second, and then he shows me how to use the app. "So after you've put in all your credit card info, which you probably have saved in your electronic wallet, you have to put this number here"—he first points to the number of the bike station and then to the number on the bike—"or you can even scan this"—he gestures to the little black-and-white symbol on the bike—"and then it will unlock." He does it, and then I hear a little click sound, and he pulls out the bike. "Easy, right?"

"Actually, yes. Thank you so much."

"Don't mention it," he says.

It wasn't easy, but it's just a matter of getting used to it. Now that I have the app downloaded, I'm sure it will be much easier next time.

"Hey and, ma'am, don't forget to put on a helmet," he hollers over his shoulder as he rides off.

If this kid calls me *ma'am* one more time . . .

"Will do. Thank you!" I holler back as I make a mental note to swing by the sporting goods store and purchase a helmet.

I take out my little bottle of hand sanitizer and attempt to clean the handles and my hands before I get on the bike.

Turns out the saying is not completely accurate. You don't forget how to ride a bike, but you do forget that your reflexes are slower, that cars are driving faster, and that pedestrians are dicks. I'm surprised I make it to the café with all my limbs intact. I also flipped off two cars and threw a hailstorm of curse words at a man hauling ass in a BMW. It was just like being in court again. I kind of loved it.

There is a place to return the bikes at the corner near the café, according to the app, so I find it and park it in the little cubby thing, and it locks. I feel pleased with myself. There's an odd sense of independence in the entire process, one that I haven't felt before, which is weird considering the last case I tried was a $37 million wrongful termination lawsuit against a major corporation and its former CEO. I went up against four attorneys by myself and won.

But this little thing—deciding to exercise, going through with it, figuring it out, parking the bike, and walking into a date—makes me feel like a giant.

"Millie?" a deep and familiar voice hollers from behind me.

"John, hi," I say as he approaches. I'm a little breathless from the biking.

"Did you come on a bicycle?" He looks over my shoulder as if he's expecting a vehicle to materialize.

"Yep."

"You never cease to amaze me," he says and then leans in, kisses my cheek, and takes my hand in his. We walk into the café together.

He looks good. No, he looks great. He's wearing a navy suit with a light blue shirt and a matching tie. His hair is not in its usual messy-but-sexy style. It's parted nicely on the side and tamed. He looks professional. He looks like the kind of man I'd love to go head-to-head with in court (and in bed). Meanwhile, I look like I just came from the gym and probably smell a bit like that too.

"Maybe when I get back from my trip, we can go to Douglass Park for a bike ride," he says. "I haven't had a chance to do that yet."

"Sure. Although I'm a novice. This is the first time I've been on a bike in more than twenty years."

"Can I admit that I'm a little jealous you can do whatever you want whenever you want?"

"Well, I am going all-out party animal these days. If you can handle it . . ." I lean closer and whisper, "After this, I'm planning a trip to the library."

"Wild," he says with a hearty chuckle.

We sit in a booth, and both of us order coffee. "You look tired, John."

"I miss sleep," he tells me with a humorless smile, and I can see the dark circles under his eyes. "I made partner, by the way."

"Whoa! Congrats. That is such great news." I am sincerely happy for him. It's an accomplishment to make partner at such a prestigious firm, even if I do disagree with the managing partners. "Why aren't you more excited? This is what you wanted. Have you celebrated?"

"I received an email this morning from Fisher's secretary, a new employment contract, and a pay increase. I also received three new cases. I don't know how excited I'm supposed to be since I'm swamped at work and haven't had a solid day off in weeks," he says.

We've been seeing each other on and off, avoiding shop talk, but it's there, the elephant in the room. It's really starting to hit me now how much I miss working. It's been about a week since breakfast with Luanne and her kids, which was such a great diversion. I need more moments like those because there's only so much hobby-ing I can do. I have an itch to ask him about work or about his cases, any case, but I don't.

"I don't miss those days. It turns out I really, really like to sleep in," I say, and he looks at me longingly. He seems overwhelmed. *Is this what I looked like?* "Maybe you can take a few days off?" I know he can't, but I ask anyway.

"I can't. I'm swamped," he says and then takes my hands in his. "If anyone knows how this job works, it's you, but regardless, I can't help feeling like I'm neglecting this relationship. I'm sorry. Hopefully, I'll have some time off for the holidays and we can get away for a weekend or something."

"It's fine. Really. I get it." And I do. I also feel bad for him now that I'm on the other side. He doesn't know what he's missing. Sleeping in. Taking walks. Not booting up your laptop for three or four days in a row . . . it's heaven.

I put my hand out. "No. No. Work is off-limits. But still, tell me what you're up to in Vegas."

He looks at me hesitantly.

"Come on, just a general idea. What kind of case, who're you up against, that kind of thing. I need a legal fix, John. Help me out here."

He laughs again. I really like him and I want to see him smile. "All right, just a taste. I'm working on a boring little breach-of-contract case."

"Can't be that boring if they hired you to fly to Vegas. There are attorneys in Nevada, you know. Must be costing the client a pretty penny. You're holding out on me."

He presses his lips together in a cute way. "The defendant is a hotel on the Vegas strip, and the plaintiff's attorney is Brock."

"Ahhhh . . ." Brock. Like Prince and Madonna, Brock needs only one name. "So it's not a boring little breach-of-contract case. It's a huge contract case; otherwise Hansel Brock wouldn't have come out of his mansion in Beverly Hills to take it." I want to know more. I crave more. Cases against Brock are never dull. But I don't ask. I know that if I do, I'll have to give my opinion, and my opinion is neither solicited nor wanted. Also, it makes me relieved. There is absolutely no way John can handle a case against Brock while taking on Phoebe. "Good luck. Brock's a bulldog."

"If by 'bulldog' you mean 'jerk,' then yes, I know."

I laugh because Brock is the biggest jerk I've ever gone up against, and John will have his hands full for a while. Even without knowing the details of the case, I know this to be fact.

Instead of digging for more information, I order a turkey melt on a whole wheat bagel while he orders a Cobb salad. I tell him about the kid, the bike app, and how I was ma'am-ed, and he laughs.

"It feels like I haven't seen you in a month even though it's only been a week," he says. It's true; we haven't talked much this week.

"You've been so busy lately. I haven't wanted to intrude. I know how taxing these big cases can be and how annoyed I used to get when I felt torn between work and my personal life. The fact that someone would even suggest dinner pissed me off—aside from Nina, of course," I admit. It made me have to put in the effort of having to decline and then feeling guilty about declining. In turn, that would make me angry with the person. I mean, Jesus, if you know I'm busy, why even ask me to have a meal? It's just selfish, in my opinion.

Or is it?

Now that I've had time to reflect, maybe I should have been more patient. After all, I did eat food. I could've taken twenty minutes and downed a sandwich with my parents or with a friend. After all, I made the time for Nina. Sometimes it was the fifteen minutes it took to wait in line at Starbucks and drink our coffee, but I made time for her nonetheless. That's not to say I didn't cancel or postpone quite often, even with her. But I now see the excuses for what they really were—just excuses. I should have made more of an effort. They weren't the bad guys for asking. I was the bad guy for not wanting them to even ask.

"Normally I do hate to be disturbed when I'm swamped, but I wouldn't be upset if you asked to spend time with me for once. You could call me and ask me to lunch or dinner. The phone works both ways, you know."

I let out a breath. *Selfish.* The word rings in my ears.

"You're right. I'm sorry, I'm kind of new to this dating thing. Look at us, two middle-aged adults who—" I freeze. His mouth is agape. "What?"

He looks around the restaurant, alarmed, and now I start looking around too. For what, I have no idea.

"What?" I repeat louder, startled.

"Just checking if there's a flying pig around," he says, and my brows furrow in confusion. "Or if hell has frozen over or—"

"What are you talking about?"

"You apologized. That's two times you've apologized to me now. Last time you apologized, you had been drinking with your sister before I arrived. But this time you're stone-cold sober and the words *I'm sorry* actually came out of your mouth, so I'm just checking to see if the Earth's axis shifted or—"

I toss my paper napkin at him and try to hold in a laugh.

Then he does something that actually does surprise me. He stands, leaning over the table, the silver napkin holder, the bottle of ketchup, and our drinks. He takes my face in his hands and lays a sweet kiss on my lips. Then he sits down as if nothing has happened. We've kissed. We've slept together. But this kiss—it's the best one so far.

"What was that for?" I want to get up and run out the door because this can't happen. We can't be an us. Also, I want to crawl on his lap and kiss him some more. I'm so torn.

"Just because." He shrugs as if he didn't just turn my world upside down. A just-because kiss is better than any other kind of kiss.

Our food arrives, and we eat while we talk about our week. I tell him about Spanish class and my cooking, feeling like we've done this thousands of times. I think that's what I like most about John; it's easy with him. I am the one who makes it complicated with my worrying. He, on the other hand, is in the present. He's not thinking (as far as I know) about all the possible reasons he and I may not work out. He felt like giving me a kiss, and he simply did. I've never met a man like him before.

"I'm surprised you're not traveling more. You light up when you talk about Cuba. Why not go? If I had all this extra time, I think I'd spend it traveling all around the world."

"Alone?" I'm not scared of a lot of things, but traveling alone—no. I don't like flying. In fact, when I traveled for work, I used to insist that one of the interns tag along. One time, I even invited my sister with me to a case in Philadelphia and called it a girls' trip. Really it was a lie so I wouldn't freak out on the plane, and I spent zero time with her. "I'm not a great traveler. I get anxious when I don't know exactly where I am or where I'm supposed to go. The thought of not knowing the language in a foreign country and getting lost gives me hives. But I have been thinking about it. Rosa has suggested it, and it would be exciting to meet my family."

"You're learning Spanish and you know people over there."

"John, your estimation of me is sweet, but you truly don't under-stand how bad I am at Spanish. I could take classes every day until

I'm fifty, and it still wouldn't be nearly enough. I'd get lost leaving the airport. That's assuming I could even talk to a cab driver first."

He chuckles. "I refuse to believe that the great Amelia Montgomery is being bested by a foreign language."

"Well, believe it. I love it, but I'm awful. Anyway, I wanted to ask your opinion about something. I want to do something for Margret. Help her in some way. What do you think I can do? Would it be okay if I spoke with her? Would she be upset you told me?"

"She's a private person. I don't know if she'd appreciate you talking about it. There's nothing she needs, Millie. I've asked her. Her insurance covers her son's expenses. She makes a good salary at JJF. Her house and cars are paid off. The only thing that she needs is time, and that's not something you can give her. I think you're going to have to let this one go."

"I feel terrible that I just thought she was a bitch all this time when she was just trying to get by." I can't even take a bite of my food because there's a lump in my throat. *Why was I so harsh with her?* I've been obsessing about all the times I made her work late or rewrite something. All the times I inwardly thought she was a bitch when she just had other things on her mind.

"I saw her get into it with Fisher's executive assistant yesterday for using the last ream of paper in the copier. I don't think any of that had to do with her personal problems."

I know he's trying to make me feel better, and I do appreciate it, but I can't help the way I feel. Or rather, the part I played in adding to her already difficult circumstances. "Damn, looks like you're surrounded by short-tempered women."

"Tell me about it."

He pays the bill, and we make our way out of the café. "I return on Tuesday morning. Maybe we can grab dinner or something."

"Sounds good. Call me."

"You sure you don't want a ride home?"

"Positive," I say, and I stand on the tips of my toes and kiss his lips. He smiles. "Try to keep out of trouble."

"I'll do my best." I wink as rainbows and unicorns fly around us and birds chirp happily as we part ways. I decide to walk home instead of taking a bike. It's a nice day, and my butt hurts from the short bike ride. I don't want to push my luck too much.

CHAPTER SEVENTEEN

~~Luanne No! Luanne~~ *Attempt #2*
~~Gary~~
Lindsey ✓
~~Jenny O.~~ *NO!*
~~Jenny M.~~ *NO!*
~~Jenny Z.~~ *Absolutely NO!*
~~Mary~~
Office MAYBE
~~Brenda~~
~~Margret~~ ~~Undecided~~
~~Jimenez~~

"I think I'm going to fail the test," I say to Z at the end of class the following Monday.

"If I fail this test, I'm going to be disowned."

That makes me laugh. I'm glad there's nothing at stake for me; there's no way I could handle the pressure. This is the hardest thing I've ever had to learn.

"I'm going to Mocha Mike's to study," he says. "Join me? We could swap notes."

"Sure," I say.

We walk together to the coffee shop on campus, talking about Professor Gonzalez and the other students and the class's general cluelessness. When we get to the coffee shop, I notice that two other people from our class have beaten us there. One is a young woman, maybe eighteen, whose name I can't remember, and the other is a guy who is about twenty-three or twenty-four, who always sits close to the front of the class. Professor Gonzalez calls him Mr. Monroe, but I don't know his first name. I've noticed them before because the guy specifically raises his hand often in class. When they see us, they wave enthusiastically, and we both head their way. They introduce themselves as Felicity and Ryder. *Of course those are their names,* I think. Felicity chose the class as an elective, and Ryder is doing his master's in Latin American Studies at UIC and decided that he needed to, and I quote, "fully immerse myself in the culture. My body is in North America, but my soul belongs in Latin America." Ryder is a Caucasian man from Denver. Never has he visited any place south of Georgia, but he is taking classes at the community college while in grad school, which is very commendable.

Regardless of the reason, we're all in the same boat. We have a test coming up on verb conjugation, and my brain is about to explode due to the sheer number of ways you can conjugate one simple word in Spanish. We are learning some of the more common ones. My head literally hurts trying to figure this all out. We order coffee and stay there, laughing, talking, and studying for two hours.

Ryder enlightens us about the rich history of ayahuasca and mushrooms deep in the jungles of Peru, which seems to be one of the reasons he is obsessed with the culture.

"We all have a reason for taking this class, but you, Millie? What's your story?" Felicity asks.

What is my story?

"Apparently I'm Cuban American. I had no idea until a few months ago. I enrolled in the class thinking it would connect me a little bit to my newfound heritage. Now I'm learning the language, trying Cuban recipes, connecting to my family." I shrug because, in a nutshell, it really has become a bigger part of my life. Between the apologies I've made and my email conversations with Rosa, my life feels pretty substantial. I'm not even obsessing over the Phoebe case anymore, although it seems to be on the news 24-7 these days. I simply turn it off and do something else. Saying all this out loud to these virtual strangers feels like a breakthrough. If Nina could hear me now . . .

"That's cool. And when's your trip? Are you just going to Cuba? Or will you also skip to the other islands or to Central America? There're some gnarly ayahuasca retreats in Ecuador. Some badass shamans that you'd love," Ryder says with excitement.

"No." I shake my head side to side. I hold back a smirk. I'm not going to go to Central America on a hallucinogenic retreat. I can barely muster the courage to go with all my faculties intact. "I wasn't planning on going, I don't think. I'm just trying to learn the language for now."

"Oh . . . ," Felicity says, sounding deflated. "But you sound so excited. You should totally go."

"Totally," Ryder agrees.

Z just chuckles and says, "Totally," under his breath too.

I laugh. "Maybe one day."

"Gotta go get my little sister," Felicity says, and Ryder asks if he can bum a ride to the bus stop.

"Well, that was interesting," Z says as the party breaks up.

"Totally," I say back, and we both burst out laughing. "I think Ryder was high."

Z sits back, his leg casually crossed, ankle on knee. "What gave it away? His twenty-minute diatribe on psychedelic mushrooms and the shamans he wants to visit, or maybe the bloodshot eyes? You know a skunk was not walking by outside."

"All of the above. God, they make me feel old," I say, putting my notes and books into my bag and then sitting back in my chair.

"Tell me about it." He laughs. "You feel better about the test?"

I exhale. "No, not really. But I've never failed a test in my life, so I'll go home, study, and say a little prayer."

"Maybe a shaman *would* be a good idea," he says, and we both laugh. We stand up at the same time, say our good nights, and head our own ways.

The next evening, I'm sitting on my couch, my class notes scattered all over. I hear my phone beep with an incoming text.

If you don't hear from me by midnight, send help. I'm going on my first official date with an online guy I just met. It's Nina. Her text is a nice distraction from the cramming I've been doing all day.

That makes me extremely nervous. Where are you going to be? What is the serial killer's full name? Is he picking you up? You better have the phone on you all night, Nina. And if he gets weird and you can't call or has a knife to your throat, the code word is "fuchsia." If you say "fuchsia," I'll know you need help.

Jeez. That got dark fast, she says, and then my phone rings. "You're not normal, Millie."

"I don't know how these dates with complete strangers go. It worries me."

"Don't worry. We're going to Paolo's on Ocean Drive, and I'm meeting him there. His name is Stuart Rivers."

"That's a serial killer's name, Nina. *If* that's even his name."

"Shut it. I'll be fine. I'll call you by midnight."

"You better."

"Will you be up?"

"Yes. I'm studying."

"Is that what you've been up to? I tried calling you yesterday, and it went to voice mail."

"I was out yesterday with some classmates, and my phone ran out of battery and I lost track of time. Nina, oh my goodness, if you met

Ryder, you'd get a kick. You'd have a field day analyzing him. He's this stoner dude who's learning Spanish just to be able to communicate with a shaman in order to get mushrooms and ayahuasca. And Z, poor Z, his family is nuts and—"

"Who are you?" she says, and I can hear the amusement in her voice. "Making friends. Chatting about 'shrooms, hanging with someone named Z, not caring that your phone has no battery."

"I know, kind of crazy, right?"

"Oh shoot. My Lyft is here. Gotta go."

"Midnight! Call me!" I yell into the phone and hope she heard me before she hung up.

I compose my first Spanish-language email to Rosa and ask her how she's doing. Then I send Luanne a quick text just to say hello and see if she's free for coffee tomorrow. We can't dive completely back into best friend territory after so many years apart, but little by little we're getting closer.

While I wait for her response, I send John a text. How's Vegas treating you?

I see the three little dots appear almost instantly. No game with this man. Vegas is Vegas. Nothing exciting to report. And you?

Trying to study for a test.

It occurs to me that I haven't heard you say a single word in Spanish.

Hola, I type out.
I am so very impressed, he replies.

That's about all you'll get from me. My pronunciation is way off. How's the case going?

219

Great. They're probably going to settle before I even depose the first witness.

Brock? Settle? You must have an ace in your pocket that he's scared you'll show.

I always have an ace in my pocket, he writes. Speaking of work. I have to go. Dinner reservations with the client.

Okay. Have a nice night.

I'm glad you reached out, Mills.

So am I. See you in a few days, John.

At midnight I receive a text from Nina. I'm home. Stuart was a dud, but dinner at Paolo's was delicious. G'night, sis.

After I text her good night, I can finally fall into a restful sleep, even if I never did hear from Luanne.

———

I just got out of my test, and I think I may have passed. I did not get an A, of that I'm sure, but I also don't think I failed. It was super difficult. *Nosotros, vosotros, usted, tú*—it's all the same thing, and I can't tell one from another. I feel like I need to drink a bottle of wine and pass out for two days just to recover.

Luanne never texted back. She doesn't have a reason to text back, and I should have no reason to be concerned. But I am, so I call her. Since we said our apologies, we've moved on. I don't think there's any lingering resentment, at least not on my part. Of course, there's still that bit of awkwardness since it's been so long since we've seen one another, but we're the kind of people who say we're sorry and then don't address it again. Otherwise, we wouldn't say we're sorry to begin with. At least that's the person I am now. I'm hoping Luanne is too.

"Hi, Lu. It's Millie. Not sure if you got my text last night. Just checking in. Maybe we can grab breakfast tomorrow. Call me back." I put the phone down and head to the mall. I don't remember the last time I went shopping. I need more casual clothes. I spend a few hours at the mall, checking my phone for a reply from Luanne.

After I get home and unpack all my bags (and make a mental note to finally purge all the suits from the corner of the closet), I decide to call her again. The phone rings twice when she breathlessly answers.

"Hello?" It's groggy, and she sounds absolutely horrid.

"Luanne? It's Millie. I called you earlier and—are you okay?"

"Yes. Everything's fine." She coughs into the phone. "Not a good time, Millie. I'm sick."

She's about to hang up when I hear another cough. This one's a hacking cough, and I scrunch my nose as if the germs are coming through the little holes on the receiver and straight to my immune system. "You don't sound okay."

"It's nothing." Cough. Cough. "Just a little sick."

"Do you need anything? Um . . . your mom isn't there?" She mentioned her mother the other day, and I know that her mom helps her out a lot.

"She's sick too. I think that's where I got it."

"Oh no. How about the kids?"

"They're in school now."

"And when they get home?"

"I don't know, Millie. I'm a mom; I'll figure it out. Moms can't get sick." There's a lot of coughing again. "I have to go. I'll call you next week. I need to take a nap before they get home." And she hangs up.

Crap.

What would an unselfish person do in a situation like this? Making chicken soup is probably not a feasible idea since I have no chicken or anything else that would go into a soup. Plus, it would take a few hours. I look through my neatly alphabetized takeout menu binder and call Latin Corner. Their chicken soup is the absolute best. I'm sure they can deliver it to her. But then I think, *What if she's too sick and going to the door is actually a nuisance?* I don't want to make things worse for her.

I could take it to her.

But I hate germs.

Regardless, I grab my keys and head to the nearest drugstore. Since I don't know what she needs, I get everything. I buy kid and adult pain reliever. I buy tissues and a thermometer. I buy Gatorade, Lysol, and a big bottle of hand sanitizer, and I also buy medical masks and gloves because . . . did I tell you I don't like germs? Then I pick up the soup.

When I arrive at her house, the one she purchased with Mitchell, I rip open the box of blue, paperlike masks and put one on. Then I take the gloves and put them on. Finally, I grab all the shopping bags and the soup, and try to balance everything out of the car and to her front door.

I ring the doorbell. Nothing.

Then I ring it again, and I hear sounds.

"Who is it?" Her voice is worse than it sounded over the phone.

"It's me. Millie."

"Who?"

Crap. The mask. I don't have a spare hand to pull the mask down, so I say it louder. "Millie. Millie Montgomery!"

"Millie?" she says as she unlocks the door and opens it. Her eyes are wide as she takes me in. Blue mask; blue, latex-free gloves, just in case she's allergic to latex—and I'm selfish?! *Pshhh*—three bags of supplies; and a big container of soup.

"I came to help."

She's still staring. Her eyes are red and bloodshot, her nose is even redder, and she looks absolutely terrible.

"I have the flu."

The flu! Shit. This is worse than I thought. It's not just a cold. I swallow my fear, glad she can't see my expression through my mask. To be honest, I'd go inside no matter what she has. I love Luanne, which is why she was the hardest person on my list to lose and to reconnect with. If I have to make a grand gesture, like contracting the flu, to make her understand how truly sorry I am for my part of our estrangement, I'll grand-gesture the hell out of her.

I've come to realize that there are people in life who deserve an apology, and there are some who do not. But then there are special people who, whether they do or they don't, it doesn't really matter. In middle school, this woman went through the disgusting lost-and-found bin to find me a sweater to wrap around my waist when I stained my pants the day I got my first-ever period. She even made sure that the sweater matched my outfit. So Luanne messed up and I messed up, and as a consequence we lost too many years of our lives being angry at nothing. We both apologized because we both needed to. But even if she hadn't, her actions throughout my life are all that I need to forgive her and vice versa.

"Lu, this is kinda heavy. Mind stepping aside?"

She does.

I remember the kitchen is to the left, so I take a left, and when I find the kitchen table, I drop everything on it. I turn to Luanne and clap my hands, ready for action. "All right. I came to help. I brought soup." Then I start unpacking bags. "I also brought Advil, Tylenol, Motrin, Nyquil—"

"Oh my God, what is all this, Millie? I have medicine. I'm fine."

"'I'm fine.' I've been told that's my go-to phrase too."

Then she sneezes and uses the back of her hand to wipe her red nose. I rummage through the supplies, find one of the three boxes of tissues, and rip it open and hand it to her. She uses it. Then I squirt some hand sanitizer on her hand. I think I see her roll her eyes, but it's hard to tell since her eyes are small, irritated slits.

"I didn't know what you had. And I got some in kid dosages too. Also, I bought chicken soup and some Gatorade."

"Well, um, that's very nice of you, Millie."

I know! Finally. Someone noticed. But I don't repeat that out loud. "I'm going to stay the rest of the day. Go sleep and let me help you with the kids."

"You are? No, I can't let you do that."

I cross my arms over my chest. "Really?"

"Yes, really," she says, matching my stance, but it doesn't have the same effect since she then doubles over in a coughing fit. I spray Lysol while she's busy coughing up a lung. I don't think she's even noticed. "My kids barely know you."

"They don't know anyone, Lu. They're tiny little people who don't know much about anything. It'll be fine."

"You don't know anything about kids."

"I know not to let them stick keys in the electric socket, talk to strangers, or fall in a pool. I know they have to eat, poop, pee, and sleep. And I know that your kids, in particular, like chocolate chip and strawberry pancakes, Mikey and Olivia, respectively. They also like cake pops."

Her eyes widen. "Wow. You remembered."

"Of course. Now, go sleep."

"Millie—"

"I also know when an old friend needs help. I know that you need sleep and you need to recover. I know that if I don't help you, you won't get better, and you'll probably get the kids sick. So please, let me help. You need help. I can help."

She seems to think about it for a moment. "They get out of school at two, and the bus drops them off about two thirty. You have to let them in and give them snacks. They'll be hungry."

"I can do snacks."

"I think I just need a nap and then a nice bath. I should be fine by later this afternoon."

"No problem, Lu. I'm not in a hurry."

She hesitates for a moment and then finally accepts the help I know she hates to need. "Thank you, Millie. I really appreciate it."

"It's fine. I got this. Go." I point to the other side of the house, where the bedrooms are, and she sneezes and coughs all the way there.

While I wait for the children to get home, I clean up and disinfect as much as I can. Then the twins arrive, and I begin to think I overestimated my ability to babysit.

"Hi. Where's Mommy?" Olivia asks while Mikey walks by me, completely unfazed that I'm in his house.

"She's upstairs sleeping. She doesn't feel well, so I'm going to take care of you for a little bit. You want to go see?"

They both nod.

"Okay, but you have to be really, really quiet. Your mommy needs to sleep so that she can feel better, okay?"

They nod, and the three of us tiptoe—literally and exaggeratedly—to the bedroom. Softly, I open the door and they see their mom asleep. That seems to satisfy them, because they thunder back to the living room.

They're cute.

Mikey starts to drag a chair, loudly, to the pantry.

"What are you doing there, buddy?"

"I am getting snacks."

He climbs the chair, and I try and hold him while he grabs the box of cookies that seems to be hidden all the way at the back of the pantry. I'm fairly certain that's not the snack that he's supposed to be eating, nor is he supposed to be climbing chairs.

"Come on, let's get down," I say. He jumps off, and I put the chair back quietly. "Now, I need your complete and total honesty, okay?"

They nod. "Do you have cookies when you get home? Is your mom okay with that?" They look at each other and are about to answer, but I interrupt them. "Wait. Before you answer, sit down." They both obediently sit, and I take the chair in front of them.

"I bet your mommy didn't tell you my super awesome secret power." Their cute little eyes are wide, and they're on the edges of their seats waiting. "I'm a lawyer. Do you know what that is?" They both shake their heads. "Well, lawyers have a special ability to know when people are lying."

"You can read my mind?" Mikey asks, his eyes wide and mouth open.

"Kind of. So when I ask you something, you can only tell me the truth. If not, I'll be mad and won't order pizza and ice cream for dinner."

"Pizza *and* ice cream!" they both yell, but I tell them they have to keep their voices down.

"So, we have a deal?"

"Deal!" they both say at once, in a very loud whisper.

"All right, so, as I was asking, do you guys eat cookies for a snack?"

Mikey looks contrite and says no. Olivia does, too, but she adds, "Mommy gives us fruit." Mikey gags for dramatic effect.

"Ah. Fruit. That sounds more accurate," I say and open the refrigerator. There are apples already sliced. I wonder what she does so that they don't turn brown. There's also some cubed pineapples and watermelon in a plastic container. I take all of it out. "Pick your poison, kiddos."

"They're poison!" Olivia says, her eyes wide. She looks legitimately terrified.

"No. No," I say quickly. "It's just a saying. Sorry. No. They're fine." I take out an apple slice and toss it in my mouth. "Look, totally fine."

The kids pick their food and show me the plates their mom uses. Everything must be exactly how Mom does it, which is so adorable, and I feel a small amount of envy that Luanne has this. I'm sure it's the most stressful job imaginable, but they love her so much. She's their superhero.

After snacks, the kids sit and bicker about everything. E-V-E-R-Y-T-H-I-N-G! By the time we've done homework, dinner, showers, and bedtime, I'm completely exhausted.

I tidy up the house and sit on the couch for a moment with a juice box because I'm too tired to uncork the wine bottle I saw on the top shelf of the pantry. Apple juice, wine, same thing . . .

"Millie. Millie," I hear faintly. Momentarily, I'm disoriented. It's Luanne, who's trying to wake me. "You fell asleep." I sit up and wipe the drool from my lip. My neck aches from the odd position on the sofa.

I yawn and then ask, "How are you feeling?"

"Not great. But I'll live. How'd you do? I'm sorry I passed out for so long. I can't believe it's this late. I'm so sorry."

"No worries. I didn't have anything else to do; really, it's fine." I yawn again. "They're funny and smart, but they're exhausting!"

"Tell me about it," she says and plops next to me, causing me to scoot over a bit to make room for her. "I can handle it from here. You can go. I really appreciate it, Millie."

I find my phone, and it takes a moment to adjust my eyes. It's a little past midnight. "I don't mind staying. Really. It's late, and I may as well make myself comfortable. I'll get them ready for school tomorrow and then take off. One less thing for you to worry about."

"No, Millie. I can't ask you to do that."

"You're not asking. I'm offering."

"I feel weird accepting," she admits.

"If we had still been friends, all these years, would you accept? Wouldn't you do it for me if it were the other way around?"

"Of course. Our kids would get married and we'd finally be related!" she reminds me.

"But I never had kids, so that dream didn't quite turn out the way we planned," I say. I'm a forty-year-old woman without a job, husband, or kids. *How did I get here?* "You're lucky, Lu. You got the house and the wonderful kids. This is what life is really about."

"They're pretty awesome," she says with a smile. "But it's hard. Doing it alone and having to count every penny."

"We're quite the pair, you and I," I say, and yawn deep. "I wasn't always selfish, was I?"

She squeezes my hands. "You held my hand and stayed with me at the hospital when Dad was going through chemo, and you kicked Joy Ramone's ass when she asked Nick Montes to prom knowing that he was already going with me. You always had my back, and then we drifted apart. Our lives took different turns. You just didn't realize how hard it was getting for me, but I guess maybe I should have told you. We've both apologized enough. Let's try to move on, okay?"

"Okay," I say. We hug for some time, and I swear to God, it feels like a huge, boulder-size weight has been lifted from my shoulders. And the worst part is, I hadn't even realized the boulder was there, which makes it even more surprising.

———

By the time I get home the next morning, I'm exhausted. By *exhausted* I mean that I barely have the energy to shower. Barely. I need to get all the flu off me, so I shower even if it takes all my energy not to drift off in the middle of it. I stick all the clothes straight into my washing machine so as to avoid cross-contamination with the rest of my germ-free clothes. When I finish, I go straight to my bed and snuggle into my comforter. I haven't had a chance to check my phone for the last twenty-four hours.

I take a quick peek and smile at a message from John: Hi. Decided to put twenty on black. Lost twenty bucks. I've never been lucky in Vegas. How are you doing? That was from last night.

Sorry. Yesterday, I helped Luanne with her kids and didn't see this text until now. But I lost forty dollars last night. Twenty for each kid, just to get them to do their homework, so it's sort of like I was in Vegas too, I type and put my phone down. There's a time difference, and he's probably still asleep.

Except that my phone rings and it's his name on the screen.

"Hi," he says.

"Hi. How's the desert?"

"Hot. How's the Windy City?"

"Windy. With a dash of snow."

"That sounds amazing. A blizzard, a nice, refreshing blizzard."

I actually laugh out loud.

"I think things are going to be okay between Luanne and me." I tell him all about yesterday.

"That's fantastic, sweetheart. I'm proud of you."

I clear my throat. "I'm happy."

"She probably really appreciated the help. You sound sleepy. Are you in bed?"

"I am," I say, and he groans.

"I wish I was in there with you," he whispers in a husky tone, and I'm suddenly a lot more awake. "I'm being summoned. I gotta run. Talk later?"

"Sure."

"Sleep well, Mills." And we hang up. Two minutes later I'm fast asleep, hoping that I don't get the flu so that John can, in fact, get in bed with me when he returns.

CHAPTER EIGHTEEN

~~Luanne No! Luanne~~ ~~Attempt #2~~
~~Gary~~
Lindsey ✓
~~Jenny O.~~ NO!
~~Jenny M.~~ NO!
~~Jenny Z.~~ Absolutely NO!
~~Mary~~
Office MAYBE
~~Brenda~~
~~Margret~~ ~~Undecided~~
~~Jimenez~~

"Dammit," I say when I see my grade.

"Whatcha get?" Z asks.

"C minus. You?"

"B," he says, and we turn to our friends. Ryder smiles and turns his exam over, revealing his A. Felicity also got a B. How the hell did Ryder get an A? He looked so lost. The class proceeds, but I'm huffing and pissy the entire rest of the hour.

After class Ryder declares, "Saturday night, I work."

"Okay?" Z says, confused, and I look at him, puzzled.

"I'm a dishwasher at La Esquinita Roja. It's downtown." The words roll off his tongue, and I'm not great at pronunciation and don't have an ear for the language, according to the teacher, but he sounds as if he's been speaking Spanish all his life, which probably accounts for that A. "The employees only speak Spanish, which is why I work there. Sink or swim."

"Oh," I say. Smart. He immersed himself in it, and he had no choice but to learn the language. This may be the one time in my life I have not been at the top of my class. My instinct would be to get upset at myself, but interestingly enough, the disappointment just doesn't come. When I'd get a B in law school, I'd double down, study, beg for extra credit, and make it my life's purpose to do my best after that. I'd berate myself for days over the imperfect grade. Now, I'm okay with my grade. No, I'm not just okay; I'm unfazed by it. And it's not only because learning Spanish isn't something that will make or break me. It's because there are things that have come to be more important than perfection. Building meaningful relationships, for instance. That's more important than that A. Also, no one seems to care if I'm the best in the class or not. No one cared in law school either. I'd never realized, until now, that it was a pressure I put on myself, and the only one disappointed was me. No one else.

"Come over on Saturday for dinner. I'll be there. The menu's in Spanish, and the servers don't speak English. We can practice."

We all exchange numbers and agree to meet at seven on Saturday for a dinner study session. I'm really excited about this prospect. Going out with other adults. Making friends. Having a little bit of fun. This is what this class has brought me. Hell, I guess I owe it to that DNA test and to the Apology Project. I haven't reconnected with all the people on the list—hell, I've only apologized to a few—but the ones I've apologized to have been meaningful, and it brought Luanne back to my life and gave me a sense of closure with others. I need to finish that list up because I think it'll be the icing on the cake. I set out to do it, and now I have to follow through with it.

Z walks me to my car. "Smart kid."

"Yeah, I have to admit, I didn't see that coming."

"Neither did I!" he says. We both laugh out loud, and suddenly I'm in front of my car. "See you Saturday, then?"

"Most definitely." I unlock my car.

"Good. I look forward to it," he says and then heads to his car. He's very attractive, but I don't get that same flutter in my belly when he's around like I do with John.

When I get home I immediately reach for the list. Who is left? I look through it and decide on Lindsey since I'm still unsure what to do about the office people. I was too harsh with some of them, but not all. Some were either inept or just nervous around me, and neither of those things are my fault.

It's been about four months since the disastrous party. It's time I tackle Lindsey because Lindsey Rodriguez is definitely someone I should apologize to.

I've been avoiding it because this one is going to be tough. Not tough like Luanne was tough, because Luanne was my childhood friend and someone I love. Lindsey isn't someone I actually know well, but someone I wronged.

Using the same super sophisticated spy technique that John used to find Brenda, I try to locate Lindsey. It isn't as simple as John's search because (*a*) Lindsey doesn't have pink hair anymore and it was hard to recognize her from her profile photo and (*b*) her profile is partially locked. I was able to scroll through her friends, and it turned out that Nina, of all people, is friends with a friend of Lindsey.

I take a screenshot and send it to Nina, who asks me a thousand questions.

Why are you asking about Lindsey? How do you know her? Since when do you have Instagram?

I don't know her per se, I explain. It's a long story and part of my Apology Project. Do you have her number?

Let me ask Joyce while I look you up on Instagram and follow you. Follow me too.

I roll my eyes and wait for her to contact Joyce, their mutual friend. Finally, after what feels like forever, Joyce provides Nina with Lindsey's email, and Nina, in turn, gives it to me.
Exhausting, right?

Tell me why you need to apologize to her.

You are such a gossip, I type, but of course, I tell her. Remember Melvin? Melvin Rogers was the only bad boy I ever dated. He was a tatted-up drummer whom I'd met at a bar. He was in a band, remember?

Oh yeah! What was the name? Dog Food or something?

No. Way stupider. It was called Catnip.

Catnip! Oh God, how lame.

Lindsey was the lead singer.

Shut up!

Yep. But it gets worse. She was dating Melvin. I never told you. It was shitty of me to do it. I liked Lindsey, she was nice, and I knew they were dating, but when he asked me out behind her back, I said yes.

You were young. We all do stupid things when we're young. Not a huge deal in the big scheme of things.

Well . . . she wrote a song about me and played it in the bar while I was there. It was humiliating. I deserved it, though.

Nice play, Lindsey.

Whose side are you on?!

She laughs and gives me Lindsey's email. I'd like to call her or talk to her in person, but this is all I have to work with. I'm not sure how much detail to put into the email or if I should just ask her to call me. I contemplate this while making a pot roast, which is not the best thing to make for one person because it's too much food and also because mine comes out more meat-loafy than pot-roasty.

After dinner I boot up my tablet, settle in bed with William, and just dive right in. The email starts mostly like it did with my professor.

Lindsey,

I know this is an odd email and long overdue. This is Millie Montgomery. We met about twenty-one years ago at Purple Haze. You were the lead singer of Catnip.

Side note: it was a stupid name. (I don't add this to the email.)

I want to apologize for what I did, you know, with Melvin.

I'm an attorney and I write important shit all day and this is the best I can do. (Again, I don't add this to the email.)

I was young and selfish, and I didn't think how it would hurt you. I don't know if you even remember the incident or if you'll even read this, but if you do read this, I'd love to invite you to coffee and apologize properly.

Best regards,
Millie

The point of the project is to apologize, not to be forgiven. I didn't expect Jimenez to write back, and she did. I didn't expect to ever hear from Brenda again, yet she's following me on Facebook and I've even "liked" some of her posts. With time, I'm sure we will speak again. We may never be best friends, but we'll be acquaintances and that's enough for me.

I don't know whether Lindsey will accept my apology or even read my email, but I did what I set out to do, and therefore, I cross Lindsey off my list and feel exceptionally accomplished.

———

It's the morning of our Spanish restaurant field trip. I can't remember the last time I went out with other adults in a social setting, aside from John, of course. I'm excited. So much so that when John calls me that morning from Vegas, I tell him all about it.

"Looks like you're making friends."

"You think?"

He laughs. "Most definitely." I tell him about the group of misfits, and he warns me to be careful with the mushrooms Ryder will likely offer me. "You don't handle alcohol well; psychedelics don't bode much better."

I chuckle. "I'm fairly certain there will not be drugs involved. Plus, Z is as straitlaced as they come. I don't think he'd be cool with it either."

"My plane lands at two tomorrow. Want to have dinner?"

"Sure."

"Don't get into too much trouble," he says.

"I'll try. Bye, John."

"Bye, babe," he says.

A few minutes after I hang up with John, Nina shows up with bagels and coffee. William, my not-too-social tabby, runs and hides under my bed the moment Nina walks in.

"Was in the neighborhood, and we're overdue for dinner."

"This is breakfast, sis."

She rolls her eyes and hands me a bagel and a little container of cream cheese. "I know. But your social calendar has been so full lately we can't seem to connect."

"My social calendar?"

"Yes, you've been busy. We've all commented on it."

"We? Who's we?"

"Just Mom, Dad, and me. You know, during our weekly 'has Millie become completely unhinged' call. Did she decide to apologize to everyone? Did she pack up and move to Cuba? Is she ever going to work again? You know . . . the usual."

I look at her with annoyance, and she smiles and shrugs. I don't think she's kidding.

"You told Mom and Dad about the Apology Project?"

"Yep. But I told them not to bother you about it."

I groan. I'm not mad about her telling them or that they know, but I don't want to be questioned about it. Not because I'm ashamed or anything, I just don't have answers, nor do I want to feel vulnerable about my reasons for feeling the need to apologize to certain people.

We take our bagels to my sofa. Both of us sit with our legs tucked away on the seat. Sometimes I think we are so similar. We look similar, except she's a bit taller than I am and a little curvier. While I have long hair, hers is in a shaggy cut, but we share the same chocolate shade of brown. But we're also so different. She's the calm to my storm. Sometimes I wish I was more like her: patient, friendly, and open. Which of course makes me wonder if Rosa is patient or fiery like me. Does Fabiola have Nina's curves or my stature? Does any of it even matter? We are who we are, and knowing them will not change who any of us are, right?

"When I was working, you guys complained that I worked too much. Now I'm not working and you're complaining that I'm having too much fun."

"No. No. No," she says, moving her index finger side to side. "I did not say we were complaining. We were *commenting*. And are you? Having fun, that is?"

"I think I am, actually. Tonight, I'm having dinner with some people from my class."

"That's great, Mills. We're all happy for you."

"Do you really think Dad's okay with me talking to Rosa?"

"Absolutely. Just because we're not interested in digging further into that doesn't mean we want to stop you from doing it. In fact, he says that Nana would be tickled by it. His words, not mine."

"I know she would," I say because I've thought about it and she wasn't the kind of person who'd be upset by it. Learning about this side of the family doesn't negate my love for her, and I think she'd understand that.

"Anything that puts a smile on your face makes us all happy, Mills. We didn't love that you were running yourself ragged at work. While you were happy, it was fine, but you didn't always seem happy."

"I guess I wasn't," I admit. "And school's been hard, but it's also something I'm enjoying."

"So, tell me more about Rosa."

"Nothing more to tell. It's hard to get through to her because her town has frequent power outages. She warned me that she'd likely not be able to get a Wi-Fi signal, so I haven't been able to email with her for a few weeks now." I hope everything is all right with her.

"What are your plans?"

I roll my eyes. Nina and her scheming. "For what? For today? I told you about dinner tonight—"

"No, not about dinner, Mills. About life. How long are you going to continue being 'retired'?" she asks, using finger quotes as if I'm not actually retired, which, for all intents and purposes, I am.

I shrug. "I don't know. I don't really have any."

"And John? How's that going?"

"He's busy with work, and it's hard to meet up. What's with the twenty questions?"

"I'm just curious is all. You've been so busy and you really do seem happy, which makes me ecstatic. I just want to make sure you're not keeping busy to avoid feeling things."

"Jesus. Now there's another layer?"

"Not necessarily. That's why I'm checking."

I roll my eyes. "I'm happy. For real. Trust me." And I am happy. I feel it—really feel it—for the first time in a long while.

"I'm so happy for you, sis."

"It's been a long time since I've been in a relationship."

"And the work stuff? That's resolved?"

"We agreed not to talk about work, and it's going well. I mean, I don't love that he works at JJF, but it's a job and I can't fault him for that. Last week, we were watching television, and the ticker said, 'As the Hugh Phoebe trial approaches, defense attorney Marc Jones . . .' and I practically tackled him to change the channel."

"Very mature of you," she says. "What did he say?"

"Nothing. It was awkward. For a moment I thought he was going to tell me something about the case or how he wanted to hear the news coverage." I panicked for that brief moment. If he had defended Phoebe or Junior, that would have been the end of the Millie-John affair. Maybe he saw my look of panic, or maybe he's just trying to follow my rules. I'm not sure. "But he just relaxed, and then we started watching an action movie and settled into a nice evening. So, yeah, we're avoiding important conversations and avoiding the news. Very mature." I chuckle, but truthfully, it's weighing on me. I can't go around avoiding everything just to make a relationship work. It's not like we disagree about what to watch on television. This company, his job, is a major point of contention, and I don't think avoiding this topic will work in the long run. Burying my head in the sand is working for now, but I do wonder if he's working on the case in any way. If he is, then this relationship is completely doomed, and I'm not ready for that to happen, so I'm going the blissfully unaware route. "Anyway, enough about me. What's going on with you?"

"Nothing much. Online dating is so much fun, Mills. You really should try it! Also, work has been so busy."

"Too busy to come with me to Cuba? If I decide to go, that is."

"Ohhhh . . . so, are you thinking about going?"

I shrug. "I don't know. There are days I want to pack my bags and go, and there are days I think, 'Amelia Montgomery, you've truly lost your mind. You don't even know those people.'"

"Well, if you feel that pull, then go. What's stopping you?"

"I don't think I'd have the courage to go through with it." I exhale, and we're in amicable silence as we have breakfast. My phone dings with an incoming text, breaking up the moment, and I guess I let out an "Oh . . ." because my sister looks at me.

"What is it?"

"It's Lindsey. I sent her an apology email and—oh my!" I read it twice and then flip my phone around for Nina to read it.

> If you think that I'm going to forgive you just so you can sleep better at night, you're crazier than you were all those years ago.

Nina's mouth opens and then closes. "Not everyone's going to accept your apology."

"Clearly," I say, reading the email again. "I guess she's still holding a grudge."

"She must've really liked Melvin."

This time we both laugh. Hard.

You win some, you lose some.

Lindsey didn't go as planned, but I have to admit, I still feel good for having apologized.

But let's not get too excited. I'm still Amelia Montgomery. Even if I've had some emotional breakthroughs lately, the urge to send her a nasty reply about how crappy her band was is overwhelming. But in the end, I don't want to stoop to that level of pettiness, even if I want to have the last word, the last one-two punch. But I don't. This is my Apology Project, not the forgiveness project. The other apologies turned out favorable, and this one didn't. I can't hold on to that because that would be counterintuitive. In fact, it was bound to happen. I can't get my way all the time, right? I feel sad for her. Having all that anger for all these years seems like a big burden to carry around. I'm letting go, and it feels very refreshing. So, instead, I cuddle back into my couch, and just out of curiosity, I check flights to Havana and different tour options. Just a little window traveling.

———

My cheeks hurt from laughing so much. A server pours me more sangria in a glass that's probably meant for water, not alcoholic beverages, but I don't care because it's delicious. I also don't care that the plates are all mismatched with fading designs on them or that the lighting in the restaurant is too bright for the evening. It's all unimportant because what is important is that I'm having a great time with Z, Ryder, and Felicity in the tiny, five-table restaurant. There's music in the background that has a salsa-like beat. A bit too fast-tempo for the ambiance, but all of it is perfectly imperfect.

I thought I ordered the rice and chicken, but instead a big paella-resembling, watery-rice plate was placed in front of me. Thank God I'm not a picky eater because I ate it and it was amazing. Apparently rice and chicken is different from rice with chicken, a.k.a. *arroz con pollo*. Things did not end up any better for Z. He thought he ordered black bean soup, but he only ordered a side of black beans. He had to order more food once the small plate was placed in front of him. Ryder got exactly what he ordered because the guy seems to speak perfect Spanish. He didn't tell us we'd gotten it wrong, but I should have known from the smirk on his face. Felicity did a little better. She is a vegetarian and ordered *fufu*, which is basically mashed plantains. Her order got dressed with *chicharrones*, though. Luckily, she isn't too picky either because she just moved the pork to the side and ate the pork-fat-covered mashed plantains. "My belly won't be happy later, but my taste buds are thanking me now," she said.

There is a Spanish tongue twister that the teacher asked us to repeat over and over to help with the rolling *r* sound.

Erre con erre cigarro

Erre con erre barril
Rápido corren los carros
Por la línea del ferrocarril.

We try to say it over and over, and the more wine we consume, the harder it gets and the louder we sound. But after about the tenth time, it starts sounding better to our ears. The amused servers don't look impressed at all, which makes us laugh even harder. Our attempt to speak only Spanish during the meal also goes out the window, as we go back and forth from English to broken Spanish.

Z is going to spend the summer packing up his entire life, wrapping up some local projects, and then he's off to Puerto Rico for his big move. We promise that we'll visit him.

After dinner we all say our good nights. My head's a little fuzzy from all the wine. Ryder and Felicity share a cab home. "Hey," Z says, and holds my forearm. "Why don't you let me take you home? I think you had too much to drink."

I readily agree, leaving my car in the parking lot and giving Z my address.

"You really should think about making the trip to Cuba. I think you'd love it. You can tie it into a trip to PR and come visit."

"Maybe," I reply. "I'm definitely thinking about it. I'm not a good traveler," I confess.

"Traveling alone sucks. I understand."

We both laugh some more as I point to my building. "You don't need to get out. I'm good."

He pulls right to the door, and I wave goodbye as I enter the building more than a bit tipsy. My phone chimes as I press the button on my elevator; it's a text from John asking if he can come over because he arrived early. Sex would be so good right now, and I'm about to text him back, but then I just don't. I can't. I'm too drunk.

This would be the exact point where my exes would have been upset and where the relationship would've deteriorated. It's not that they were jealous; it's that I didn't prioritize the relationship. I like my space and independence. Wanting to sleep off this hangover doesn't mean I like John any less, and I really hope he knows that because, instead of calling him, I faceplant right onto my bed, not even changing out of my clothes. William purrs as he cuddles into me. And I don't go to bed content. I go to bed feeling happy.

CHAPTER NINETEEN

~~Luanne~~ ~~No!~~ Luanne ~~Attempt #2~~
~~Gary~~
~~Lindsey~~ ✓
~~Jenny O.~~ NO!
~~Jenny M.~~ NO!
~~Jenny Z.~~ Absolutely NO!
~~Mary~~
~~Office~~ MAYBE
~~Brenda~~
~~Margret~~ ~~Undecided~~
~~Jimenez~~

The fact that John is a constant reminder of my old life is becoming an issue.

I explained to John that I just wanted to go to bed after dinner last night and he understands, even though he does tell me he missed me while he was away. He also tells me he hates that we go entire weeks without seeing each other. I agree, but it's the nature of the job. Although I've come to realize that it's not just the nature of his job; it's that I'm pulling away. I like him a lot. I do. But as the Phoebe trial gets closer, it's on the news round the clock, and it's becoming harder and harder to avoid. I regret not having done more to help the victims, which in turn makes me feel conflicted about John. If we're dating, how can I not bring these feelings up?

This Saturday, he stays the night. And all of Sunday. We have coffee on my balcony wrapped up in a thick, soft, faux-fur blanket. When we're inside, William sits on his lap most of the day.

"What a traitor," I say as William purrs while John pets him in the exact perfect spot.

"You still have the office left." John points to the apology list on my fridge door, which has everything else crossed off.

"I know. I'm not sure what to do about that."

"What do you mean?"

"Do I even need to apologize to them? I saw some people at the Halloween party, and they didn't seem mad at me or anything."

"Only you can decide that, Millie."

"I think I do," I admit. "I was abrasive."

"Then do it. Get that off your chest."

"Logistically, how would I even do it?" I'm careful how I word the next sentence. "I prefer not to see any of the partners, and I can't just start calling up thirty people."

"Maybe if you came over for lunch, to see me, it would break the ice."

I don't know. I don't think I want to step foot in that office ever again. The NDA doesn't specifically ban me from entering the building but . . .

"Let me think about it," I say, and he nods. "When do you have to go back to Vegas?"

"I don't. We reached a settlement. I'm going to prepare everything tomorrow from the office and send it. If everyone signs, the case will be closed."

"I'm impressed!" I say, surprised that he was able to close a case of that magnitude so quickly.

"Coming from you, that's quite the compliment."

We spend the day on the couch watching movies and vegetating. It's the most relaxed I've seen him. "I have a recipe for a dessert I want to make. It's for a chocolate mousse."

"Is that code for chocolate chip cookies?"

I chuckle and then stand up and head to the kitchen. "We'll see after I'm done." I busy myself cooking and even serve the mousse in fancy martini glasses.

"Mills, this pudding is delicious," he says, eating it all up.

"It's not pudding. It's chocolate mousse."

He looks down at his almost empty glass, and his brows furrow. He shrugs and keeps eating. "Are you sure about that?"

Blerg!—my mousse is pudding. Then we go back to vegetating on the couch like a real couple who's been together for some time. I feel comfortable with him in a way I don't think I've felt in any other relationship. Regrettably, it doesn't go unnoticed how he quickly changes the news when they start talking about the upcoming Phoebe trial. I also know that he knows that I caught that.

Damn, I really like John, but I wish he didn't work with my nemesis.

Unfortunately, he leaves for work early the next day because he has to run home and change first.

I grumble when he kisses me to leave. Not because I don't like being kissed and having sweet words whispered in my ear. It's that I don't like anything whispered in my ear before ten. Funny how easily you can get used to sleeping in. For twenty years I woke up at six in the morning, sometimes earlier if I had a trial. A few months of not having to worry about an alarm, and anything before ten seems like a crime against humanity. Anyone who tries to wake me gets a prickly Millie.

———

Hi. It's a text from Luanne.

Hi, I text back.

Mitchell decided to bless us with his presence. He's taking the kids for the weekend.

Oh. Well, that's nice, I write back, because I'm not sure if it's nice or not, or if this is something she's upset about.

This is the first time in years I have an evening for myself. Is it sad that I don't know what to do?

I laugh. No. It's not sad.
Would you like to have dinner? she asks.

Sure.

I know it's last minute, and if you have plans, I understand, she says. I do have plans. John was going to come over later tonight.

No, I'm good. Let's do it.

Great! she says. How about Oasis?
Oasis! Is that place still open? I ask. It's our old stomping ground. We went there so many times when we were in our early twenties.

It is! I bet they still have those crappy wings and watered-down drinks.

I hope so! I say because I do. The food and drinks sucked, but the music was great and so was the vibe of the place. I can pick you up. How about eight?

Perfect, see you later.

I'm so excited. I pick up the phone and dial John.

"Hey, you," he says when he answers.

"Luanne called me and asked me to go to dinner with her because Mitchell showed up to take the kids for the weekend. Typical male, showing up to take kids to a fun place, leaving her to be the broke bad cop, but I digress. I know we made plans, but Lu asked me for dinner, John. Dinner. She called me! Can we have a rain check?"

He chuckles into the phone. "Take a breath, Mills."

I do. I inhale and then exhale.

"It's fine. No problem at all. I have to catch up on work anyway. Have fun. Don't drive if you're going to drink, and maybe we can meet up tomorrow."

"Yeah, tomorrow," I say and hang up almost as an afterthought. I think I hear him chuckle on the other line as I disconnect.

I want to find my old ripped jeans, the ones that I used to wear at Oasis. And maybe those black, pleather platforms with a thick band on the front and a little strap at the back.

I pull up at her house, and she's already waiting for me outside. She looks just as excited as I feel. "You haven't changed a bit. I swear you look younger than I remember," I say as she jumps into my car.

"Seriously?" She pinches her belly and then her arms. "You're sweet, but you know that's not true. There's at least thirty extra pounds on me."

"You had two kids! You look great, Lu." Maybe the jeans are a little tighter and her cleavage is more pronounced, but I think she looks fantastic. "And I absolutely love the shorter hair. Do you think I can pull it off?" I ask as I make a left at the light.

"Yes. But don't do it. I had to cut it because my hair started to fall out after the twins were born."

There's awkward silence. "Luanne—God, I wish I had been around for—"

She cuts me off. "Don't. We've moved on, right?"

"Right." I want to ask her one more thing. Something that's been niggling at the back of my mind, an issue we skirted during our Starbucks meeting. "You never did tell me. Mitchell didn't like me much, did he? I always got that vibe."

She exhales. "No. He kept planting seeds in my head. I'm not putting the blame on him. I'm a grown woman; I should have called you. I should have told you that you were acting like an ass instead of avoiding you. But yeah, he wasn't a big fan."

What a dick. I don't say that out loud now, but if I ever run into Mitchell, I will.

"Well, tonight is about us," I say as I park.

As soon as we are out of the car and face-to-face, we hug. It's a very long overdue hug. "I love you," she says.

"I love you, too, Lu." And I can feel a tear rolling down my cheek.

"No. Don't you dare cry. I get at least one crying fit a day from my kids; I will not put up with it today, on my day off!"

I sniffle and pat my cheek with the back of my hand, careful not to smear my makeup. "Okay. I won't cry."

Oasis is pretty empty and a little sad. It's not like we remembered. It's actually dilapidated and looking old. The fried bar food tastes exactly the same, and wine is wine, especially if you order a bottle, which is opened in front of us.

"So, tell me what's with you? Why aren't you working? The real reason," she asks. She still knows me. She doesn't buy that I wanted to retire.

"It's a long story, one that I can't get into. But what I can say is that I came out with a nice chunk of change and I'm trying to figure out what I'm going to do next."

"You should travel! If I had money and time, that's what I'd do. God, how nice would it be to go on a cruise or maybe to Napa."

"Everyone tells me the same thing! Not about the cruise or Napa, but about traveling. My sister told me to take a trip to Cuba."

"Cuba? That's random. I'm sure it's nice, but it's—"

"Oh!" I laugh loudly, liquid sloshing over the rim of my glass. "I didn't tell you! I found out I'm Cuban. My father's biological mother is Cuban, and I've found my great-aunt."

"What? Cuba? Great-aunt?"

"My mom gave me a 23andMe test for my birthday. There was a DNA relative match on the site, and I reached out to her and we've been chatting. I really like her. I have a bunch of family over there and everything. This big booty wasn't just happenstance, Lu. It's my Cuban side!"

She laughs heartily. "Whoa! You've been busy."

"But I think I'm going to skip the trip. I don't like traveling alone. Maybe I can figure out a way of FaceTiming with them."

"Why not go on the trip? You wake up and do all the sightseeing you want at your own pace. You eat where you want without having to ask anyone's opinion. Seems like a dream."

"That's because you're knee-deep in Cheerios and sleep deprivation. You need alone time. I need . . . I don't even know what I need."

"You need to do something exciting! That's what you need, Millie. Go on an adventure."

"I don't know . . ." I sigh.

"I think you should consider it," she says. "Can I ask you something?"

"Sure," I say.

"I always pictured you with kids. What happened?" As soon as she says that, she seems regretful and quickly adds, "Oh . . . I'm sorry. That was insensitive. You never know these days with all the infertility stuff you hear about."

"No. No. It's fine. It's not that I can't have children. I mean, I've never tried, but everything works correctly, as far as I know. Life got in the way, and before I knew it, I was forty."

"I get it. Days and weeks and then years go by and before you know it, you're married with two kids and your dickhead of a husband is cheating on you."

I laugh because it's just ridiculous, this entire conversation. "Mitchell sucks."

"Mitchell does suck," she agrees wholeheartedly.

Even though I always felt fulfilled in my professional life, now that I have no professional life, I realize I've missed out on a lot of things. "The baby train has passed this station already." I've never said that out loud, and for some reason the realization, the fact that I'm voicing it—it doesn't feel good. It actually makes me sad. Heartbreakingly sad.

"No!" she says, pointing a finger to my face. "Those better not be tears."

"No." I swallow. "I have something in my eye is all." I signal for the bartender to bring us another bottle.

"You're still young. People have kids nowadays well into their forties."

"I know. I'm just thinking of you and your kids and then my dad's mother who apparently wanted him so badly she fled the country! I never really thought about having kids, but now it seems I know so many amazing moms, and I feel like it's weird that as a woman, I didn't think about it until like right now."

"Kind of," she admits.

"Hmm. Well, I was busy, you know, and that was always something I thought I'd get to. And now I'm forty and never got to it."

"Maybe this new no-job situation came at a good time then."

I never thought of that. Not at all. Interesting.

"Anyway, enough about me. Tell me about you. What's happening with Mitchell besides his affliction of being an asshole?"

She tells me about how Mitchell comes in and out of their lives at his convenience. They have fifty-fifty custody, but Mitchell always misses his days. It hurts the kids, but they get so happy when they do see him, she doesn't have the heart or the money to tell him to go to hell or to get an attorney and fight for a revision of the custody arrangement.

"I could help you if you want," I say. I'm not practicing at the moment, but for a friend, I'd be willing to help. "You have to wait about six more months, though, unless Mitchell lives more than ten miles away. That's part of the agreement I made with the firm. I cannot practice law for a year within ten miles of the firm."

How nice to annihilate Mitchell in court.

"I think I'll keep that offer in my back pocket for now. I don't want to stir the pot too much just yet."

By midnight, we are blasted. So much so that I leave my car in the parking lot and call a cab to take us to my house, where we will basically pass out on my bed.

"Hey, Lu?" I say, my head resting on the back seat of the cab.

I turn my head, and Lu looks much like I do. Her head is back, and her eyes are closed. We're going to regret all the drinking tomorrow morning.

"Yeah?" she says, not bothering to open her eyes.

"I like this new me." I used to drink an occasional glass of wine, and now I'm leaving my car in parking lots and having to be driven home.

She doesn't respond, and I think she's fallen asleep. A moment later, as we're pulling up to my apartment building, she says, "This is not a new you. This is the same you as always. Amelia Montgomery has always been awesome."

And I smile.

———

"Is this 1997 all over again?"

I moan when I hear my sister's voice. I open one eye and find her standing by the door of my bedroom with an amused look on her face.

"Is that Luanne Chase?"

Luanne groans and flips to her stomach, shielding her face from the harsh light seeping in from the window. "Hey, Nina."

There's a knock on the front door.

"I'll get it," Nina says, and I hide my head under one of the pillows. I feel Lu rolling out of the bed and into the bathroom.

"I'm having déjà vu." I hear John's voice coming from the same place Nina's was a moment ago.

"Sister, darling, your boyfriend's here," Nina says, and I make a mental note to kill her. Boyfriend. How could she! We haven't had this conversation before. Also, isn't there some sort of sacred sister code about not letting a hot guy see your sister in this unkempt state? I whimper into the pillow, unwilling to see him, but I feel a dip in the bed and smell his familiar scent—soap and aftershave and pheromones.

"You had a fun night, I see," he says. He lifts the pillow, but I have preemptively placed my hands over my face. He chuckles and pries my hands off myself. "Do you make a habit of drinking too much and waking up with someone else in your bed?"

"It's only happened twice. This is the second time. But this time was platonic."

"Glad to hear it." He kisses my lips. Poor guy. He probably got drunk just from the fumes seeping out of my pores.

"I'm Luanne," she says, walking back into the room. She looks as hungover as I do.

"It's nice to meet you, Luanne. I'm John"—he points to himself—"the boyfriend." I scream internally, and Nina and Luanne giggle. He's a good sport, thank God. "I've heard a lot about you. I'm glad you two reconnected."

"Me too."

"Why are you here?" I ask John.

"Just because."

"Aww . . . ," both Nina and Lu say together, and I realize they're watching us intently.

"Nina, do you think you can give me a lift home?" Luanne asks. "I need to shower, and then I need to go back to sleep."

"Sure," Nina says. "I left bagels and coffee in the kitchen. Don't do anything crazy, kids!" Nina yells as she walks out.

"It was fun, Mills," Luanne says. "At least I think it was fun. I'll call you tomorrow and let you know when the headache goes away."

John and I chuckle, and then we're both alone. He leaves and comes back with coffee and an aspirin. I sit up and take a drink. "Can you stick around? I'd like to shower."

"Sure. I'll just chill right here with William."

"Great. Make yourself at home."

"Do you mind if I use your tablet to answer some emails?" he says, looking through his phone.

"Sure. It's right there." I point to it and then head to the bathroom.

I jump off the bed, and it takes me about half an hour to get myself together. When I finish, I'm feeling much better.

"That crazy hungover person you saw a little while ago . . . that was a figment of your imagination."

He chuckles. "So that other person wasn't my"—he lifts a brow with a smirk—"girlfriend."

I groan. "You can't let one go, can you?"

"I'm very astute. I like to read people."

"And make them uncomfortable?"

"Does it make you uncomfortable?"

"Does it make you uncomfortable?" I ask back.

He chuckles. "This is why attorneys can't date each other."

"You didn't answer the question, counselor."

"Neither did you. But I'm not scared of you, Madam Lawyer. I will answer the question. Does it make me uncomfortable to be referred to as your boyfriend? Yes. Because I feel we're too old for that particular vernacular, don't you? I think what we have is something different. Something akin to boyfriend/girlfriend but with a lot of wild adult sex, houses of our own, careers, no curfews, no sneaking around."

I chuckle. "I like your interpretation. For now, I guess boyfriend will have to do." Even as I say it, I'm worried I'm taking too big of a leap.

CHAPTER TWENTY

~~Luanne~~ No! ~~Luanne~~ ~~Attempt #2~~
~~Gary~~
~~Lindsey~~ ✓
~~Jenny O.~~ NO!
~~Jenny M.~~ NO!
~~Jenny Z.~~ Absolutely NO!
~~Mary~~
~~Office~~ MAYBE
~~Brenda~~
~~Margret~~ ~~Undecided~~
~~Jimenez~~

Hola Millie,

Our computer broke and that is why I have not sent you an email. Everything here is good. I'm catching up on your emails from a friend's computer that looks like Frankenstein. The computer not my friend. Her son put it together with parts he found. I hope you had a nice Thanksgiving. It was my favorite holiday when I lived in the States. Oh goodness, I miss turkey. We don't have turkey over here.

We received your package and are so grateful for your kindness. You did not have to send all of that. I don't know how I'll pay you back. I've shared everything with the familia and they say thank you and extend an invitation for you to come visit. We can take you to Varadero using your cousin Yovani's ID, since he works in one of the hotels and gets a special tourist permit. It is the most beautiful beach you will ever see. I promise that to you. Marta and Fabiola thank you for your books. I am happy to report that Fabiola is still working! Her husband is furious, but she just smiles and keeps going every morning, she's even stopped making him dinner when she comes home tired. She says: "He has two hands. He can make it himself." It is quite a scandal. But he loves her and he will have to figure it out, or starve. You know how men are . . .

Anyway, I will try to connect again soon. I am getting a new mobile phone from a friend in Miami who is coming to visit and then when I have a number I'll let you know so that we can talk instead of write. I would like to hear your voice. It would be nice, no?

Un abrazo,
Rosa

What a relief. I had been thinking of her all through the holidays. It had been over a month since I'd received an email, and I was worried. John spent Thanksgiving in Portland with his sister, and I spent it with Nina and my parents.

The time between Thanksgiving and Christmas has been a whirlwind. John's been working long days, and I've been mostly shopping for presents. Unlike past holidays when I bought everything online without much thought, this time I actually made a list and have really enjoyed buying the perfect gift for everyone. I don't think I've ever done that before. Ironically, I've spent less money than any other year. Before, I overcompensated with the extravagance of the present to make up for the fact that I didn't put any real thought into it. Of course, I included something for Rosa. I know she's going to think it's too much, but I have the money and I wanted to buy it. It's a tablet with a camera and mic so we can chat and actually see each other. Really, it's for the entire Roybal gang since they don't have a computer and I'm sure they can use one.

I send Rosa a quick email. I know she can travel to the States, unlike most Cubans. She is, after all, a US citizen.

Rosa,

I know it is difficult for you to leave your sick mama, but if you can get away for a week, I would love to buy you a ticket to come to spend the holidays with me and the family. Would you consider it? On me.

Also, I'm thrilled about Fabiola. I'm starting to think I got my independent and stubborn nature from the Roybals. It's interesting to discover that men are the same everywhere. There are a few good ones, however. My dad, for one. He is wonderful and caring and perhaps he got that from his parents—both real and biological.

Let me know about the trip!

Love,
Millie

John decided to stay in town for the holidays, and my parents decided to take a transatlantic cruise this year, so I've decided to host a Christmas Eve dinner. Since my failed party last spring, I've been hesitant to even say the *p* word.

"Are you sure you don't need any help planning this party?" Nina asks.

"It's not a party! It's just an intimate holiday dinner."

"Fine. Let me know if I can help," Nina says before hanging up.

Dinner was supposed to be just Nina, John, and Luanne because the kids were going to be with Mitchell this year. Last minute, however, Mitchell decided it was too much "stress" on Lydia, his girlfriend, so he "asked" Luanne if she minded taking the kids.

Of course Luanne didn't mind. Good parents don't "mind" when their kids are around for the holidays. Feeling embarrassed about the two additional guests, she called to cancel, but I would have none of that, and now Mikey and Olivia will be joining us.

Children change the dynamic of things, so I am now rearranging the dinner table. Actually, I'm not rearranging the dinner table; I'm rearranging furniture because I have a special, smaller, kid-friendly table just for them that I want to make sure fits in the same general area as the adult table. The decoration on the dining table is formal, in elegant blues and silver, and the decoration on the kids' table is fun, red and green and festive. I went to Target and basically purchased everything from that dollar section right by the door, the vortex of overspending. I got them little Christmas puzzles and arts and crafts. I want them to have fun even though I have no other remotely kid-friendly items in my house.

Initially, I was going to cook everything myself, but at the last minute I changed my mind and had everything catered. I didn't want to make any mistakes. I want everything to be Pinterest perfect. My last party was a disaster, but it was also something I should never have attempted. I invited people I didn't even care about. I was doing it to prove something. To show people another side of me. This time, I'm hosting this not because Nina convinced me or because I'm proving something to someone, but because I want to do it and I want these people—my favorite people—here. It's my way of apologizing to them for all the years of missed birthdays and parties and anniversaries.

I move the beautiful honey-baked ham from the aluminum tray into a brand-new ivory-colored Christmas Spode platter that I purchased yesterday just for this purpose. I place the creamy mashed potatoes in a matching Spode bowl. I also ordered salad, rolls, and a green bean casserole. There's red and white wine, and now there are juice boxes too. I even take out the fine china my mother gifted me years ago. She would be so happy if she saw it. I take a photo of the beautifully made table with the china and text it to her. Interesting how useful my mother's gifts have suddenly turned out to be.

I've texted Luanne a dozen times about her children's likes and dislikes. She keeps telling me not to worry, which makes me worry even more. I run to the grocery store and get frozen chicken nuggets, bread, cheese, peanut butter, strawberry and grape jelly, potato chips, and popcorn. I run home and heat up the nuggets in the oven and make cute little grilled cheese sandwiches and some PB and Js. I also bought an apple pie to go with the blueberry pie I had already purchased. I remember the face they made at blueberry pancakes when we had breakfast months ago, but everyone likes apple pie, right? I also bought ice cream just in case.

I step back and look at the table one final time.

Perfect.

I quickly change into a pair of high-waisted, wide-legged, black trousers and a red blouse, which I purchased for the occasion. I fluff my hair, put on some light makeup, and I'm ready for my guests. I swear, I have PTSD from my birthday because I sit and look at my watch a hundred times wondering if anyone will show up, which is ridiculous. Of course they'll show up.

My phone chimes with an incoming text. Don't get mad. Kevin's coming along. He didn't have anywhere to go, and I felt bad. We're not together now.

What!—I start to type out, but my doorbell rings. I get up and open it to see Luanne and the kids.

"Hi!" I say. She looks apologetic and I whisper, "What?"

"I brought Mom. I hope that's okay. She was going to my brother's, but his wife had the flu and—" She stops and mouths, "Sorry."

"No, it's fine. Of course she's welcome." I look over Lu's shoulder. "Nancy, hi. Long time no see."

She looks just like she did the last time I saw her. After we exchange hugs, I herd them all inside. "Come in. Make yourselves at home. Mikey, Olivia, come meet William," I say as Luanne and Nancy, who I hadn't noticed had two bags each, place them on my counter and start to take out food.

I make a mental note that I need to add two more place settings, but then there's a knock on the door, not a ring. I furrow my brows and go see who it is. Turns out John's hands were full, so he used his foot to knock.

"Oh, hi. What's all this?" I ask, taking things out of his hands.

"Flowers for you," he says, giving me a kiss on the cheek. "I also brought a cake. I know you said you didn't need anything, but it's made of Nutella so . . ." I smile and kiss him on the cheek. "Oh, and wine. I brought wine."

My sister walks in with Kevin before I even have a chance to close the door behind John. "Howdy ho, everyone!" Nina says. "Oh, Nancy, it's been ages." She walks right in and says hi to everyone. "Luanne, Nancy, this is a friend of mine, Kevin." John already knows Kevin from the office, and they, too, greet each other.

"Mills, this looks beautiful," Luanne says, looking at the table. "And oh my God, look how cute, Mom." She examines the kids' table. "You shouldn't have gone through all this trouble, Millie."

"It's no trouble." The kids run around the house playing with William as Luanne and her mom take out plates of cheese, a casserole, and a bunch of delicious-looking food—lumpy mashed potatoes, a sweet cornbread hash, jalapeño poppers, and even an ambrosia salad. I wasn't sure how William would react to children since he's never been around them, but I gave him a good talking-to before they arrived and he seems to have listened because he's being uncharacteristically playful.

My beautiful Spode platter is pushed aside to make room for the aluminum trays holding other food. Nina brought a salad in a clear plastic container, which she places next to mine.

"At this rate, we're going to need a bigger venue for your forty-first birthday party," Nina whispers, placing her arm around my shoulder as we watch everyone chatting, laughing, and reorganizing my table, which now looks perfect.

"Don't even think about it." I side-eye her.

"Why?" she whines. "Because of one little failed party? Look how successful this has turned out."

"Epic failed party. Not little fail. And this isn't a party."

"Yeah, I think it is. Anyway, you're in a much better place now. Isn't that the point of the Apology Project? I thought you wanted to have guests for your party."

Even as she says it, I feel horrible that I ever contemplated that. "Well, now that I've thought about it, I don't need a party. The friends I have and the people I've been meeting, they're enough. I don't need two hundred people at a party I don't really even want. I'm good with a handful of friends and acquaintances coming in and out of my life. I don't think a big party is what I want."

"Aww . . . look at my little caterpillar blossoming into a beautiful butterfly."

"Is that what you tell your patients?"

"Only the big kids," she says and plants a wet kiss on my cheek.

I look around. John's in the kitchen talking to Nancy about the wine or the juice boxes, I'm not sure. Nina and Luanne are trying to wrangle the kids, and Kevin's eating a roll that's supposed to be for dinner.

My Pinterest perfection is now completely covered by aluminum and plastic. The kids' puzzle pieces are everywhere, but there's laughter in my house. A lot of laughter. Right before we begin to eat, I stand up. "Thank you all for being here. I hope this, in some small way, makes up for all the years I missed out on important events in your lives." I turn briefly to Nina. "I wish Mom and Dad were here. I know this is just dinner, but it means a lot to me that you're all here sharing Christmas with me. I just . . . I just wanted to say thank you, and I hope this is the beginning of many more holidays spent together." *Thank you* is the antithesis of *sorry*. It's easy to say and only brings joy to people. I need to say it more often.

There's a round of "awwws" and "Merry Christmases" and "hear, hears." John kisses me briefly on my lips, and Nina winks at me proudly from across the table. I feel so light and joyous right now that I want to cry. Happy tears, of course.

Best Christmas ever.

I hope the Roybals are enjoying their evening too.

———

Querida Millie,

I am sorry that I had not replied to your email. Mama passed away last week. We are all devastated, but she's at peace now. You did not know her, but I told her all about you and I think she understood. I am sorry to have to give you the sad news on an email.

I also want to thank you so much for the present. It
is too much, Millie. You spoil us.

Love, Rosa

I feel like someone I've known my entire life has died. Tears slide
down my face. I didn't know MariRosa, but she was the closest connection to my biological grandmother. How many stories has she taken
with her? I want to tell my father even though he's been holding himself
back from my search. I try to call my parents, but just as I expected, it
doesn't connect. They're still on that cruise. I leave them a message and
then send my father an email asking him to call me.

Rosa,

I cannot express to you how sorry I am for your loss.

Sending you my love,
Millie

I mope around my apartment for the next two days. It's already
January, and it's freezing; I haven't left the house in two days, and I need
human connection.
Lunch? First I text Nina, then Lu. Neither answer. I text John next.

Can't. I'm swamped. Going to have to work through lunch.

How about I take you something? You can eat it at your desk. I
don't even have to stay.

Isn't this exactly what I hated for people to do? Disturbing me was
the worst possible offense. What an asshole I was.

You are an angel, he says.

Not really. I'm trying out a new recipe, and I need a taste tester. For some inexplicable reason, I don't want to talk about MariRosa. No one will understand. Heck, I don't understand. I didn't even know the woman.

He sends me the same emoji my sister sends me, the one with the green face. I roll my eyes.

It's delicious. Trust me. Baked ziti with homemade meat sauce.
I've been slow cooking the sauce for the last four hours.

My stomach just made a very loud noise.

You shouldn't fart at work.

LOL. You really are a very special kind of weird.

So I take it as a yes for lunch?

Hell yes! If you are comfortable coming into the office. I can meet you downstairs at the atrium of the building.

I'm not exactly comfortable, but I'm not going to let JJF dictate whether I can take lunch to John, and the NDA doesn't say anything about going to the office. If I happen to see any of the partners, I'll take the high road, which basically means not elbowing anyone in the face. I'll quickly wave and then continue on my way. I doubt that they'd engage in any conversation with me anyway since anything they say can put the NDA in danger. We'll freeze down there. I'm okay. You were right, I need to break the ice and going there to meet up with you is a good reason.

Okay. And, if it puts you at ease, none of the partners are in today.

It does put me more at ease. Great. I'll be there in an hour.

I remove the ziti from the oven and then take a big spoon to pour it into a container, but it is a little firmer than it should be. It looks more like a lasagna than it does baked ziti. I shrug and add another piece and some garlic bread. I take two cans of soda and put everything into a little lunch box that I used to use when I worked there. I change into jeans and a nice blouse and, of course, my scarf. I must say, my jeans are fitting a little better than they did before. I'm still the same size and my weight hasn't changed much, but I think the daily walks, occasional bike rides, and Pilates are doing something to my body. I brush my hair and then put it up into a nice, neat ponytail. I sprinkle on a bit of makeup and slip on some cute flats as I walk out.

The security guard at the front of the office building, the same person I saw every day for almost twenty years, asks me for my ID.

"Carl, it's me. Amelia Montgomery," I say as I hand him my license.

"Amelia?" He looks at me carefully. "You look different."

"I'm not in a suit."

"Yeah. And you're smiling." Was I that much of a shrew? "I don't think you've ever said my name. I didn't even think you knew who I was," he says.

"Sure I did."

"Nope. Pretty sure you didn't," he observes.

"Well, then. I'm sorry about that, Carl."

"It's not a problem, Ms. Montgomery. Please go ahead," he says, letting me through the lobby. I walk to the set of elevators but look back at Carl. *How did I go about life so oblivious to everyone and everything?* I *knew* Carl. He's married and has a seventeen-year-old daughter, whom I remember from a take-your-child-to-work day. He's a pleasant enough man who said "good morning" every day and "good evening" as I left.

I suppose I never reciprocated the sentiments. By the time I'm at the seventeenth floor, I feel like crap. I make a mental note to order a box of Crazy Cleo's Cookies and have them delivered to Carl tomorrow.

Then the elevator opens, and I'm hit with a one-two punch of nostalgia. The sound of people talking and typing, the familiar smell of the office, and the lighting—everything hits me all at once. Hard. My legs feel like lead, and I'm having trouble taking steps out of the elevator.

"Ms. Montgomery?" Jackie, the receptionist, says from across the room. "Ms. Montgomery?" she repeats, louder.

Hesitantly I step out of the elevator.

I clear my throat. "Everything looks the same," I say, mostly to myself.

"Pardon, Ms. Montgomery?" she repeats.

"Sorry. I was just talking to myself. Anyway, hello, Jackie. It's been a long time. How are you doing?"

She looks taken aback by my nicety. "Uh . . . fine?"

"Fine, as in you're not sure if you're well?"

"No. Sorry." She clears her throat. "I'm fine, thank you, Ms. Montgomery. And you?"

"I'm great, Jackie. I'm actually here to see John."

She nods and picks up her phone. "Mr. Ellis, I have Amelia Montgomery here to see you. Yes. Okay."

She hangs up and then looks up at me. "He's in his office. It's the one across from your old one. I can take you—"

"No. I can find it myself. Thank you, Jackie."

She nods and sits back down, flustered.

I open the door that leads to the rest of the offices, and it hits me again. I think I never saw it from this angle. I was always so deep inside the trenches with my head down, working or arguing or shouting orders, that I never really looked up. I see the pool of cubicles with four paralegals typing furiously into their computers. There's Margret's desk, but she's not there. I walk toward the row of offices, all with glass walls, but no one looks up from their computers. I see Helen, Mo, and Najib, three associates at JJF, all immersed in their work as I walk by them. My old office looks inhabited; there are papers strewn messily over the desk, a jacket on the chair, and a mug on the table, but no one is sitting there. I'm looking in when I feel a hand on my waist. I turn, startled, and I see John's smile. "This way," he says and leads me to his office, which is directly across from my old one, like Jackie said.

"If I still worked here, you'd be seeing my face every time you look up," I note.

"I know. Unfortunately, since that's not the case, I get the wonderful privilege of having to stare at Bruno Jennings all day. And before you ask, yes, he's as beautiful as you are." He winks and then gestures to the chair in front of his desk.

"I don't think I've met him, but if that name is anything to go by . . ."

"Exactly." He laughs. "Must be bizarre being here. Did you see the old gang yet?"

"It's surreal. I saw familiar faces, but they were working, and I didn't want to interrupt."

I look around. There are files and boxes everywhere, the name Phoebe written with a Sharpie on the front of all of them. "Knee-deep in Phoebe," he says, and I start to hyperventilate. Why are all those boxes here in John's office? It's Junior's case, not John's, right? Maybe he's just helping out? My mind starts to race, and I remember what Nina said about half truths. I'm imagining the worst-case scenario because I don't know what exactly is happening. Except that I'm starting to feel ill.

"Yuck." Regardless of our opinions on the case, Phoebe is gross. I don't just mean this because I don't like him or what he did, but also because in the context of social norms, he is unattractive and skeevy. Needless to stay, the thought of being knee-deep *in* Phoebe makes me want to gag, and by the look on John's face he agrees, whether he believes Phoebe is guilty or not.

"So, what did you bring me?" he asks, motioning to the lunch box I place on his desk and obviously not realizing I'm having a small aneurysm. "I'm starving."

"Um . . . ," I say, shaking my head side to side, trying to shift the cobwebs from my thoughts. "I hope you'll like it."

"I hope so too. I skipped breakfast."

"I think I've really improved."

I take out the containers, the food still warm, and hand it to him, my eyes drifting to the boxes but then back to the task at hand.

"You're not going to join me?" he asks.

"I had a late lunch, and I was planning on eating this for dinner. I'm good. But please eat up." I place the utensils I brought and the soda in front of him. "I can go if you want. I just wanted to bring it." I want to leave. Gather my thoughts. Not jump to conclusions.

"No, please stay. I'd love the company."

I smile with effort, and luckily he's not looking as he opens up containers. I'm sure I have all my emotions playing out on my face right now. The last place I want to have this discussion is here in this office. He studies it for a moment. "I thought it was baked ziti." He stabs at the pasta and then picks up the knife to cut a piece. "Isn't ziti supposed to be sort of liquid-y?"

I bite the inside of my lip. "It's good, though. Taste it." I tried it and the taste was on point. The texture . . . well, not so much.

He hesitates and then takes a big mouthful.

I wait.

"It's really good. It's more like lasagna, though. Or maybe like . . . I don't know. It's a little weird. But it does taste good." *Breathe, Millie. Don't overreact. There is a logical explanation to this.*

I smile, instead, with effort. "Like the braised short ribs that turned out soupy. You and Nina thought it was beef stew."

"All right, so your problem is that you're setting yourself up for failure with the title. Don't name the dish. Had you told me you were bringing lasagna, I would not have been surprised by this." He takes another forkful. "Sorry about the mess in here, by the way. There's construction in the filing room, and they've stuck boxes in everyone's office. You should see the conference room. It's a mess."

I exhale in relief. The boxes are just being stored here. I can feel myself start to calm down a bit. Clearly I need to work on my cooking skills. Luckily, the ziti still tastes good.

"So, what's on the menu next?" he asks.

"Tomorrow I'm supposed to be learning how to make risotto with shrimp, so you can prepare yourself for seafood gumbo."

He snorts out a big laugh, and I follow him. As we dip into chat about the week, I'm trying to overlook the files around him. Even though I feel relieved they're just here for storage, I want to know about those victims. I wish I could peek inside and see what their strategy is going to be. Did anything I said to Junior penetrate his thick skull? I doubt it. But I want to know so badly. The anxiety of knowing what those women are up against is almost too much to bear. I really can't fathom that Junior's going to destroy their testimony by using their sexual proclivities when they were in their early twenties to justify Phoebe's disgusting actions. Or use, for one particular victim, her addiction to painkillers five years earlier to discredit her statements. The thought alone makes me livid.

John takes my hand in his and asks, "You okay?" He's so sweet and thoughtful. He's put up with my occasional rule-breaking, judgmental fits of anger without making me feel like I'm nuts.

I'm falling in love with John even as I fight it. The more time I spend with him, the more it's going to hurt if this doesn't work out. I stopped myself last week from saying "I love you" when we hung up the phone. I said some sort of garbled, nonsensical thing instead, trying to cover my almost mistake.

I've avoided anything JJF-related in months because that's what we agreed we'd do. Unfortunately, the other side of me, the one who practiced law for twenty years, the one who elbowed Junior in the face, the one who isn't lovestruck, the one who was already partner in this same law firm, wants to tell him all the reasons he should charge into Junior's office and demand that he treat the victims in the Phoebe case with respect. Demand that he tell the partners to drop the Phoebe case altogether. Maybe since John's a man, they'd listen to an alternative defense strategy. But I also know that asking him to do that is ridiculous. It's my plight, not his. Luckily, there's a knock on the door, and we're interrupted before I say something I know I'll regret.

"Hey, you want to grab a quick lunch—oh, never mind," the familiar voice says from behind me as John takes a bite of food. "Guess you're already eating."

I swivel my chair around. "Hi, Mo."

His eyes open wide. "Amelia? Whoa. I didn't recognize you." He steps farther into the office. "Hi. How have you been?" Mo's a longtime associate at JJF. We weren't exactly friends, but we were friendly. He's been second chair on a few cases with me through the years.

"I'm good, thank you. And you?"

He looks a little surprised, much like Jackie in the reception area. "I'm fine. Fine. Working hard. Took over some of your cases."

"Hope you're keeping my defenses solid."

"I had shoes to fill," he says. "I, uh . . ." He looks between John and me as he realizes that I'm not here for a work meeting, that this is purely social. "It's a little disconcerting seeing you like this."

He says it with his eyes roaming me from the top of my head to the tips of my toes. It's not in a sexual way but in a surprised manner.

"Like what?"

"Like . . . not scary." He shrugs. "Leave you guys to it," he says, and walks away.

"I'm not scary. I just wanted people to do what they were paid to do. Not more. Not less."

"You're intimidating, Millie," John says. "Your reputation precedes you. You're confident; you're no nonsense, unapologetic, and gorgeous. Plus, you aren't exactly the most approachable even on your friendliest of days. People are inclined to walk on eggshells when you're around. And you want perfection from people because you strive for it. Not everyone can get up to your level."

"I was nice to you."

"You weren't. If you recall you tried to kick me out of your party."

"Well, you slept with me anyway."

"No one ever accused me of being stupid."

"What do you think about me bringing lunch for everyone in the office tomorrow? Just to clear the air between us and so that I don't feel uncomfortable when I come visit you."

He wipes his mouth with the napkin I packed him. "I think it's a good idea. Can't hurt, right?"

"Well, it can actually." I bite the corner of my lip. "I was super difficult to work with, John. Maybe no one wants lunch if it's coming from me." As soon as it comes out of my mouth, I think of my failed birthday. *What if no one shows up?*

"That's not going to happen, I promise. People never say no to free lunch," he says, and of course, again . . . failed birthday party pops to mind.

I let out a big breath. "Okay. I'll do it. Fingers crossed."

"Can I give you a suggestion, though?"

"Sure."

"Don't cook. Use a caterer."

I roll my eyes. Christmas was a real hit, but just because I catered that doesn't mean I'm going to stop cooking. I try to hide a smile. "You ate every last bite. Couldn't have been that bad."

"I plead the fifth on this one, Millie."

272

On Friday, which is usually the firm's least hectic day, I have lunch sent for the entire office. It's placed in the lunchroom in big aluminum trays. I don't want to cause too much of a distraction, so I decide to serve it myself instead of having one of the caterers assist.

"Thank you, Ms. Montgomery," a paralegal says as I hand her a plate.

"Please, call me Amelia."

"This was very nice of you, Ms. Montgomery," one of the junior interns adds and takes a plate.

"Amelia, please."

"Hello, Margret. I got a separate vegetarian dish for you," I say, pointing to a smaller container.

"Uh . . . wow, thank you. I didn't know you knew I was vegetarian."

I smile and don't tell her that John told me this morning when I was ordering. There're a few other vegetarians in the office.

I take the empty chair next to Margret, and we chat and make general small talk. John comes and sits by us. "So, Margie, how bad was she? Tell me. Did she really make a law clerk cry?"

I elbow him.

"Two of them. They were bad, though. Probably deserved it."

"Come on, Margret, the name She-Demon was a bit over the top. Tell the truth, I wasn't that bad," I say with a touch of amusement. She's being friendly, and I'm feeling more relaxed. Yet she skews her face in a way that says I was worse than all of them, and John bursts out laughing. I shake my head.

"Smells delicious. Did we buy lunch for the office? What's the occasion?" The too-familiar voice sends the hairs on the nape of my neck right up.

"No. Amelia catered lunch for the office. Isn't that nice?" says Dean, one of the administrative assistants, and I turn my head around toward the door.

"Amelia? Amelia Montgomery?" His voice hardens, and I put the knife down because I shouldn't have a knife on my person when I'm dealing with Marc Jones Jr. I wipe my hands clean on a paper towel and stand up.

"Mr. Jones." I used to call him Marc, but after my elbow came in direct contact with his face, I'm thinking we are not on a first-name basis.

"What the hell are you doing here, Montgomery? You know you're banned from coming inside this building." His baritone voice booms, and everyone who had been cheerily chatting stops talking. All eyes and ears are on us. You could hear a pin drop.

"I most certainly am not. But of course, you probably didn't read your own agreement, did you? Maybe you should get a competent lawyer to explain it to you."

People gasp. I'm teetering. I'm a sliver away from breaking the terms of the NDA, but so is he.

But he doesn't intimidate me. This adversarial scenario doesn't faze me one bit. This is just a normal day at the office, and apparently just stepping foot inside is enough to wash away nearly seven months of self-improvement. I'm already stooping to his level.

"You better have not touched one file in this office," he yells.

I lean casually against the table behind me, trying to keep the cool I've already so clearly lost. "It has recently come to my attention that I wasn't the most pleasant colleague at the firm, and I thought I'd bring lunch and take an opportunity to apologize to a few individuals. You should try it sometime, Marc."

"Have her escorted out!" he booms. "You think that this changes anything? You left the firm and dropped your caseload on us because you had a little hissy fit, and you think the millions you cost us in upset clients and severance payments and the aggravation will be overlooked with—what is this . . ."

Someone murmurs, "Shrimp scampi."

Someone else: "And filet mignon."

Then a third: "There's also two vegetarian dishes."

But none of that matters. I see John standing near me, conflicted. When Junior's voice booms again, John takes a couple of protective steps toward me.

"You cost all these people their Christmas bonus, you know?" says Junior, leering. Everyone gasps.

"No, Marc, *I* did not." And then I step forward. "Would you like to tell them what really happened?" I eye him like I've eyed countless plaintiffs and juries in courtrooms across the country. "I'd stop while you're ahead."

"Your severance—"

"You do not want to start disclosing the terms of our agreement. Once you do, I can do the same." I look him right in the eye. Maybe this is what people mean by intimidating. My shoulders are squared, and my head held high. I will not let this fool scare me off. I'm sure he scares others, but he will not scare me. He exhales, knowing that I'm right.

"I heard rumors about you two," Junior says to John and me. "John, I want to see you in my office. And I urge you to remember that you have an oath not to disclose any confidential client information."

"We don't discuss work," John says from behind me. No, not behind me, but next to me. He is making it clear that we are together. I want him to tell Junior to take his job and shove it.

"So, tell me, is it that you didn't have the balls to do the work yourself? You bitch at me for Phoebe, but you're okay with your boyfriend doing the dirty work. He's going to bring those women to the stand and rip them apart just like you were instructed to do. Instead you took the easy way out—the big payday. Now you're sitting on your throne judging everyone else, letting the men do what you didn't have the balls to do," he spits out, and the blood drains down my body. The rug has been ripped out from under me, and I think I even sway a bit. But I hold myself together. I look at John, and he goes from looking pissed-off at Junior to looking . . . what is that? I can't even tell what that emotion is on his face.

"We don't discuss work or JJF, but thank you for breaking that NDA just now. It's going to be truly wonderful watching your little empire crumble when I tell the world all about the toxic work environment at this firm."

He smirks. "If anyone's toxic, it's you. You think some food is going to erase years of you being a She-Demon?"

Damn, that hits hard.

I'd been here to cross out the last names on my list, and I ended up in another brawl with the man I despise.

I take a step away and then another as I feel the tears start to clog my nose and move up to my eyes.

But if I leave right now, I'll never forgive myself. "I wasn't easy," I start as I look at Junior, but I'm mostly talking to the office staff on tenterhooks. "I know that. I acknowledge that. I wish I could take some of it back. I was trying to do my job, and I never ever did anything to purposefully hurt anyone's feelings or demoralize anyone. You're right, I can't make anyone forgive me. But I can try and be a better human being. Unfortunately, you'll never be anything but the shadow of your shitty father, Junior." Just like Marcus, he will never be a better person because his father taught him to be a narcissistic, sexist jerk. He'll never apologize to anyone because it doesn't even register that he's done something wrong. Sad that I had not thought about possibly having hurt Luanne or Gary or anyone else on my list until I took a step back and pondered it. But once I did think of it, I quickly realized what a jerk I'd been. Junior could have the rest of his life to think over the damage he's done to me and everyone else he's crossed paths with, and he'd never own up to his wrongdoings. That is the biggest difference between us. I have a heart. I have self-awareness. He, on the other hand, is an entitled narcissist with no remorse whatsoever.

I'm so disappointed in John, but right now I have bigger fish to fry. Actually, I'm frying so many fish at once, I feel my face heat up. I want to vomit. But I refuse to give Junior the satisfaction of me having a breakdown in front of him.

Phoebe is a sonofabitch who deserves to lose, and those victims, who are claiming almost $70 million in punitive damages, should get it all. Every single penny and more. But Junior is a great litigator and so is John, and between the two of them, I have no doubt Phoebe will win. And the fact that John can stand there and take on this case and not see what I see . . . my feelings completely shift. Completely.

John doesn't come to me. That brief moment of solidarity is gone. John may be standing next to me. He may have developed feelings for me. But his job is still his priority, and he's going to sit and talk to Junior when I leave, and they are going to discuss the case, and, if he has to choose me or his career, there is no doubt in my mind that John will choose his career. And then when this is all over, he's going to call me and try to win me back and make excuses, and I'll just take him back—or at least, that's what he thinks will happen. A few months ago, sadly, I'd have chosen the job too.

"Margret, call security and have Ms. Montgomery escorted out of the building immediately."

"Marc." John takes a step in front of me. "That is not necessary." But I walk around John to face Junior directly. I don't need John's help. He's not the hero here.

"It is," Junior says, exerting his power. "I want her out of this building now!" His decision right now is to squash me. Squash me in front of all my peers like a dumb alpha bear.

I will not cry. I will not cry. For two decades I've managed to keep my emotions at bay. I will not give Junior or anyone else the satisfaction of seeing my heart crumble into pieces. Who the hell have I become?

As a rational, intelligent woman, I understand that it's not fair to John to have to fight this fight, but it doesn't mean that I don't want him to. I wish he would have quit the moment he saw the Phoebe file. I wish he'd put Junior in his place and chosen me over work. Heck, I wish he'd elbowed Junior in the nose in defense of my honor. He does look torn, though. I'll give him credit for that. I swallow down the lump that's choking me.

I turn to Junior and I hate—hate!—the way my voice quivers when I speak. Not because of him—I couldn't care less about Junior—but because of John and the fact that he's made me break in front of my ex-colleagues. It's as if all the emotions I haven't felt in twenty years are all coming out right this second. "I'm leaving. No need to call your guards." I grab my purse, and a room full of people is watching me leave. "One thing I will never apologize for is my integrity," I say to Junior, but I'm also looking at John. John, who sold out.

Everyone's wide-eyed, watching everything unfold like a telenovela. "You know the saying about men who have to exert their power over women?" I whisper to Junior as I walk past him. When he looks at me questioningly, I put my thumb and index finger together, the universal sign for something small. It's petty, but I feel pretty damn good about that last little dig.

I'm shaking by the time the elevator door opens, and I'm relieved no one's inside. The entire Apology Project feels stupid now. Junior was able to cut me deep by bringing out all my insecurities in front of everyone. *She-Demon.* That's what I am and what I'll always be to everyone in this office.

"Wait!" I hear John say from behind as he runs to catch up to me.

Even as the elevator doors close, I hold out hope that it was all a dream or a misunderstanding. But it's reality. John watches me as I watch him, sadness in both our eyes as the doors close and then he's gone. I guess that's how our entire relationship has been—me holding out hope that he'd make a decision he was never going to make.

Not all love stories end with a big gesture of love. Some just end.

CHAPTER
TWENTY-ONE

~~Luanne No!~~ Luanne ~~Attempt~~ #2
~~Gary~~
~~Lindsey~~ ✓
~~Jenny O.~~ NO!
~~Jenny M.~~ NO!
~~Jenny Z.~~ Absolutely NO!
~~Mary~~
~~Office~~ MAYBE ~~FAILED! FAILED! FAILED!~~
~~Brenda~~
~~Margret~~ ~~Undecided~~
~~Jimenez~~

Of course. My parents choose this moment to FaceTime me. I pull over into an empty parking lot and answer.

"Hi, honey. Is everything okay? We got your message."

I wouldn't be able to hide my devastation even if I wanted to. I wipe my eyes and look at the two faces staring back at me from the tiny screen. "MariRosa died."

They look at me questioningly for a moment. "Rosa's mother?" my father asks.

"Yes, your aunt," I add.

Biologically, she is his aunt, but he has never met these people; the connection is just not there.

"I'm sorry, dear," my mom says. "I know you've grown attached to them."

"That's terrible. At least she's at peace now," my dad says in condolence, and I know he doesn't feel anything but sadness on my part.

"You're really taking it hard," my mom says as I wipe my eyes and runny nose.

"Well, it's that and also"—now I sob—"I went to the office today and I saw Junior, and we had a big argument. It wasn't good."

"Oh, honey . . ."

"It's fine," I say, but it's not fine. Not at all. And then there's John too. It's a lot.

"What can we do? You're worrying us," Mom says.

"Nothing, Mom. I just needed to talk is all. But I'm okay."

"You don't look okay, Millie," Dad says.

"It was a rough day. I'll tell you about it when you get home. I just wanted to tell you about MariRosa, but then the work thing happened just now."

"I'll call back in a few days, okay? I hate having to let you go," Mom says.

"This call is probably costing you a fortune," I say with a watery smile. "Don't worry about me. Have fun on the rest of your trip. Love you guys."

"Love you," both of them say before the call disconnects. I feel just like I did on my last day at JJF. Lost. Sad. Hopeless. Except now I feel stupid for making an effort at trying to become a better person.

What good did that do? I apologized to people . . . big freakin' deal. I'm still all alone, and now I'm also heartbroken. It was so much easier when my heart was sealed up tight.

John and I got along well but also avoided talking about his work, which is a huge part of his life. Mine, too, even if I don't work at JJF anymore. I still have opinions. I still have a brain and beliefs, and the fact that we couldn't discuss them is a problem. It would have never worked in the long run. Better to find out now than when I'm truly invested, although I fear it's too late for that.

But now as I arrive home, tears falling down my face, I'm overwhelmed. The trial starts next week, and I can't be here for it. It'll be impossible to keep from attending the trial, which is open to the public, from screaming at the news for covering it, from feeling horrible for any part I may have played in the case. But most of all, I can't watch my opinion of John crumble to the lowest lows.

I call Nina, who doesn't answer, so then I call Luanne.

"Hello," she says breathlessly.

"Is this a bad time?"

"It's always a bad time. Mikey, Olivia, go do your homework!" she yells. "What's up? I'm all ears."

"What do you think about taking a little trip with me? All expenses paid. Two weeks. Anywhere you want to go. Bring the kids."

"What?!" she says.

"I need to get out of town. Maybe a cruise, but I don't want to go alone. Say yes. It'll be so much fun."

"Did something happen? Are we going on the lam?" She's sort of laughing but also sort of serious.

"The trial that I told you about, John's on it now, and he didn't even tell me. I don't want to be here for it. I need to get out of town and get my mind off everything."

"Oh, uh . . . well, that seems a little extreme, but I guess it's also better than storming into the courtroom with a bat."

"Exactly!"

She gets me.

"I wish I could, Millie. Seriously, I need a damn break. But I can't. Mitchell will never let me take the kids away for two weeks, and I can't leave them with him for two weeks."

My heart deflates.

"I understand. It's okay."

"Don't think about it so much. Go online right now and book yourself a cruise. No Wi-Fi. Middle of the ocean. Warm breeze. Booze. You can play bingo with other people, or shuffleboard. You won't feel alone. It'll be wonderful. I'm jealous just thinking about it. Do it, Millie."

I exhale loudly. I may actually do it. I am so anxious to avoid this trial that I may in fact just get the hell out of town. Alone.

"Thanks, Lu. Maybe I will."

"You won't regret it, I promise."

As soon as I power up my tablet, the last email from Rosa, the one about MariRosa's death, pops up, and I have instant clarity. It's kismet. I don't even think about it. I book a trip to Cuba. I'll be missing the last week of Spanish class, but it's fine. I wasn't getting a degree in the class anyway. I am going to Cuba alone. And because I overthink everything, I book it for three entire weeks so that I can't go back and change it after I've thought about all the pros and cons later. Truth be told, I have enough money that I could just buy an overpriced ticket back home if I'm truly that miserable, but in spirit, I've made a solid decision that feels like something I can't undo.

Three weeks feels long enough that I'll be able to truly avoid the trial and also truly disconnect, since they don't have much in terms of technology over there. I'm scared out of my mind, though. It's not even a fun trip. From what Rosa has described and my research, there's nothing luxurious about where I'm going. I could afford to stay in one of the foreign hotels in the touristy parts of town, but that's not *why* I'm going. I'm going to visit my family, pay my respects to my great-aunt, and learn more about my Cuban roots. But mostly, I want to get out of Chicago as soon as possible.

When Nina finally calls me back on FaceTime, she immediately knows something has happened. My puffy eyes, the trembling of my lips. "What's wrong?"

"Everything. Everything's wrong. I screwed everything up."

"How?"

"John's working on the Phoebe case. I should have asked. How could I have pretended it didn't matter that he worked there? I was so stupid."

"You're not stupid, Mills. It was a tough call; I understand why you did it."

"It's more than that, though. I was at his office trying to follow through with that stupid Apology Project. I regret it so much." I'm so mad at myself. "No one gives a crap if I apologize to them. I'm not that important. I was so stupid and humiliated, and then my boss, who's really not my boss but sort of is in the sense that he's one of the Js from JJF, walked in and was his normal, nasty self and . . ." I say it in one long breath and then break down in a sob. "I'm such an idiot."

"Millie. Oh, Millie." She sounds like she wants to run to my home and hug me. "Nothing you've done is stupid. You're only trying to do right by everyone. You have such a good heart. Don't let a spineless prick let you question yourself, honey."

I wipe my tears. "I'm going to go to Cuba for MariRosa's funeral."

"For the funeral or to escape your problems here?"

"Both," I admit. "I don't want to be here during the trial. It's already on the news all the time, and if I see John on the news, too, I'll probably break the flat-screen. I need a change of scenery. I need to think."

She exhales. "I get it, and I support whatever you decide, but I'm worried. This isn't the right headspace to make a rash decision."

"It's not that rash. I've been thinking about it."

"I know but—"

"But nothing. This gave me the kick in the ass I needed. I can't see the big picture if I'm in it. I need to step away. I need to think about what I'm going to do next with my life. I need perspective on the Apology Project, and I really, really want to meet Rosa and the rest of the family."

"I love you, Millie, and if you feel that strongly about it, then do it."

"I just spoke with Mom and Dad, and you know it's hard to get a hold of them unless you email first. I don't want to scare them by sending them an email letting them know that now I've fled the country." She smiles. "I'm going to leave it vague, and if I don't speak with them again before I leave, can you explain things to them?"

"Yes, of course. But please be careful and send me all the information of exactly where you'll be."

"I will. I love you, Nina."

"Love you more, Millie."

Next, I send Rosa an email, but I don't even know if she'll get it before I arrive. I have the address from when I sent the package, and I give it to my father, just in case this all turns out to be a big catfishing scam and they can't find me. With my luck these days, I wouldn't say it's implausible. Clearly my judgment-of-character feature is broken. I preemptively ease his fears by sending him a report about the crime rate, which is low, and I also beg him to finally read the emails from Rosa as well as all the research I've done. The Roybals are real, and even on the off chance that they're not my family, I've developed an attachment to Rosa.

Luanne's going to watch William, and her kids are really excited about that.

Next order of business is John.

I don't even call before I go over. Actually, I almost don't go over at all. I don't owe him a goodbye, but I owe myself closure, and that's why I decide to go. He opens the door in gym shorts and a white T-shirt.

His hair is standing up in odd places like he's been running his fingers through it. He's called me a hundred times, but I've ignored them all.

"Millie," he says as I walk in.

"We need to talk."

"No," he says and closes the door behind me. "We don't." He cups my face in his hands. "No. I don't want to talk because I know what you're going to say, and I don't want to hear it. We can separate things. We have been doing it. Work is work; us is us."

"Bullshit, John. You are your job just like I was my job." My voice breaks. "This isn't going to work. Hell, it never was going to work."

"Of course it wasn't!" It's the first time I see an actual chip in his armor. "You always had one foot in and one foot out. You were waiting for me to screw up, and now you think I have, and bam—you bolt."

"No. That's not—"

"We're good together, and you know it. You have tried hundreds of cases; not all of them have been exactly squeaky clean. You've dug up dirt on people. You have squashed victims and plaintiffs. Now you've had this moral enlightenment, and I'm expected to have one too? It's not fair of you to do that, Amelia."

"You lied to me!" I say through gritted teeth.

"How the hell did I lie to you?"

"You didn't tell me you were on this case."

"You told me not to talk about work! I didn't know this particular case was the problem! I thought your issue was with Junior." He runs his hands through his hair.

"Don't you get it? My problem with Junior was about the *Phoebe case*. I don't have to tell you that what you and Junior want to do to the victims is screwed up. It's evil. It's wrong. I shouldn't have to tell you to have integrity. You should just know."

He looks like I slapped him in the face. "That's fucked up, Amelia."

"It is. It's very, very fucked up. Which is why I can't be here to witness it."

"You're being unreasonable. I don't even know what the hell Junior's strategy is, and you're already assuming I'm going to do the wrong thing. I was only just appointed. I don't even get the benefit of the doubt? What is it that you want? Do you want me to march up to Junior and quit?"

"No, John. I don't want you to do anything. You can choose to stay exactly as you are. You can keep doing everything like you've been doing it. I just don't have to be part of it. I was wrong. This rule about not talking about work, it was wrong. This shit about apologizing to everyone, it's stupid. I'm always going to be me. I'm going to be assertive. I'm going to get in your face. I'm going to yell and curse, and sometimes I might hurt other people's feelings."

"I've never had a problem with that. You are the one who has had a problem with that."

He's right, but I refuse to acknowledge that, so I continue my rant. "The only way you and I will ever work is by shutting out a part of our lives, and I'm not willing to do that anymore. The man I choose to be with should know what I stand for. He should stand for the same thing, and I should not have to apologize for that."

"You know more about me than anyone." He exhales loudly, and I think he's having a hard time getting words out too.

"Not everything, obviously."

"Millie, I'm trying to prep for a career-defining case that is just days away from starting and that I am just getting a handle on. I have Marc up my ass, and even if I'm pissed off about what happened at the office . . . I can't just walk away."

I don't know if he means me or the case, but it doesn't matter. "I won't cause you any more additional stress."

"Then don't," he says, his voice booming, his hands clenched, his nostrils flared, and his lips pressed into a straight line. This is the first time I've seen him so upset. A big case will do that to a person. There's so much weight on his shoulders, the pressure can be overpowering.

"Don't break up with me, sweetheart." He reaches for my hand, and it feels so familiar and safe, but it's also a big farce because I've lost so much respect for him after what happened at the office. "Forget Marc. Forget the case. It's almost over, and then we can move on and I'll take cases that—"

"Stop. Just stop. It's over." I swallow and let go of his hand. "I can't keep doing this."

"You're just going to walk away?"

"I'm going on a trip."

"What?" His eyes are wild.

"I booked a trip. I don't want to be here while the trial's happening. It'll be good for me, but I think it'll be good for you too. You can focus on that and not have to think of me and my big opinions while you're working."

"Once the case is over—"

"No!" I yell because he's not listening to me. I want to grab him and shake him and make him understand. He reaches for me, but I sidestep him. "You're wrong!" Tears start spilling out. "Once the case is over, it'll be worse! There's a little part of me that still believes you'll do the right thing. But if you don't—I think I can't ever look you in the face again."

"The right thing for who, Amelia? For the plaintiffs? Those are not my clients!" He's getting frustrated, and he's louder now as he paces around trying to understand. "It would be unethical for me to help opposing counsel. I could lose my license. You are being completely unreasonable!"

"You don't have to help them. You just don't have to make them out to be the bad guys. He tried to rape one of them, for God's sake!" I pound my palms on the counter.

He throws his hands up in the air. "He was acquitted!"

"So was O. J. Simpson, John. Just because he beat the criminal justice system doesn't mean he has to win in civil court."

"Amelia, don't do this. This is crazy. We have fun together. Don't do this."

"I wish things were different. I can't be with you if you put those women on the stand."

"You can't give me an ultimatum. You can't tell me how to try my case, Millie, damn it."

"Then you're no better than them."

"Than *him*," he corrects me. "Than Phoebe, or are you talking about Marc?"

I wipe the tears from my face with the back of my hand. "Both! I can't even look at you right now knowing that you're about to do something I feel so strongly against. I know I shouldn't put that pressure on you, but there it is. That's what I need from you, and that's why we can't be together. Because you cannot give me that." He doesn't say anything. He doesn't have to.

He runs his palm down his face. "How long will you be gone?"

"A while," I say, not wanting to commit to a time period. I don't know if I'll want to talk to him when I get back.

"Promise me we'll talk when you get back?"

So no, I can't date a man that thinks this is okay.

"After the trial, I'll hate you," I whisper between sobs.

He flinches at my words because he knows that it's really over.

The next day, I'm on my way to Havana.

CHAPTER
TWENTY-TWO

As a privileged woman who's never had to struggle, I know that this trip is going to be eye-opening. I need to find some sort of connection, and I think spending time with Rosa would help. I've researched as much as I can, and I know that this is not going to be a ritzy getaway.

I'm way out of my comfort zone.

But I need to go. I need to step away from everything else going on around me. I need to finally meet the Roybals. Maybe a new perspective from these family members will help. And if not, at least I can say I met them, and that'll be enough. I've been doing too many things to please others, and now I need to do something for myself.

Ordinarily, I would take a sleeping pill, but since I'm traveling alone, I'm scared to fall asleep and wake up confused and groggy, and I need all my faculties when I arrive in Houston for a brief layover. I don't so much as drink a glass of wine, which means that by the time I land, I'm pretty jittery. I'm so overwhelmed, in fact, that I'm running through the airport in a full-blown panic because I can't find the terminal. And I'm still in the United States!

I go to the restroom in the airport and splash water on my face, take a deep breath, and regroup. Once I've calmed down, I find a map of the airport, and within minutes I'm at the terminal, already boarding for the second leg of the flight. I pity the person sitting beside me, since I spend most of the flight uncontrollably bouncing my foot up and down and moving anxiously in my seat.

When we arrive, José Martí International Airport overwhelms me. Cubans speak fast and loud. It is nothing like the Spanish I "learned" in class. Plus, there are a lot of military-looking people standing about, which just boosts my anxiety to another level.

The airport is small and not sophisticated, especially compared to O'Hare. I don't see any signs for where I'm supposed to go. To top it off, when I left Chicago it was thirty-six degrees, and I was wearing a fairly heavy coat and a long-sleeve shirt. The moment I walk off the plane, the heat and humidity hit me square in the face, and I feel like taking everything off and splashing water on my face again.

I want to turn right back around and go home. Instantly, I regret making this rash decision and almost break down in tears when I find myself being spoken to and not understanding a single word.

"¿Señora, está bien?" a lady with a badge attached to her shirt asks. *Perdida, perdida?* I think that means lost. *Am I lost?* Yes, emotionally and physically, but I don't think she needs to be part of my emotional breakdown.

"Sí. Sí. I'm trying to figure out where to get my luggage. *Los bagajes.*" I point to someone's luggage, and the lady smiles and patiently points to where I need to go. I thank her profusely and head that way.

With bags in hand, I look around on the off chance that someone is holding some sort of sign with my name on it, or that I'd have some instant, familial pang of recognition, but there's nothing. I expected this, I tell myself. I knew there was a possibility that Rosa would not get my email. I take a deep breath and look around. Okay, there are people yelling "taxi," but no one is in any kind of uniform, and the taxis look like beat-up old cars.

I am not completely ignorant, though, and I did do my homework. I took out cash, since I knew the ATM and debit cards didn't work here, and I also researched how to get from Havana to Matanzas, which is about two hours away, according to Google Maps, back in Chicago. Here, I don't get reception, but that's what it said online before I left. There's a bus system that doesn't always work, and there are taxis and people who offer rides, but there's no Lyft or Uber. Although the crime reports seem to be favorable, this is also a country known to be pretty hush-hush about anything off-putting, so if I'm going to risk my life, I'm going to risk it with a taxi or what looks like a classic car with a yellow box held to the roof with a rope that goes through the window and says "Tax" because the *i* in "Taxi" has peeled away. That seems pretty legit, right?

"Hola," I say to the pudgy man standing against the "taxi" talking to another "taxi" driver. I think he's talking, or maybe they're arguing. I'm not sure because they're so loud and gesticulate a lot. But when he bowls over in laughter, I realize they're not arguing.

"Excuse me? *¿Con permiso?*" I try again.

I've caught him by surprise, and he stands up straight and tosses away the cigarette he'd been holding. "Matanzas?" I say and show him the address I have written down. "Can you take me here? *¿Me llevas a Matanzas?*" I ask.

"Matanzas," he draws out, and it sounds nothing like what I said, but we're on the same page. We negotiate a price, sort of. He says one amount, and I say no; then we go down in increments of five dollars until I'm finally done and just say, "Okay." He helps me with my luggage and holds the door open. I slide in, and when I try and close the window because all the heat is seeping into the car, I realize the handle is missing and there is nothing electric in this car.

"Yo soy Armando."

"Armando," I repeat. *"Mucho gusto,"* I say. *"Yo soy Amelia."*

292

He repeats it, and it doesn't even sound like my name. He pronounces Amelia with a short *e* like in "elephant" rather than a long *e*, like in "easy." Amazing how the sound of one letter changes the entire name. It's actually rather beautiful the way he says it.

"Welcome. Welcome," he says in broken English, and I smile. I lean my head back and close my eyes. It's been a long day, but the moment abruptly ends when the car jolts. For a moment I think we've lost a wheel, but then it happens again, and I realize it's the potholes and the very bad roads. I should have brought a sports bra because this is going to be a very bumpy trip. Which, incidentally, makes the two-hour trip four hours long.

He parks the car on the street in front of a house that is equal parts royal blue and baby blue, not for aesthetic reasons, but because those may have been the only colors available to do some sort of shabby plastering so that the house doesn't fall in on itself. Despite the state of the neighborhood, there are people sitting on their front porches in rocking chairs just chatting the afternoon away. An unfamiliar car, however, turns heads. I hand Armando the money, and some extra for getting me here safely(ish), and he helps me with my luggage. "*Espere aquí,* please? *¿Por favor? Más dinero.*" I want him to wait a moment so that I can make sure I'm in the right place.

"Sí. *Dale,*" he says, and I smile and turn toward the house.

The two gentlemen on the porch watch me as I approach. "Hola."

"*Buenas,*" one says, and stands up. He has a kind smile but a questioning look.

"Rosa? *Estoy buscando a Rosa,*" I say, hoping I'm asking for Rosa.

The other gentleman bolts up. "Amelia?" he says, the same way Armando pronounced it earlier. I love the way it sounds!

"¡Sí! ¡Sí!"

"*¡Tía! ¡Tía!*" he yells over his shoulder, and the two men start speaking to each other super fast. One takes my luggage and says something to the taxi, who is waved off. They knew about me, which has to be a good thing.

"*¡Rosa va a estar tan contenta de verte! Yo soy Pancho y este es Rey.*" They introduce themselves and confirm Rosa will be happy to see me.

"Oh, Rey. Husband de Fabiola," I say because I do not know how to say "husband" in Spanish.

"Sí, sí," he says. I also recognize the name Pancho. He is the husband of one of my cousins, but I cannot remember which one. There are thirteen, and I cannot keep them straight just yet.

"*¿Qué pasa?*" A woman whom I instantly recognize even though I've never actually seen her walks out while wiping her hands on a dish towel. She has paint all over her hands and clothes. "*Ay, ¡dios mío! ¡Amelia!*" she says the instant she sees me, and she runs down the steps, the dish towel falling to the floor. She envelops me in a tight, warm hug, careful not to get paint on me. Just like I have no reason to recognize her, she has no reason to recognize me, but it's immediately apparent that we know each other. Be it from the emails of the last months or from the blood relation running through our bodies, there is an instant connection.

"Rosa!" I say, embracing her back. Other people from inside the house and from neighboring homes start to come out to see the commotion, and some hug me and kiss my cheeks. Others ask rapid-fire questions, but I'm overwhelmed and do not understand most of it. Rosa shoos them off so that I have breathing room.

"What are you doing here, *mija?*" she asks with just a trace of an accent. "I was working on a new painting. I'm a mess." She tries to fix her hair, but she just makes it worse, which is actually adorable.

"I . . . I . . ." And then I break down into sobs. Why am I here? Because I have a broken heart, MariRosa died, I'm unemployed, the Apology Project was a failure, and Phoebe's ugly face is plastered all over the news. They all look at me for a moment, but then they go into action. The men—some are cousins, some are husbands of cousins, some are just neighbors—disperse after my bags have been brought inside. They don't want to deal with a sobbing woman.

Some of the women leave also, but two of my blood relations, Elizabeth and Lari, stay. Lari proclaims, *"Voy a servir café."*

"Yes. Maybe a little café after her long trip will help," Rosa says in English. She's being gracious enough to help me with the language barrier so that I don't have to think. I just need to cry.

I wonder if they have Nutella.

The front door opens and closes. *"¿Qué es todo este escándalo?"* Scandal? Scanning? I'm not sure what the person is concerned about.

"Mira quién está aquí," Elizabeth says toward the door, indicating that I've arrived.

When the woman rounds the corner, my eyes widen. Oh. My. God. She is the spitting image of me! Her hair is shorter, and her cheeks are a bit fuller and her skin a bit darker, but there is absolutely no question we are related. That makes me cry even more.

She drops her bag without thought and sits next to me. *"¿Está enferma? ¿Qué le pasa?"* she says and touches my forehead to check my temperature.

"Esta es Amelia, ¿no?" she asks Rosa and then looks at me, and in very broken English she says, "You are Amelia, ¿sí?"

"Yes, and you are Marta," My cousin, the nurse.

She smiles and then says, "What is the matter? You sick? ¿Por qué lloras?"

"No. No. I'm not sick," I say. "Maybe tired. I think I'm tired."

"Está cansada," Rosa translates for the other women. "Let me get your room ready and you can lie down. We'll talk later."

I want to talk now, but I also don't, so I just nod in agreement. The four women fuss over me, and I'm shuffled to a room with open windows and a refreshing breeze. The room is packed to the brim with knickknacks, but the bed is wide and the linen is crisp and clean and calling my name.

The flight was eight hours, and the drive to Rosa's house was four, not to mention having to arrive at the airport early. It had been a long, draining day, and by the time I fell asleep, the sun was starting to set. Now as I wake up and get my bearings, I see the bright sun coming in through the curtains. I must have slept through the night. But it's not the brightness of the room that wakes me.

I wake up because I am so damn hot. I look around the room and see there is a fan, the kind that has the blue blades and plastic cover that you connect to the wall so that it can turn slowly. This is not a Dyson or a remote-controlled ceiling fan. This is the kind you have to stand in front of to get any air.

It's fine, though. I've slept long enough. I've confused and worried these people long enough. And mostly, I hope that I didn't put anyone out of their room last night with my sobbing and tired drama. I hear voices coming from the other room, which I think is the living room. But before I go out and face anyone, I need a shower. I may as well cash in on all this hospitality and go out looking presentable.

There are folded towels on the sink, which I think is Rosa's way of giving me permission to take my time and freshen up. I take a cool shower, not because I necessarily want to, but because the pressure from the hot water is dismal. When I finish, I rummage through my bag and change into a light linen, casual dress, gather my damp hair into a ponytail, slip on some sandals, and then head out to officially meet my family.

"Buenos días," I say when I find Rosa and Marta in the kitchen. The women, who are sipping coffee and eating toast, stand up to help me to a chair like I'm sick or frail. I must have caused quite the ruckus last night.

"How do you feel this morning, mija?" Rosa asks as Marta pours me a small espresso or café. Unlike an espresso, this potent sucker has a lot of sugar in it.

"I'm so sorry I caused such a scene. I don't know what got into me," I say, embarrassed.

"Agotamiento," Marta says, and I look at her, confused. I don't know that word.

"Exhaustion," Rosa clarifies.

"Oh, yes. I was so tired and maybe a little overwhelmed," I admit. "I am sorry to have imposed myself on you. Did I take your room? I'm mortified," I say.

"No. No," Rosa says, gently patting my arm. "That was Mama's room. It's not being used. It's all yours for however long you'd like to stay. You will stay here while you're on the island. I insist."

Oh boy, I'm in the room of a recently deceased woman. I don't know how I feel about that. I slept well, though, and I didn't see any ghosts, so the room will have to do. "That would be so great. Thank you. I did not book a hotel or anything. I just packed my bags and flew over." I scrunch my nose. "I probably should have thought things out better."

"You are welcomed here," Marta says and then turns to Rosa. *"Dile que la familia siempre está bienvenida aquí. Que se quede cuanto tiempo quiera."*

"She says to stay as long as you like. Family is always welcomed here."

"Gracias," I say to both ladies, and then Rosa stands and starts to crack some eggs into a bowl. There's the smell of oil heating and then eggs being scrambled. She places some thick slabs of bacon into another pan. I know that food is scarce, and I feel uneasy taking the little they may have, but also I don't want to offend or embarrass them, so I graciously take what they are offering, which is delicious. I think it's been twenty-four hours since I've eaten anything.

"When you're up to it, I'll take you next door to Lari's house, and you can meet everyone again. You might not remember everyone who was here yesterday," Rosa says.

"That would be great. Gracias."

The morning turns out to be very nice, and my nerves abate. I'm not sure if they are giving me space because they're scared I'll crack again, or because it's the middle of the week and people are busy doing their own things. It turns out that Rosa is an artist. There are paintings she's made all over the house. Of course I didn't know this; I barely know her.

"Have you always painted? They're beautiful." I'm staring at a watercolor painting of a bowl of fruit. It's simple but very intricate in the brushstrokes.

"No. I started when I moved back here. I felt useless, and taking care of Mama wasn't enough. I needed to keep busy."

"So you just started painting. One day to the next?"

"Pretty much. I used to draw when I was little and then became busy with work, and then I came here and I couldn't be idle. One of our neighbors had these paints that no one was using, so I asked if I could have them and she said yes. Now it's become my favorite thing to do."

I guess we're not that different. You're never too old to start something new. It gives me joy that she paints, just like it's brought me joy to find her and the family and learn Spanish and rekindle my relationship with old friends. It's been only a day since I arrived, but already I'm feeling a little better.

Around midday Marta leaves for work and gives me a kiss on the cheek on her way out. Rosa asks if I'd like some lunch at Lari's house, but if not, she could make something here at her home.

"I'm good. Really. I'm sorry again about yesterday. I really was just exhausted. I don't know what came over me."

"It's no problem, mija. I think it's more than that, though. You seem troubled. Maybe you'll be up to talking about it later."

"It's just been a rough few months. But I'm fine." There are my go-to words. I know that just the fact that I said them means I'm not fine. There's no reason to lie; it's obvious something is going on. "Rosa, I don't think I'm fine," I try again. "But I will be, and I think being here is a good start."

She hugs me and says nothing more about it. I cannot tell you how comforting it is not to be pushed to talk right now.

We walk next door and go right inside. "Hellooooo," Rosa says, and a bunch of replies fly fast and loud, cascading over each other. Don't get me wrong; I love it and I want to understand, but right now I just hear noise with a few recognizable words like *frijoles, pollo, visitante, prima.*

"Prueba, flaca," Lari says, handing me homemade *croquetas* and *empanadas.*

"¿Prueba flaca?" I repeat, and Rosa translates it for me. "*Prueba* means 'try this,' and *flaca* is a term of endearment, but its literal translation is 'skinny.'"

I point to my very full bottom, which is very similar to some of their full derrieres, and I say, "No *flaca*," and they all burst out laughing. Then I ask something that's been lingering in the back of my mind. "Are any of you allergic to pineapple?"

Rosa eyes me curiously, and I hear murmurs of *"¿Cómo?"* which means "what," and Rosa translates.

"Rey is allergic to aspirin, and Fabi is not allergic to anything, and Lari is allergic to lobster and shrimp and . . ." There's a cacophony of people yelling out their allergies. It's quite hilarious actually. No one has even bothered to ask me why I've asked such a random question, but now I know everyone's allergies, and I also know that even though we have many things in common, we don't have everything in common.

Eventually the conversation of allergies turns into conversations of different ailments, mostly from the older people—neck aches, gout, arthritis. All the while people come and go from the house, bringing food and taking food and joining in the conversation, as random as it may be. It's like this is Union Station, and they pool their resources for a great family meal. Lunch or *almuerzo* is their heaviest meal, they explain, and we have *lechón asado, arroz con frijoles*, and then Elizabeth brings over *platanitos maduros*, and someone else brings an avocado, which they cut up to make a salad with some onions.

They don't always eat this well, Rosa explains. Sometimes there's no lechón, but because of the funeral of MariRosa a few days before, they still have a lot of leftover food from neighbors and friends. Normally, it's a lot of beans, plantains, and chicken or eggs.

I am starting to understand them better. I've met most of my cousins now except Fabiola. Apparently, she was at work when I got in yesterday and left early this morning, but I've met her husband and everyone else. There are children and older people, some with dark skin and some as light-skinned as me, and they're mostly related one way or another. Everyone kisses on the cheek and hugs when they come in and when they leave, as if it's been years, not hours, since they last saw each other. I'm used to my subdued and unaffectionate family, so it's all so very different from what I'm used to.

After lunch, we walk back next door, my belly so stuffed I think I'm going to explode. I know the ocean is nearby because I can hear it crashing into the Malecón, and I can smell the saltiness in the air. "I think I'm going to go for a walk. Would you like to join me?" I ask.

"This old lady's knees need a rest. But you go. It is safe. Stay along the path so you don't get lost," Rosa says, and she points to a patch of dirt that has deepened into a trail from people's continuous steps.

I stroll toward the sound of the ocean. A rooster scurries past me, which causes me to chuckle. There are a few dogs wandering the streets too. Mostly though, there's a lot of people out and about. For the middle of a workday, it's odd for me to see so many people just hanging out calmly on their porches, chatting, playing dominoes, laughing.

I am enthralled by the old cars on the streets—*old* as in beautifully kept antiques, but also as in dilapidated, twenty-year-old Toyotas—and the cars are much like the houses. They are beautiful if you take a quick look and focus on the vibrant colors, but if you look carefully, they are actually in pretty bad shape.

The poverty here is obvious. The entire island looks like someone pressed a pause button in the 1950s and forgot to unpause it. I reach the Malecón, the seawall, and sit on a nearby chunk of concrete that at one point may have been a bench, and look out at the vast ocean and inhale the clean ocean breeze.

If I had still been working at JJF, I would have never gone on this journey. I would never had had the opportunity or time to go on this trip or learn Spanish or rekindle my relationship with Luanne. I would have never felt a need to apologize to anyone because I would have still been the She-Demon. Junior can say whatever the hell he wants about me, but I know I'm not that person anymore. I'm still Amelia, but I'm also Millie, and maybe my temper is short, but my apologies have really meant something to me and those people I've apologized to, Lindsey notwithstanding. Much like this island, stuck in another century, I've been stuck in the past, and it's time I move on.

I sit here for a long time. So long, in fact, that a woman startles me when she sits down next to me. "Hola, Amelia. Yo soy Fabiola."

"Oh. ¡Hola!" I say, and she gives me a kiss on the cheek and a hug. I'm taken aback by how much she looks like Nina. It's uncanny.

"Rosa sent me," she says slowly.

"You speak English?"

"*Un poquito,*" she says. "Rosa worried. You here a long time."

"Sorry. *Perdón.* I got caught in the moment." She looks at me, confused, and I point to the horizon because I have no idea how to translate that. "*Muy bonito el océano,*" I say. "*Estoy* relaxed."

She chuckles at my Spanglish. "I come here too. Gracias for the books and DVD."

"*De nada.*"

I look at her swollen tummy, and she smiles and wraps her arms around her belly. "One month more."

We sit in mostly silence, and then it's time to go. We walk back to Rosa's home, and she points to different things—Elizabeth's home and a friend of a friend's and another cousin's. Everyone lives more or less in the same neighborhood.

Rey is waiting for her by the door, and he waves at me. "We go to beach on Saturday, okay? All family," she says, and I give her a thumbs-up. She hugs and kisses me goodbye, and then she disappears inside with her husband, and I cross the street to Rosa's house.

And that's more or less what happens the entire three weeks. I use American dollars to miraculously buy a lot of food that was supposedly unavailable but became available when they understood I had money to spend. Rosa was uncomfortable accepting, but I explained that if I had to pay for a hotel, I'd be spending a lot more than what I just spent on food for the entire family. So we eat very well the rest of the trip because when I saw food running low, I sneaked to the market for more.

I learn to get around the town, and by the end of week two, everyone knows me. "¡Amelia! ¡La gringa! ¡Flaca!" is the town's nickname for me. Every afternoon, I take a stroll, and on the first weekend, we go to the beach, which is magnificent. The water is crystal clear and barely thigh-deep for as far as the eye can see. My chaotic cousins join us, and we set up camp and stay there until the sun sets, drinking beer and eating delicious fried food they brought from home.

I am able to call Nina and my parents a few times to tell them I'm okay and having a good time.

On my last week, I am able to procure us some Havana Club rum, and we drink and eat and dance right on the front lawn of Lari's house. Most of the neighborhood comes out to join the festivities.

"Fabiola, por favor," Rey's voice booms, and I can tell they are arguing. She rolls her eyes and continues doing some salsa moves. What I've learned is that there is a form of machismo here, but it's not the same as what happened to me with Junior or Phoebe. Yes, I'm sure there are plenty of sexist pigs on the island, just like there are everywhere, but there's a difference that I hadn't known before. Rey is demanding and has a certain expectation of how things are "supposed to be." He grew up in a place where he, as the man of the house, is supposed to be caring for his wife. Fabiola constantly rejects that offer to help, and yes, he gets upset and I hear some Spanish cursing under his breath, but it is so obvious to anyone who sees these two people that it is all said and done with love. His method of showing her he loves her is by trying to keep her safely home and provided for. She takes him his beer because she loves him, and it is not about sexism and gender roles. It's about the two of them.

And I see this a lot here. The men are loud and boisterous, but it is a matriarchal society where the men think they rule, but they don't. Not at all. The women don't care whether the men know it or not, because in reality they are the ones in charge of their homes and their lives. I may be a little tipsy that evening when I'm sitting outside on a wicker-and-wood rocking chair with Rosa and Marta. We all have cups of rum in our hands. "I shouldn't have let Junior affect me. At the end of the day he knew he was wrong, and I knew I was right. Everyone knows Junior is a jerk. I don't have to show them that; he showed them that himself."

"*¿Quién es Junior?*" asks Marta. I don't know if my Spanish has gotten better or her English has, but we've been communicating just fine.

I finally tell them everything. I tell them about the NDA, the trial, Phoebe, John, the Apology Project, my disastrous party. Everything. They probably understand 50 percent of what I've said; even Rosa, who speaks English, probably can't keep up with everything.

"You had a bad year, mija."

"No, I had a good year," I correct her. "I've been focused on all the wrong things. A lot of good things came out of a bad moment."

"That is a beautiful way to see it," Marta says.

"Did I tell you that I didn't speak with Mama for five years?" Rosa says, and her eyes get watery. She tips back the rest of the rum and wipes the bead of sweat from her brow. "I wanted her to come to Miami with me. 'I mean, how can anyone live like this?' I used to say. In Miami I had a job; I could afford to buy her anything. She would never be hungry or hot or in need of anything, but she refused. She said she was old and all her family was here. This is the house she was born in, and this is the house she would die in. I was so mad. I am her only child, and she chose this place over me. We didn't speak for five years. It was a long time ago, but now that she's not here anymore, that's all I can think about." She wipes tears from her eyes, and Marta pats her back.

"I never said sorry to her. You know that? She got sick, and I didn't hesitate to come back home to care for her. She accepted me back as if nothing had happened, but I should have apologized."

"*Ella lo sabía*, Rosa," Marta says.

I nod. "Yes. I'm sure she knew you were sorry."

"But there's always that little doubt, you know? I wish I could have said it. I was too proud to say it. *Perdón*. One stupid word."

I think of the Apology Project; I'd allowed one insignificant man to make me question myself. I had said those words: *I'm sorry.* Those words were for me, not for the other person, and I would not have to go through life feeling regrets. I don't say this out loud, obviously. Instead, I pour us all more rum, and we hold it up. "To MariRosa," we say, and we tip it back in a single gulp.

It's my last day. I leave at the crack of dawn tomorrow morning, and this is my last opportunity to say my farewells. I'm wearing a long and flowy blue maxi dress with sandals, and I have my hair up in a ponytail. I've gotten used to the sticky heat and perpetual sun beating down on my skin. I find it fascinating that the Cuban women, even if they have little food and money, always have their hair and nails perfectly done and dress in styles similar to those of American women. So I try and look as presentable as I can, considering I seem to always be sweating in this country.

I've sneaked in more food and some extra bottles of rum and cases of beer. I paid a neighborhood vendor an extra hundred dollars to bring it to the house today. I wish I had more to offer them.

I don't think I can ever go back to the American version of Amelia. Can we change the way our names are pronounced? After forty years? I ponder that for a second.

They have made so much food, it's insane. I didn't get all this for them to indulge me, but then I see things I didn't buy, like yuca and tamales and *congrí*. I've shown them some photos that I have on my phone, but I had Nina send me more, which I downloaded when we had some Wi-Fi yesterday.

Why I didn't bring albums of photos, I'll never know. Well, I do know. I left like I was fleeing the country and did not plan accordingly. Anyway, I show them photos of my parents and of Nina. They are so absolutely fascinated by my father. Apparently he looks just like Mercedes. They bring out black-and-white and very old photos that they've found of Mercedes, which they give me. This is my father's biological mother! It still feels unreal. There's even one right before she fled the country where she is clearly pregnant. She looks so young and scared, and even through the photo it is clear she is trying to cover up the belly.

"Every Sunday she'd lock herself in the small closet, kneel, and pray the rosary. She could've been arrested, you know? Catholics were forbidden from joining the Cuban Communist Party, and anyone who was not part of el *Partido Comunista Cubano* was considered a *traidor*."

"A traitor?" I say, shocked.

"Yep. She could've been arrested, but she was so headstrong. Amelia, think of what you were doing at fifteen, and then picture yourself pregnant and a stowaway on a boat fleeing to America!"

It chokes me up. "I can't."

"I know," she says.

"She was so brave," Marta says and hands me an old rosary. "For you."

"I couldn't," I say.

"Please. We insist. For you to remember your Cuban family," Rosa says.

As if I could ever forget. It is a lovely evening, so when it's time to part ways and go to bed, I'm rather sad and wistful. I feel a genuine connection to these people, and that "thing" that I had felt was missing, I think I found. I cannot thank them enough, and I promise to visit them since they cannot visit me. They will never know how much coming to Cuba has meant to me, how much meeting them has made me feel hopeful again.

———

By the time I arrive at O'Hare, I feel triumphant. I've tackled one of my greatest fears, and I am beyond proud of myself for doing it. Nina picks me up from the airport. "I want to tell you everything, but I'm so tired," I say.

"Aww. Promise to talk soon?" she says as we arrive at my apartment.

"When I wake up in a week, I'll tell you everything and show you all the pictures."

She laughs and says, "Okay. That's a deal." She helps me unload the luggage and carry the suitcases upstairs. "Have you heard about the case?"

"No. I avoided it. Even if there had been any access to American news in Cuba, I haven't even checked my emails."

"Well, I think you should google it or ask someone. After you've caught up on your sleep."

"Why? What happened?"

"Something about a settlement. You should check it out." She sets all the luggage in my room, kisses me goodbye, and then she's gone.

It feels sublime to be back home. I love the familiar smell of the linen candle I always have around, the kind that smells fresh and clean even when it's not lit. Everything is exactly the way I left it, yet it feels so different now. It's like I've been gone for months instead of weeks. I know I have a lot to catch up on, and leaving for three weeks didn't do anything to lessen my hurt and anger, but it did make me feel even more sure I made the right decision this last year. And now that I'm back, all my problems are still right where I left them, just like my unlit candles and those old 1950s cars all over Cuba. They looked perfect on the outside, but were falling apart on the inside. I'm still jobless and uncertain about my next steps, and I'm still devastated about John, but in the midst of the sadness, I feel stronger.

But Nina left me with that little nugget about the trial, and even though all I want to do is go to sleep, I can't just forget about it. Damn it. I had hoped I could avoid this for a few more days; I never thought I'd be googling it the moment I entered my house.

Settlement Reached in the Hugh Phoebe Sexual Harassment Lawsuit. I click the link, and there is headline after headline. One says $30 million, another $100 million. The amount wasn't disclosed, and the media is speculating. There are also stories about how various directors of Phoebe Enterprise and its subsidiary have stepped down. Turns out the trial never happened. I piece together everything I read, and it seems like a settlement was reached between the parties the morning of the trial, just two days after I boarded my flight to Havana.

I have so many missed calls, texts, and voice mails from John, but I delete them all. It's over. There's no need to dwell on the inevitable. I am curious about the settlement, but it's not my problem anymore. I wonder what new piece of evidence the plaintiff uncovered that caused Phoebe to accept a settlement. He had been adamant that he would never settle. The bastard, through it all, never really thought himself guilty. He always thought he was above the law.

My mind reels with all the possibilities. Maybe there was a video or another witness or witnesses? Maybe an old text message or email? Something monumental must have triggered the last-minute change.

The new information doesn't change how I feel about John. The settlement was a fluke; new information forced Phoebe's hand. It doesn't negate the fact that John would have tried the case and vilified the victims. It makes me sick to my stomach all over again.

—

My sister is coming to dinner tonight so I can tell her all about the trip. I forewarn her that talking about John or Phoebe is prohibited. I want to enjoy dinner drama-free.

I'm showing her the photos one by one. She's the kind of person who enjoys watching them and asks questions. Some people don't want to see a bunch of photos of a trip they didn't go on, but she does. "Oh my God, she looks just like you!" she says when she sees a photo of Marta, and she brings the phone closer to her face. "Same nose, same eyes. Wow."

"Wait until you see Fabiola. You two could be sisters." I show her the photos, and her eyes widen.

"Oh, wow," she says and stares at the photo of her Cuban twin. Then she continues flipping through some group photos. "You don't look like you belong with them, but you look like you wouldn't belong anywhere else. Bizarre, right?"

"Exactly!" She's finally understanding.

She flips from picture to picture as I finish making dinner.

"Okay, it's a quiche. I swear it's going to taste and feel like a quiche."

She laughs, puts my phone to the side, and takes a bite. "It's a quiche! Amelia! It's a quiche that is a quiche, not a quiche that is an omelet. I'm so proud of you. It's delicious."

"Finally!" I'm so happy with the accomplishment that I find myself crying.

Nina puts down her fork and runs around to where I'm sitting and holds me. "Millie? What's wrong? Are you choking? Do the universal sign, Mills!" she yells and puts both hands around her neck. "I can't perform the Heimlich unless I'm sure you're choking!"

"I—I'm n-n-ot choking. I—I—I'm crying!" I am ugly crying now, and I think Nina is starting to worry.

"Crying?" She plops down as if I've taken two years off her life. "You were just laughing a second ago!" she yells, shaken up by my complete mood swing.

"I know. I'm just so happy about the stupid quiche."

"Oh, honey, I'm pretty sure it's not the quiche. But we'll go with that if you'd like," she says and wraps her arms around me, and I snort out a little laugh while crying.

This is a victory, and this dumb little quiche makes me feel like everything is going to work out. I'll find a purpose. I'm going to be okay because I'm Amelia Montgomery *and* Millie Montgomery. I'm strong even without a career, and I'm also a good person with a lot of love to give, even when my patience runs thin.

Finally, I feel complete.

———

The following week, I'm walking out of Pilates when I happen to bump into someone. When I look up, I see Mary Wallace. She's on my list. Actually, she happens to be the last person on my list. It takes me a moment to realize it's her. She still has the short bob that she had when I went up against her ten years ago in front of Judge Costa.

"Hey! Watch where you're going!" she says and bends down to pick up her phone, which fell upon impact. "The least you can do is apologize," she huffs.

"Apologize? For what? You bumped into me," I say, because it's true. The woman was texting and not looking where she was going.

She looks up from fiddling with her phone, which doesn't seem to be broken. "The nerve of—hey, wait, I know you. We tried a case together once. Monterrey something?"

"Montgomery," I correct her. "Amelia Montgomery." Mary was on my list, but I crossed her out as soon as I realized I was not apologizing to any more undeserving people.

"Yes. That's right. You lost that case, and I had the judge hold you in contempt because you were late to trial."

My mother had had a car accident as I was on my way to trial, and yes, I was twenty minutes late, but I was also a nervous wreck, not knowing if she was okay or not. It wasn't a frivolous cross-country meet like with Jenny M. This was a true emergency. I was not on my A game for that trial, and Mary knew it and took advantage of it.

"You're lucky my phone didn't break," she says as she finishes inspecting the device and then makes a stupid little noise. It's snooty and arrogant, almost like a villainous laugh. "I'm sure you'd hate to lose to me again for something as silly as a phone."

I had to pay a $500 fine because of her motion to hold me in contempt, and as soon as we walked out of court, I called her some very nasty things.

"I called you an evil bitch if I remember correctly."

She looks up at me. "Yeah. I hope you've learned to be a little classier."

"I have, thank you for your concern. But, Mary, you're still an evil bitch." And I walk away.

Sometimes people are just evil bitches who deserve to be called out, and no number of apologies or niceties will make them less bitchy. I feel completely okay with this decision.

The Apology Project wasn't something I ever thought I needed to do, but I'm so glad that I did it. It set me free. This interaction with Mary feels like the closure I needed.

I can't help but think about John, because it all started on the day we met. I want to call him and tell him all about it and have a good laugh together, but then I remember what a complete disappointment he turned out to be, and my desire to call him goes out the window. Every time I think about him, I get angry at him and at myself for getting so emotionally attached. When I get home, I crawl into bed, and William curls into me and purrs. I may not be able to share this sense of accomplishment with John, but it's okay. William is happy for me too.

CHAPTER
TWENTY-THREE

"Maybe you can use your big severance to open a restaurant, Mills," Nina says as she gets a second helping of lasagna. Lasagna that was made to be a lasagna.

"Nah. I've actually had a thought. I may get back into law, but on a smaller scale. I want to pick my cases and take only those that inspire me."

"I like it. I think that'll be a good use of your time."

"I think so too. I need to get back into researching. I need to put my brain to use."

"Have you heard from John?"

I've been back for two weeks now, but just hearing his name hurts. I feel as if I've had closure on everything, but that pain in my heart when I think about John just doesn't seem to want to go away. "I blocked his number. He called a lot, but what's the point? Why make it harder than it needs to be?" Secretly I was hoping he had read the file, seen the light, and somehow brought down the case from the inside. But he didn't do that. The texts I did read when I came back from my trip were just I'm sorry and Call me, please. He was issuing blanket apologies and assuming that I'd just forgive him once the case was over. He was so very wrong. Another thing I learned throughout my Apology Project is that the apologies have to mean something; they have to be genuine and specific.

"I hate this for you."

I shrug. "I hate it too."

"I'm back with Kevin."

"I figured. I heard him in the background last week when I called."

"He asked me to move in with him," she says.

"Whoa!" I say, surprised. This is a big step for them. She's been wanting this for a long time. "That's great, Nina."

"I know. I'm so excited. I love him, you know."

"I know," I say, hugging my sister. I'm so happy that she is finally getting what she wants. Kevin may not be my favorite person, but Nina is, and if she loves him and he treats her well, I'll eventually warm up to him. Then one day she'll get married and have kids, and I'll be the best aunt in the world.

Maybe I'll never have the things I thought I wanted, but at least the people I love are getting their happily ever afters. And it turns out the things I thought I wanted have changed. The trip to Cuba opened up a thirst for adventure I didn't even know I had. I'm already thinking about my next trip.

———

To: Amelia_montgomery@gmail.com
From: Johnny83@gmail.com
Subject: Legal Services

Ms. Montgomery,

I am in need of legal services. It is a complicated matter but one that I think you will find interesting, if not challenging. I received your information from a mutual friend, and he said that if anyone could assist me, it would be you. I understand that you are currently retired, but if you'd find it in your heart to listen to my story and at the very least point me in the right direction, I'd very much appreciate it.

Sincerely,
Johnny

The name immediately makes me think of John, but it's such a common name, and John would never email me for legal services. There's something about the email, though. I figure, why not listen to the man?

To: Johnny83@gmail.com
From: Amelia_montgomery@gmail.com
Subject: Re: Legal Services

Johnny,

I can meet at the Starbucks on Eighth and Miller, next Tuesday at ten a.m. Full disclosure, I'm not currently practicing law and cannot promise you anything. However, you have piqued my curiosity, and I am willing to meet with you and offer advice if I can.

Sincerely,
Amelia Montgomery

Meanwhile, I send Brenda a DM through Facebook because if I'm going to do anything law-related, I'd like to know my options and I may need some help.

> Hi Brenda. I love all your FB posts, and your children are beautiful. Wondering if you're still practicing law. I'm thinking of starting a new venture, mostly pro bono work, and I'd love to pick your brain about that or if you'd be interested in doing some pro bono work yourself. Would love to catch up in a less embarrassing setting than at your brother's wedding.
> —Millie

The next day I have a bubble on my phone with her picture on it letting me know she's replied:

> Girl, you have not posted anything other than your profile photo. Post something. It was admittedly unexpected and a little strange seeing you, but I'm glad I did. Let's have lunch soon. I have a small firm and do some pro bono work, but like you said many moons ago—pro bono doesn't pay the bills, so I haven't been able to grow that part of the business to where I'd like. Let's talk.

We make plans to meet next week for lunch, and suddenly I'm excited about the possibility of having possibilities! Where I felt hopeless that afternoon at JJF, now I see options.

———

Starbucks is packed, but I arrived early and was able to snag a table off to the back where there is less noise and a little more privacy. I have a legal pad and a pen on the table. I'm wearing a pair of trousers and a button-down shirt. Last week, when I made my decision about starting to practice law again, I donated most of my suits to an organization that helps victims of domestic violence get back on their feet, which includes preparing them to enter the job market. I did keep some of them because you never know, but I don't think the kind of law that I'm planning on practicing will require the insane number of designer suits I owned.

I'm sipping my black coffee, waiting on Johnny, when in walks John. My heart expands in my chest, then deflates when I realize it's him, and he's not mine, and he screwed up, but he's still so handsome, but he's also a pig, and . . .

He sees me from across the room and walks straight to me. He's casual in jeans, a polo shirt, and Adidas sneakers. He has his hair messy the way I love it. He doesn't wait for me to say anything; he just pulls the chair out and sits down.

My heart picks up speed, and damn it—why can't I hate him?

"Kevin told me you're thinking of practicing law again, and I need an attorney. The best attorney," he says.

Kevin, of course. My sister and her big mouth . . .

"You need an attorney? For what? Oh, are you Johnny83@gmail.com?"

"Yep. JJF is suing me."

My eyes widen. "Suing you? For what?!"

"Well, it turns out that once I realized exactly what the defense was on the case, I changed my entire strategy, and when it was my turn to question one of the victims, I didn't do what I was told to do."

"You sabotaged the defense?" My eyes are surely the size of saucers.

He nods. "Luckily, because of the settlement agreement I all but forced Phoebe to make, Phoebe ran out of money to sue the firm for improper representation. Unluckily, or luckily, depending on how you view it, he also ran out of money to pay his legal fees. Plus, it would be bad for his ego to say he was strong-armed into settling. But JJF doesn't give a shit. They're suing me. Oh, and also, I punched Junior in the face, so I was arrested."

"What? Oh no!" I probably look like a fish out of water, with my mouth opening and closing and my eyes wide. My heart feels as if it's going to come out of my chest. I gulp down my emotions. "I need more information." I clear my throat. "I just can't take any silly old case."

He smiles, and I can see some of the tension between us start to melt. "Right before the trial, Marc said something very distasteful about one of the victims. Something I won't repeat, but it involved the words *she wanted it* and *bitch*. It made me feel wrong. I hadn't heard him say anything like that until that point, Millie. If I had, I would have walked out of the firm a long time ago; you have to believe me. I told him I didn't like it. I need to know what he did to you. I know he did something. Tell me."

"He made a disgusting remark about women, and I elbowed him in the face. It was actually sort of an accident, but still, it happened, and it wasn't worth explaining since I was on the verge of slapping him anyway. I think I may have broken his nose. There was a lot of blood."

His mouth is open wide.

"But then I threatened to sue for sexual harassment, and we settled."

"You are amazing," he says.

"Well, keep talking because right now you sound pretty amazing yourself. What happened next?"

"The sonofabitch did something he'll regret until the day he dies."

"What?" I'm on tenterhooks.

"He said something offensive about the woman I love, and that's not something I take lightly."

My heart. Oh God, I can't take it. "The woman you love?"

"Millie, you should have told me why you left the firm. I thought you and Junior just didn't get along. You have to know I would not have accepted him talking to you that way. Talking to any woman that way. And you must know I would never represent Phoebe the way Junior wanted you to. No way would I do that to any victim!"

"You know I couldn't, John. If I could, I would have."

"Turns out, Junior isn't such a stickler for the confidentiality agreement. He said you quit because, and I quote, 'She's a weak woman who probably likes it rough in the bedroom just like the plaintiffs in the case. Once she gets it rough, she gets embarrassed and yells rape just to save face.'"

I gasp and then cringe. "Yep, that's pretty much what caused my elbow to connect with his face."

"Except that I got arrested."

"John!"

"But the charges were dropped."

"Oh, good," I say in relief.

"But then I got called to Springfield by the Illinois Bar. Turns out that what I did at the last minute went against a bunch of ethics rules as well as rules of conduct. I had to go in front of a panel and almost lost my license. Thank God I didn't, but I was sanctioned and suspended for a month."

"John!"

"*Then* I was fired. But we knew that was coming from both the assault and the last-minute withdrawal of the case."

"Why didn't you call me?"

"I did!"

"Oh yeah, I blocked your number."

He lets out a deep breath. "I'm pissed at you, too, you know . . ."

"At me? I was right all along."

"But you didn't trust me to make the right decision," he says. "It took you twenty years to figure out that JJF was toxic and leave. You wanted me to make that determination the moment I stepped foot inside."

Maybe he's right.

"You should probably also know that since Margret was there when Marc said all that shit, she quit, and then half the office quit, and now everyone feels they owe you an apology."

"I don't want it."

"No. But you deserve one."

He stands up and comes around the table. He takes my hands and helps me to my feet. "Amelia. You've apologized to a list of people—"

I interrupt him. I know it's not the time, but I do tell him anyway. "Not quite. Mary was a dick, and I didn't apologize to her. I actually did the opposite. I called her an evil bitch. But I swear, John, she deserved it. And the Jennys were just awful at their jobs, so I didn't apologize to them either. And—"

He laughs. "See, that's exactly why I love you."

Oh God . . . my eyes water.

"So, as I was saying, you've apologized to a bunch of people, but now I owe you one."

"You really don't. I missed—"

"Amelia, babe, please shut up and let me finish."

"Oh. Please. Proceed."

"Amelia Montgomery, my love, from the bottom of my heart, I'm sorry."

"I accept!" I say and kiss him hard, but he's apparently not done.
"You don't even know the extent of it. Let me finish."

"Oh, okay. Go ahead."

"You were right. Phoebe didn't deserve to be represented, and that's a tough thing to admit. Those women shouldn't be used as pawns for him to get away with those despicable actions. And lastly, I filed a formal bar complaint against Marc."

"We can leverage that to get you out of the lawsuit," I add.

"So you'll help me?"

"Of course I will."

"You should know, before you decide to take me back, that I'm currently unemployed and will probably be homeless when my savings run out. Hopefully you have cheap legal rates."

"Honey, nothing about me is cheap, but luckily for you, I would do this one for free. Plus, also lucky for you, I've come into a lot of money, I have a great big apartment, and I'm willing to help you get back on your feet." He smiles, but I add, "For a price."

"There's always a price."

"You know it." I kiss him over and over right there in Starbucks. "You have to go into business with me: Montgomery, Ellis & Associates."

"I don't think I like that."

"If you think I'm putting your name first—"

Then he really, really, really surprises me. He steps back and gets on one knee. I vaguely hear people gasping and aww-ing. I never in all the years of my life expected something like this. He takes out a box. "How about we make it Ellis, Ellis & Associates?" I'm in tears now. Full-blown tears. "And before you say no, I do know you'll probably want to keep your last name, and I'm fine with that, if that's what you need. But for dramatic effect, I'm going with Ellis."

And it turns out that apologizing really does set you free. It's not about the person you've hurt; it's about letting it go so you can move on. And most importantly, it's about acknowledging when you are wrong, which I have been many times. Learning from your mistakes is a powerful thing.

And I have certainly acknowledged that.

ACKNOWLEDGMENTS

2020! Is it over yet? It was difficult to write a sexy romance during these challenging times. So I stopped trying and wrote a book with real characters and messy lives—just like reality.

My lovely readers, you are reading the final version of many drafts, many tears, and a lot of yelling. It's almost like Amelia wrote it herself, isn't it?! And, in many ways, she did. Amelia is the most relatable character I've written. She's tough, feisty, and misunderstood, much like me, but also quite sensitive, something most people never get to see. I hope everyone can see a bit of themselves in Amelia and in Millie.

With that being said, I want to thank my husband most of all because he's always seen the Millie in me—even when I'm being a She-Demon. I can't even put into words how grateful I am. I love you! And my kids, for being so patient and understanding when I'm on a deadline. One day you'll understand (I hope). I love you, kiddos. And my parents and grandmother for always being around to help me when I'm in my writing cave and need to do laundry or feed children. I have the best support system.

Sarah Younger, my friend, my agent, and my sounding board: How many times did we edit this book? How many f-bombs and sexy times did we delete? But if it weren't for your spot-on advice, we wouldn't have made magic happen. So truly, from the bottom of my heart, thank you. Love you. I owe you more bubbly. #LadiesWriteNight: Tif, Annie,

Rachel, and April, how far we've come. When we met, we had not released a single book. We've come so far, and we've not even started!

Finally, Chris from Lake Union. Listening to you talk about this book and Amelia makes me teary-eyed. *You get it! You get it!* There's nothing more an author needs than someone just "getting it," and you did from day one. And Krista, you and Chris together are truly a dream team. You've been so organized and thorough, you've made my job easy when everyone knows edits are the hardest part of writing a book. You challenged me with your edits, but I'm grateful for it because it's made me a better writer. So thank you, and I hope to have many, many more chances to work together!

And to my readers . . . if I could hug each and every one of you, I probably wouldn't because we have to keep six feet apart and we have to wear masks. But, in an alternate universe where it is still 2019, I'd hug you all one by one! I know how invaluable your time is, and just for the fact that you took the time to read my book—I THANK YOU!

Gratitude. Gratitude. Gratitude.

ABOUT THE AUTHOR

Jeanette Escudero worked as an attorney before picking up a pen at thirty years old to write something other than legal briefs. Being published fulfilled a dream and gave her an outlet for her imaginative, romantic side. Writing as Sidney Halston, she is the *USA Today* bestselling author of the Panic series, the Worth the Fight series, the Iron-Clad Security novels, and the Seeing Red duet. In addition to writing and reading, Jeanette has a passion for travel and adventure. She and her family have been to the Galapagos Islands and have hiked Yellowstone, the Shenandoah mountains, and the Great Smoky Mountains. Born in Miami, Florida, to Cuban parents, she currently lives in South Florida with her husband and her three children, in whom she's instilled a love of nature and an appreciation for the planet. For more information visit www.sidneyhalston.com.